Death in Athens

Also by John Xiros Cooper

Pillar of Faith
The Serpent's Dish
The Cambridge Introduction to T. S. Eliot
Modernism and the Culture of Market Society
T. S. Eliot and the Ideology of Four Quartets

A Panos Akritas Mystery

DEATH IN ATHENS

John Xiros Cooper

This edition published in 2020
by Norman Carney SA Editions.

Copyright © John Xiros Cooper 2017, 2020

The moral right of the author has been asserted.

*All characters and events in this publication
other than those clearly in the public domain
are fictitious and any resemblance to real persons,
living or dead, is purely coincidental,*

All rights reserved.
No part of this publication may be reproduced, stored
in a retrieval system, or transmitted in any form or by any means,
without the prior permission in writing of the publisher, not to be otherwise
circulated in any form of binding or cover other than that in which it is published
and without a similar condition including this condition
being imposed on the subsequent purchaser.

Norman Carney SA Editions
Montreal Vancouver Athens
normancarneySAeditions@gmail.com

I think the slowness of the gods in punishing sinners is particularly awkward.

> Plutarch

/1/

The old man rested quietly on his comfortable leather sofa watching the television news. Nassos Archontas was ninety-one and he was dozing as the blue-eyed blonde read the news droning dead-eyed about the day's doings. Archontas looked up and noticed three masked men staring down at him. For a moment he didn't believe they were there. Recently, he suffered from what the doctor had told him were 'waking dreams'. They were hallucinations, but the doctor had done his best not to panic his patient. Unfortunately, the three men, holding guns and wearing ski masks, were all too real.

Archontas ignored them as if they weren't there. One approached the old man grabbed him by his shirt collar and yanked him up. They certainly were there. It's amazing how men, robust and blooming with health in their middle years, could be so wafer light in old age. Perhaps this is what's meant by the phrase 'lightness of being', the lightness in fact of being old, skin like crumpled paper, bones of fragile porcelain, and flesh as air dried as finely sliced *louza* ham left out on the counter too long. The old man sputtered something incomprehensible and one of the intruders smacked him hard across the face.

"Shut the fuck up," he said his voice hissing.

"Who arrh . . .?" Archontas gasped.

The second man punched him in the stomach. Then he punched his face three times. The crunching third blow shattered the porcelain of his left cheek.

The first man let him drop and Archontas lay on his Persian rug gasping for breath. The third man came over and kicked him in the ribs. More broken porcelain. The heap of skin and bones let out a painful whimper.

The second man extracted pliers from a side pocket on his military style trousers, reached down, and in one movement yanked out the thumbnail on the old man's left hand. The old man's scream sank into yelps and whimpers as blood reddened the pulpy thumb. The third man came forward, holstered his pistol, and pulled out a slim blade. He reached down, grabbed the old man's white hair, pulled his head back, and drew the knife across the crumpled paper of his throat making sure to slice the external jugular. Blood spurted out and slowly soaked the Persian rug. His assassin gripped his white hair for a moment longer watching the blood gush making sure none of it soiled his trousers and then let his head drop. Archontas was dead before his head hit the floor with a damp thump.

The intruders walked into the large white bedroom and emerged a few minutes later carrying a small canvas bag. As they let themselves out, the first man stopped, looked around the apartment one more time and then, satisfied of a job well done, tossed a piece of letter-sized paper into the room. It floated back and forth a couple of times before settling noiselessly on the floor. He closed the door behind him. He hadn't bothered to put out the lights.

Sounds from the shadowed road below blighted the dead silence. Somewhere in the distance, the dead man, had he been able, would have enjoyed the drumming from the half dozen merry African timpanists entertaining tourists in Monastiraki. On the mantelpiece, a gold clock ticked its melancholy way into the future, loudly sounding the seconds as they passed, now beyond earshot of Nassos Archontas. On the television screen, the news had ended and been replaced by a young man flying through the air like a winged Hermes, thanks, it seems, to the contract he had just signed with an international mobile phone company.

Ten minutes passed and the front door began to open. A well-dressed young man entered. He left the door slightly ajar and walked over to where Archontas, a man who had made hundreds suffer in the past, now rested past suffering on the blood-soaked Persian rug. The young man stopped and looked down at the corpse. He didn't need to check to see if he was dead. Turning, he went back to the front door.

"You'd expect more blood," he said quietly. "Hey," his voice brightening, "look at that vase. It'd look great with flowers in my place."

He pulled the door open a little more and a woman in high heels entered.

"You know sometimes you talk too fucking much," she whispered.

She looked around and then walked over in her high heels and stared at the dead man. Her gaze surveyed the spacious sitting room, with its Roche Bobois furniture, the antique engravings on the walls, the small sculptures and ceramic vases that decorated several shelves and a long low bureau by one of the walls.

Then she turned and looked at her companion and smiled. In the meantime, he had taken out his iPhone and was flicking his fingers over the screen. She began to undress. She lifted her skirt over her head using her elbows to make sure not to disturb her carefully disarranged hair. She placed the skirt over an armchair near the sofa. Then she unbuttoned her white blouse and put it in the same place. She stood in the middle of the room in her high heels, black lace bra, and a black thong with a triangle of lacework over her pubic hair, at least the triangle that hadn't been shaved. She was in her late thirties, on the tall side with curved hips rising to strikingly shapely breasts. The young man lifted the iPhone and took several photos of her standing over the corpse. Some from the front and a couple of her from the back leaning over the dead porcelain doll. As she dressed, they both laughed.

"Wait til I get you back to my place," he said.

As they were leaving, the woman looked back at the apartment with a smile on her face.

"Tell me again what you're going to do to me when we get there."

She closed the door, cutting off his words to save the old man, a broken, bloody bundle, the embarrassment of hearing the crude reply.

/2/

Police Captain Panos Akritas, homicide detective of the Hellenic Police, the *Elliniki Astynomia*, was only half listening when his good friend and colleague Lieutenant Costas Psarros told him that a 91-year-old man was found murdered in his apartment in Plaka, Athens' oldest quarter. The victim's housekeeper telephoned at 08:12 to say that Nassos Archontas, her employer and retired civil servant, was lying on the floor of his second floor flat in a pool of blood. His throat had been cut and it looked as if he'd bled to death. His body had suffered what looked like torture before dying. Akritas sipped at his coffee and kept on reading his newspaper. He was a man in his late forties, lean body, average height, dark hair combed straight back, with gray traces near his ears, colouring like a suntan that never goes away, dark, thoughtful eyes touched, depending on the light and time of day, by melancholy.

He still scanned the newspaper in the morning with his coffee but he never remembered anything that he'd read five minutes after he'd read it. Except the football results . . . PAOK 3 Lamia 1, Olympiacos 4 – Xanthi 0 . . . There was nothing wrong with his memory. He had an exact memory and an excellent eye for detail . . . Tripolis 0 Panathinaikos 2, Atromitos 1 – AEK Athens 3 . . . He could recall even the smallest things without effort. No, he couldn't remember what passed before his eyes in the news because most of it was rubbish. But the printed news still wasn't as hollow as the blue-eyed blondes who read the news on the private TV channels. Their bland, artificial voices made his skin crawl. He always thought that if he heard one word more, he would stop being Panos Akritas, unique human being, and become some stereotype, a cliché, infected as if he had a chronic disease. He told himself that it was important to watch the TV news for five minutes every evening because that way he'd know what it's like to have a stroke.

The news of course was always the same. The usual mix of politics, celebrities, and violence. The politics were the normal antics of politicians whose activities flip-flopped between making momentous decisions that further ruined the lives of the powerless and acting like clowns, minus the big red noses and the floppy shoes. The fat man, the current Minister of Defense, came to mind. As for the celebrities, one was always getting a facelift because she thought she looked 'too Armenian', another had leased half of Venice, the fashionable half, for his wedding, and one more was wearing a big red nose and floppy shoes for a charity event in Geneva, one of the most expensive cities in the world, to help poor people in Gabon. As for violence, it was so widespread that the newsreader, looking as bland as a very pale slice of veal, took an awful long time before she reached the end of the wars, rapes, murders, and mutilations. After the last massacre, turning her carefully coiffed and made-up head to camera three, she would smile brightly and say, 'And now here's Fotini with the weather'. Akritas could never quite manage the transition without seeing the sunny graphic over Athens beaming down on the last pile of corpses.

It was what Psarros said next that made him look up.

"That's number six in the last month."

"Six? Six what? You mean the old men cases. There are six already?"

He put the paper down and looked at his colleague. Costas Psarros was a veteran detective who often partnered Akritas on difficult cases. Lately he'd been sidelined by the chief of detectives because of an imagined slight to the chief's authority. He'd been given cases well below his pay grade and his experience. This had rankled, but Costas Psarros was a patient man and did what he had to do. He'd learned a valuable lesson about the chief. Aris Boutsekes was a vain man and like all vain men a vigilant auditor of small slights. Psarros had recently angered his boss by making an unauthorized arrest. It was a simple oversight, and thoroughly insignificant. The arrested man was obviously guilty –indeed he'd confessed – but Boutsekes insisted that his detectives 'keep me informed'. This was the chief's version of the papal offering of a hand for the compulsory kiss. Psarros had thought the case was too trivial for the full performance of papal obedience. As a result, he'd been given the criminal dregs – pickpockets, pimps, and petty thieves – to work with.

"What are we dealing with here? A serial killer?" Akritas asked.

Psarros shrugged and grimaced, giving his head a slight shake.

"To be honest, Costa, I haven't been following what's been happening."

"No-one has," Costas answered with what in a patient man passes for a scowl. Akritas paused and looked up at his colleague. Psarros' usual cheerfulness was gone. He's a good cop, Akritas thought, unhappy that nothing was being done. He had the look of a man who'd been let down. He knew the look. It was only a matter of time and circumstance, being let down one too many times, before concern would finally flop over into indifference.

"This is serious, isn't it? Damn, maybe I should keep up with the massacres."

He flicked the paper and checked the front page. There would be nothing about today's murder but one might expect a story about the investigation of the others. Not a word.

"That's the problem," Psarros said, "the papers have nothing. It seems weird that the papers and TV are more or less ignoring the whole thing."

"The fact is that we haven't made a big deal about it," Akritas offered. "Where are the press conferences, the media scrums, the outrage, all the usual bullshit, so the brass can get their faces on TV? There's got to be a reason."

"Gun down a sixteen-year-old kid from Halandri," Psarros said with a touch of bitterness, "and they burn Exarchia, kill six old men and everyone, says, oh really, yawns and goes back to solving the country's problems over coffee. This one was in his 90s, the other five all in their 80s."

"Hey, Costa, one of our guys killed the sixteen-year-old, that's why they burned down Exarchia."

"Come on, Pano, you know what I mean."

"What're you saying? Our guys are responsible for this too?"

Psarros ignored him.

"So, who's got the case?" Akritas asked.

"Xiloudes."

Hearing that name, Akritas sighed and went back to the paper. In these last few years of the debt crisis in Greece, he was doing a lot of sighing. In this aspect of personal expression, he was no different from millions of other sighing citizens in the country. This was the seventh year of the debt crisis and everyone was hurting. Meanwhile, the fat cat politicians, their relatives, and their rich friends were still laughing all the way to their off-shore banks and, if they were sighing, it was because they had just eaten a very good meal, or smoked a lovely cigar, or been blown by their trophy girlfriends. The last time Akritas had sighed because he was in a good mood, apart from sultry evenings spent in his girlfriend's bed, was . . . . . damn, he couldn't remember. He took a sip of coffee. It was cold. He wanted another but did he want it bad enough to get up and take the elevator down eight floors to the coffee shop on Alexandras Avenue?

The coffee could wait.

He remembered fondly the time, not that long ago, when they could make coffee in the office on the old stained hotplate with one of the half dozen *brikis* in the cupboard. The department had cut back on 'unnecessary' expenses and no-one out of his own pocket would stoop to go buy the coffee an old guy in Karytsi Square roasted to order in his tiny *kafekopteion*. Among the department orators, this refusal to go out and buy some coffee was seen as an act of political defiance against austerity. The International Monetary Fund and the European Union could go fuck themselves was the general sentiment. The IMF, the EU, but especially the central government, unfortunately, had not yet noticed the rebellious boldness of its unhappy detectives. As a result, one of the small pleasures left in crisis-ravaged Athens – walking into the little square, with the big church dedicated to St. George of Karytsi, and breathing in the aroma of roasting coffee beans – was gone. And now no-one volunteered to go get the coffee as a matter of principle. Since their salaries were either cut or frozen, everyone was on strike as far as making up the shortfalls for stuff that used to be provided by the fucking state. No, Akritas was not in a good mood.

"So what's the connection?" he asked not looking up.

Psarros shrugged. "Xiloudes thinks it's robbery. The old men had all their money in their houses and this guy, the thief, found out, got in, tortured them until they told him where it was. Then he slashed their throats. Like the latest guy . . . seems the thief got away with lots of cash in a bag the guy had under his bed. Everyone these days has cash stashed away at home.."

"Do you?" Akritas asked looking up.

"Well, no. I don't have any savings, but that's what the papers say."

"And you believe all the garbage they print?"

"Damn, Pano, don't be such a fucking cynic. Why are you even reading the goddamned paper?"

"Yeah, you're right, I should maybe just look out the window at the blue sky. It kills the time."

The two men looked at each other.

"And so," Akritas said, "it's better to have some cash stashed under the bathroom tiles than let the politicians fuck you over?"

"Yeah, that's right," Psarros snapped. "This is Greece Pano. Your chances of holding on to your money are better under your mattress than thinking it's safe in the bank."

"What do you mean?" Akritas asked.

"You know what old people are like, especially these days. They feel safe in their homes. This is a safe country at the end of the day. Are you surprised they don't trust banks or the government. Keep their shit under a mattress. Or the fridge."

"I've got some money in the National Bank, should I be worried?" Akritas asked, knowing the other heard the pinch of mockery in his voice.

"Why not?" Psarros replied. "Look at what happened to those poor suckers in Cyprus who trusted the fucking banks. Do you really think anyone trusts that little shit of a Finance Minister we've got now?"

Akritas stared at his colleague for a moment. He nodded and pursed his lips. He remembered that he was supposed to call Katarina at some point. He sighed again, this time more audibly.

"You all right?" Psarros asked.

"Yeah, yeah, yeah."

"What's Xiloudes got?"

Psarros shook his head. "The perpetrator's good, leaves nothing behind."

"Nothing at all?" Akritas asked, sounding skeptical.

"Xiloudes hopes the guy gets enough money soon and fucks off out of the country. Or if he's a Pakistani, he either gets taken down by the Dawn or picked up and put on the plane back to Kalahari."

"You mean Karachi."

"Oh yeah, Karachi."

"How come no female victims?"

There was a moment's silence. Somewhere in the distance a siren sounded. Down the hall, they could hear someone shouting.

"What kind of question is that?"

"Just men? Seems a little strange. Old women don't trust banks, governments, their nephews, the good-for-nothing son-in-law . . . and they put their money in the fridge as well."

"I dunno Pano, maybe they don't have as much money. Better ask Xiloudes."

"I will."

He folded the paper, picked up the landline on his desk, and dialed Katarina's number. No answer. Try her mobile? He hesitated and then put the handset down. Did he really want to talk to her just yet? Damn, why had he promised to call her? It was 10:43 in the morning. The familiar, but still odd, emotion seeped through him again – the formless discontent of not really knowing someone, even after you've been with them for a while.

Why no women, he thought? Maybe it's easier to get to know the old guys. They would spend most of their time down at the *kafenion* with their mates complaining about their health, the Germans, the fucking politicians, and the fact that their wives were spending money like there was no tomorrow. The tale of woe would be counterpointed by idle conversation about the bubbly blonde talking heads with the big tits on the TV talk shows, or how clever they'd been when they were buying and selling plots of land in their villages, and how much money they had hidden away, out of reach of the finance ministry. The old women would not be sitting around most of the day nursing one cup of coffee and talking trash on a terrace. Well, at least not man trash. They had trash of their own to talk about. And most of that would be done in their darkened sitting rooms or down at the church.

Old people, Akritas thought, there's something strange about them and yet they are so damned obvious. They've lived so long they've internalized all the clichés and banalities served up by society, the media, priests, neighbors, hairdressers. Yet with the years they also grow bizarre. Strange and familiar all at the same time. Akritas remembered his own father's last years in Patras. How bizarre he seemed. He had fought in the resistance during the German occupation and this had set his personality in cement. He typecast himself as the noble communist partisan long after the war ended. It kept him forever young. It was who he was. Yet his best friend, another old communist, was the local loan shark, the guy you went to when the bank turned you down. His father railed against the banks like all the good communists but saw nothing wrong when his old friend bled the destitute of their last drachma.

Caught in a time warp, Stavros Akritas could not conceive of a time that wasn't like the drama he'd lived during the German occupation, Civil War, and the white terror that followed in the 1950s when all the idealism and dreams of the war generation had been shattered. Men and women who had sacrificed so much in the resistance suddenly found themselves the losers of history, just as they had begun to celebrate their victory over both the Germans and the home-grown fascism that had supported the occupiers. The history books said that the Civil War had ended. But look deep enough and you'd find it was still the source of the country's anger and pain. For most Greeks it still raged inconclusively in the shadowy gap between memory and vexation.

Stavros had not been happy to see his son become a policeman. Like many ordinary Greeks, especially those with left wing views, he believed the police were little more than fascist scum. As a teenager, he had fought with the communist resistance, ELAS, in the war and followed that up with the communist led Democratic Army in the Civil War. The resistance fighters of Italy, France, Holland, and Denmark were treated as heroes after the war. In Greece, he never failed to protest, they were shot down like dogs and left on their doorsteps to crawl in their own blood. Meanwhile, the men against whom they had risen in defense of Greek honour were dressed up after the war in new uniforms and could be heard singing the royalist anthem, 'The Eagle's Son', as they roamed the dark cities, rank with sweat and terror, looking for reds and their sympathizers.

"I am your father and you will listen to me," the old man cried out one day after a particularly turbulent argument concerning Panos' plans. He was fairly quivering with rage. The old fighter was usually quiet, smoking his cigarette – the habit of a lifetime that would eventually kill him – head up, taking in the blue sky and the mountains north of the Gulf of Patras, lost in his thoughts. Panos had never seen his father in quite this state of agitation. As he spoke, the son listened but, in the background, in his father's voice he could hear other sounds, the thunder of old wars, the cries and whispers of dying men, or worse, the screams of men and women mutilated in the dungeons of the white terror. He could hear the songs he'd heard as a child like the steady, weary *tragoudia* of resistance and redemption by Sotiria Bellou or the Cretan defiance of Nikos Xylouris. He knew in his heart this was the old man's last appeal to an indifferent universe, one in which the best of men and women were killed or silenced and the worst presented themselves before an uncaring God as smirking victors, vicious to the core.

Stavros told him that he would rather see his son blind and lame than wearing the detested uniform of fascist goons. Panos would see soon enough, his father said, that the national police were not what he thought they were, loyal defenders of order and justice, dedicated to the preservation of the peace and the enforcement of the laws. He would see that they were dogs, worse than dogs, the shock troops of the capitalist ruling class. If they defended anything, it was to keep the big families and all their hangers-on at the top of the social and political pyramid. No son of his was going to devote his life defending the indefensible. Let the bastards rot in hell, Stavros shouted, no longer speaking to his son but directing his bitterness towards a deaf heaven.

Panos tried to convince him that things had to change and the past must be allowed to fade away. He told his father something his high school literature teacher had taught him. She'd said that one of the great contributions of the ancient Greeks to civilization was not democracy necessarily, but the idea of impartiality, so that Homer, in the *Iliad*, a Mycenaean Greek was able to praise the heroism of the Trojan warriors in exactly the same terms as those he applied to the heroes on his own side. Impartiality and independence from politics and, particularly Panos insisted, independence from the buying and selling of favors, freedom from the system of influence-peddling and nepotism known as *rousfetia*. That must be the way of the future.

Stavros was too angry to listen.

"Do you know who brought honour and liberation to our land?" he roared. "Not the tax collectors and *gendarmes*, the bastards who served the Ottomans and the big landowners. It was the *kleftikoi*! D'you hear me, the *kleftikoi*! Understand? They were called bandits but they were our liberators. Do you understand? It was the so-called bandits, men of honour, who knew the difference between dignity and shame, they were the ones who civilized us."

"Yes, father," Panos began quietly, holding his ground, "but they were also the ones who uncivilized us."

"What do you mean, you little idiot?"

The old man surged forward, starting up out of his armchair as if he were going to confront his son, even smack his face. This was the way of the old Greece, the one in which fathers dominated their children by shouts and blows. But he fell back and stared, blinking. Panos had not moved. Neither flinching nor cowering, the son had been ready to accept the old man's assault. It never came. The old man had seen something in his son that stayed his hand.

It was Panos' directness of gaze, a wide-eyed gravity, innocent of malice. Stavros saw that the boy's eyes had a peculiar and special intensity, dark yet mild, steady like a *caïque* under sail in a strong wind. Courage and sympathy were there. This Stavros was wise enough to glimpse and to know that it was a rare thing. Had this been the previous century, the century of honour and courage, Panos' eyes might have drawn many men to his side and many women too. But this was a new century, a century of calculation, an undignified time that rewarded the canny, the astute, the people with interests to exploit and defend. His son would grow to be a man who would no doubt make demands on others, but they would be demands on their goodness, not their self-interest. It was all there in his eyes. The father saw it.

Eventually the storm in Stavros subsided and the old man lit another cigarette. Panos was shaken by the outburst but said nothing. As he turned to go, his father caught his arm gently and told him that he would not say another word, but if Panos loved his father and his family, he would find another line of work, something honest, something clean. The old man's eyes were glistening with tears. Then he let his son go. He smoothed his black moustache and put the cigarette to his lips. Head back, he exhaled the grey smoke, and sought comfort in the sky's blue detachment. As he walked away, Akritas realized that his father was not actually living in the present, he was back there in the year war crushed his country, 1941. The arrival of the Germans – their tanks rolling down Panepistemiou towards Omonia Square – was the moment from which he would never escape. Anger and humiliation chained him to that year and the occupation years that followed. The Civil War doubled and tripled his anger and humiliation when he found himself on the losing side against the home-grown fascists, their bourgeois allies, and their American and British paymasters. Every year after that did not really exist. Yes, time passed, but for him, whether it was 1954, 1988, or 2016, it was always 1941. Endlessly.

Panos had stopped explaining to his friends and relatives why he was a detective in the detested *Elliniki Astynomia*. He saw how difficult it was to change centuries of custom, habits of thought, and the deep-seated distrust of authority. He had believed in something else for his country. After twenty years he found that he could no longer believe. For the next five years he disbelieved. Greece would never change. The old habits of mind and custom were like a strange iron cage. You always found your way in, but when you looked for a way out, you could never find the door. The day you realized there was no door was a dark, bleak day. How did you ever get in? What was left? Belief, disbelief, and now a new feeling that he couldn't name. He wondered to himself what remains when even disbelief has gone? There was no answer to that question, but, strangely, he was surprised to feel completely free for the first time in his life.

/3/

If you wanted to find the old women with money stashed in the fridge you had to go to the church. Where else? On the other hand, maybe men were easier targets. Women would never volunteer anything about their finances, but, men, men, Greek men especially, could they possibly sit there and not boast about the rewards of their hard work or good fortune, even if they'd not done or had either.

   He walked over to the window of the squad room and looked down at the traffic on Alexandras Avenue. For a moment his mind went blank as he watched the noisy, disjointed cavalcade below jerking along east and west. He realized how much he loved Athens, the noise, the chattering voices, the sun, the crowds, the lumbering articulated buses, the women, and the city's perfume on a hot day, a heady mixture of cigarette smoke, diesel fumes, and Chanel No. 5. To the left a distant flank of Mount Hymettos rose and fell between the buildings. To the right and a block down, he could see the green walls of the Panathanaikos football stadium across the street. Past the stadium walls decorated by hardcore fans with the team's three-leaf clover and the Gate 13 logo, a design crudely belligerent and contorted, he could just make out the range of hills, the Oros Egaleo, to the west. Hit men were fond of disposing their corpses among the stunted trees and rocky ridges, if they didn't feel like driving all the way to Parnitha, the mountain of choice for more discerning killers.

Gate 13 was the entrance at the west end of the stadium where all the most ardent 'greens' sat and chanted, waved flags and set off fireworks and flares. When he was in the squad room on a Saturday night and Panathanaikos were playing, he would hear the rhythmic chanting and singing with the occasional gunshot of a firework in the distance. He sometimes envied the fans their sweaty community of throaty bawling. Akritas looked up at the blue sky and knew that he was not cut out to stand shoulder to shoulder with others and bellow nonsense at the top of his lungs.

He had grown up in a traditional community in Patras but when he signed up for the police he had, without meaning to, taken a step away from his beginnings. He could understand his father's coldness, but what surprised him was that his whole family, a brother, two sisters, several cousins, and a variety of aunts and uncles, all, without saying much, seemed to have cut him off a little as well. When he sensed the chill, he had tried to explain and cajole, they nodded and said they understood, but no one really wanted to listen. Only his mother still radiated the old warmth. He would visit the old home on Ladonos Street but he knew as he approached the house with the red tiles and the phoenix and fan palm trees that it was no longer his place. When she died he was pretty much left alone in Patras. Oh, people who knew him still greeted him and stood him coffee now and then, everyone seemed friendly, but he could feel their coldness and their distrust. Did they really think he was a fascist?

He was a good cop, in both senses – he was not corrupt, and he was effective in his job – and so he persisted in those years thinking that he was doing something constructive. He liked the idea that others saw him as a man of principle. But then maybe he liked it too much. Self-congratulation was dangerous. The glow of self-admiration made you forget your weaknesses and he had his fair share of those like other men. His first posting as a detective was in his hometown. Then after several successful investigations and convictions his superiors grew wary. Making difficulties for some of their business friends marked him out as not only a successful cop but a dangerous one to have around. The tipping point was reached when he nailed a wealthy friend of the Police Chief for dealing in contraband, bribery, and accessory to murder. Akritas had enough to convict him, but just as he was about to make the arrest, the Chief moved in, yanked the case out of his hands, gave it to another, more reliable, detective who promptly dropped the charges for 'lack of evidence'. Akritas was indignant, rendered speechless by the bare-assed audacity. He was composing his resignation letter when his partner, Yannis Panetsos, a thirty-year veteran, found him fuming at the keyboard, explained the facts of life, and eventually talked him out of it.

After that Akritas was a marked man. His superiors had him transferred to Athens where he fell in with the other detectives for a time. Unfortunately, he found most of his new colleagues unbearable company and so had, without choosing, chosen the path of solitude. He was always surprised when, years later, he remembered his youthful naïveté, wondering what being a police officer would be like. Now he had to agree with his father. Some of his colleagues were fascist scum. But some, like Xiloudes, were just plain thick, well-meaning but not very swift, not attuned to the strangeness of life and the fickleness of the ordinary gods who preside, just out of sight, over our affairs. Of course, many of the criminals were equally stupid and fell into easily discernible patterns of behaviour.

His favorite story was the one about two bank robbers from Nea Smyrni who managed to get past the airlock door system of a branch of Alpha Bank in Kaisariani, steal about €2000, and then immediately head back to their neighbourhood and start flashing their new found wealth around. It only took about two hours for someone to put in a call to the police and report the two losers who never had any money and were suddenly buying rounds of *tsipouro* and *raki* at the *kafenion* and giving the guy behind the bar a €50 tip.

He turned from the window and looked at the telephone. Then there was Katarina. They had been together for over two years. At thirty-three, she was still a part-time lecturer at the National and Kapodistrian University of Athens. The debt crisis had blocked all paths to advancement in many areas of life. Young people especially suffered. Many immigrated, most shuffled from one low paying job to another, or to no job at all, and lived on whatever their families could provide. The rest slept in the streets and begged. Katarina had hung on the fringes of academic life for almost ten years. She was lucky to have her family and enough part-time work at the university to manage.

She also did odd academic jobs for her former teachers at the University. They would toss her teaching and editing jobs now and then. She insisted on calling them her 'mentors', but for mentors they hadn't done a great deal for her in the mentoring department. She was intelligent, wrote beautifully, and was, he'd heard, an excellent teacher, but in wisdom about the ways of the world – and especially the ways of the academic world – she was as green as an unripe olive. In that respect her mentors had failed her badly. One of them, Dimitris Koutoulis, the celebrated media intellectual, and his wife, Lila, who was also something of an academic, especially relied on her services as both a badly paid research assistant and unpaid secretary. Friendly with the right government ministers, Koutoulis was never short of research cash, even as the debt crisis deepened. Half of it went to what he called research but the rest went for holiday travel and to re-decorating his two residences.

There were some perks to be had. Katarina was always invited as a summer houseguest to their beautiful villa on the island of

Aegina. There they entertained and were entertained in turn by a former Minister of Administrative Reform whose wife had inherited a beautiful villa from her industrialist father that had once belonged to Nikos Kazantzakis, the novelist. Katarina also attended the splendid, and frequent, dinner parties in their flat in Neo Psychiko, where she could hobnob with the cream of university society. Akritas never really fit in all this high-powered university milieu, but he did his best to please Katarina by pretending to be interested in the academic gossip and the asinine ideas many of these people had about how the world worked. Most often at these noisy dos he would end up sipping his drink, admiring again the night skyline of Athens from the Koutoulis' picture windows wondering what the hell he was doing there.

It looked like another fine autumn day. He glanced at his watch. About forty-five minutes more to wait before his appointment with the deputy prosecutor. He turned towards the window again. This was his favorite time of year, sunny and with a yielding breeze moving the trees and flags. He looked forward to the evenings. They were particularly beautiful in early October with the sky to the west washed in gold, rose and cream-coloured streaks running through the wispy clouds over the hills. A glass of Jameson's Black Barrel on a seaside terrace down in Kastella seemed like the ideal way of concluding another day at the office. He winced, knowing he needed to put in another call to Katarina. As he reached for the phone, he hesitated. This was their usual night out. She would want to go out to eat at her favorite taverna for a plate of their celebrated chicken and okra in a rosemary and thyme sauce. But first he had to decide whether that's what he wanted to do, and if he didn't, he had to come up with a good excuse or suggest a different place.

He wondered how long this relationship was going to last. Lately, it had been tough going. Her mind had accumulated its impressions of men from books and films. That's how her imagination and life had been shaped. These images were a little blurred and more or less unreal. Akritas presented a sharper focus. This sharpness of outline had captured her because he seemed more real than any man she'd known. For the hundredth time in the last month a thought formed itself in his mind: why was he still with her? It was like a tune stuck in his head, made out of the same three chords, repeated over and over. Why? Still? Her? Those three chords. He knew that if the chording changed, he would lose the thread and be gone. It was as if the two of them observed each other through a single telescope. She looked through the proper end and saw him up close; he through the other end and saw her further away. Was it because he was, at heart, a cold man, unable to open himself to another? Was it his job that had closed him up like a clamshell? Once during an argument she had castigated him for having lost his idealism.

"We are all optimists today, aren't we?" she had said.

"I am a pessimist," he snapped back. "But I'm new sort of pessimist, drunk on the squalor and idiocy of the world. The more I see it, the more I like it."

She hadn't spoken to him for three days after that.

He put his palm up to his forehead and rubbed for a few seconds, sighing. At least, the sex was good and for about three-quarters of the time she didn't seem to mind that he was a policeman. For the other quarter he had to put up with her often silly views about authority, politics, what was wrong and right about their country, and, of course, the warmed over social theories of her favorite thinkers, theories in which the police were more often than not villainous curs and the actual villainous curs pathetic trauma victims in need of therapy. You can't punish sick people, she'd say. And he'd say, yes you can darling, if they've committed the crime. And then he'd get the look. From that point on, their evening was done and she'd say she had to mark student papers and he'd make his way back to his little flat in Galatsi alone. Park the gray Skoda and, when settled in his banged up armchair, he'd reach for a book and the Jameson and pour himself a glassful of amber forgetfulness.

/4/

He was aware someone else had entered the large room where the detectives had their desks. He turned from the window and found Lieutenant Andreas Xiloudes standing behind one of the desks staring at him. His face was very dark, unshaven, dented. He was nonetheless oddly handsome, the way men from Xanthi are handsome. Square jaw, prominent forehead, and black eyes that have a way of scouring and scurrying over the floor as if looking for something small and lost. But he had big ears and his handsome head looked a little lopsided like a jug with prominent handles. It was an unfinished look and the office wit, a surly, bad-tempered detective with small angry eyes, would sit back in his chair whenever Xiloudis entered and everyone in the room would smile to themselves remembering what he'd once said about the hapless man, "when God made Andreas, he forgot to finish the job."

Costas was the first to stir. He looked up from his newspaper and greeted the new arrival. Then it was Akritas' turn.

"Andrea," he said, "how are you?"

"Good, good," Xiloudes nodded, as he sat down at his desk and started opening and closing the drawers. "I'm good. What's up with you?"

"Not much."

"Have a case going?"

"Yeah, I've got a mugging that went wrong. The victim fought back and got himself killed."

"Drugs?" Xiloudes asked, slamming a drawer shut.

"Yeah, I've got the guy in remand, but the deputy prosecutor wants to see me before we go to court."

"You're lucky, Pano," he said, violently slamming another drawer shut. "I've got these old guy murders busting my balls and all I'm doing is waiting for the next one to drop in my lap or for the guy to mess up and give me a break."

"You looking for something in the desk?"

"There was a weird looking drawing left at one crime scene but I can't remember where I put it."

"A drawing?" Akritas asked.

"A drawing's been found at each place."

"Really? What kind of drawing?"

"Hard to describe. You know just a drawing."

"Whadya think it means?"

"Probably nothing. Guy's just tagging his work. You know, like the graffiti boys."

" You mean he's leaving a signature?"

"Something like that." Xiloudes finished shuffling some papers and opened another drawer. Odd, Akritas thought, thieves don't usually tag the scene. They grab what they can and get out. Drawings? Sounds premeditated. He was about to mention this, but stopped himself. He could see that Xiloudis was flustered and not in any mood to listen.

Akritas wondered why the brass had given him the assignment. Catching serial pickpockets and protecting tourists from the rip-off artists in Monastiraki was his usual beat. He had only recently been transferred to homicide by the boss. It was a feature of Boutsekes' management style that he seemed to favour mediocrity. His appointments to the homicide unit had one particularly disagreeable trait: they all seemed mildly concussed when speaking. As for their thinking, it had the monotonous character of a one-way street. Surrounded by ingeniously constructed human-like automatons, Boutsekes must feel less vulnerable in the bureaucracy rat race, Akritas had concluded. Not one of these guys was ever going to go after his job.

"Last time we talked," Akritas began, "you thought it was robbery. Still think that?"

Before Xiloudes had a chance to answer, Costas looked up and said:

"Hey, Andrea, that's one of Pano's questions about your murders."

"What question?" Xiloudes said looking at Akritas.

"Are you sure theft is the motive? Are there any other possibilities? Like a serial killer?"

"Nah, I'm pretty sure it's not a maniac. The victims were all well off, wealthy-like. Not a serial killer type pattern."

"Uhmm, maybe you're right," Akritas said, waggling his head back and forth in the time honoured manner of the halfheartedly convinced. "You're sure then?"

"Well, what else have I got? The latest guy lives, uhh, lived, in a pretty nice place in Plaka and you know what a place there costs, once it's renovated, at least a quarter mil. He had pretty expensive shit around the house. Nice furniture, expensive clothes, the big plasma TV alone must have cost €1000, ceramics everywhere, lots of art on the wall, that kind of stuff. All of them been in their eighties except for the last guy. He was ninety-one. The youngest was eighty-four. Easy targets, I guess. Six in all."

Xiloudes was damn good with numbers, Akritas thought. It occurred to him as the other man finished speaking that the absence of women victims may not be so odd, but what was odd was the fact that the victims were all about the same age. If it were robbery, a 65- or 75-year-old would have been as just vulnerable and in some ways an easier target. After all, a 75-year-old probably can still get around on his own, whereas many people in their 80s and 90s are apt to be rather sedentary and when they're out be accompanied by some kind of minder, like a relative. He didn't want to complicate Xiloudes's life any more than it already was, so kept quiet.

"You getting any help?" Akritas asked.

"Nah, not really. They've given me a couple of uniforms to check around with neighbours, that sort of thing, but no investigators."

That was damn odd, Akritas thought. Six murders and only one guy assigned. He'd never heard of that happening before. Was there a manpower shortage?

"And you know what uniforms are like," Xiloudes continued, "more interested in making sure their uniforms are looking good and talking to floozies."

"What about Boutsekes, isn't he pushing you?"

"None of the brass is taking much interest in some old dead geezers."

"But aren't there relatives who want to know what happened to these guys?"

Costas looked up and nodded his head. He put down the newspaper and listened.

"Now," Xiloudes brightened a little, "that's the one very interesting thing about it. The relatives I've talked to, sons and grandsons mainly, seem not to want to know why or who. Just when are we going to release the body and will they have to answer any more questions. I don't understand why. Most people would want to know, don't you think?"

By the time he reached the end of his little speech the light had gone out once again.

"Yeah, that is odd," Akritas said. "Why don't you ask Boutsekes for another investigator? I know that Niko hasn't got anything right now."

"Why?" Xiloudes snapped, sounding surly, his eyes going from bleak to burning and back again in an instant. "I can handle it."

"Maybe more pressure on the relatives might shake them up," Akritas said, trying to sound conciliatory. "What about all those cases where family members kill their relatives and then try to pretend it was a break-in and robbery gone wrong? As soon as you start asking questions, the fake evidence usually falls apart like the meat off a well-cooked leg of lamb."

Xiloudes looked at him and frowned.

"Yeah, but Pano," Xiloudes suddenly brightened up, "they come along one at a time not six in row like this. Maybe I should look into it a little more though. I'll ask Boutsekes for more hands on deck."

Akritas decided to stop troubling him with awkward questions for now. "Well, I'm off Andrea, good luck with it. See you, Costa."

"You seeing Katarina today?" Xiloudes asked.

"Yes, we'll probably go somewhere for a bite later tonight."

Akritas looked at him. He'd kind of suspected for a while that Andreas paid a little too much interest to his relationship. Whenever she was around, he would talk to her, and stare at her breasts the whole time. The staring gave that game away. But he said nothing. Closing the door behind him, Akritas decided to walk and began the eight-floor descent to the ground, one chipped marble stair at a time.

/5/

A blue and white articulated bus lumbered by with its load of office workers, students, and migrants headed west on Alexandras Avenue. The bus was surrounded by a swarm of yellow cabs darting here and there like demented hornets, weaving in and out of the traffic as the bus made its patient way, unmoved by the buzzing activity. Akritas walked in the opposite direction towards Panormou Street, turned the first corner and disappeared down into the underground parking garage beneath the massive police headquarters. The grey Skoda bumped up the ramp and out into the traffic heading west. Damn, he thought, I should have called Katarina again before I left the office. But he sensed somewhere behind the conscious thought, the subconscious dodge.

He drove west along Alexandras passing in front of the police building. The next block, and directly across from the football stadium, he spotted the small marble slab erected by the Communist Party to commemorate the fighters who died in the opening battle of the Civil War – 'Honor and Glory to the Heroic Fighters of the KKE and EAM-ELAS who fought in December 1944 against the Bourgeois Class and British Imperialism'. Akritas always felt a pain in his heart as he drove by. He never failed to remember his father whenever he passed this melancholy, yet dignified, reminder of smashed hopes and lost illusions.

Behind the slab, the ghastly ochre faces of the *prosfygika* turned their baked façades to the blazing sun. The eight apartment blocks, erected in the 1930s to house refugees from Asia Minor, had been allowed to deteriorate to the point of no return. Listed for their supposed architectural interest, they were never demolished even though they had become uninhabitable. Not fully alive but not allowed to die, they existed in a state of comatose decay, stretching for several hundred meters up the hill derelict and empty or occupied by gypsies and other squatters. When he first arrived in Athens to work he was shocked to see this decrepit monument to civic folly still standing, looking like a broken down, old beggar baring his toothless gums at a pitiless sun.

One evening, when investigating a mugging, he found himself walking among the long, gaunt shadows cast by the buildings. He had come upon a confrontation between a snarling feral cat and the biggest rat he'd ever seen, and he'd already seen his fair share running around the Patras waterfront. It was a fight to the death. The cat triumphed in a few seconds of furious aggression. The rat's back was soon a splodge of brown fur and blood. The attack was so vicious, it exposed the rodent's white backbone. The filthy white and orange cat, well-satisfied with himself, flung one nasty look at Akritas, flicked his tail in the air, then sat quietly beside the mangled corpse and began cleaning himself languidly with his long, red tongue. Akritas could not drive past these buildings without always remembering this little scene of carnage and triumph, bloody brutality and self-satisfied repose. It summed up something about the world for which he could never quite find the words. Or, perhaps, he could, but refused to speak out loud that which he knew.

He turned right on Killirou Loukareas, coming up beside the modernistic, vaguely neo-classical façade that encases the Athens

Court of Appeal and Prosecutor's Office in all the columned, marmoreal splendor that the state thinks conveys to its citizens a pleasing sum of gravity and dread. The usual line of yellow taxis lined the sidewalk by the entrance and drivers lounged around smoking cigarettes while fiddling with their phones. Three or four were involved in an animated conversation with plenty of finger jabbing, snorts of disbelief, and those slight head tosses that tell the speaker he is a complete fool to believe the bullshit he's spouting. All in all it was a friendly talk, an Athens scene repeated a thousand times a day in a thousand places across a talkative city. Akritas turned into the parking area for officials, showed his warrant card and the machine gun toting guard waved him in.

Entering the cavernous lobby, he walked past small groups of citizens clustered around their well-dressed lawyers who were patiently explaining to them the legal niceties of their cases. The clients were holding sheaves of letters, forms, and other documents all decorated with signatures, stamps of all colours and kinds, some inked, signed, confirmed and reconfirmed with emblems of the Greek state in bright colours, but mainly blue. Akritas had always wondered why his country's bureaucracy was so addicted to forms being stamped, re-stamped, signed, co-signed, confirmed by further stamps, reconfirmed again, stamped again, and otherwise disfigured by repeated assessments of their authenticity. He knew in the back of his mind that no functionary actually believed what he was being shown by the wretched applicant. Unless the document had been stamped, signed several times, countersigned by the section chief, and had one more stamp affixed and franked, the prevailing bureaucratic belief was that the applicant was trying to get away with something. Every citizen was a potential swindler, cheat, or imposter and every bureaucrat a forensic examiner with a pencil thin moustache and narrowed eyes. In the end, the thick layer of official stamps, signatures, and what-not absolved individual bureaucrats of any responsibility whatsoever should the case go sideways. That was the point. All those pretty blue stamps, franked, unfranked, signed and countersigned told you all you needed to know about what the Greek state thought of its citizens.

If you were visiting from Mars you would have to say, going by the looks on people's faces in the great hall, that most of them were either being informed of the death of kinsmen or that the court had decided that they were to be shot at dawn. In the seconds it took Akritas to walk through the shadowed entrance lobby, the unfortunate listeners seemed to move from crestfallen to totally gutted to suicidal in quick stages. He recognized the effects that the Greek legal system visited on its victims. The simple grimace gave way to a short excursion in barely controllable rage before it settled finally in gloom and apathetic despair. The saddest thing about this whole scene was the fastidious, but still hopeful, care with which the defeated supplicants folded up their documents and forms slipped them cautiously into the jacket pockets of their baggy brown suits and walked away. Ah, he thought, everything is working as usual – Kafka would have been impressed. He reminded himself not to let irony drift slowly into unredeemable sarcasm. That way madness lay. Well, if not madness, then immigration to a different civic culture. Some orderly place like Copenhagen. But would he be able to learn Danish before retirement age? And no doubt Katarina would want to come with him.

For a reason he always wanted to forget, Katarina admired the Danes above all other foreigners. This agitated him, this love and admiration for the Danes. He knew why it upset him so much. Its name was Eleni Konstantinou and she was the cause. It was whenever Denmark or the Danes came up that he remembered her, the first great love of his life, Eleni Konstantinou, and the disappointment of losing her to another man never failed to flood his mind again like watching a spreading stain of blood soak a man's shirt after he was shot. Was this the source of his uncertainty about women?

He met Eleni when they were students at Athens University. After their first coffee, they were inseparable. They were happy together for many months. Of course there were the usual ups and downs of a relationship, but they were always genuinely glad to see each other. His desire to become a policeman troubled her because she shared the common opinion, especially among young people, that the police were hopelessly right wing and that anyone who wanted to be a policeman was either a fascist or mentally unstable. The subject disappeared from their conversations in the interests of harmony. They made love, they talked, read poems, talked some more, and found themselves discovering the pleasures of sex through trial and error, sometimes embarrassing, other times comical. Then Eleni was encouraged by one of her professors to enter an essay she'd written into a European Union competition for young writers. She did. She won and the whole thing went to her head.

To receive the prize she was invited to Copenhagen for the award ceremony. It was an all expenses paid two weeks in the Danish capital. She was thrown into a milieu of writers, intellectuals, and artists. It was the first time she had been celebrated so lavishly for her intellectual work. She was twenty that year and in Copenhagen she met a Danish writer with whom she felt an immediate affinity. He was sixty. A distinguished bearing, an impeccable record as a political activist (he counted Vaclav Havel in Prague as a friend), and a long career as a noted writer and intellectual ended up turning the young woman's head. He courted her and she responded. She didn't cheat on Panos but when she returned it was very clear to him that her mind was trained on Copenhagen rather than Athens. Of course, she told him about everything that happened, even her interest in the Dane. Things began to unravel and when Panos learned that the lordly

Dane was to make a visit to Athens to see Eleni, he got angry, then morose, finally coming to rest in despair. He didn't want to say it out loud but he knew, he sensed, that it was all over. A new world beckoned her and he, the aspiring cop, wasn't up to her change of status.

The periods when they were apart grew longer and longer. The Dane arrived, stayed for a week, a week when Panos neither saw nor heard from her. It was hell. The Dane left and still he heard nothing from her. It was all over. He kept his feelings to himself. The ache stayed with him for a very long time and he found it difficult to open himself to other women. The fear of rejection had never entirely left him. To forget Eleni he studied hard, graduated, and began to take the practical steps for entry into police work. Eleni was gone, but the other thing, the little tremors of anxiety, never left.

As these thoughts were circulating quietly through his brain, he noticed Greg Martinson sitting on a bench, elbows on knees, holding a sheaf of stamped and franked papers before him looking as if he was about to burst into tears.

"Hey, Greg, what're you doing here? You look terrible. Did Haris Alexiou just get run over by a bus?"

His friend looked up and drew his lips in a straight line, his face taking on a pained grimace. Greg's blue eyes had that doleful, but strangely blank look that Akritas always associated with the crusader knight in Bergman's *Seventh Seal*. They said silently, OK buddy, joking aside, this is a bad day, if my favourite singer has died as well, I'm in a worse mess.

Akritas had known him for almost fifteen years. Their paths had crossed when the Englishman was interviewed by detectives in a case involving the murder of a rich industrialist. Greg had been the man's English tutor and was one of the last people to see him alive. Since then, he had become Akritas' closest friend in Athens.

Martinson was paunchy, in clothes that embraced an accidentally fashionable slovenliness. Middle-age grunge rocker minus the drugs and minus thoughts of self-destruction. He did play the electric guitar, but as an artist he was stuck back somewhere in the fag-end of the Spencer Davis Group era. He didn't always play in key but had learned how to orbit near enough to a key to keep the song airborne. His most exciting moment in music occurred when a guitar string he was changing snapped and almost took out one of his eyes. At fifty-one, he had been in Greece for twenty-five years teaching English in language schools, to private students, and to his various Greek girlfriends.

He had followed a sultry, studious Greek girl he'd met while they were both studying at the university in Birmingham, his hometown. They had arrived in Athens and immediately been immersed in her enormous circle of garrulous female and male friends and, of course, her watchful, skeptical family. Gradually at first, and then quite suddenly, she underwent a personality change that astonished him. The reserved young professional woman who was studying business administration in the UK reverted to her Greek self, outgoing and somewhat loud. She spent more and more time drinking coffee and gossiping with her friends than with Greg. As summer came on, she wore fewer and fewer clothes.

Then one July day, he saw her going out the door to meet one of her friends, a smirking, curly-haired, unshaven young man on a motorbike. Her midriff was bared from her navel to just below the lower curvature of her breasts. As she mounted the back of the bike, her nipples firmly planted in the guy's back, he realized his mistake in following her to Greece. He packed up and moved out. Broke, he found work teaching and promptly fell in love with the country. He stayed and made a very good life for himself on the Mediterranean. After twenty years, he met Katia Kallergi, a speechwriter and public relations professional in Athens. They were still together after five years. It was Greg's longest relationship, and hers.

"Why the long face?" Akritas asked as Greg rose to meet him.

"My goddamn lawyer just told me I owe her another €500 because she has to take my case to a different court that I didn't even know existed."

"Not *another* fucking court," Akritas sighed.

"She says the government created it last Wednesday and now everyone who has a problem with one of the ministries has to make an appeal at this new place. On top of that, there's a six-month delay so they can set it up."

"Why am I not surprised?"

"Of course, she wants the money now. I'm not even sure she's not lying to me or just has no clue what's going on."

"Isn't she Katia's friend?"

"Yeah, so it can't be a scam. Can it? My god Pano, when will this end?"

"When you die Greg, when you die. Ever thought of plying your trade in some place like Denmark?"

"Don't joke with me. They all speak English in Copenhagen already."

Then he laughed and put his hands on Akritas' shoulders.

"It's nice to see you, bro. What are you doing here? Come to arrest the Interior Minister? I just saw him go into the Chief Prosecutor's office." Ever since spending six weeks in America last summer, Greg had picked up a few expressions and Akritas was too good a friend to spoil his pleasure in sounding like a cartoon American.

"If only. Nah, I'm here to talk to a deputy prosecutor, Argyro Kanellopoulou, about a case she's taking to court."

"She's drop-dead stunning, man, she went into her office about fifteen minutes ago."

"I arrested the slimeball we're prosecuting and now she's wondering if we've got enough evidence. She wants to go over the whole case."

"Ever thought she's making a play for you, you balding but still handsome sonofagun?"

Akritas looked at his friend and snorted.

"Hey, Greg, look at me, I'm old enough to be her father."

"That never stopped you in the past. Remember that 20-something you were with before you met Katarina?"

"Eleftheria," he said thoughtfully, "that was different. She was young in years but she seemed older than Katarina. Eleftheria was not naïve, she wasn't watched over by her family twenty-four hours a day. She may have been twenty but she was older than the rocks she sat among."

"Pano, old man, you are something else. When the hell did you read Walter Pater?"

"Never mind, I'll tell you another time. I have to go now, I'm already late for the appointment and the gorgeous Argyro can't be kept waiting, can she?"

"Adios. Hey, wait, what are you are doing tonight, or should I say what are you and Katarina doing tonight. Want to go to Nikitas for something to eat? I'm meeting Katia at 7. We could meet at 8:30, 9, 10 whenever."

"Sounds good. I'll call you after I've had a chance to talk to Katarina."

And with that he walked over to the door of Argyro Kanellopolou and knocked. He heard a muffled voice on the other side of the door say something like come in. She stood up as he entered. She wore a black dress of some kind of satiny material, very much pinched in around the waist. A loose gold-coloured chain outlined her hips. White lace trim defined the black V down to her breasts, revealing just enough cleavage to make a point and no more. A neck choker of intertwined white and black lace fondled her throat and her masses of black hair were held up by two crossed ebony hair sticks. Her lips were a precisely applied crimson. She had a pen in her hand and she waved it at Akritas to sit down. She never took her elegantly mascara-ed eyes from his face. He shook hands with her and sat down in front of her desk. He'd always wondered how old she was, maybe about thirty-five was his guess.

"Nice to see you again, Pano."

"Nice to see you too."

"I asked you to come here under false pretences. I don't really want to talk about the case I mentioned over the phone. I want to ask your opinion about something with the police that's bothering me."

"What's that?" he asked.

She was looking at him intently as if she were sizing him up, for what exactly, he couldn't tell. When she spoke he could just make out the tip of her tongue now and then between her very white teeth. The sun coming through the tall window behind her lit up her hair as if it were a nimbus of black light. Was she beautiful or not beautiful, he thought? Maybe with her professionally applied make-up she looked a touch vulgar like the presenters on the private TV channels. He wondered what she would look like in the morning before applying the mask. What was behind the steady gaze? And why did he feel unrest coming from her, rather than what she could so easily pull off with her good looks, her irresistible glamour? Perhaps it was the way she fingered the pen. He felt compelled to look at her.

"Have you been following the serial killings of old men over the last month?"

This again, he thought, taken off guard.

"Not really, but I did hear about the latest one this morning. I even had a chat with Xiloudes about them."

"Good. I'm glad you know Xiloudes. I'm concerned about his investigation. It seems to be going nowhere and the brass down the road aren't pressing him hard enough to get some results."

"Xiloudes has a theory that the motive is robbery," Akritas said. "The old men are easy pickings. I don't know the case that well, but it's a theory."

"Listen Pano, there are rumblings about these killings and Xiloudes seems to be deliberately ignoring them."

"Deliberate? I don't think so. He's not the kind of guy who picks up on anything that isn't solidly based on material evidence."

She laughed and her whole bearing softened. She leaned forward smiling and lowered her voice a tone.

"Well put, Pano, you mean he's a bit stupid."

"I wouldn't say stupid, methodical, cautious . . ."

"Stupid," she insisted, smiling.

He looked at her and wondered what her game was. He'd cooperated with her before on cases in the courts and at police headquarters, but not like this. Her usual professional briskness had disappeared. For the first time, she was coming across as a woman rather than a slick lawyer.

"I'll tell you what I think," she said, straightening up and becoming serious again, "he's been put on the case to make sure the truth never gets out."

"What? Are you sure?"

"Yes, I am."

"Why? What do you know? And why am I here?"

"You're here because I'd like you to look into the case for me. Confidentially, of course. I know you want to know why. Why is this important enough for me to get involved?"

"And why is it?"

"The rumblings are not just in legal circles. The politicians seem more concerned than usual about what, *prima facie*, looks like a simple criminal case.

"You don't think it's just a criminal matter?" he asked.

"Something's going on behind the scenes and I'd like to know what it is," she said.

"You must have other investigators you've used before. I don't see why you've picked me out."

She got up and walked in her black pumps round to where Akritas was sitting. Her calves were sheathed in black nylon. She leaned back and rested against the teak desk, the silky fabric of her black dress taut across her hips. She looked down at him; some stray hairs fell across her cheeks. She's taller than I remember, he thought, looking up, but then maybe I've never been this close to her. He was close enough now to breathe in traces of her Voyages d'Hermès scent.

"I've seen a lot of cops come through this office, Pano, but you're the only one I feel will tell me the truth, no games, no punches pulled, just the plain and honest truth as you know it."

She paused and looked down at him. He couldn't read her face. There was an intention there. It could have been sly mockery, or something like seriousness.

"You know you have a reputation around here, don't you? . . . and also down at headquarters. If you've got something nasty to hide, don't tell Akritas. He'll make life difficult."

"Me? Reputation? You can't be serious."

"Look, I'll be dead honest, I'm with PASOK and there are political implications about this case which trouble me and the party."

"Why don't the politicians use a private investigator instead of a serving policeman?" he said, hoping she hadn't heard the pinch of irony as he said the word politicians.

"Impossible," she replied briskly. "We need someone inside but who is an independent mind. And that, my dear Pano is you."

The hint of sarcasm when she mentioned his name was unmistakable. Yes, he thought, she'd heard it.

"OK, but do I have a choice? Can I just say thanks for the vote of confidence, but I've got a couple of hoodlums to catch. Can I get up right now and walk?"

"Of course, but you haven't heard everything I have to tell you."

"Okay, go ahead, I'm listenting."

She then proceeded to tell him about the men who'd been murdered. The story dated back to the latter days of the German occupation and to the Civil War that followed it. All six, as teenagers and young men, had been members of Security Battalions, Nazi sympathizers, recruited and organized into fighting units by the Germans and their Greek collaborators. They had been active in detaining, torturing, and killing ELAS men and women who fell into their hands. As well as whatever Jews, gypsies, and homosexuals they came across.

So, thought Akritas, that's why the men were all about the same age. While his father was fighting to liberate Greece these men were securing the nation for the Germans. But he remembered his father saying that men like these were also preparing the ground for the postwar where they would be in control.

"In the Civil War they were actors in the White Terror," she said.

"You mean they served the Papandreou government?"

"Of course," she replied. "When Papandreou arrived in Athens in October 1944 from Cairo with the support of the British, Archontas and his men performed the same services against the Democratic Army of the left that they'd performed for the Nazis. They were feared and loathed by just about everyone in Greece, not just the communists."

"Wouldn't they have been decommissioned after the Civil War?" he asked.

"From active military service yes, but they were installed in various government offices as a reward for services rendered. They did no real work except keep an eye on the rest of the functionaries making sure none of them were serious leftists or communists. Their colleagues learned to keep clear of them and the few who didn't and who expressed any leftist or even liberal sympathies were dismissed, or in three cases murdered outright, although the medical examiners reported them as suicides.

"Were they there in the 1960s during the Colonel's regime?"

"Yes, they were. During the dictatorship they plied their miserable trade again and more men and women were broken in the prison islands of the Aegean like the one at Makronisos."

Argyro Kanellopoulou walked around her office growing more agitated as she spoke. Akritas could see there was more to this than a prosecutor just doing her job. At times she seemed distraught and even looked for a moment as if she might just break down and cry. But she didn't. Like a great tragic queen, she was going to get through this with dignity intact, without letting mawkishness have its way with her.

"Listen, Ms Kanellopoulou . . ."

"Argyro, please."

"OK, Argyro, why are you so interested in this? You seem to be taking it personally."

"It is personal, Pano," she said, picking up the pencil again and walking to the window where the sun lit up her face as her voice trembled with emotion. "According to the testimony of other prisoners, my grandfather was tortured on Makronisos and, when barely alive, taken up in a helicopter and dropped into the Aegean."

"Was his body ever found?"

"No," she whispered and turned to look out the window. She moved her arm and Akritas thought she was wiping away a tear. "It must have been weighed down with heavy stones. His remains are somewhere at the bottom of the sea. And his brother, my great uncle, was also tortured and spent the rest of his life in a wheelchair."

"Are you saying that the man responsible for both of these crimes is Archontas, the one they found this morning?"

She turned and looked at him. Her face had all the drama wrung out of it. It was hard, clear, and garishly white. She was very still, her body stiff with what was either dignity or anger or both. The sunlight brought out faint gold hues in her black dress. She looked down and nodded her head. She moved around to the front of the desk and looked down at Akritas.

"I see," he said quietly looking up into her face.

"My family comes from Agia Triada in Evrytania. I don't know how familiar you are with that area."

He shook his head.

"It's west of Lamia. During the occupation it was a main stronghold of resistance against the Germans. ELAS operated in central Greece under the leadership of the EAM delegate in the village. You can imagine how often the Nazis, the Security Battalions, and then the Greek army and the paramilitary *Chites* campaigned up there during the Civil War."

"What happened when the left was defeated in the Civil War?"

"My grandfather and his brother were arrested, interrogated, and tortured."

She looked at Akritas for a moment, turned and put the pen down on the desk. She picked up some papers, looked through them slowly. Then turned and faced him again. He could see the tears and the smudging of her mascara. Her voice seemed to stand on tiptoes like a child to speak.

"Excuse me, Pano."

"Take your time."

She walked slowly around her desk, found some tissues in a drawer and fixed her eyes, using a small cosmetic mirror. She looked at him again.

"Yes, it's personal. All six so far are connected by this history and I want to know who's killing them and why."

There was a long silence. For a moment, her voice was a distant sound in his head.

"Pano?" she prompted.

"Sorry. My father was ELAS too but in the Peloponnesus."

"Well, then. Listen, will you think about what I've said? What is it today, Tuesday? Call me at this number on Friday and let me know what you think."

She handed him a slip of paper with a mobile number.

"And listen," she said in a voice that sounded conspiratorial and pleading both at the same time, "please don't tell anyone we've had this talk."

He stood up. They shook hands again and he walked out of her office.

/6/

Greg was still in the lobby staring at his papers.

"You still here?" Akritas said approaching his friend. "You waiting for the lawyer?"

"Nah, she came and went. I just don't know what to do now. Last week I picked up some more work and I need it. The crisis has really cut into my money. But if I teach without this new certificate from the ministry, they could fine me."

"Greg, Greg, my friend, don't worry about that, just do your thing. If they haven't set up the office yet, do you really think that they'll be looking for violators any time soon?"

"You sure?"

"You've been here long enough to know how things work. Or don't work. Come with me, I'll drive you to wherever you want to go."

"Thanks. How was the magnificent Argyro?"

"She's taller than I thought," he said as they walked out into the parking area.

"You straightened out the case with her?"

"Oh, yeah, no problem. She's ok with the evidence now."

Back on Alexandras Avenue driving west towards the junction with Patission, they drove without speaking for a few minutes and then Greg began a long story about one of his students who'd been studying English with him for a year and yet still couldn't say more than a few words. The man lived in Nea Filadelphia and that's where Akritas was driving him. He was an electrical engineer with some British firm and he said he needed to learn English to advance his career. In the end Greg thought he was just lonely and wanted to have someone, anyone, come by for a visit. Greg's company cost him €40 once a week.

"Cheaper than getting married, I guess," Greg shrugged, "but sort of pathetic."

After dropping him off, Akritas made his way back to the office and the first thing he wanted to do was call Katarina. She answered after four rings.

"Hi, sweetheart," she sang out when she recognized his voice. She was in a merry mood.

"Why are you so happy?" he asked.

"Dimitri appointed me to teach one of his courses next term and he's given me a free hand choosing what to teach. He doesn't have time to teach because he wants to work on his new book."

"Good, good," he said without too much enthusiasm in his voice, hoping that she hadn't noticed. He wondered whether the new book was going to be as flat and uninspired as the last one.

"Are you busy, dear?" she asked.

"Yes, I am," he exclaimed a little too quickly, "I was just calling about tonight. Greg and Katia want to go to Nikitas for something to eat after 7 some time. Do you want to go with them?"

"Yes, that'd be nice, but can we make it around after 8:30?"

"Yeah, I'm sure that'll be fine. I'll call Greg. I'll pick you up around 8:30 then."

"OK," she answered, "I love you."

She hung up before he could return the endearment. He looked at the handset for a moment and then replaced it in its cradle.

The detectives' room was empty. He sat at his desk, leaned back in his chair, and stared at the cracks in the ceiling for a few minutes. It was a disorderly network of lines like the canals of Mars examined through a telescope. Traces of ten thousand cigarettes smoked in the room teased his nostrils. He replayed the scene with the prosecutor. Could he trust her? Could he trust anyone with lips that shade of red? Was there more here than the bare outlines of the story she told him? And what about his so-called 'honesty'? His so-called reputation for telling the truth? Sounded too much like flattery, or a trap. Was it meant to reassure the rabbit before getting him ready for dinner? She was obviously headed for bigger things in the system and particularly in politics. She was a comer all right. Not very many voters would be able to resist those red lips. Or the way the black lace choker made you notice her white throat. At least she was a helluva lot more interesting than the thin fuck and the fat fuck who were running the country nowadays. So, how did these murders fit into her battle plan for advancement? There was no doubt she was damned ambitious. It was there clinging to her skin like the scent of her perfume. He tried not to think of that damned choker round her neck. Getting up suddenly, he knew that he had to look for Xiloudes and ask him a few more questions. The problem for him now, if he were to join in the investigation, even informally, was that he hadn't had a look at the crime scenes. He hadn't had the chance to pick up all the clues, all the tiny ones, the ones that often gave the game away. Outside, the afternoon light was failing like the light in a dying man's eyes.

The phone started ringing. He looked at it wondering if he should pick it up. It rang four times and then he reached over and put it to his ear. It was the chief inspector, his boss, and he wanted to talk to him. Could he come to his office? Now.

What the fuck does he want, Akritas murmured to himself as he walked down the hall towards the office of Police Major Aris

Boutsekes. He had been promoted, against the wishes of the commander, Police General Solovos, during the last New Democracy government because he was reliable politically. He hated communists with a visceral disgust and that included SYRIZA and the mildly left-of-centre PASOK. It was rumoured he had comradely relations with the leadership gang of the neo-fascist Golden Dawn party. But he was too crafty a political animal to queer his larger ambitions by letting those connections sully his good name. His good name was, as he never failed to say, more important to him than a pile of gold. Whenever he heard this from his boss's lips, Akritas would imagine not gold but a hot pile of steaming shit.

Absolutely uninterested in police work, Boutsekes saw his position as a platform for further self-promotion and self-enrichment. It was rumoured that he had extorted money from some politicians and their families because of the dirt his detectives had dug up about them. These 'donations' to the 'policemen's benefit society' – he was the only policeman who ever benefited – were promptly laundered through third parties and then used to buy and sell properties all over Greece. The word in the squad room was that he had 58 such properties, one more than the Prime Minister, the thin fuck. He also had, it was said, a pile of money in a numbered account in a Swiss bank.

Boutsekes was a tallish man, about Akritas' height, but running to stout. Not superficially vulgar, in spite of his love of gold, he had perfected a kind of charming old world façade via his contacts with the old money families settled in Kifissia and Paleo Psychiko. He declined to consort with 'the rich filth', as he called them, in the *nouveau* suburbs of Ekali and Rea. His patrician manners and personal style had by the age of sixty been completely absorbed into his body as a second nature and his first personality, the tough kid from the wrong side of Pireos Street, thoroughly submerged, indeed, violently drowned in a bucket of ice cold water. His face never betrayed the faintest smile, nor was there any trace of self-consciousness or anxiety in his bearing given his origins. It was as if the old self had simply ceased to exist. He was extensively bald with a fringe of iron-grey hair resting on his ears. He had only one feature that one might call vulgar, his puffy, wet hands. The calm exterior was disarming. What was going on inside was anybody's guess. It was not possible for a man to be freer from unintended grimaces and accidental wrigglings. Also it was perhaps not possible for a breathing man wide-awake to look less animated. His bearing inclined to languor and indifference. But it was dangerous not to take him seriously and it was doubly dangerous to believe that he was actually indifferent. He was all eyes, like a spider. You cannot understand such a man from externals alone, because he is well hidden from view. You may recognize the alphabet, but you are not sure of the language.

As Akritas entered the outer office and said hello to the Chief's secretary, he hoped that he wouldn't have to shake the man's hand. Could he resist the urge to dry his palm on his jacket?

"Sit down Akritas," the Chief said indicating a chair by his desk.

Boutsekes leaned back in his own chair and with elbows on the armrests, brought his fingertips together, and then slowly let his forefingers fall to his lips. Akritas was not one of the detectives he'd appointed. His predecessor as chief had tried to enliven the culture of the homicide squad by bringing in officers who had something on the ball. Akritas and Costas were both earlier arrivals. Boutsekes preferred officers disposed to a certain uniform sluggishness. It's as if his men had all eaten of some root that compelled their brains to the same narrow monotony of thought and action.

"What can I do for you, Chief?"

"We'll have to see what you can do for me in a moment, but first I want to ask you whether you've been kept abreast with developments in the murders that Xiloudes is working on?"

What's this, Akritas thought, an hour ago I was playing footsie with the deputy prosecutor about the case and now this.

"I just had a talk this morning with Andreas. So, I don't know anything much, just the fact that six old men have died and they found the last one this morning in Plaka. That's about it."

"I see," Boutsekes said, "do you have any opinion about how the investigation is going? Xiloudes seems to think the motive is robbery. Do you agree?"

"I can't really disagree as I know very little about it."

"You're an experienced officer, you must have some idea."

"Not having examined the crime scenes, not knowing any of the physical evidence, and not knowing anything about the victims, I'd say I'm completely out of it as far as the investigation is concerned."

Boutsekes looked at Akritas with a slightly exploring gaze, but without changing expression. There was a pause and then he spoke.

"What if I told you that Xiloudes doesn't really know what he's got a hold of in this case?"

Where have I heard that before, Akritas thought.

"Like what?"

"What if I told you all these men were connected in some way, knew each other from a very long time ago, would that change the current theory?"

"Well, it would open up new possibilities, wouldn't it?"

"What one thing about the case, as you know it so far, sounds strange to you?" Boutsekes asked.

"One thing?"

"Yes."

"Why are the six victims all so close in age and on top of that why are they so old? I mean men in their eighties and nineties? Why no-one in their seventies?"

"Good, good. Excellent point," Boutsekes said. "Go on."

"They are just as vulnerable as targets for robbery as a ninety-year-old."

"Let me get to the point, Panos, how would you like to switch cases with Xiloudes? He'll take whatever you've got and you can take the lead in the old men case?" He leaned further back in his chair and seemed to be kissing his forefingers.

How bizarre, Akritas thought, first Kanellopoulou and now Boutsekes. And he called me by my first name for the first time ever. He answered carefully, watchfully.

"Well, yes, it would be fine with me. It sounds a lot more interesting than what I'm working on at the moment. But won't Andreas be put out by the switch?"

"It's none of his concern and he'll do what he's told."

"But he'll ask me why you chose me. In fact, why are you doing this? Andreas is a perfectly good cop."

"I'm doing it because I think you have more experience with complex cases. And I think, like you, that there's more here than meets the eye and I'm not sure Xiloudes will be able to see it."

"OK then, who breaks it to him? You or me?"

"He's coming in to see me in half an hour. I'll tell him then and he'll bring all his notes and whatever else he's got. He'll brief you and then you'll brief him on what you've got on tap and that will be that."

Except for the jealousy and bad feelings and resentment, Akritas thought. Boutsekes was making motions of dismissal by shuffling papers on his desk and turning to the laptop by his side.

"I'll see you later," he said.

Akritas got up and was out the door before any outstretched hand could be offered.

He was puzzled. I wonder, he thought, why they swung into action today with the sixth murder. Maybe there was something special about the sixth man that rang bells all over Athens. If they all served together in a Security Battalion maybe the sixth man – what was his name? – served as leader and the others just foot soldiers. The first thing he would have to do was dive into the police and public archives and see what he could find. He would also have to go to the newspaper archive in the National Library. This sixth man, as the catalyst, may have made it into the newspapers of the day. He'd need Katarina's help at the Library. She knew everyone there and she loved being in the position of opening doors normally closed to *hoi polloi*. The latent busybody in her would be in its glory for a day. He smiled, imagining her moving surely among the wooden desks and the Ionic columns in the main reading room, absorbed in her work and unconsciously raising her arms to fix her hair. That lovely bit of her just where her upper arm and shoulder descended to the upper slope of her breast would be taut and exposed.

Back at his desk, he took some time checking the Internet to see if Archontas' name popped up in the pages devoted to the occupation, the December days of 1944, the Civil War, the prison islands, and the aftermath. He re-familiarized himself with the history, but all it gave him was context. Nothing on the dead man. Then at about 6 PM, Andreas Xiloudes appeared at the door looking as if he'd been run over by a tram. White, stooped, and thoroughly beaten, he slumped down and looked over at Akritas. He tried to say something but his brain and mouth seemed clogged up. He stuttered thickly.

"Have . . . have you . . . beh . . . been told ?"

"Sorry Andrea, I was just informed an hour or so ago. I'm sorry."

"It isn't . . . you," he said, pulling himself together. "Anyway, I . . . just resigned. I'm heading home to Xanthi. I've . . . I've had enough of this bullshit."

"What? You've quit?"

"It's not for me," he said more steadily. "Never was and never will be. Big mistake to take off the uniform. Big mistake. Never really took to the job."

"But you're a good cop," Akritas insisted.

"I'm 51 and was only waiting for my pension. If I'd hung around another four years, I would have got more, but I've had it."

'You're still young. What'll you do?"

"Don't know." He hesitated and then went on in a rush. "I'll pick up some security work back home. I'm going to live with my mother. She needs me around the house now that my father's gone."

"Are you sure you've done the right thing?"

"Yeah, I'm sure. I should have probably done it a long time ago. Boutsekes told me to brief you on the case. Do you want to do it now or wait until tomorrow? I'll be around for the next couple of weeks while they do my paperwork."

"What would you prefer?"

"Tomorrow. Early, say 9?"

"OK, and, Andrea, I'm very sorry."

Xiloudes shrugged, picked up his coat, and walked straight out. He had been Boutsekes' man. The boss lost interest in him and, just like that, Xiloudes was gone, crushed. Akritas sat there staring at the door, then picked up a pencil lying on his desk and threw it hard against the wall. The mark it left was soon lost among its many weary companions, like when a suspect plunges into a crowd and vanishes, but is still there, somewhere, unseen, or like when grey-eyed Athena becomes a swallow and is lost to sight, but is up there on a branch watching. He remembered he had to call Greg. They arranged to meet at the restaurant at 9. He needed to go home, shower, and change clothes before picking up Katarina. As he left the building, lost in his own thoughts, he didn't see the red Honda motorcycle across the street start up as he headed into the underground parking for the grey Skoda.

/7/

He arrived at Katarina's just after eight. Some minutes before she came to the door, he could hear her talking on the phone. When the door opened, she still had the phone in her hand. It was clear she wasn't ready. She gave him her harassed-and-I'm-doing-my-best look. She disappeared into her study and he looked around the spacious, but cluttered, front room. A large dining table and eight chairs dominated one side by the windows. A sitting area with two couches, both uncomfortable, one not-so-easy chair, and another antique wooden armchair that was Katarina's pride and joy took up the central space. Books covered two walls. There was a fireplace and an antique chest of drawers under an opening in the wall that looked into the small kitchen. Her voice came from the study down the hall. Outside the flat he could hear two or three dogs barking. A motorcycle drove by and then stopped just up the street. It was almost completely dark outside. He closed the wooden shutters and pulled the curtains.

She'd asked him on a number of occasions whether he wanted to move in with her. Several times he almost said yes, but in the end thought better of it. He loved her in his own way, but there was something smothering about her that stayed his hand. Her very traditional family lived upstairs in the upper flats. Her mother and father were fine people but their only concern seemed to be Katarina's marital prospects. What she really needed, they told each other and all their friends, was a husband, not just another live-in man like the dentist, who had insinuated himself into the first-floor flat and stayed for five years before Katarina plucked up enough courage to get him out.

Her younger sister, Anna-Maria, also lived in one of the flats. She had worked in her father's business ever since leaving the technical college she'd attended in Thessaloniki ten years earlier. When the father, Theo, retired she would inherit the home furnishing business. Anna-Maria was considered by everyone to be spectacularly beautiful. And no doubt about it she was a tall, olive-skinned, dark-eyed beauty, with a model's figure, and long black hair that fell down her shapely back like the thickly combed mane of an Arabian thoroughbred. But for all that, there was something a little affected about her. Maybe it was her voice, a bit too high-pitched, a bit too forced and sounding as if she were auditioning for a part in a show. She seemed to think playful ingenuousness made her sound cute and witty. It was neither, just grating. When walking, she moved as if she were always being looked at or at least expected it. Not unintelligent herself, she hung out with idiots as far as Akritas could tell. Expensive male hairdressers with names like Matty and Rudolph, good-looking but dim bartenders in Kolonaki, and the kind of suntanned dolts who spent all summer on the beaches of Vouliagmeni with no visible means of support except for the fact that they drove Porsches and wore Dolce and Gabbana sunglasses. But perhaps he was being a little harsh. She had, over the years working in the family business, become something of a shrewd businesswoman. She didn't let her tougher side reveal itself too much in her personal life. You mistook her penchant for playboys as weakness. It was protective colouring, almost as if she needed their flashy nonsense as a way of concealing her steel.

Several dogs barked out their raucous farewells as a motorcycle outside roared into life and was off down the street. Akritas looked at his watch. It was 8:15. He sent a text to Greg telling him they'd probably be there after nine. For the hundredth time he looked at her books. Most he didn't know but a few he recognized from when he was studying history at university. He wondered what a so-called 'life of the mind' would have been like. He sometimes liked to flatter himself thinking he might have been able to make a creditable contribution to the study of Greek history, but he had no real sense of what it would mean to always be involved with ideas, the presentation of those ideas, and the debates and discussions that would follow. Was there any pleasure or sense of having done something significant in all that? He didn't know. But then again wasn't all life a life of the mind even for those who the world thinks are mindless. Katarina's 'life of the mind' was a kind of privileged sanctuary where thoughts circulated like fluffy clouds in a blue sky. His life of the mind was so down to earth he could never quite get all the dirt off – bodies and their various oozings, DNA samples, fingerprints, traumatized victims, scatter-brained witnesses, decomposing corpses among fragrant pine trees on Pendeli, the smell of oregano mixed with human sweat. This for him constituted thinking, or at least what is called thinking for a policeman.

What she called thinking amounted to a kind of sensuous pensiveness and that comprised half her life. The other half was her body. That too had a mind of its own and its own superb sensuousness. Perhaps the body was a better organ for thinking than the brain. The body's mind – the hidden treasure – he knew and understood. It had come with the years, the years of looking at bodies, the all too solid flesh of the living, the dead, the sullied, the bruised, and the decomposed. Abstractions and concepts stir the brain only. It only needs those skeletal, ghostly things. The genius of the body defies them. He thought of the Nike, or Victory, of

Samothrace that one of his professors, Yorgos Koukougiannis, had once thrilled an entire lecture hall by describing. He had said its glory was the body of the Nike, not the thought of victory in the abstract, but her body under the folds of her gown that made our loins feel their own heat, our feet know swiftness, very much like when we read the *Odysssey*, and are launched out on the sea so that our bodies know the swell of the wave and our hair and scalp the salt wind.

Katarina was an intellectual. Yet her body at the age of thirty-three was fully alive and ripe, fully the greatness of an adult woman coming to glory. She emerged from her bedroom and held out her arms to him. She was so beautiful that at that moment he would have done anything for her, anything. And then the little inner voice crackled into life in his head, the little voice that always checked the flight of feeling, 'even live with her'? They kissed each other's lips and held each other for a long moment.

When they first met he was attracted to her instantly. Something in her voice made him take notice. It was a normal voice, a contralto, but there was something more there to which he'd never been able to put a name. He heard it most clearly when they were talking on the phone. Nothing hard or strident, simply a tone of voice that communicated heart-revealing intimacy. That sometimes she spoke nonsense about politics or society or, worse still, homeopathy, to which she was devoted, did not erase the glad kindness of the voice, nor cancel the inner courtesy that was its source. He was also struck by her hands. On the small side, they had a delicacy that would have suggested an artistic temperament for some, but he saw only tenderness. He remembered the first time they sat talking wanting to take them into his own hands and feel their softness. In a phrase, her whole bearing seemed quietly gentle, yet she was not some small, slim, repressed woman. Black hair framed her face with its long-lashed eyes and sensuous lips. Her nose with its little upward curve suggested a certain touch of mischievousness that never actually came to light as mischief. It was not in her temperament. Her skin had tha light olive colouring of southern women. It was warm and when they first went out all he wanted to do was caress her, her arms, her shoulders, in fact, her whole body. Also there was something assertive about her, something clear and unhindered, but not crude in any way. Unlike her sister, she did not see herself through others' eyes. She did not have the look of someone who knew she was being watched whenever she moved her body. She had a wonderful way of extending her hands and tilting her head questioningly when she talked. Her intelligence absorbed her smile. Her eyes and mouth took pleasure, now and then, in a touch of irony, but it never coarsened into mockery or contempt. Her dominant character-trait, however, was sympathy and, as a result, she was, to a degree, naïve.

In the car, she was chatting about her new course at the university when Akritas noticed a red Honda motorcycle start up and fall in behind them some 25 meters back. He wasn't suspicious at first. It was just a beautiful looking machine. About five blocks down Veikou Street he noticed it was still there, the same distance behind them, but thought nothing of it. Veikou is a major through street. It is one way of getting into the centre. When he finally turned on Patission after winding through the streets of Galatsi, he saw the flash of red in his rear view mirror and knew that the Honda was following them. He wondered if when they stopped he should take his service pistol from the glove compartment, just in case. Should he tell Katarina what was happening? No. It would just spoil the evening and her happiness. He kept his eye on the helmeted motorcyclist behind them. The faceless rider was no longer one more headlight among the flash and glitter of cars, neon shop fronts, and the yellowish glow of the sodium street lamps in his rear view mirror.

"Are you listening to me, Pano?" she asked.

"Yes I am, darling, but the traffic is bad tonight and I'm a little distracted."

She put her hand on his neck and caressed him.

"You pay attention to the road and don't worry about me. Let's get there safely. I wonder if Katia bought those shoes she told me about yesterday."

As he was parking the car on the pavement-vendor end of Ermou Street, he noticed that the red motorcycle was nowhere to be seen. The last time he'd spotted it was as they were coming down Athinas after Omonia. He helped her out and, hoping that she wouldn't see it, slipped the Heckler and Koch pistol in his belt at the back. As they walked arm in arm into Psirri, he started getting very tense and alert. It was dark and the recesses and shadows were worrying. Katarina picked up on it right away.

"Try to relax darling, it'll be a very nice evening, you'll see."

"You're right, it's just I had a tough time at work and it's made me edgy. I'll be fine." He could feel the hard metallic object digging into his spine.

When they spotted Greg and Katia at the restaurant, Akritas relaxed a bit because the narrow road was well lit. Nikitas' outdoor terrace abutted a church and there were only two approaches. Akritas looked up and down the road wondering whether the motorcyclist was somewhere in the shadows watching them. Nikitas was crowded and Christos and Anna, the brother and sister who owned it, hurried back and forth among the tables.

Katarina and Akritas apologized for being late, with Katarina taking all the blame. Her sister had called her about some love affair she was having with a Greek-American who'd been in Athens for a few months but now wanted to go back to the States, to live in 'a less chaotic society'. Anna-Maria was both heartbroken that she wouldn't see him and pissed off at the man's attitude towards Greece. And when Anna-Maria was in turmoil about men, it was Katarina who had to hear the whole story.

"Yeah, well the man's right, this is a chaotic society," Katia volunteered, pushing a few stray hairs behind her left ear.

Katia was a woman blessed with lustrous, shoulder-length brown hair and cursed by a childhood from hell. Her father was a lawyer without an ethical bone in his body and an alcoholic, her mother an out-and-out bully. That Katia turned out as well as she did all but defeats the theory that our domestic circumstances form us into the adults we become. She was self-possessed, intelligent, and loyal. She did have a body-image problem and as a result always wore loose-fitting clothes that effectively hid her body. Her shoes had just enough heel to put her at eye-level with most men. In a crowd she would probably pass unnoticed, but in a room where business was being transacted she always held her own. She had a reputation of being something of a cynic and to some extent she was, but there was another side, more idealistic and caring. Katarina and Katia had been friends for about fifteen years having met when they both worked on a left-wing newspaper. Although their careers had taken different paths they remained the best of friends and their passion for social justice had never left them.

After the white wine, *tsipouro*, beer, and a dozen *mezedes* had arrived, Katia and Katarina fell into a hushed conversation about a mutual friend who had just split up with her husband. Greg looked at Akritas, rolled his eyes, and raised his glass.

"Here's to chaos," he said with a wry smile on his face.

"To chaos, and may it have a long and happy life in Greece" Akritas saluted and took a long drink of his *tsipouro*. He knew that what foreigners and, he supposed, some diasporic Greeks, took to be chaos in the life of his country was no such thing. It only seemed chaotic if you didn't understand it. When you took the plunge and compelled yourself to open your eyes in its blue depths, Greek life was as orderly as any other and more so than most. It was just more complex and involved than the superficial orderliness of, say, Britain or America, places where the surface calm obscured the dark anarchy of its depths. The group at the next table saw them raising their glasses and joined in the toast in comradely fashion.

"Shall we tell them what we're toasting?" Greg whispered.

"Excuse me," Katia said looking up suddenly, "what are you two talking about?"

"Chaos," Greg said mock solemnly.

"Some call it chaos, I just call it Monday," she retorted with a straight face. "Hey, I just had a thought about Anna-Maria's guy. When Greg and I were in America it seemed pretty damn chaotic as well. Remember all the homeless people in San Francisco, Greg, and how hopeless their lives seemed. And all those fucking rich people stepping over their bodies like they were bags of garbage. And then everyone armed to the teeth. What do you call that if not chaos?"

"I'm not sure that's chaos," Greg interjected. "It's more like a civil war, then again it just might be craziness."

"At least the craziness here is disarmed," Katia said. "What do you think, Pano? You deal with the chaos here…"

"To be honest when I was in Baltimore years ago, I was astonished that the criminals and drug dealers were often better armed than the cops. It seemed like that part of America – I mean the war between the cops and bad guys – had reached a state of perpetual armed struggle, not exactly what Trotsky had in mind, but lethal and senseless just the same. The whole place seemed schizophrenic to me . . ."

"You and me both, mate," Greg interjected.

". . . – a well-regulated, calm surface," Akritas continued, "and permanent warfare underneath. We Greeks are probably schizophrenic in some other way and Anna-Maria's guy never got the hang of our two faces."

"You mean our four or five faces," Greg said. "Our chaos is a little more complicated than most people's."

Katia laughed and put her hand on his arm. "You're right, each culture has its own kind of chaos. Or maybe it's all on a continuum. Like the British and Germans are chaotic in their own way at one end of the scale and the Italians and us are at the other end." She laughed again and then took a sip of her white wine. "You know," she continued, more thoughtfully, "one of the things I learned being in America was not about America as such but something about Greece. I hadn't realized how Americans always want to improve things – themselves, their society, their beer."

"Especially the beer," Greg murmured.

"We Greeks don't need improvement. For the simple reason we think ourselves perfect already. We might be totally miserable, like we are now because of the crisis, but our vanity has always been stronger than our misery."

Her three companions looked at her more intently. There was something in her voice that compelled their attention, something approaching vehemence.

"You know why we're pissed off with the Germans these days? Sure they want us to change, to reform our economy, and worse they want us to atone, to suffer for our profligacy. Hell, aren't they mainly Protestants? What do those Americans say, Greg, . . ."

"No pain, no gain," he answered.

"Precisely, but here this means not only changing a few economic policies, it means reforming our whole culture, our character, our everyday understanding of who we are. And it means each of us changing one at a time. And you know what pisses us off the most about these demands?"

She paused to let the question form more fully. Then she spoke.

"It upsets our illusion of being perfect. This is the source of the chaos here. The sense of superiority we feel dazzles our eyes. Do any of us ever really change, or think that we ought to change for the better. No, not at all. But we don't call it what it is, we call it

69

pride, and are bloody well satisfied, but, you know, you know in reality, it's just plain old blindness."

And with that she stopped and seemed to be trembling. For a moment, she seemed close to tears. Thinking about Greece these days inevitably brought up the general disaster – debt, unemployment, foreign loans, migrants, the whole gamut of humiliation and despair that hung over the country like a bad hangover. Katia picked up the glass of wine and brought it slowly to her lips. She set it down without drinking. Akritas recognized the somber mood. If the Greek mind were a weather map, the forecast would be 'continuous overcast with occasional short, sunny periods for the foreseeable future'. They sat in silence for a moment.

"How can outsiders understand us?" Katarina asked. "Every time they arrive here with their plans and demands, they think all we need to do is change our minds. What you're saying, Katia, is they want us to change our souls."

"Something like that."

"I'm not sure that will ever happen," Katarina said gently, but with a note of determination in her voice.

Akritas looked at these two good women and wished that Dimitri, the celebrated media intellectual, were there to hear them. If he had any wit at all, or virtue, he'd lower his head abashed. For a few minutes, they ate in silence. All around them people were eating and talking. They were all Greeks after all and they were determined not to let the economic catastrophe facing the country get in the way of a good meal and genial talk. This was one of those short, sunny periods. Katarina was describing the course she would be teaching in the new year. Akritas listened but he was also keeping an eye out for whoever it was that had followed them. No-one suspicious was to be seen. He sipped his *tsipouro* and for the first time that day felt happy and content as the liquor warmed his throat.

"Katarina," Greg said during a pause in the conversation, "I've been meaning to ask you this ever since we met. Why did your father give your sister and you what sound like Italian names? Like, why aren't you called Ekaterini?"

"Oh, Greg, he adores Italy. Milan is where he learned about the home furnishing business. When we were kids he would always take us with him to Milan, the Lakes, and the Alps for holidays. Dad would leave us at the hotel or the lake and visit his business contacts in the city."

"Oh, so that's why so much of the stuff he's got in his shops comes from Italy," Greg said.

"Yes, thank goodness he didn't get into some German business because then he might have called Anna-Maria Brunnhilde and me Sieglinde or something even more potato dumpling-y."

Greg laughed. "Makes sense. Shall we have some more *mezedes*? Something sweet maybe?"

Akritas relaxed, but still kept one eye on the approaches to the tables. The conversation was convivial and friendly and when they were done Greg suggested they walk over to the Oscar Wilde Irish pub in Thissio for a nightcap. They paid, said goodnight to Christos and Anna and began to walk back towards Ermou Street. When they emerged from the narrow lanes of Psirri, the first thing that Akritas noticed was the red Honda parked a block away facing towards Metaxourgeio. He noted the license plate, repeating it several times in his head so that he'd remember. The motorcyclist was nowhere to be seen. Akritas looked back for a moment at the narrow street they'd come from. A dark figure moved without haste into the shadows of a graffiti-spattered colonnade. It was then he realized he was meant to see that he was being followed. Why would a tail who wanted to be invisible ride a powerful *red* motorcycle and allow himself to be seen so obviously following them? What was the message here? Did it have anything to do with the six dead men? Of course it must, he thought.

Greg led them across Ermou into Agiou Filippou Street, past the Thesis 7 jazz club where they could hear the burly, bearded Yiannis Nikoletopoulos belting out Greek songs to a crowded, smoky room. A right turn and half a block away, they could see the golden harp on the green awning of the Oscar Wilde Irish Pub.

/8/

Leaving Katarina's building early the next morning, he heard the mournful coo-coo-cooing of doves, a series of reverberations most people found comforting but which he always found ominous and unsettling. It wasn't really birdsong, was it? It was more like the sound a well-oiled machine might make if it had been tooled to emit soft, dove-like sounds. He looked up at the balcony of her first floor flat and imagined her sleeping peacefully in the bed they had just shared. He was glad he hadn't woken her as he dressed and helped himself to some breakfast. Out on the street, he headed for the Skoda. There was no sign of the red motorcycle. A tawny-coloured dog was sleeping on the pavement a few meters from his car. As Akritas approached, he raised his head, took a long look and then slowly returned to his slumbers. Bitter *nerantzakia* oranges lay on the ground beside the gate of the driveway. Katarina's father hadn't yet left for work. He looked to see if Anna-Maria's black Peugeot was parked on the street. It wasn't. She hadn't come home last night.

On the way to the center, he decided that after meeting with Xiloudes he would go to Plaka and take a look where Nassos Archontas died. First, he stopped at his small flat in Galatsi, showered, changed clothes, and then headed to Alexandras Avenue.

Xiloudes was already there and seemed in a hurry to get the briefing done. He had pulled himself together. Akritas was surprised how little information there was to hand over. Xiloudes' notes were so cryptic, even their author couldn't remember what some of them meant. Akritas remembered some of his own notes when he first became an investigator, totally undecipherable after an interval of time. There was very little physical evidence, no murder weapons, no signs of struggle, most of the DNA samples collected matched the victims. Some didn't, but the traces were inconclusive, or they could be dismissed as belonging to a relative, the cleaner, or a cook. The killer or killers had entered the apartments, done their worst, then disappeared without leaving anything – professionals, Akritas thought. Xiloudes was curt and offhand. It was clear he'd lost all interest in the case and Akritas did not lengthen the interview beyond the basics. The whole thing took about twenty minutes and when it was done Xiloudes grabbed his jacket from the coat rack and was gone without a word of farewell. He wasn't sure whether he'd ever see him again.

At the Archontas flat in Plaka, he saw that the bloodstained rug and floor tiles had not yet been cleaned and everything had been left more or less as it was when the body was discovered by the housekeeper the previous morning. Minus the body, of course. He looked at Xiloudes' notes and apart from the brief description of the scene there was nothing, except for a cryptic note that read, 'p bsde bdy, op hds'. Something beside the body? He shrugged and started looking around the flat. The window looking out over the street was partly open and he could feel a breeze coming in through the narrow gap. He could see a building across the narrow street and a shuttered window. The shutter opened slightly and then closed quickly with a bang. As he turned back to the room, he heard a man and woman walk by on the street talking noisily about money.

Archontas seemed to be a lover of ancient Greek art. Copies of ancient vases, *amphorae, kraters,* lovely white *lekythos* pieces, and a magnificent black *glaux skyphos* were arranged to be seen to good advantage in several rooms. Akritas was no expert but he could see that these traditional ceramic pieces were magnificent specimens of ancient art. There were other art works as well, some modern paintings, engravings of Athens in the nineteenth century when the city was making itself into one of the most elegant cities in Europe – before the post-war construction industry began to turn Athens into a viciously ugly concrete jungle while making a number of political families immensely wealthy. There was one splendid rendering in yellow and peach on cream-coloured paper of what in the early years of the new state was the royal palace, now the Greek parliament building in Syntagma. The architectural painting was large and expensive looking. Surely someone bent on theft would not have passed it up.

The man's bedroom had clearly not figured in the crime. It looked as if the victim had not gone to bed. The bed was made, his dressing gown was still hanging up on a hook behind the door, and his pajamas were neatly folded on a small armchair beside the double bed. Arrian's *History of the Anabasis of Alexander the Great* lay open face down on the bedside table. The former fascist torturer looked as if, in his old age, he were re-living the glory that was ancient Greece. Akritas was pretty sure the old bastard must have justified his crimes in the name of a magnificent Hellenism that the bestial communists and socialists were bent on betraying.

When would a 91-year-old man retire? Probably early. As there was no forced entry, the old man must have let his killer in. Or the killer had a key. The medical examiner would be able to estimate the time of death. He opened and closed the drawers in a white dresser. Neatly folded clothes brought to mind a fastidious, fussy man. Under some some socks, carefully rolled up as tight little cylinders, he noticed a white letter-sized, sealed envelope. Taking his handkerchief, he pulled the envelope out and turned it over several times. No address, no marks, nothing to indicate what was inside. He took out his small penknife and slowly slit it open. He found a half-dozen five hundred Euro notes, fifteen one hundred Euro notes and a folded letter-size receipt for the Dolder Grand Hotel in Zurich. "Banking," Akritas murmured to himself. Strange, he thought, why hadn't the killer found this? He seemed professional in every way but to overlook €4500 that was just sitting there under some socks suggested rank amateurism or maybe just bad luck.

Back in the front hall, he noticed that the entry phone for the building had a small screen and that perhaps, if it were a more recent machine, might even have a recording of the comings and goings. Taking out his handkerchief, he lifted the receiver. The screen lit up but was blank, so it looked as if the unit or the camera downstairs wasn't working. Or the killer had disabled the system.

Walking back into the sitting room with its chocolate brown leather sofas and armchairs, very tastefully arranged around an antique coffee table covered almost entirely with coasters, small gold-coloured squares in patterns on the surface, he stopped and got down on his knees. He looked under the coffee table, the side tables, the sofas and armchairs. The sofa nearest a fireplace built into one corner of the room looked as if it had been moved. Not much, but moved. It was a little askew from its alignment with the other, meticulously placed pieces of furniture. He looked at the sofa carefully, reached in behind the cushions, and felt down into the linings. On his hands and knees, he looked under the piece and saw something white on the floor just beyond his reach. He marked the position of the sofa, with a light pen mark, and pushed it back a little until he exposed the corner of a piece of paper. He pulled it out carefully, making sure not to tear it or spoil any fingerprints.

The paper was an A4 letter size sheet with a drawing on it and an inscription in ancient Greek.

The drawing in a fine point, black felt pen depicted what Akritas recognized as the shape of typical grave *stele*, the kind of headstone ancient Greeks used to mark the burial places of the dead. He remembered Professor Koukougiannis's lectures on Greek funerary and burial practices from ancient times to the present. The lectures had been lavishly illustrated with slides of grave monuments and the professor had seemed completely fascinated by the scenes carved in stone or marble. Usually these depicted the dead in touching moments of farewell with the living, usually parents or children, and occasionally even their dogs and cats. Akritas always remembered the point that his professor had made. The ancient Athenians had invented and discovered much in the way of politics, the arts, and science, but these grave *stele* showed also that they had, for the first time in the ancient world, understood and been able to depict in their art the concept of subjectivity, of the intersubjective intimacies between human beings, those fluid emotional ties between people, that are as essential to human existence as breathing.

The drawing that Akritas was holding in his hands was very different from anything he had seen before. It had the right shape but there were no figures under the shallow pediment at the top. He wondered if it was a rendering of an ancient *stele* at all or just a drawing made to look like one. But the inscription in three separate lines was in ancient Greek, ΖΩΣΙΜΗ / ΗΡΑΚΛΕΩΝΟΣ / ΑΠΑΜΙΤΙΣ. The first word, Zosime, was a woman's name, and the second word indicated she was the daughter of Herakleon, but the third word, Apamitis, meant nothing to him. Below the inscription, the open palms of two hands were rendered in low relief, filling a good half of the area.

Then he remembered Xiloudes' note, 'p bsde bdy, op hds' – yes, 'paper beside body, open hands' – so he had seen the sheet of paper. Did this mean that he found the sheet there on the floor beside the body? It must. But why was it under the sofa? He called the office and asked if anyone had Xiloudes' mobile number. Xiloudes confirmed that, yes, there was a sheet of paper on the floor beside the body when he arrived. Why it ended up under one of the sofas, he didn't have a clue. It was what he was looking for in his desk the day before. He volunteered that the slight misalignment of that particular sofa must have happened when the crime scene investigators were taking photographs and collecting samples. Someone must have bumped into it. There were quite a few people in the room and maybe that's how the paper got under the sofa as well. But before Akritas could ask if there had been similar sheets left with the other victims, Xiloudes hung up. Yeah, he murmured under his breath, your mother needs you in Xanthi, Andrea.

He looked around the apartment a little more and then decided he'd seen enough. In the Skoda downstairs he knew there were some evidence bags in the back seat. He carefully put the sheet of paper with the open hands into a large plastic envelope and laid it on the passenger seat. Then he slipped the envelope with the cash into a second evidence bag. As he drove back to Alexandras Avenue, he kept looking at the sheet beside him. There was something very peculiar about it that he couldn't quite put his finger on. What did it mean? Who could he ask? He thought of his old professor, but almost thirty years had passed since his student days and he wasn't even sure the old man was still alive. Certainly he'd be retired. He'd check with the university anyway. Maybe, if Koukougiannis was gone, there'd be someone else who could help.

On Patission, the traffic was heavy. It was the usual mix, cars, motorcycles, yellow taxis, buses, delivery vans, and adventurous pedestrians darting in and out among the moving vehicles. Akritas never understood where people got the confidence to believe that all those drivers either making phone calls or checking out the big-breasted redhead walking by were paying attention to the road.

He was inching past the graffiti adorned walls of the Technical University when a red light brought him to a full stop. As he looked down again at the drawing on the passenger seat he glimpsed a red flash, a motorcycle pulled up beside him. Glancing at the helmeted driver, he saw a brown leather jacket riding on the back. In that instant, the passenger drew a 9mm pistol. Akritas flew down onto the seat. The explosion was deafening. A cascade of shattered glass filled the Skoda. The red Honda roared off and Akritas got up in time to see it turn right after the National Archeological Museum and disappear into the warren of narrow streets that is Exarchia.

Akritas was not hit. The bullet had passed through both windows, hitting the side of a blue bus that was stopped beside him on the driver's side. "Fuck me," he said in a low voice, "that was close." He'd been fired at before but not at such close range. Through the ringing in his ears, he heard people shouting and someone nearby screaming.

He brushed bits of glass from his hair and clothes. All the traffic around him was immobilized. People came running over, shouting and waving their arms, as he got out of the car. He identified himself, and although he remembered the license plate of the bike from the previous night, he asked if anybody noticed the license plate on the motorcycle. No one had. Both windows in the Skoda were shot out and bits of glass were scattered all over the passenger seat and the envelope with the drawing. Within minutes he could hear police sirens approaching. Someone had called the emergency number. The young bus driver, who had one phone bud in his ear and the other dangling down to his knees, asked if he could carry on.

"Get everyone off the vehicle and leave it where it is," Akritas told him. "And pal, you shouldn't be driving with those things in your ears."

"OK, OK," the driver replied, still very much in shock.

Pandemonium reigned. A man ran by waving his arms in the air. An older woman chattered non-stop, then stopped, and sat down on the pavement. The sirens were getting louder. Two police motorcycles arrived first, blue lights flashing, with the usual uniformed officers riding in tandem on each machine. They began to untangle the enormous traffic jam clogging up the street. Then a police car with siren at full blast arrived. Two uniformed officers jumped out and dealt with the crowd of people standing around. Within minutes, more police cars arrived. One of the newly arrived officers asked Akritas if he was all right. Above the shrill wailing of sirens, car horns honking like angry geese, raised voices, the man had to shout to make himself heard.

"Yeah, yeah, fine," he yelled back. "Call in and tell them to notify all units to be on the lookout for a red Honda motorbike, license plate XPB931, with possibly two riders last seen heading east through Exarchia. But they could be going in any direction. They're armed and dangerous."

"Anything else, sir?"

"I need an arms specialist. There's a shell stuck in the side of that bus over there. There may also be a shell casing lying around on the road. Start looking for it, over there, on that side of my car."

He walked over to where bus riders and passersby were standing and watching. He asked if anyone had had a good look at the men on the motorcycle. Both men were helmeted, so no-one was able to give a description, although one well-dressed matron described the clothes they were wearing in some detail. When he asked her why she'd noticed how they were dressed, she replied that it was because of the brown leather jackets they were wearing. Her nephew wanted a leather jacket for his birthday and so she was in the habit of looking at them whenever someone was wearing one. He thanked her and went back to the car. It would need new windows. Damn, he thought, there's a week without the Skoda. The department would have to give him one of their crappy cars while the repairs were being done.

Then suddenly a TV crew arrived and started filming. He asked them to stop. They ignored him. He walked over and yanked the camera from the man's shoulders.

"I told you to stop, didn't I? You can have this thing back when we're done here."

He checked the 20 or 30 seconds of video they'd shot and deleted the file. He handed the camera to one of the uniforms and looked around for the TV guys. One of them was on his mobile, the other was holding the sound equipment and some other gear. He walked over and stopped in front of them.

"How did you know to come here?"

"None of your fucking business," the guy with the phone said.

"How did you know to come here?"

"Fuck off and give my man here his camera back."

Akritas could put up with a lot from civilians, but journalists were a special breed of pains-in-the-ass. His experience with them had never been good; he'd learned early on that the media organizations they worked for were never that interested in either facts or the truth. Seeing that the country's media owners were mainly businessmen-politicians who were only in the media business to promote their own commercial and political interests, most of their employees were spineless underlings doing their boss' bidding. And those who weren't lackeys were either crazy conspiracy theorists or had put their skills in the service of one ideology or another. In twenty-six years of police work, he'd only met three or four working journalists who treated their work as a calling, respected facts, and were clearly interested in getting at the truth of a story. He'd kept in touch with one of them, Philolaos

Manolakos, and the thought occurred that perhaps it was time to give him a call. Having an honest reporter alerted to what was going on might help. He worked for a conservative newspaper, but it was the most serious and reliable in the country. There were other honest journalists around, good investigators and reporters, but they were toiling on the margins, the alternative media, or writing unread blogs ever since the big money media companies had put honesty lower than bootlicking on their inventory of vital journalistic values.

Akritas called over two of the uniformed officers and told them to arrest the two guys, put them in handcuffs, and sit them in the back of the patrol car.

"You can't fucking do that . . .," the mouthy newsman began before he was hustled off and shoved into the patrol car. Akritas could hear him yelling from the back seat about getting a lawyer . . . . blah blah blah, Akritas thought.

"Keep the assholes there until I say they can come out," he told one of the young cops.

When the crime scene unit arrived, the traffic chaos had eased a little. The ballistics guy got to work on the bullet stuck in the bus. Another officer had found the casing and put it in a plastic baggie. Once all the evidence had been collected and statements taken, the bus was allowed to go. Akritas drove the Skoda to headquarters and parked on the street so that it could be picked up by the garage. At his desk upstairs on the eighth floor he stared at the drawing of the hands and decided to call Argyro Kanellopoulou.

"Pano," Argyro said, when he identified himself, "what is it?"

"Two things, Boutsekes has yanked Xiloudes off the case and put me in charge and someone just tried to kill me."

Silence on the other end of the line.

"Did you have anything to do with either of those events?"

"No. Are you all right?" She seemed concerned.

"I'm fine. What about Boutsekes? After I talked to you yesterday, he called me in and told me it was now my case. Why is that?"

"I don't know, Pano. But I told you that these murders have rattled a lot of people. What about the attempt on your life? What happened?"

He explained, telling her also about being followed the previous night while out with friends. And then he asked if there were anything else he should know about this case that she hadn't bothered to mention before. She was silent for a moment.

"Yes, there are a couple of more things. But I don't want to talk on the phone. I'm not sure how secure my office is either. Can we meet at the Dioskouroi café up the hill from Monastiraki near the back entrance of the Agora? Tomorrow?"

"What time?"

"Seven."

"See you there," he said and hung up. A couple of other things? Of course, there would be a couple of other things. There are always a couple of other things when someone tries to put a bullet through your head. He knew the café in question. It was probably a good place to talk because it was outdoors. You could sit right beside the fence of the Agora and only have to worry about an approach of 180 degrees rather than 360. And also the presence of tourists all over Plaka meant that assassins would be a little more circumspect. Local assassins don't want foreigners and their embassies involved. It makes everyone nervous.

Leaning back in his chair, he began to relax a little. Wound up like a metal spring, he let out his breath slowly, uncoiling. He realized that he felt as if he'd been holding his breath since seeing the flash of red and hearing the explosion. He was frigid and beginning to shiver. He knew it was shock, the effects having taken their time to arrive. Your nerves let you get on with the job first, before becoming icy splinters. His hands were shaking.

Looking down, he realized why so many of his colleagues smoked, or drank. He stood up and walked around the room. That usually calmed him down. Looking out the open window at the blue sky, he heard the doves collected on the cornice calmly cooing .

The door opened behind him and a handsome young man walked in. Fashionably unshaven, an expensive looking leather jacket cut high on the waist, designer jeans and sunglasses, he had police ID dangling from his neck on a lanyard. Akritas looked at him without speaking. The guy might have been thirty at a stretch, but more like twenty-five.

"*Geia sas*," he began, "Captain Akritas?"

Akritas nodded, walked back to his desk and sat down.

"My name is Anatolios Statiris, I've been assigned to assist you on the murder case. Call me Tolio."

"By whom?"

"Eh?"

"By whom have you been assigned?"

"The Chief, well not the Chief himself, his assistant."

"And who exactly is that?"

"Afroditi Zoulinaki."

"You mean the blonde who works downstairs? She's his assistant?" Akritas tried to mute the sarcasm.

"I guess so. She's the one who told me."

Akritas looked Statiris up and down and wondered why they'd assigned a guy like this to help him. What the fuck could he do with a playboy? Well, he'd have to put up with him until he could suss out if he was any good. Nothing ever happened that didn't have a back-story. And if you could front it with a pretty face, all the better.

"OK, Tolio is it?"

"Yes, it's Tolio."

"What do you know about the case?"

84

"Not much. The dead men, the theory that it's robbery, and no leads."

"OK, what do you make of this then?"

Akritas handed him the open hand drawing. He looked at it for a moment, knit his brows in an impersonation of thinking, shrugged his shoulders, and handed it back shaking his head. Katarina's sister, Anna-Maria, suddenly went through his mind. This guy reminded him of her hairdressers and the sun-tanned dolts from Vouliagmeni with no body hair. He'd need to keep a close eye on this particular Vouliagmeni-man.

"Listen Tolio, this is going to be a complicated investigation. There's lots here that needs looking into. I'm going to need a bigger team than just the two of us. I'll get in touch with Boutsekes about getting some others assigned. Xiloudes had some uniforms helping him. We'll keep them. Have you ever investigated a murder before?"

"No, I haven't, but I did the training course."

"Good. Now, what I'd like you to do today is get out all the files on the six killings and go through them. I'd like you to look specifically for things that repeat."

"You mean like patterns and similarities?"

"Yes, like did each victim have this drawing or any kind of drawing left at the scene? Stuff like that. Medical stuff too. Do you understand?"

"Yes, yes I do. I'll get on it right away. Uhmm. The files will be where exactly?"

Akritas looked up at him and was about to say why don't you look under Afroditi Zoulinaki's pillow.

"Where they're usually kept, down the hall in the active records room. I'd like to see you at about four this afternoon, here, with a report on what you find. I haven't seen these files myself. I was just assigned to the case yesterday, so I want a clear and detailed report from you including reading every word of each of the medical examiner's reports. Got it?"

"Yup, yup, anything else?"

"No, that's it for now."

As Tolio retreated towards the door, Akritas saw that he was wearing what looked like very expensive shoes, sleek, brown, Italian things, very fashionable and no doubt up in the €200 range. He wondered how this guy, in his twenties, and on a cop's meager wages, could afford to be so well-shod?

Was he a plant? Or just a dolt deliberately assigned to him as one more big stone to roll up the hill. Detective work often resembled the myth of Sisyphus. You roll a big stone of evidence up a hill thinking that if you push hard enough you'll get it to the top, only to find half way up that's it's the wrong stone. He'd seen a lot of big stones rolling back down the steep hill in his time.

As he sat looking at the open hands, he knew in the pit of his stomach that this was going to be a dangerous case. This had the makings of something very nasty, involving not only hit men on red motorcycles, those animals he could handle, but bigger personalities, political people maybe with friends everywhere including the upper reaches of the Hellenic Police. It was just after noon and he looked out of the window at the changing sky. White clouds with darkened undersides were drifting slowly from east to west. Winter was a ways off but it was definitely coming. He could feel it. Shuddering slightly, he remembered the searing flight of the bullet meant for his head and he realized how shocking that moment was and, suddenly, he felt ice cold again as if he were already a corpse.

He hadn't yet put in a report on the attempt on his life and hadn't made the compulsory appointment with a department psychologist for counseling. But first he needed to assemble a team. There was this Tolio and he thought he'd need at least one more experienced detective and two more uniforms. That would do for beginners. He'd have to see how the investigation was going before making any other personnel requests or changes.

One thing had emerged as he'd thought about the six killings. They were all spaced evenly in time. One every three or four days. Six killings in about four weeks. It didn't seem like a series of robberies to him. Not after that morning's event. Perhaps this was your standard-issue serial killer. If he stuck to his timetable then there were three or four days before he struck again. Akritas had that amount of time he reckoned to get a handle on what was happening if that were the case. But robbery and serial killings did not seem right. Why did Kanellopoulou and Boutsekes suddenly want to get involved? If these were political murders and Archontas was the one that caught the attention of the higher ups, then perhaps the assassin was done, assuming there were no others in line for liquidation. But he'd learned over the years that once a detective began penetrating a case, digging more deeply into it, the case would begin to change to take into account his presence, just like the scientific truism about the experiment changing because of the presence of the experimenter. Xiloudes had not got very far into the workings of the experiment and his steps were so predictable, the killer hadn't needed to adjust his methodology.

There was a delicate balance in police work that he'd rarely been able to get across to some of the younger officers who'd been assigned to him. His first partner and mentor in Patras, Yannis Panetsos, had made him aware of how fine that balance is between letting things show themselves as they are and barging in changing everything. Panetsos had never put it into words but Akritas had been able to get the gist by observation. He had the gift of putting it into words, but most of his colleagues did not have the gift of understanding what he was talking about. Which is why he liked working alone on most cases. This one was different. He needed to spread the work around, but also the risk. If he were alone he would be the single target. If there were more people involved, the increase in the number of targets created for each of them a greater degree of safety. Not only from hit men but from the people in the background who were pulling the strings. And he was convinced that there were string pullers somewhere in the vicinity. You could silence one policeman easily enough, but you couldn't silence five or more without attracting attention.

Later, he booked himself in to a counseling session with the psychologist, a very nice man named George, who was half Swiss and half Greek. George saw him right then and there. They talked for an hour but all that he took away was that the Swiss and Greek parts of George hadn't integrated very well. The man went back and forth between two personalities, one that marched briskly along like a shiny new Rolex and the other with a glum face, that had less edge, was more dolefully sad, and seemed about to burst into the wail of a tragic song. Akritas found it difficult to know which George he was addressing. He wished that the other psychologist, the black haired one with the high cheek bones, from Metsovo – Christini was her name – had been available. At least there was one and only one of her. Back at his desk, he was tapping out the report on the assassination attempt on his life when Tolio walked in looking a little more flustered than he'd been in the morning. Akritas looked at his watch and Tolio flushed. It was 4.47.

"Sorry, sir, I'm really sorry, there was more in these reports than I could finish by four. I'm sorry."

"OK, yeah fine, don't worry about it. What'd you find?"

"Each victim," he began by reading from his notes, "was killed early in the evening, between 6 and 8. In four out of six cases the victims were bound, their mouths taped shut, tortured by being cut with a sharp instrument like a razor blade. The thumbnails from the left hands of all of them had been pulled out, with pliers probably. A two-inch builder's nail was driven into the right eye of one, a

Nektarios Vekres, while he was still conscious. Tolio pulled out photocopies of the corpses. All had been brutally mutilated.

Akritas took a look, got up and walked over to the window. Tolio paused in his recitation. Akritas motioned him to go on.

"Each died from a knife wound. Throats were cut with a nine-inch blade and they were left to bleed to death, which seems to have come quickly, probably because of their age. In each case there was evidence of torture and the killer or killers stood around watching them die before leaving.

"Were there any signs of forced entry?"

"No. In each case it looks as if the killer or killers left the way they came. No fingerprints were found of anyone other than the victim and others like relatives and cleaners who have all been cleared. The victims all seemed to be very well off. Not wanting for anything.

"That's why Xiloudes thought it was robbery," Akritas said walking back to his desk and sitting down.

"But then why did the killers leave drawings?" Tolio asked.

"So there were more?"

"In each case, there was a drawing on A4 paper found either on the body or near the body. I made photocopies of the ones that came back to the office. One of them was misplaced and seems to have disappeared. So, with the one that you've got, here are four more." He placed them on the desk.

"What about interviews with relatives, neighbours, etc.?"

"Difficult to follow the notes in the files, but the investigating officer didn't seem to have much luck."

"Thanks, Tolio, that's good. Do you think I should go and take a look myself?"

"I don't know, sir, you might find something that I missed."

"Well, if I can find the time I'll take a look. But thanks, you've done a good job. Listen, Tolio, there's only two of us on this case right now, oh yeah, and two uniforms that were helping Andreas. I want one more detective and two more uniforms. I'm going ask Boutsekes to assign Costas Psarros. Do you know him?"

"I think I know the name but I'm not sure who he is."

"OK, listen, you can go now but tomorrow I'd like you to make a complete list of all the people who've been questioned about these murders because I want us to question them all again. Come by here at four with the list and we'll work out a timetable and discuss the kind of questions we're going to put. Got that?"

"Yes sir. See you at four tomorrow and I promise to be on time."

Akritas laughed and Tolio smiled back. Who knows maybe Vouliagmeni-man will work out, he thought, as the kid closed the door behind him. He picked up the phone to call Boutsekes. The Chief immediately agreed that Psarros would be assigned to the case. Akritas called his colleague and told him to be at the office at nine sharp in the morning.

It was 5.33PM. He wondered if anyone was in the archeology department at the University. He gave it a try and was put through to one of the senior archeologists who was still at his desk. After Akritas described the drawing, the man said it was certainly possible that it was an ancient *stele*. He could probably say a few things about it but Alritas should consult the real expert in Athens on these artifacts and the inscriptions on them, Dr. Polyxeni Zavvou at the Epigraphic Museum, attached to the big National Archeological Museum on Patisson. When she answered the phone and he told her what he wanted, she suggested he come over in an hour and she'd take a look.

/9/

As he waited, he looked at the four new drawings laid out before him. The first was an old man with a beard and hat and what appeared to be winged boots. Ah, Hermes, Akritas said to himself. In his left hand Hermes carried a scale, like one might use to weigh things. On each pan of the scale there were small male figures. One pan had sunk lower than the other and the little man on the lower pan looked as if he was about to fall off. There was an inscription but Akritas couldn't tell what it said. His ancient Greek was a bit rusty.

The second drawing depicted a bearded man with long hair, naked, and tied to a wheel. Ixion, he remembered from his schooldays, punished for . . . what was it? . . . desiring to screw Hera, the queen of Olympus? Her husband, Zeus was not pleased. Astonished at the effrontery and especially as he had favoured Ixion earlier by pardoning him for the murder of a relative, Zeus was not about to turn the other cheek. For desiring Hera there was no forgiveness and Ixion was tied to the turning wheel as punishment for eternity.

The third was a very odd thing. A naked man standing upright had his arms bound behind his back. But his head was turned 180 degrees to the back, so that it looked as if his head was on backwards. Strange. He'd never seen anything like it before. The fourth was also what looked like an ancient headstone with an inscription on the horizontal cornice of the pediment, ALKIUS PHOKEUS. It sounded like a man's name. The drawing was of a naked warrior with helmet, shield and spear advancing to the left but stepping on the shoulder of a dead man, a man he had just killed in battle, who was lying on the ground. Moving in his haste, the warrior had let his robe slip from his shoulders. It trailed over the corpse as he rushed forward.

The niggling thought he had had earlier suddenly came into focus. Drawings? Why would a thief with a nasty violent turn take the time to draw a picture? And not just anything. Some depictions of ancient classical subjects? Your run-of-the-mill thief might defecate on the carpet as a way of tagging his work. But carefully drawing funerary *stele*? Not bloody likely. What was the message? The deputy prosecutor said it was revenge. Looks as if she's right, he thought, but these drawings were a sophisticated twist that puzzled him.

Just then his phone buzzed. It was a text. Katarina wanted to know if he would come to her tonight. He looked at his watch. They'd shared some wonderful moments last night and he wanted to see her again. He texted her back. *Yes, I'll be there between 8 and 9. Is that OK?* He waited. In seconds, the phoned buzzed again. *Of course, darling, anytime will do.* In moments like this he loved this woman and his musing on whether this relationship would last was forgotten. But he knew also that the darker mood would be back. Better grab this while it lasts, he thought.

Driving over to the museum in a department Opel, his phone buzzed. It was Katarina again. *Mother has given me some chicken with macaroni, don't eat out.* He smiled. Her mother was always dropping by with food and he had to admit most of it was very good in a traditional Greek way, except for a soupy thing made with chick peas that had a foul taste he couldn't stomach. It was definitely the baking soda she put in the dish. Once he talked Katarina into making it without the soda. It was delicious.

He parked the car behind the museum on Bouboulinas Street and took his handgun with him. He checked the whole area around him as he approached the entrance. Inside the outer gate, he was met by a uniformed security guard who told him that Dr. Zavvou was waiting for him in her office. It was 6:53. Polyxeni Zavvou was a well-dressed woman in her late 50s he guessed, with short black hair that was on its way to gray. Her broad face was unpainted and lively. She had a large, generous mouth with laugh lines in tiny arcs around her lips. Hazel eyes looked at you steadily. Full bosomed and sturdy looking, she greeted him with a smile and a wry twinkle in her eye.

"Well, Detective Akritas, what have you brought me?"

No polite chit-chat with Dr. Zavvou. She wanted to get at the job at hand immediately. She was already eyeing the sheets in plastic envelopes under his arm.

"These are photocopies, Dr. Zavvou . . ."

"Call me Xeni, if you let me call you Pano."

"OK," he said smiling.

She took the sheets, extracted them from their envelopes, and laid them out on the table beside her desk.

"Aha," she said looking at the open hands and tapping it with a forefinger, "you're in luck, Pano, this is a drawing of one our pieces in this museum. It's a grave *stele*. As you can see, the inscription reads Zosime, daughter of Herakleon, and then the word Apamitis. They were one of the multitudes of foreigners from the East who resided in Athens in Hellenistic times. The ancient city had its migrants too, just like today. And with all the same problems. So, the dead person was an Apamite."

"I've seen these *stele* before, but never one like this."

"They're rare," she said. "The raised hands suggest that Zosime came to an untimely and violent end. Probably murdered. The open hands symbolize an imprecation and invocation to the gods to avenge her death."

"So, it's about getting revenge."

"Yes. The image frequently appears with curses and prayers for justice or vengeance. Usually addressed to Helios, the great judge in many Eastern cults. He is asked to expose and punish the guilty. The galleries are closed right now, but if you come by during the day I can show you the original."

"Well, perhaps I will."

"This one with the warrior stepping on the dead man is also in the National Museum next door. That's the name of the dead man – it's not clear whether it's the man lying on the ground or someone else. Most scholars think that this is an episode from the Peloponnesian War, which means the *stele* dates from the end of the fifth century B.C. Probably someone who fell during the fighting."

"Is there any suggestion in this one of vengeance like the open hands?"

"Not likely," she said. "It commemorates a fallen warrior."

"Why is the live warrior actually stepping on the dead one?"

"Probably signaling dominance. Disrespect perhaps. Like one might desecrate a corpse if there's hatred or scorn for the fallen."

"You mean like Achilles desecrating the body of Hector at Troy?" Akritas asked.

"Yes, precisely. Now this one with the figure of Hermes and the scales reminds me of a black-figure *lekythos* in the British Museum. If it's the one I'm thinking of, it was painted in an Attic workshop about 500 B.C."

"What do the scales represent?"

"They are part of an old belief that as death approached, especially when two men were dueling, Hermes would weigh their souls to decide the outcome. It is referred to as *psychostasia* or *kerostasia*, the weighing of souls. I can't remember the exact details of the vase that this reminds me of, but it's clear the warrior on the lowered pan is doomed to die in the duel. It's probably Achilles and Hector, but I'm not sure."

"So, there is a kind of judgement involved?"

"Yes, I suppose that's true, but I'm not sure the ancients would have given this a moral or legal meaning."

"What do you mean?"

"It was more like a man's time on earth had run out and the gods had decided it was time for him to go. Indeed he may have been a noble and dignified hero like Hector."

"Do you mean the gods had no specific reason?"

"Why or how they came to these decisions is a mystery. I like to think it was caprice, which is part of their charm. When your time was up, no matter who you were in life, there was no appeal from the judgment of the gods."

"You mean they just got bored with you?"

"Yes, they just lost interest in you in the same way one might lose interest in a main character in a play and leave after act two."

Akritas realized he was beginning to like this woman very much.

"I see," he said, "what about the Ixion one?"

"So, you recognized the punishment of Ixion. I'm not sure what ancient original this has, if it has one, but it is certainly punishment meted out to Ixion by Zeus."

"What about the inscription?"

"Nothing, it's double-dutch, nonsense. And why it's like that, your guess is as good as mine. Now this final one you've brought me is a curiosity, isn't it? It is an Athens piece. I have seen it next door in the National. It is a curse figure like a voodoo doll, about 12 centimeters high."

"Why is the head on backwards?"

"It probably symbolizes something done in the past, the criminal with his arms bound being forced to look back at his crime. But I'm guessing. On the original there's some lettering that probably refers to the name or names of the intended victims of the curse. This is definitely a vengeance piece. The drawing is not that good, but what it represents is perfectly clear. Whoever possesses the figure wants someone punished."

They talked a little more and the curator added more detail, some of it quite technical, that Akritas noted in his small red *tetradio*. It was mainly information about workshops, dates, materials and such like. Finally, it was time to go.

"Thank you so much, Dr. Zavv . . . Xeni. This fills in some detail in our investigation."

"I'm happy to be of help, Pano. Would it be worth me asking what the investigation is about?"

"We really don't like talking about ongoing investigations. But when we get to the bottom of things, I'm sure the papers will be full of it."

"You mean full of shit like they usually are?"

He laughed out loud and knew that one day he'd be back for his tour of the collection with this very good and amiable woman.

"You mentioned that I could come by and see the original of the open hands *stele* when the museum is open."

"Of course," she replied, "give me a call before you come and I'll take you to it and show you some other wonderful things we have. It's been a pleasure, Pano, come to me any time you want."

She held out her hand. He shook it and thanked her again.

Outside, he stopped for a moment to check the pedestrian area between the museum and the Technical University. It was empty. One desultory *nerantzaki* orange lay on the ground by a dusty tree where a dog was sleeping. Patission about fifty meters to the right was jammed with evening traffic. Cars, buses, trolleys, taxis made their noisy and slow way north towards the suburbs. He would be joining this tide in a few minutes. It was out on Patission just in front of the University where the attempt on his life had happened earlier in the day. For an instant it all came to him in a strident flashback, the red streak, the charcoal grey pistol emerging from the rider's pocket, the detonation, the sudden stillness, then the screams and the surging roar of the bike as it sped away. His hands shook. The thin extremities of his watch pointed to 7.45. Time to go to Katarina's warm arms and her mother's chicken and macaroni. He wondered if she'd remembered to close the wooden shutters.

/10/

Thursday dawned with the sun flooding Katarina's living room. Akritas sat on her uncomfortable sofa *cum* day bed drinking coffee. She was still in bed dreaming of little mermaids under a full moon. He knew that soon she would be stirring. They'd had another wonderful night together. Even after the love-making they hadn't had enough of each other, so they slept with the lengths of their bodies touching. And when he'd woken during the night he caressed her while she slept. She stirred and moved closer to him. As he took a sip of coffee, the thought went through his mind that he should ask her to marry him. He'd never been married and he wondered how that might change not only their relationship but who they were. Then he remembered he was a cop and had been shot at the day before.

Should he subject her to the usual anxieties of a cop's wife? He had seen many marriages fail because of the spouse's anxieties about the dangers of the job. The irregular hours didn't help either. Maybe she needed a man who was safe, reliable, could provide for her because, even at the age of 33, she still had no steady income, and also a man who could give her the intellectual support she needed.

But then maybe she wouldn't want him as a husband anyway. That he was more than fifteen years older didn't seem to bother

her, but there were other things. The fact he was a policeman had never sat well with her, for all the usual reasons Greeks have for hating the police. Yet she'd made the distinction between cop and man and stuck with it. Only occasionally did his position come between them and over the time they'd known each other they'd learned how to avoid that minefield. Marriage might change the nice balance they'd achieved. When his job came between them, he couldn't bear to have that look she gave him as an unavoidable part of their lives.

The thing was that she'd never found a man who could satisfy her physically as well as he could and he felt the same about her. He'd never been with a woman who was, in bed, so . . . he struggled for the word . . . so womanly. He closed his eyes against the sun and remembered the night. The dim light in the bedroom illuminating that lovely plunge down her flank, across her hip, to the front and the descent from her lower belly to the tangle of dark hair at the apex of her tanned legs. She never failed to arouse him whenever he saw her naked. Everyone she knew, her family included, thought that Anna-Maria was the family beauty. Katarina was the bespectacled intellectual. But one night when they were in each other's arms and he looked into her face he saw how beautiful she really was and told her. In his eyes, Katarina was the family beauty. Her sister was very good-looking, even sensationally so, but it was the touch of vulgarity that spoiled the effect. Katarina had a clarity about her, like an archer's tightened bow, but leavened with sensuousness. She was intelligent, never afraid to speak out, to give her opinions, and hold firm to a principle. Even after the look and the quarrels and his doubts about how long they could last together, he always wanted to be with her again. Not just to sleep with her, but to hear her voice, see her playful eyes, and see, also, the dreaminess of her face when they were lying in bed together after making love.

Although, he'd had a number women friends ever since arriving in Athens, Akritas had never connected with any of them to quite the same extent as Katarina. As he sipped his coffee, his mind went back twenty-five years to Maria Euklidou, a voice teacher at the Athens Conservatory. She'd helped him solve a particularly tricky case involving a murderer who was in the habit of humming an old folk tune as he killed his victims. They'd been very close for about a year until she met a French horn player from the Athens Symphony and, that day when he received the bad news, Akritas retreated to the Galaxy bar in a dim *stoa* off Stadiou Street to lick his wounds. He'd had girlfriends after Maria, some more serious than others, but none had lasted more than a year, and in some cases just a couple of months. You could say he was an experienced man, but he had always had commitment problems. And that had always brought these relationships and flirtations to an end. Women wanted more than a part time boyfriend. They wanted husbands, mates, children, maybe a nice roomy flat in one of the leafier suburbs, two weeks in the islands in the summer, some property with olive trees in the countryside, and a steady pension after the man died to support them in their widowhood.

The exception was the young Eleftheria. She was a street-smart young bohemian living in Exarchia but originally from the village of Thiva north of Athens. As an 18-year-old she'd come to university in Athens to study archaeology, but had fallen in with alternative people, so-called anarchists and the like, and stopped going to school. Her family kept sending her money, thinking she was still pursuing her studies, but she had taken a job as a waitress in a hip bar just off Kolokotroni Street on Kalamiotou. Akritas would drop in for a coffee and to read. At that time he'd been working on a case out of the local police station on Leoharnous Street. He'd been served by her a few times and the two had bantered back and forth now and then. She was upbeat, clever, and he liked the look of her, even though her hair was dyed a bronzy red with green fringes that, with the masses of costume jewellery she wore, made her look a little too much like a Christmas tree ornament.

One day, he came into the café with his book under his arm, saw her, and ordered his coffee. She said sorry, but she had just finished her shift and someone else would have to serve him. In that case, he said, if you've got nothing to do, come and join me I'll buy you a coffee or a drink if you want. Not here, she replied, the guv doesn't like us fraternizing with the 'enemy'. So, they went to another bar down Kalamiotou Street and started drinking whiskeys. In an hour they were in his flat making love. It was wild, passionate, and totally intoxicating. She was 20 at the time and had broken out of the usual claustrophobic Greek upbringing in Thiva: the 'family as penal colony' was his term for it. Athens was her great escape and she was taking full advantage of it. They would meet at all hours of day and night, both of them working odd shifts. It was an unrehearsed and improvised relationship. Neither knew from one day to the other what was going to happen next, except sex. This went on for about seven months.

Then one cold winter day in February, they'd been to a club just off Athinas Street to hear some Greek guys and two Cubans play Afro-Cuban jazz. They drank some whiskey, they danced, they drank some more, danced some more, and at 3 in the morning they were on their way to his place, when in rooting around in her bag, the whole thing slipped from her lap and everything in it spilled on the floor of the car. He pulled over, got out, and started helping her pick up her things when his hand touched a soft plastic baggie. White powder. Give me that, it's mine, she said in a cold, hard voice, suddenly very sober. He looked at her, opened the baggie, wet his finger, tasted the white stuff and realized it was heroin. The rest of the paraphernalia he found on the floor. And that was that. He took her home, told her to get off the stuff, that he couldn't see her again, and that he would neither arrest her nor report what he'd found. He told her he didn't think he was doing her a favour by keeping quiet, but he just couldn't put her through the hell of a charge for drugs possession, a trial, jail, and the humiliation for her family. Just get off it he said and get your life straightened out. He never saw her again.

After that it was a series of nice professional women, a lawyer, two business managers, and a female naval officer he sat beside in the Metro one day. After a month of dating her, he realized what he'd really liked was her crisp white uniform and the cute officer's hat women wore in the Hellenic Navy. It ended when she put out to sea for a six-month tour with NATO in the Indian Ocean.

Then he met Katarina. He had to admit that what attracted him at first was her bottom. It was exactly the kind of bottom that drove him crazy. He tried to feel ashamed of himself for being so superficial, but he was an honest man and in the end he'd just accepted that that was what it was. His interest was not exhausted there of course. He'd come to love her tenderness and her passion, not only for love-making, but for ideas and for justice. It's just that some of her ideas were a little too dreamy and impractical. Cynics might have said she was unrealistic, but they would have been wrong. She was pensive, capable of thinking very clearly, and of being decisive, but there was a side of her that disliked what is called knowledge of the world. And sometimes she shrank from it and seemed deeply unhappy that any of it had been thrust upon her. She spoke in a fine contralto that, when he first heard it, made him suddenly hear all other voices as the discordant clucking of poultry. Her voice brought to his heart's ear the deeper notes of a thoughtful viola against the mindless chatter of a banjo. There was a whimsicality about her too that was utterly lovable and he could not see how he could live without it. Yet, there was also something that made him hesitate in taking their bond that one more step that would have made it permanent. He wasn't sure whether that obstacle was something in her that repelled him or something in him.

Katarina came into his life while he was investigating the murder of one of the university professors. The man was gay and it seemed he'd been cruising, picked up a man who'd strangled him with his bare hands and then robbed him. Katarina had been one of the last people to see him alive. She'd been out with a girlfriend at a coffee bar in Kesariani when the professor and had entered with a young Romanian migrant, sat near them and ordered coffees. She knew the professor usually stuck with gay postgraduate students. This was the first time she'd seen him with a young man who was clearly not one of the university crowd. She didn't know why, but she felt anxious about the little scene being played out at the next table between the two men. She'd never seen the professor so forward in his advances. Constantly touching his companion's arm and thigh, at one point even trying to kiss him. To Katarina he seemed drunk. The young man had responded with a crudeness that Katarina found distasteful, indeed the whole little episode was verging on the repulsive.

When the naked professor was found dead in his bed the next day, it was Akritas who had to interview those who could account for the man's movements the day before. She came forward and told him what she'd seen. And she was able to give a good description of the Romanian. After an hour's conversation with her – he stopped taking notes after ten minutes – he asked her out and she accepted. Three years had passed since that day and they were still together. This was about as long a relationship as he'd had.

She'd once told him that falling for a policeman was the last thing she'd ever thought would happen. But fall she had and mostly she, she said, she just stopped thinking of him as a cop. For one thing he was well-educated enough and knew stuff, especially about history, of which she was somewhat ignorant. Her training had all been about media, politics, and cultural studies, theory and practice, but mainly theory. She'd had one longer relationship with a man, a dentist, before she met Akritas.

She'd met him at a party, hadn't had a man for some time and just wanted someone to touch her body. He seemed like a nice enough chap at the time, quite good-looking according to a couple of her friends who met him, smiling, and friendly. He had started hanging out at her place a lot and eventually in a moment of weakness she suggested he move in with her. This he did with an alacrity that surprised her. Once inside the flat, she began to see other, less pleasing, sides to his character. Impatient to a fault, he also had an anger problem and when angry he would be verbally abusive, calling her stupid and brainless because she was a 'humanist', a word he'd spit out like the chewed fragments of a rancid almond. But then that would pass and he'd be pleasant again, even fawning and self-deprecating. This hid his real character, which was threateningly arrogant and controlling. She started to be afraid of him because of this Jekyll and Hyde behaviour. The anger would always return and so would the shouting.

She grew more afraid and, then one day when she found she was pregnant she didn't tell him but immediately checked herself into a clinic and scheduled an abortion. She did not want to marry him and have a child. She thought he would be a terrible father and, anyway, she didn't love him and had grown, in fact, to dislike him. She would have preferred to get him out of her home, but whenever she'd begin to broach such a possibility, the shouting would erupt and she would be cowed into submission. They stopped having sex and he grew more aggressive until one day he hit her across the face with an open hand when she refused to sleep with him. That was it. She told her father what happened and he and her uncle came down and, in effect, threw the dentist out. Five years had passed. When he left she was 31. Three months later she met Akritas.

He took a last sip of his coffee stood up and was on his way to the kitchen when she came out of the bedroom, stretching her arms above her head and yawning.

"Hello darling, how's my man this morning? Want to come back to bed for an hour or two?"

She held out her arms and he put the cup down and embraced her. The warmth of her sleepiness enveloped him and almost drew him back into the bedroom. Almost, but not quite.

"It'll have to be tonight my love. I've got to get to work. They've put me on a new case. By the way I've got to do some research about the occupation, the Civil War, and what followed in the 1950s. Can you give me a hand at the National Library at some point in the next few days?"

"Of course I can, *agape mou*, just let me know and we'll go together. What's the case?"

"Some murders of old men who were involved in those old battles 60 years ago. I'll tell you about it later. Now I've got to get dressed and get down to the office."

"One more kiss before you go," she said.

They held on to each other for a long time until she pushed him away and told him not to be late for work and when could she expect him that night.

"I'll call you later when I see what's happening. I've got to meet someone at 7 and I'm not sure how long that'll last."

On the way down to Alexandras Avenue, he stopped and picked up an espresso and a brioche. He sat in the car munching the pastry and drinking the espresso in one gulp. He walked into the detectives' room at nine. It was loud and animated. Costas was already there and other detectives were at their desks working on reports or on the phone, getting ready for the day's work.

"Pano, thanks, for getting me assigned to your case" Costas said. "I need to work on something with a little more meat than the thin piss they've been serving up lately."

"To be perfectly honest," he began in a low voice, "you and General Solovos are the only ones in this department I trust. You know how to handle the office shit that's sure to flow when we begin to open up this toilet."

"A toilet? Really?"

"Listen, let's go down for a coffee, and I'll fill you in. I don't want to talk in here."

They walked towards the lift.

"Do you know a guy called Tolio Statiris?" Akritas asked.

"No, who is he?"

"A young guy. Boutsekes has assigned him to work the case as well. Looks like a south coast playboy, but he seems to have some smarts. I think he'll be ok. We'll see."

After they'd ordered their coffees at the *kafeneion*, Akritas brought Costas up to date on all the facts and developments of the case so far. He told him about Argyro Kanellopoulou's interest and the coincidence of Boutsekes assigning him to the case not an hour after he'd talked to the pretty deputy prosecutor.

"And what about the guy who shot at you?" Costas asked, taking a sip.

"Have no fucking idea. Total mystery."

"What about Kanellopoulou?"

"I'm meeting her at seven to hear about the things she forgot to mention the first time we talked. She's a slippery one, Costa. Be very careful when she's around, she's smart."

"Have you got a theory?" Costas asked.

"Well, after talking to a Dr. Zavvou yesterday," Akritas said, "I'm pretty sure it's got something to do with vengeance for stuff these guys did when they were young."

"If my father and uncle had ever got their hands on them, they'd be dead now," Costas added.

"You know how things are. Question in my mind, why did the perp wait sixty years?" Akritas asked.

"Opportunity maybe," Costas offered, "or maybe the killer wanted them to feel real safe. They'd stopped looking over their shoulder."

"Like Plutarch says, when Zeus is slow in punishing the wicked."

"I guess so. But if he says that the wicked get complacent and start thinking they're home free and easy, then yeah."

"That's if the motive is revenge," Akritas mused. "Let's not jump to conclusions just yet."

He wasn't sure why this had suddenly occurred to him. Revenge certainly seemed like the most obvious motive. Kanellopoulou's story had opened up that path and the story the drawings told seemed to confirm her suspicions. But, but, there was something . . . that he couldn't quite put into words. All he knew was that the obvious was often as much in need of scrutiny as the problematic.

"Do you think there may be something else?" Costas asked.

"If revenge is the motive why did someone try to kill me? And why didn't they go after Xiloudes?"

"Right, it's odd," Costas murmured. He reached for a cigarette, lit it, and blew the smoke over his right shoulder. Several people entered the *kafeneion*. They both looked over as the new group sat down at a nearby table.

"I have absolutely nothing to go on," Akritas said, lowering his voice, "but I was taught long ago never to rush a conclusion, even if everything you've got so far points to it."

"It's early. The fog will lift eventually."

"Yeah. Revenge is the strongest possibility right now, so we'll go with that before moving elsewhere. We'll need some solid evidence to change course."

Akritas explained the first steps they were going to take. All the people who'd been interviewed would be interviewed again. The relatives would be asked point blank why they didn't seem too interested in who had committed the crimes and in bringing the perpetrator to justice. It was also necessary to get a clear sense of how closely the victims had been connected as young men and later over the years when their war activities had receded into the past.

On the way back up to the squad room, Akritas and Costas were stopped by a uniform who gave them a note. It was from Tolio. He'd been working in the records office when he received a message that the red Honda had been found on a small side street, the Odos Ermagora, in Kolonos, just west of Metaxourgeio. And it was still there, being guarded by a motorcycle unit. The two detectives immediately turned around and were out of the building.

/11/

Come praise Kolonos's horses and come praise the wine-dark forest shadows, the thick-flying nightingales will deafen the light there and the immortal ladies will tread the earth dizzy with the bird's sound. Athens, first of cities, have pity upon this miserable ghost, old Oedipus, now blind and lame. The words of the old play came to Akritas as they drove towards Kolonos. Must read it again some time, he thought, better still, Katarina and I must see a performance at Epidaurus with the sun setting and the trees restless. *The words will rise again from the marble ground to mourn the daughter as Athena stares down, grey-eyed and sombre, from her great height.* Kolonos, he wondered, what would it have been like then? Now it was a working class suburb where killers dropped off their used hardware.

"Maybe this is the break we need," Costas said, interrupting his reverie.

"Yeah, maybe. Let's hope. This is the bike that followed me to and from Katarina's place two nights ago. The guy made it pretty easy for me to spot him and I keep wondering why, if the plan was to kill me, why would he make it so obvious?"

At first, they had trouble finding Odos Ermagora. Costas had to lean out of the window of the Opel and ask a woman walking by where it was. A couple of left turns and they were there. It was a tiny, narrow, one-block road that ran between Alamanas and Dimosthenous Streets. It had a couple of multi-floor apartment blocks, relatively new, some older buildings from the 1950s and a really lovely one-storey dwelling that must have dated back to old Athens, when it was one of the most charming cities in Europe. The windows were boarded up like all the best things in the city. They saw the two motorcycle cops smoking cigarettes standing beside the red Honda.

The two cops explained how they and another motorcycle unit had been driving down Keratsiniou Street nearby and been called over by a man who said there had been a break-in on Ermagora. The break-in was in a garage right across the street from the Honda. At first the cops didn't notice the bike, but one of them remembered the description from the day before and called in for the license plate. They matched. The police tow truck was going to arrive any minute to pick up the bike. Akritas thanked the two men and looked at the red machine. Costas checked the saddlebags, empty. The bike was relatively new and seemed well maintained. Akritas looked around at the buildings and the neighbourhood. He wondered if it would be worth going door-to-door to see if anyone had seen who had parked the bike there. As he was looking up at the apartment block nearest to them, a man came out on the first floor balcony and lit a cigarette.

"Hey, buddy," Akritas called out, "any idea who this belongs to?"

"Nah, it was left there yesterday afternoon by two guys in helmets and leather jackets. I was out here having a smoke – my wife doesn't want me smoking inside – and they just drove up, parked the thing – it's a beauty isn't it? – and walked away down that way."

As the man was speaking and pointing, the police tow truck turned the corner and stopped in the middle of the street. The driver got out accompanied by a uniformed officer.

Akritas thanked the man on the balcony and turned to greet the new arrivals.

"I've got the authorization-to-impound form, sir," the uniformed cop said.

"OK, go ahead," Akritas replied.

"Sir," the uniform continued, "I also have information about the bike. It was stolen in Preveza four days ago but not reported until yesterday. The owner only used it on weekends and didn't realize it was gone from his garage until yesterday."

"I see," Akritas replied, "is that all?"

"Yes, sir. Can we take it away now?"

"Sure."

Akritas and Costas watched as the tow truck guy with the help of the other cops got the Honda on to the flat bed. When they were gone, Costas asked if they should go door to door in the immediate vicinity and see if there were any other witnesses. It took about two hours for them to ring bells and ask about the bike. Nothing more than what they'd learned from the man on the balcony, although one man who'd been on the street thought it was a little odd that the two men who'd just left the bike still had their helmets on as they walked past him. He said that one of them, who had a slight limp, seemed to be speaking with a foreign accent, he guessed maybe German or Dutch.

It was about two by the time Akritas and Costas got back to Alexandras Avenue. Neither of them had had anything to eat. They went into a local souvlaki place and ordered a half dozen *kalamakia*, some bread, and a *horiatiki* salad. As they ate, Costas told him about his marital problems. He'd been going through an ugly divorce for the last eighteen months. Stavroula, his ex, was going to get their two kids and she was trying to restrict his access to them. He was bummed out by the rancour and bitterness of the whole process, but his brother and his wife were helping him stay sane.

"Hey, Costa," Akritas told him, "if you need time off or any help, let me know we'll arrange something."

"Thanks, the best thing is to work, stay busy, keep things on an even keel, and let my lawyer deal with the ugly stuff."

He looked at his friend and thought of old, blind Oedipus led to Kolonos by his daughter Antigone. *Endure what life Zeus gives and ask no longer span. The bride is carried to the bridegroom's chamber through torchlight and tumultuous song. Celebrate the kiss and watch entanglements grow. Endure. Even the grey-leaved olive-tree was bred like a miracle out of living stone.*

Back in the detectives' room, Akritas sat down and started writing out the questions he wanted his guys to ask when they interviewed the principals in the case. At four, the others on the team began arriving and Akritas got the meeting underway. He went over all the recent events and provided the background. He said that he'd be doing some work on the victims' histories, who they were, what they'd done during the Occupation, the Civil War, and the years of the Junta. Revenge seemed to be the motive. It was also confirmed, more or less, by some of the higher ups with whom he'd spoken. The word was that the sixth murder had set off alarm bells in political circles for some reason and that's why, suddenly, Xiloudes had been pulled off the case and a new group assembled with more resources. What the political ramifications were, he couldn't say. But they seemed serious enough that an attempt had been made on his life. There was no telling if the killer or killers would strike again. All they could do was be vigilant, carry on with the investigation, and wait.

He handed out the sheet of paper with the names, addresses, phone numbers and the questions he wanted asked, emphasizing that each of the witnesses should be asked to provide at least one more piece of information that they hadn't mentioned in their first interviews. He also wanted to know why the relatives did not seem to want to know who the perpetrators were. He wanted pressure put on them. Why did they seem to want to sweep the murders of their fathers and grandfathers under the carpet? What was it about the dead that the near relations didn't want resurrected? Were they embarrassed, afraid, or what?

"Don't settle for bullshit," he said. "Press them. We're going to get to the bottom of this."

Then he looked at the list made by Tolio and he assigned the four uniformed men to question the cleaners, cooks, maids, and neighbours. Costas and Tolio would tackle the relatives, friends, and associates. He'd come in after the preliminary interviews. If someone could be squeezed for more information, he'd come in and do some of the squeezing.

Before leaving, one of the uniformed policemen stopped him and thanked him for including him and his mate in the investigation. Xiloudes it seems had more or less ignored them and they'd spent most of the time sitting around smoking and playing with their phones. When he'd left, Akritas looked at his watch. He had an hour before his meeting with Kanellopoulou. He called Katarina.

"*Agape mou*," she said affectionately, "I thought you'd never call."

"Busy day. We got a break and found the red motorcycle."

"What motorcycle?" she asked.

He winced. He'd not said anything to her about being followed or the attempt on his life. The shooting had been reported in the media but he had not been named as the intended victim. She may have heard of the incident but there was no reason to connect it to him.

"Sorry, honey, it's the case I'm working. I thought I told you about it. Will you be staying in tonight?"

"Listen, Pano," she said noticeably worried, "I heard on the news about something involving a motorcycle. I think it was a shooting. Were you involved?"

"Yes, I'm in on the investigation. I'll tell you about it when I see you. In fact, I'd like to come by tonight, say about nine, to find a time for us to go to the newspaper archives. Maybe tomorrow, if you can manage it."

"You're not in any danger, are you?"

"Well, no more than usual. There's always some danger. But this isn't America, so don't worry my love. I'll be fine. See you tonight then, about 9?"

"OK, but Pano please take care."

"I always do. See you later."

How to bring her into the case without alarming her? Do I have to lie, he thought, or should I just tell her exactly what's happened? He didn't want to put her in danger but perhaps even being associated with him had already put her in harm's way and he should at least warn her. What am I dealing with here? And what about this woman, Argyro Kanellopoulou, could she be trusted, or did he have to watch his back with her around? He looked at his watch, 6.30.

He reached Plaka at seven but couldn't find a parking spot right away. Fifteen minutes later, he finally found himself at the Dioskouroi. The café hugged a twenty-metre stretch of the Agora fence as it ran up the Acropolis hill. Coming up the hill, his eye followed the long row of tables. At first he couldn't see her; then there she was behind a couple of men who were sitting directly in front of her. She was perched on a wooden chair with her legs crossed. He apologized for being late.

"It's OK, Pano, I just got here myself, parking was something awful."

He sat down opposite her, a little metal table between them. She was looking a little less like a lawyer today and more like a well-to-do thirty something who should have been making the rounds of Kolonaki lounges rather than sitting in the somewhat disreputable Dioskouroi with a bunch of black clad anarchists and unshaven pseudo intellectuals all around her. Hair down, lighter shade of red on her lips, and a cream-coloured jacket over her dark brown dress made her more attractive – less hard and self-possessed. But he knew that under the new camouflage she was still sharp as a stiletto. No choker today, less of a distraction, Akritas thought. He ordered a glass of whiskey, Jameson's Irish.

"Pano, why not have one of their single malt Scotches," she said, "it's on me."

"Nah, that's OK, I'll stick with the Jameson's. Thanks anyway."

She was drinking a glass of white wine. They talked a little about the weather until his drink came. He raised his drink to her, they clinked glasses, and he took a good pull on the whiskey.

"We found the red Honda today," he began, "the one used yesterday. One tidbit of information from a passerby when the two guys dumped the bike in Kolonos. The witness thinks one of the guys was foreign. He was speaking with an accent, maybe German.

"It was Danish," she said.

"Say again."

"It was Danish," she repeated. "The government has received information from Copenhagen that a Danish man, well known as an assassin, arrived in Athens two days ago."

"Why didn't you mention this yesterday?"

"We didn't know why he was here."

"But how did you know who he was?" Alkritas asked.

"He's worked Athens before. Contract killer."

"And he's just walking around loose?" Akritas said, looking away to mute his exasperation. "And . . . anything else?"

"It seems he's known as The Little Mermaid," she answered. "His favourite way of killing people is drowning them. He seems to like holding them down as they struggle for their life. But he also shoots people and cuts throats."

Akritas got the distinct impression she enjoyed telling him how this man killed people. Especially the drowning part.

"The last guy, Archontas," he said, "was cut with a nine-inch blade according to the medical examiner's report. Is the Dane our man then?"

"Probably not," she said, "he doesn't get involved in the details. He's here to clean up some loose ends after the fact."

"Oh, I see, he tried to kill me because I'm a loose end. And why did the red motorcycle driver let me notice he was on my tail the night before?"

"I don't know," she said, "but let's start at the beginning. You wanted to know what else is involved in the case. I'm sorry I didn't go into detail the other day, but I wasn't sure you were going to stick with this. But now that I see you've got your people together to carry on a proper investigation, you need to know some things."

The sun was sinking over the Agora to the west and lighting up the Temple of Theseus in that magical way Pentelic marble glows as the sunlight falls on it in a shower of gold.

"Our office," she began, "has confirmed that the six victims were all killed as revenge for things they'd done during the war and after. It isn't a single killer. There's a conspiracy of young left-wingers who've identified these men as particularly brutal in their dealings with the KKE and leftists in the years after the occupation. They are well organized and hidden. They don't seem to make mistakes and they know how to get in and out of people's houses without leaving a trace."

"Apart from the fact it's an organized gang, what you're telling me I could have told you."

"Yes," she said, "but what you don't know is that they are being financed, we believe, by a man, now also in his nineties, who was a communist in the 1940s, fought with the Democratic Army during the Civil War, was arrested and tortured on a prison island and recanted his communist sympathies. He signed the government's loyalty document and after a year more in prison he was released. After this he went into business and opened a shop that sold cloth. If I mention the name, you'll know it. I'm sure your mother even bought cloth and fabric there when women still sewed the family's clothes."

She paused, took a sip of wine and looked around the terrace. He took a quick look himself, but nothing seemed out of the ordinary. The outside tables were about half full.

"You expecting someone?"

"No," she said.

"OK, go on," he said.

"His business increased in the good years and he ended up owning an entire chain of shops all over Greece. He became very rich and it seems that now as an old man he's decided to get even with his old enemies."

"If you know all this, why hasn't anyone tried to stop him?"

"No evidence that will stick in court. For example, his recantation document has disappeared from the archives and it's believed the group he's paying are totally loyal to him."

"Is he with the communists?"

"The KKE, we've learned, have nothing to do with him, or these actions. It's an operation entirely independent of any party or organized political formation. They are a tightly-knit cell and our security people have very little idea of how it operates."

"Wait, if that's the case, how do you know any of this?"

"The little we do know points right at him," she said, showing signs of irritation at being interrupted.

"So, it's all circumstantial," Akritas said, leaning back in his chair.

"We're pretty sure the old man is the source of the funding, but, as I said, we have no concrete evidence and because of his social position we can't very well arrest him."

"Where is he located?"

"He lives in Plaka, very near where the last victim was killed. His wife is there with him. A daughter lives in Kifissia where the family have another large home, but she doesn't seem to be involved. She's an amateurish painter who only gets exhibited because she's got money and buys her way into galleries. You know who I mean of course."

"Yeah, I do, Klopas Karavias, and yeah, my mother did buy fabric from his shops in Patras. But tell me, why did he wait all these years?"

"It seems that recently he sold the shops to a Dutch company for quite a lot of money, which is safely tucked away in several Swiss banks. It seems that with the crisis people are buying fabric again and making their own clothes. The company has been making a good profit, again"

"So he's suddenly swimming in cash?"

"Now that he's liquidated his holdings, he can act without jeopardizing his business. If he'd started his campaign earlier he might have compromised his commercial interests and robbed his family of a fortune. Now their future and his wealth are protected and as far as he's concerned he can't be touched."

"What you're saying," he interrupted, "is that we're dealing with speculation here, mainly, and very little fact."

"A little of both," she said, "we know his money is now out of the country. We know that the recantation document has disappeared. We know that the group responsible for the killings has as much money as they need to carry out his will without being tempted by any other offers, that is to say, offers by the government for example to pay them more than he can. In the present crisis, the government no longer has the sort of resources to throw around and turn people. There are too many EU and Eurozone accountants sitting around government offices these days watching how every penny is spent."

She stopped and sipped at her wine. Two women from the day care next door to the café walked by talking. Akritas watched them pass.

"The killers," she continued, "are young and ideological. They've been brought up on the stories of how the left were betrayed and butchered in the aftermath of the war. This is their way of showing solidarity with their old mentors."

"So, what have we got here then, another November 17 type assassination cell?"

"In a way," she said, "but they only have one mission and that is revenge on all the remaining actors in the White Terror."

"At this stage, how many of the old-timers remain?"

"Not many and that's why Karavias had to act now and not wait any longer. After all, he's 94 as well this year and although by all reports still in good health for a man his age, how long can he go on?"

"Why are you so concerned about this, or the government for that matter? If he's settling scores, it'll end when they're all dead and that's probably going to happen soon. So, why didn't you just let Xiloudes muddle on with this until the whole thing blew over? Let the old bastards fight it out among themselves. What does it have to do with us, now?"

"That's a very good point, Pano, it's just that we can't let this become a precedent for others. My family suffered, as you know. But old rich people can't go around recruiting kill cells to settle private scores."

"But these aren't really private, are they? Injustices were committed that have never been redressed. If the government won't do it, then why not a private citizen with the means?"

"I'm a little surprised, Pano. You have a reputation for being a stickler for the law, and this doesn't quite fit the picture."

"Maybe it doesn't, but there are things that don't make sense. It seems both a kind of romantic adventure on the part of an old man and completely irrational. Well, maybe they're the same thing in the end. Listen, a man with Karavias' business smarts was anything but a romantic or irrational in his day. He couldn't afford to be. People get over this kind of stuff, especially if they've become multimillionaires in the meantime. It's just got a weird feel to it."

"You really can't tell what goes through an old man's mind," she retorted, sounding a little more exasperated with him.

"And then there's the arrival of this Dane, whose first act seems to be that he wants to kill me. I don't even know anything about this so why?"

"That we're not sure of yet," she said, "and that's the question we're hoping you can answer."

"You keep saying 'we' – who's 'we'?"

She frowned and looked over towards the distant Temple of Theseus framed by trees, but said nothing.

"Well?" he prodded.

"That information, Pano, must await developments."

Akritas sighed and looked at her for a long minute. He drank a little more whiskey. She sipped at her wine, turned in her chair and crossed her legs.

"What else do you need to tell me?"

"Just this," she said, "watch out for Boutsekes. He's involved in this in some way but we're not sure what his interest is."

"Why would he care? He assigned the wrong guy to investigate? And then after you spoke to me, he changed his mind. Is he part of the 'we'."

"No, absolutely not," she declared.

"So?"

"He's very upset that the six dead men were all men of the right and he thinks there's a wider left wing conspiracy here that will soon target others on the right, not just for settling old scores from half a century ago. Be careful what you tell him, he's a dangerous man."

Akritas weighed her words carefully. He knew that Boutsekes was not a man one could trust, but she was PASOK, he was New Democracy and the thought crossed his mind that he was being caught up in a dispute that was certainly not going to turn out well for the chump in the middle. But this didn't make sense either because with the rise of SYRIZA, New Democracy and PASOK, especially PASOK, no longer had the political smack they had in the past.

He also knew that a man like Boutsekes had no real principles. His only real political party was the party of himself, so why should he care about a *vendetta* from the past. The interview seemed to have come to an end.

The light was fading fast. He wondered how quickly he could get away for the drive up to Maroussi and Katarina. He was beginning to stir when he heard a commotion behind him. He glanced at his companion's face. She looked startled. She took his arm in a way that signalled trouble. He turned and saw a short, thick-set man advancing up the hill towards them with what looked like a .45 calibre pistol in his hand. Ten meters before the man reached them, a young guy, tattooed, head-shaved, stood up from one of the tables. The man shot him in the chest. On the quiet slope the gunshot sounded like thunder. The young man went down. Everyone ducked for cover.

"Get down," Akritas barked at Kanellopoulou. Then he shouted, "police, police, I'm the police. Everyone get down."

Down on one knee with his pistol in his hand, he pulled the metal table in front of him. Their glasses shattered on the stone. More thunder, but the bullet pinged off the tabletop. Akritas fired back hitting him in the right hip. He staggered and went down but was still able to shoot and another shot twanged off the tabletop before he was tackled from behind by two young men who'd been sitting nearby. They struggled to get the gun and eventually had him pinned down.

He looked around for Kanellopoulou. She was crouching behind another table, holding it like a shield, her back to the fence of the Agora. Suddenly from the side street, another gunshot ricocheted off the tabletop. Akritas turned and fired into the shadows. Another shot came from there and missed him. He fired again but nothing. Then there was one more detonation from the side street, but this time it was aimed at the first gunman, who was being held down by the two patrons. The bullet tore a hole in his skull and bits of flesh, bone, and blood were splattered over the two guys. They fell back unhurt, but the first gunman lay motionless on the stones with his head open to the night. Akritas peered into the shadows and heard footsteps running and he knew that the second shooter was gone. If he didn't move quickly, it would be impossible to find him in the labyrinth that is Plaka, now dark and shadowed. Shouting at Kanellopoulu to stay down, he sprinted into the narrow street from which the shots had come. It was dark and silent. In the distance he could hear faint drumming coming from Monastiraki. He stayed close to a wall on his left and moved carefully down the narrow street. A movement up ahead stopped him in his tracks. Not wanting to present an easy target, he went down on one knee and looked into the darkness. Crouching as he moved, he held his gun with two hands, barrel up. There it was again, someone moving in the shadows. He stopped, listening for footsteps. Nothing. Sweat beaded his upper lip and temples. As he rose he heard footsteps again up ahead receding quickly down a staircase and knew that the gunman had decided to make a run for it and would soon be long gone. A shadowy movement on his right made him turn. The cat's appearance took him by surprise. A sudden urge to laugh . . .

he shook his head and smiled. He lowered his weapon and the cat black as coal, walked up to him, black tail waving slowly, and rubbed it's side and back against his leg. Pitiless, yellow eyes looked up at him and the cat made a sound, wrapping itself around his feet. "Hungry?" he murmured. "Sorry, got nothing for you, Mephisto."

He stood up, holstered the pistol, and walked back to the café followed by the cat. He looked for Argyro. She was still crouched down behind an upturned table. Fright had turned her face white, eyes staring wide open. The other café patrons were also all in shock. Someone had called the emergency number and within minutes several uniformed police arrived from the vicinity of Monastiraki Square. Akritas helped Argyro to her feet.

"You OK?" he asked.

"I…I…think…so."

"Sit down and have some water."

He went over to a table that was still upright, picked up a glass of water, and gave it to her. She took a sip and looked up at him frightened and trembling.

"My God," she said, "what . . .!"

"Someone was trying to kill you, or me, or both of us. And the second shooter was there in case he missed or in case the guy was captured and needed to be disposed of."

Several more officers arrived. Akritas identified himself and the deputy prosecutor. She was still standing and in no condition to say very much. She was shaking and Akritas took off his jacket and wrapped it around her to keep her warm. He carefully got her seated. More police arrived and he asked an officer to go into the café and get a blanket, or tablecloths, or something to put around the woman to keep her warm. He crouched down beside her in the chair and took her in his arms and held her as tenderly as he could. He knew that people in shock after an act of violence just needed to feel human contact, someone to treat them gently, and to keep them warm. After a few minutes, the trembling subsided and she just looked open-eyed into his face. She tried to speak but couldn't.

"Sshh," he said, "don't speak."

An ambulance crawled up the hill as more people from the neighbouring streets began to gather quietly to see what had happened, murmuring to each other. After the loud detonations and the scramble of bodies and screams during the firefight, the whole area was now very quiet and still. People were moving around but in slow motion it seemed.

Akritas was still holding on to Argyro, who was breathing in short gasps. Shudders shook her body every so often. She was looking down into her lap where her hands where knotted together as if about to start praying. Her hair shrouded her face; shock was slowly giving way to anguish, the usual series of emotions. The anguish would be replaced soon enough by apathy, a kind of lassitude that would eventually lead the mind to want to sleep and let recovery come through the healing power of dreams and the galloping horses of the night.

Tomorrow would be another day and it would bring strange memories. For a long time she would not be able to remember whether the memories were of real events or the spectral episodes in her dreams. Odd, unrelated dream images would come to her, seaweed caught in her hair, her body naked at dawn wearing only the double earrings of the Incas, Salonika sleeping under red lights. There would be constellations passing overhead, gunshots from the shadows, the weather would be calm and then a tattered rag, a croaking voice, and the stillness. She would find herself up against the fence of the ancient market staring at darkness, the black, leaf-gorged trees in the distance, and standing out like a golden lamp the Temple of Theseus under a pale moon the colour of bone.

/12/

The Dioskouroi was flood lit like a stage set as a dozen police in and out of uniform moved around collecting evidence, interviewing witnesses, and scouring the area for anything that might help in the investigation. At about 10:30PM, Akritas called Katarina apologizing for being so late. He told her something had come up at the last minute and that he'd be by in about an hour or so.

"Of course, darling, you've got the key, come when you can. I'll be waiting for you."

Argyro had been taken to Evangelismos Hospital for treatment. They'd probably give her a sleeping pill and two policewomen to take her home and stand guard. Akritas would check in on her the next day.

He was sitting drinking coffee at one of the small metal tables that had saved their lives . Night sounds drifted up from streets below and the Temple of Theseus across the shadowy Agora presided calmly over the darkness. He was trying to piece together what had happened. It all seemed mad. Why did the first gunman come storming up the hill with his gun drawn for all to see? It seemed more like a terrorist attack than a serious assassination attempt. Professionals would hit without being seen and be gone before anyone knew what had happened. Exposing yourself was suicidal, especially as one of the targets, a policeman, would be armed and probably able to handle a frontal assault. One more piece of a puzzle that increasingly didn't make sense.

"Are you well enough to go home?" one of the detectives asked Akritas.

"Yes, fine. This is the second time in two days I've been shot at. I'm getting used to it."

They both let out bemused snorts that were meant to be laughs. Akritas got up, checked he had his pistol and slowly made his way down the hill towards his car, refusing the offer of an escort. He descended towards the lights where the restaurants and cafés were in full swing. Over in the old square, the African drummers were entertaining the tourists with their racket. As he walked among the restaurant tables he was struck how garish and noisy all this seemed. People forking meat and fried potatoes into their gaping mouths. Others were trading obscenities at their friends. He'd always marveled how well the Greek language bestows a rich collection of insults, and curses. Aging women with too much make-up smoking and eating at the same time: first a forkful full of food, then a drag on the cigarette leaving red traces on the white tube. There were hot cascades of fake diamonds and frocks mailed with sequins. A young man had his hand on his girlfriend's thigh as he tore at a skewer of meat with his teeth. He looked up at Akritas with tiny scheming eyes and a mouth full of pork. A group of men, obviously drunk on *raki*, were picking at plates of French fries, olives, and *keftedes*, laughing and declaiming to no one in particular their sour view of the world. The whole place seemed a broiling, luridly lit cavern, inhabited by slatternly savages. None of them were aware what had happened not two hundred meters away a few hours earlier. Lucky them, he thought, as he turned into the darkness.

Plaka at night is a place of light and dark. It embodies perfectly the two faces of the typical European tourist trap. The sociable, shiny smile that masks the brooding, dismal scowl absorbed in calculating profit and loss. The main passages lit brightly for commerce, consumption, and the human comedy. The narrow back lanes, black with shadows and frightened cats. He found the department Opel in a murky side street and was just opening the door when he heard a gravelly voice from a darkened doorway.

"Akritas," it croaked, "don't make a move. I've got a gun on you and I'll use it if you try anything stupid. Listen to me. You were not the target tonight. It was the Kanellopoulou bitch we wanted. I don't know what bullshit she's been feeding you. Don't believe a word of it. She's playing you like a cheap accordion."

"Who are you?" Akritas said in a low voice realizing after he'd spoken how brainless the question.

"Shut up. We'll get her eventually. Now, get in your fucking car and go. You've got ten seconds then I shoot."

"Why did someone try to kill me on Patission the other day?"

"Shut the fuck up and go."

He got in his car and slowly moved away from the pavement, looking into doorways. In one, he thought he saw a figure but he couldn't be sure.

It was quarter to twelve when he arrived at Katarina's flat, shutting the door as quietly as possible. Taking off his jacket, he put the pistol in the pocket and hung it up with the other coats. His body sagged as weariness crept through his frame. He left his shoes by the door and went into the living room. One small lamp was still lit. He knew she was in bed and probably asleep. She never had any problems falling asleep; in that one way she was like a child. He'd been having difficulties falling asleep for years. Sleeping pills had helped now and then, but he didn't like the metallic taste they left and the fact that if you took them regularly you developed a serious drug problem. That had happened once and he'd gone through very unpleasant withdrawal symptoms when he stopped.

In the bathroom he took off his clothes and stared at himself in the mirror. He looked haggard, unshaven, and lost. He washed himself, brushed his teeth, and came out into the corridor, startled to see her standing there in her nightdress.

"Welcome home my love," she said smiling and holding out her arms.

They embraced and, leading him by the hand, she took him to her bed. A small lamp on the bedside table cast a dim light in the room. She took off her nightdress and lay down beside him. He was too tired for love-making and she knew it, but they both wanted their two naked bodies to be tangled together. And then, before she could turn out the light, she saw that his eyes were glistening.

"What is it, *agori mou*? Tell me. Has it been a difficult day?"

A few tears came quietly, without drama, until he was done.

"Yes, it was a bad day. Let's sleep now and I'll tell you about it when we get up. Have you made any yogurt?"

"Yes, it'll be ready in the morning," she whispered. "And the nice lady in the shop down the street promised to bring me some of her lovely bread as well."

"Good, because that's what I want to have when we get up. I love you, Katarina."

"I love you too Pano. Let's sleep."

And with that they lay together, touching each other's nakedness, and quietly fell asleep. The dim light burned all night.

A generous spoon of thyme honey, some orange slices, and walnuts covered the yogurt she served him in the morning. It was delicious. The bread the nice Albanian lady brought over tasted as good as ever, as did the Dutch butter Katarina bought at the Central Market on Athinas Street. Akritas had woken up very hungry and helped himself to two or three servings of everything. The Greek coffee washed it all down. He made a second cup for himself and sat at her kitchen table watching her as she washed up the breakfast things. Every so often she would look back at him and smile. When she'd dried her hands, fixed her hair, and sat down opposite him with her tea and a glass of water in front of her, she asked him about yesterday.

He had decided she should know everything. He began with his being parachuted into an investigation being led by another detective, who, when he'd learned he was being shoved aside, had promptly resigned. He told her about his first meeting with Argyro Kanellopoulou, his meeting with Aris Boutsekes, the fact that when they went out with Greg and Katia they were followed by the red Honda, the drawings with the open hands, the assassination attempt on Patission, the very nice Dr. Zavvou, his forming a team to investigate, and the events last night during his second meeting with the deputy prosecutor. She sat in her chair growing increasingly alarmed as he spoke.

"This is turning into a very dangerous case," he said

"Dangerous? Of course it's dangerous. What's going on?" she demanded.

"I'm not sure what's going on exactly."

"But are you in danger?"

"Look, Katarina, I am concerned about my safety, but I'm much more concerned about yours."

"Mine? Why?"

"I think the red motorbike began following us from here. I'm trying to think of a way of protecting you until the whole thing is cleared up. Do you think you could sleep upstairs with Anna-Maria for the time being?"

"Yes, of course I can. She'd be happy to have me. In fact, sometimes when she's lonely she comes down here and sleeps with me. But Pano, what about you? Can you get some protection from the department?"

"I have Costa with me most of the day and I'm very wary now of being out in public. I'll take all the precautions necessary.

Whoever is doing this had a chance to kill me last night, but didn't. It's possible I've just been caught in the crossfire in a war between two sides."

"You mean like in a civil war?"

"I've been led to believe it all goes back to our Civil War in the forties. That's why I want you to help me at the Library."

"What do you need to find out?"

"The dead men were active then and I want to see if there's any information about them. I'm really interested in the most recent murder. He seems to have been more prominent and he may have been mentioned in the press of the time."

"Have any idea who this killer is?"

"That's just it. There isn't one killer here, but at least two and they are after each other. I'm not sure why yet, but now I have a better idea of what we're facing. It seems that after the six old men were killed," he said, looking into her face, "someone is now fighting back. I really don't know what's going on."

She stood up and walked over to the fridge and poured herself a glass of water. She turned and looked at Akritas lost in thought.

"You know, Pano," she said, "the Civil War has never really ended, has it? Maybe civil wars never do. If only they hadn't killed Lambrakis. How different our country would be. Do you think these six old men were involved in his murder?"

"I don't know," he said, thinking back to what he'd read about the 1963 assassination of the popular left-wing politician.

"If only we'd had honest police then, maybe Lambrakis would still be alive."

She looked at Akritas as she spoke and an icy look began to stiffen her face. He was a cop after all and she seemed to be withdrawing emotionally from him as she remembered police complicity when Lambrakis died.

"We are trying to change things," he said quietly. But he sensed as he spoke that he was struggling to believe his own words.

"I know," she said, softening. "Is there anything you want me to do?"

"No, you mustn't be involved in this. In fact, we'll need to limit our contacts for the time being."

"Pano, that's terrible," she said.

"Don't worry, this will be over soon and then I'll get back to the boring cases I usually have."

"Pano," she said in a mock-scolding voice, "I know you. You love these cases, the more complicated and dangerous the better. Maybe, one day soon, they'll promote you and give you a desk job in that big building on Alexandras and then maybe we can get married."

She was struggling to set the bond again.

"But what about all your university friends who think all policemen are fascists? What would they say if you were married to one?"

"Fuck them," she said in a low, sweet voice and with a delicate little smile on her lips. She was back.

If at that moment she'd offered to go down to the city hall and get married then and there, he'd have helped her on with her coat, grabbed his jacket, and driven to Kotzia Square as quickly as possible.

They talked a little more and agreed that when he came over for the night they would sleep in her flat. When he wasn't there she would sleep upstairs with her sister and when she was working in her study, she would never open the door to her flat to anyone whom she didn't know. As they were talking, his mobile buzzed. It was Costas enquiring after him.

"I'm fine. Where are you? Where? Yeah, I know it. I'll see you there soon."

"Be careful," she said.

"I will. I'll call you later about tonight."

As he drove down into the center he thought again about the revenge angle. It was still good. There was certainly plenty of evidence for it. But he also began to wonder how the warring factions fit into a revenge scenario. And what did killing him and the deputy prosecutor have to do with it? Unless it really was a right-left struggle, where the right was now mobilized to challenge the left kill-squad delivering retribution for past crimes. But, but . . . . There was more here than he could see for now. At least he'd managed to understand an important dynamic of the case. Two killers, not one, and at war with each other. But what did they represent?

Costas had told him to meet him at the depot in Aghios Nikolaos where the police impounded vehicles used in crimes. He wanted to show him something about the red Honda. Akritas saw his colleague crouched down examining one of the red side panels. As Akritas approached, he looked up.

"Look at this," he said. There were two thin lines like one could make with a sharp object, a key or a blade, but lightly scorched. "Someone's fired on the bike. I'm sure ballistics will confirm it."

They both crouched down and stared at the lines. Here was further evidence that some kind of armed struggle was going on around the six dead men. Someone was shooting at the shooters.

"What do you think?" Akritas asked.

"Here's a thought. These are near misses, fired, it seems, from behind. The bullets were too low to hit the rider in a vital spot, but could have wounded him in the leg, don't you think? Maybe we should be looking for a man with a leg injury."

He paused and looked at his partner.

"Remember the guy," Costas continued, "who said he heard a foreign accent on Ermagora Street? He thought one of the men was limping."

"Good work, Costa. How did you know to come here and take a look?"

"One of the guys who works down here, Marios over there in the shed, is a mate, he noticed it. He called me."

"The bike was stolen four days ago," Akritas said, "so if these marks weren't made before it was stolen, whoever was shooting at the shooter was doing it very recently. How are the interviews going?"

"Interesting stuff. You're right, the first guy I talked to, son of the first victim, just clammed right up when I started pushing. Definitely something they don't want to talk about."

"I wonder how we can scare them into talking?" Akritas asked.

"I don't know. They seem like solid citizens. The guy I talked to today lives in a very nice place in Ekali. He's not some lowlife who's been in and out of trouble all his life."

"Hey, how about we threaten them with the tax collectors?" Akritas said smiling. "If they're rich, they've definitely cheated on their taxes. If we move in with the threat before they can organize their political friends to defend them, maybe they'll be more co-operative."

"It's a worth a try. What probable cause should we give?"

"Tell them, we've received an anonymous tip about their taxes and we're wondering if the death of their relative is connected, something like that. Tell them the Finance Ministry guys will follow up later with their own questions."

"Got to love those anonymous tips," Costas chuckled. 'That'll make'm concentrate."

"I should check to see how Kanellopoulou is doing. She was in shock last night after the attack. See you later Costa, good work on the motorbike."

He called the hospital.

"She's not here," the duty nurse answered. "Checked herself out in the morning and as far as anyone knows she went home to rest."

He pulled out the paper with her number and called.

"*Ela*," she said, answering on the second ring.

"Akritas here. How are you?"

"Not quite myself," she said, "but otherwise, calm. I'm home."

"Yeah, I know, I called the hospital. Mind if I drop in?"

"Not at all, please do, I can use the company. When I got back here it seemed awfully cold and empty. Yes, I'm at 34 Gennadiou in Kolonaki, number three on the second floor."

"OK, I'll be there in thirty minutes."

On his way over he wondered why he wanted to see her. She'd told him all she wanted to tell him the night before. What he wanted was to see what shape she was in because it was clear to him now there was something going on and she was one of the targets. He had been targeted by the other side on Patission. The other side didn't want him on the case. But which side was that? Why hadn't the man in the shadows last night finished her off when the first gunman was drawing all the attention? That would have been the plan, wouldn't it? Get the cop with her focused on the mad gunman and then put a bullet in her while she was defenseless. But the shot from the side came after she was crouched behind the metal table; the kill moment had passed. The only loose end was the first gunman being held down by two café patrons. The second shooter didn't miss the kill shot. What went wrong then?

She was not wearing any make up when he entered her spacious and luxuriously furnished flat. Everything in the place oozed money. The Boca do Lobo sofa and armchairs, the Parian marble floors, the €5,000 Hirst carpets, the art on the walls, the €1000 lamps, everything.

"Come into the nook," she said, bringing him into an area with a table and chairs near the gleaming, stainless steel kitchen.

Nook, he thought, damn, this is the size of my living room.

Without cosmetics, she actually seemed more attractive than when she had the mask on. She wore a dressing gown of a material that looked like silk, jet black with very brightly coloured butterflies all over it. It was like the darkest night crowded with brilliant, fluttering creatures. They weren't printed on the fabric. They were hand sewn with fine threads. But several didn't look like butterflies at all, more like dangerous things, like angry dragonflies, except for the beautiful, quivering wings. There's another €500, Akritas thought. Where did all this money come from?

"Do you want anything to drink, coffee, something stronger?"

"Coffee will do thanks. Greek please."

"None of that foreign muck, eh, Pano," she smiled.

"Already had an espresso this morning, that's enough foreign exoticism for one day."

She busied herself in the kitchen with the *briki*. For a moment Akritas thought that she's so far removed from the way ordinary people live maybe she won't know how to make it. After a few minutes she produced a rather good cup of *elliniko*. She served him and herself as well as two tall glasses of ice water and sat down.

"How did it go last night at the hospital?" he asked.

"They were very good. They gave me something that calmed me down. Half a sleeping pill and I was out for five hours or so. When it was dawn, I just wanted to leave and come home. The policewomen drove me and stayed all night. When they left, they said the department will want to give me police protection. What do you think?"

"Of course, after last night you've got to have protection. My sense is that you were the target and for some reason they botched it. So, a police guard outside on the street will be the right thing to do. If they've tried to kill you once, they'll try again."

"Maybe you're right. How do I arrange for that?"

"Don't worry, I'll take care of it when I get back. Have any idea who wants you dead?"

"How can you be sure it was me they were after and not you? They tried to kill you on Patission, why would they now switch to me?"

"Listen, Argyro, we don't have much to go on, but it's just a hunch at the moment. Over the years I've learned to take them seriously, especially if they have an edge on them."

"An edge? What do you mean?" she asked, looking at him with her eyes narrowed slightly.

"It means that there are anomalies in this case and the more they multiply the edgier I get."

He decided not to tell her about the man in the shadows who warned him about her last night as he was getting his car. She had held back on him and was probably still keeping her cards close to her butterfly-adorned chest. Time he did the same.

"You're not married, are you?" she asked.

"No."

"How about a steady girlfriend?"

He hesitated before answering.

"Not really," he lied, "I play the field, that's the expression, isn't it?"

"I see," she said looking directly into his eyes. She knew he was lying.

He got the impression that if at that moment he reached out, pushed the dressing gown aside, exposing her naked leg, and ran his fingers along the length of her thigh from hip to knee and back to her hip, they'd be in bed in ten minutes. Trauma victims sometimes were not entirely in control of their emotions. She looked as if she'd pulled herself together, but he'd seen this before. Perfectly calm exterior, but still a great deal of turbulence inside, that poked and prodded you into rash acts and misjudgments. He knew it was time for him to go.

"Take it easy for a couple of days. I'll get the department to put a man downstairs and don't you open the door of your flat to anyone you don't know, not even any city personnel who suddenly show up out of nowhere wanting to check the water pressure in your pipes. Refer them to the guard downstairs."

"I was planning to go back to work tomorrow."

"Look, tomorrow is Friday, take it off, and then you've got the weekend. Go back to work on Monday, everyone will understand. But, in the end, it's your call."

And with that he stood up to go. She reached over and took his arm and held on to it, looking up at him.

"So soon?"

"I'm afraid so, Argyro, get your doctor to send you a couple more of those pills and don't wander around outside."

What could these dead men have in common, he wondered as he entered the police building, other than their activities in the aftermath of war and during the dictatorship? So far as he could tell political revenge was still the primary motive, but it was also only a hypothesis. What if the hypothesis were wrong? What else could be at issue? In his experience, it had to be one of two other thing that usually incite people to kill. Sex and money. Or both together. The idea of 80- and 90-year-olds and sex brought a smile to his face, although he recalled what a lover man his father had been at 70 with Roula, his mother, when she was in her 60s. His smile broadened into a grin. Stavros and Roula had never hidden their lovemaking from their children and that went on right into their old age. But somehow the idea of sex being a factor in this case seemed pretty remote. Then, if politically motivated revenge wasn't the spur, it had to be money. Boutsekes and Kanellopoulou came to mind. Both of them seemed to be rolling in dough, but he had no idea how they got it. Whoever was behind these murders had to be strong enough or high enough in the national power pyramid to divert attention from themselves. But this seemed fanciful guessing.

Revenge for past crimes still seemed the best path to follow. How could theft be a factor when the one crime scene he'd examined did not contain much or any evidence that robbery was the principal motive. Unless of course the killer was looking for one particular thing, had found it and then was gone. In that case, he would have knowledge of the victims and of their residences. He needed more information about how an old fascist like Archontas had ended up so rich. Time to put in a call to Petros, he thought. Petros Cleomenes, the cynic, worked as a financial adviser and was always in the know, about what the Kifissia-Psychiko money mafia was up to.

Back in the detectives' room, he saw Tolio writing at one of the desks.

"Tolio, what's up?"

Tolio looked up and Akritas was sure that he was blushing. He put down the ballpoint and looked up at him with a pained expression.

"I think I may have put my foot in it, boss."

"Oh yeah?" Akritas said, as he sat down opposite the younger man's desk.

"I was talking to the grandson of the second victim, a Mr. Xeniades, when I said something innocuous like 'I'd put my money on . . .' I forget what it was – I think I was trying to say that robbery didn't seem to be a factor in his death and that 'I'd put my money on another motive' – yes, that's it. I don't think Mr. Xeniades heard me right because he then got very defensive and frightened. He said 'What do you mean? It's got to be robbery, what else could it be? Is there other evidence?' Without thinking I said 'Yes'. Then I realized I shouldn't have been so positive. So I backtracked and said something like, all kinds of evidence gets thrown up in an investigation and everything needs to be looked at before making final decisions about motive, perpetrators, etc. But I'm not sure he was convinced. He came back again to other motives several times. I'm very sorry but I hope I haven't blown anything in the investigation."

"Best to keep your cards close to your vest."

"Damn," Statiris said.

"Who knows, this guy might be an accomplice and you've just shown him a card in our hand."

"It was an honest mistake, I swear."

"I know. But it may be OK in the long run. If you throw a crumb out now and then just to see what reaction you get, it might help. Understand what I'm saying?"

"Yeah, I think I do. Like a tactic to get something moving."

"That's exactly what I'm saying. But, and keep this in mind for the future, when you're deliberately tipping your hand, timing is everything. OK, anything else?"

"Yes, when I was leaving, I looked back and he was already on the phone and looked as if he was having pretty angry words with someone."

"Good, we're going to see something soon. Take care, these killers don't take prisoners."

As he walked to his desk, he thought about the young Tolio. Not the cleverest of guys but he gave the appearance of being competent and, more importantly, being able to learn stuff. The problem with most of his colleagues was that they thought they knew it all already. And that for a cop was fatal.

About a half hour later his mobile rang. It was Katarina.

"How are you, *agori mou*?" she said.

"Good, good, and you?"

"Missing you, but otherwise ok. I wanted to ask you when you wanted to go to the National Library?"

"Let's see it's Thursday today. I need to put some of this material in order. How about Monday? It gives me a chance to think about what I want to look up."

"As far as I know I don't have anything scheduled, but I'll check. How long do you think this might take?"

"I'm not sure, but we don't have to do it all in one day. I'll have six names and I'd like to see if they show up in any media accounts from the 1940s on. We can do searches like that, can't we?"

"Yes, if they've been in the news they'll pop up. OK, one more thing."

"Yes?"

"Dimitri and Lila have invited us over tonight for dinner. I know it's a last minute thing but that's how they are honey. You will come with me?"

He had murders to investigate and a poxy party with some self-important eggheads was not on the agenda at the moment. His immediate reaction was to say no. But realistically what could he do to further the investigation at night?

"Yes," he said, "if you want me there, but you know what these university people are like when there's a policeman around."

"Let's not worry about that sweetheart. I think they're used to the idea of us together by now. You're almost one of the family."

Someone who didn't know her might have heard her last comment as somewhat mocking. But he knew her better than that and for all its misguided good heartedness she was being serious.

"What time should we be there?"

"They said nine."

After they hung up, he wondered what sarcastic or ironic remarks he was going to have to put up with at the Koutoulis' place. He hoped none of those pretentious bastards from ERT, the state broadcasting service, were there. Relax, take a deep breath, and hope that Katarina didn't start talking to any of that bunch. Relax, take a deep breath, and sip Dimitri's excellent *tsipouro*.

/13/

Petros Cleomenes fairly snarled '*Ela, ela*' in his most cynical and exasperated voice when Akritas rang him up. This was a man who knew that men and women learn wisdom with extreme slowness, and are always ready to believe promises that flatter their secret hopes. It had made him a successful businessman but had not yet extinguished an even deeper and incongruous belief in the goodness of humanity.

"I see you're in a good mood again," Akritas said.

"Ah, Pano, it's you. Nice to hear your voice. It's been a bitch of a day, thank God it's Thursday as those fucking Americans like to say. I bet you've got a bitch of a case and you want to talk to me about it because it involves money. Am I right?"

"Of course, you . . . you old Armenian moneychanger. And the Americans say Friday, not Thursday."

He'd meant to say Jew but had, at the last moment, remembered that Petros was Jewish on his mother's side.

"Details, mere details."

"Look, can we meet today?" Akritas asked.

"Ah! It's an emergency, is it?

"Yes and no. I've had two attempts made on my life in the last two days. That kind of makes me want to get to the bottom of who's trying to kill me. And no, it could wait til tomorrow."

"OK, how about To Kafeneion in Kolonaki at 2:30? Let me buy you lunch you sad, underpaid civil servant. I've got a pocketful of 50 Euro notes that need to be spent on propping up the civil authority."

"See you there and I'll pay for my own lunch."

"Like hell you will. Bye."

And with that he banged the phone down so hard that it sounded like a gunshot.

At 2:45 there was no sign of Petros. Akritas sat sipping at a glass of white wine and enjoying the old world charm of the restaurant that had survived the smart-phone bar and lounge culture that had invaded the area. Years ago, Petros had introduced him to the Loukianou Street establishment and he always enjoyed eating there. The food was traditional Greek fare but excellent and the surroundings always put him in a good mood because it recalled the style and beauty of an older Athens. Then along came the 'entrepreneurs' and their money-grubbing clients and the old city went down under a heap of modernistic looking rubbish. He sat there wondering what it would have been like being a detective in those old days when gentlemen wore linen suits, could quote Cavafy, sported silk ties or cravats, strolled with silver-topped walking sticks and wore white hats and elegant shoes made by Greek shoemakers who knew what they were doing. And then when the EU came, the old shoemakers who knew what they were doing were driven out of business by the Italian multinationals who made, it had to be said, damn good-looking shoes which, unfortunately, hurt your feet and left blisters on your heels. The shoes made by the Greek shoemakers fondled your feet like your mother long ago when she had you in the bath and was washing your toes. Then his reverie evaporated as a raspy voice called out to him from the door.

"Pano, you old devil!"

It was Petros and it was almost three. Only a half hour late. It must have been his Greek half. And then he remembered that Jews were also always late. So, he assigned fifteen minutes to each of Petros' two halves. His friend was a burly, balding man. Measured by chairs or doors, he was of immoderate physical dimensions. He exceeded the average in height, stoutness, and bluster. He didn't just occupy a room he dominated it and everyone else felt, inevitably, like an intruder.

"Good thing you're here," Akritas said, "I'm already into my second glass of wine and I was thinking of going home for a nap before getting back to protecting the Greek public from pickpockets, real estate agents, and bankers. How are you, you old Jew?"

"Fine, fine. Sorry I'm late but a billion euro deal came up at the last minute and had to be attended to."

Akritas rolled his eyes.

"And then of course," Cleomenes grumbled as he settled himself in his chair, "the Minister of Finance rang up for a little advice on how to get the German banks off his back. So tedious, so damn tedious, Pano, you have no idea."

A strikingly beautiful woman stared at him from a corner of the restaurant. She caught his eye.

"It always surprises me," he said turning to Akritas, "to see beautiful people out and about. They wander about in life just like ordinary folk."

"What of it?" Akritas asked glancing at the woman.

"Dear boy, they should be isolated from *hoi polloi* like lepers, or a cache of dynamite."

Akritas laughed out loud and motioned over to the waiter to bring Petros a drink. The waiter didn't need to ask what he was drinking. The red martini with lime arrived within minutes and the two men ordered some food. It came quickly and they set to eating without talking. It was part of their ritual, enjoy the food, then talk business. They shared a dish of lightly sautéed zucchini, some *fava*, and bread. Then Akritas' veal with peas in a succulent tomato sauce arrived and was superb. Petros dug into his lamb and roast potatoes with gusto. A smile spread across his face like a thick wedge of soft butter on a slice of rough peasant bread. When they were done, both men leaned back in their chairs and nodded. Their coffee was served decorously by an attractive young woman. A house sweet was produced rounding off the meal. Both of them enjoyed these ceremonies. It was an Athens thing.

"Now," Petros said, "tell me."

"You ever heard of a man called Nassos Archontas?"

"And what's it to you?" Petros asked.

"So you have. He's dead. I need to know what you know about him."

"What do you know already?"

"My various superiors are trying to tell me that he was in the white terror death squads during and after the war and that he was killed by some new red terror death squad out to get even for all the old crimes sixty years later.

"Did you believe them?"

"I was willing to listen and all the evidence they've offered seems to confirm the revenge idea."

"But?" Petros asked.

"Yeah but, the whole thing doesn't hang together. I've got my suspicions there's something else here. I think it's got to do with money but to be honest I'm not sure. Anything?"

"Plenty. Nassos Archontas amassed an enormous fortune over the last fifty or so years. Most of it is, or was, in cash in Swiss banks, some gold, and a few works of art. I'm not sure the cash is still there because money like this gets moved around to whiten it up."

"How'd he get it?"

"No-one I know is quite sure how. There are half-a-dozen theories but all of them are gossip. You know what we Greeks are like. We make up fanciful tales whenever there's no evidence. I deal only in facts my friend."

"So, what are the facts?" Akritas asked.

"There aren't many. I know pretty well all the people in Greece who are in business and making loads of money. I know how they came to have their filthy lucre. And I know where they've got it hidden."

"But, Archontas must have had business dealings with others."

"That's the problem Pano, no-one I know has ever had any business dealings with him and he doesn't seem to have had any dealings with commercial interests outside of Greece."

"How did he come by his money then?"

"Right, how did he? And without seeming to have done anything? It's only in myth that Zeus turns himself into a shower of gold. And that only so he can have his way with Danae of the delicious hips. Archontas is no Danae, so how come he had a shower of gold fall on him?"

"And?"

"Many people in Athens wonder the same thing. But you say he's dead. When did it happen?"

"Three days ago. The *Astynomia* is being tight with the information. I've been to his flat in Plaka and he certainly looked loaded. Do you think the revenge angle from decades ago is a possibility?"

"It could be."

Cleomenes hesitated.

"No, fuck that," he continued, "not really, those old battles make for great *tragoudakia* in the music clubs at two in the morning but not for those of us who live up to our necks in the present. They're for the intellectual hacks up in Exarchia and the University to worry about. Money, my friend, has no memory. It moves on, always looking to the future, always on the make, like the young nowadays."

"Which in that respect," Akritas interjected, "they are very much like the old."

"You're are wise beyond your years Pano," his friend grinned.

"Was he holding the money for someone else?"

"Some people say it's rotten money that needs a front man to 'own' it. Archontas was, it is said, that man. But who's behind it, is a bit of mystery."

"Even for you?"

"Even for me," Petros said, "as hard as that is to believe. However, I personally don't thing he's fronting for someone else. He's the man in charge. But all these are rumours, but rumours in my game are important whether they're true or not, because it means no-one believes the publically available explanations. But it's Greece, isn't it? Does anyone believe anything anyone says when it comes to money? Or politics? Or sex for that matter? Also, unless it's all been decided already, I imagine there's going to be some fallout in the struggle to see who gets the loot."

"This sounds like a falling out among thieves."

"Unfortunately, Pano, the line between organized crime and commercial enterprise can be a little blurred."

Akritas leaned back and looked at his friend. He toyed with the spoon that came with his coffee and took a bite of the semolina sweet.

"Any idea where I should start looking into his money affairs?" he asked.

"Call my friend Haniotis at the National Bank of Greece. He knows more about how the money flows in this country than any man alive. Tell him I've referred you and he'll do all he can to help you. I'll have my secretary call your secretary with the number.

"My secretary!" Akritas exclaimed. "You scoundrel. How you like to rub it in! I'll get you back one day you old cynic. Us idealists, we'll inherit the earth you know. Eventually."

Cleomenes laughed out loud and the other patrons of the restaurant looked over at the two of them. The owner of To Kafenion, who knew Cleomenes well, looked over at them as well and smiled.

"You idealists, my good man, make our work so much easier. Which is why, by the way, we erect statues to you in the public gardens, like that one of Byron down the road. No-one will ever put up a statue to me and my kind. You idealists do us a great service because, while you're at it, we get on with the job. If there is anything financial behind your murder, Haniotis will know what it is. OK, now I must go, I have to get back to shoveling money into my clients' pockets."

"Are you planning to shovel any of that money into government tax coffers to help the economy?"

"Are you mad? They'd only give it to their relatives, at least the part they don't put in their own pockets."

"Incidentally, have you ever heard of a man named Aris Boutsekes or a woman Argyro Kanellopoulou?"

"The man's name means nothing to me. The woman is a prosecutor or something in the justice system, isn't she?"

"Yes, she is."

"I don't know anything about her other than she's supposed to be very good looking. Why are you interested in her?"

"She was the first to drag me into this affair."

"Sorry I can't help you. But I'll see what I can find."

"What about this man Haniotis' number?" Akritas asked.

Cleomenes wrote it down on the back of the receipt for the meal and handed it Akritas. The waiter brought the change from the

147

crumpled hundred euro note the financier put on the table and after a handshake and quick goodbye, Cleomenes walked over to the beautiful woman, talked to her for a minute, then was gone. Akritas sat at the table looking at the door of the restaurant and wondering why he'd never arrested his friend. Deciding finally that he couldn't arrest him because he never understood what the man was doing. In the meantime, the beautiful woman got up, paid her bill, and left.

Instead of going straight back to his car and over to headquarters, he went for a stroll in Kolonaki in order to let the fine lunch settle and to think further about what he'd learned. Had he learned anything from his friend? He walked on looking into shop windows. Window shopping was something that he did not do, but as there's very little else along Iaokim Patriarchou Street except shops, he started looking at what was on offer: shoes and boots, handbags, jewelry, expensive luggage, designer dress shops by the dozen, and one shop for men with Armani suits in the window. And there's an economic crisis on in this country, he thought, as he strolled along? Not in this part of the world. These people live on a different planet. And Nassos Archontas seemed to be living on that planet as well.

He spotted what looked like a reasonably unfashionable coffee bar on a side street and went in, sat down and ordered a double espresso. It came with a glass of water and a little saucer with two small biscuits, one blonde, one brunette. Although it was still a bright day outside, the room was rather dark and it took a minute for his eyes to adjust to the dim light. As he looked around, he suddenly realized that Katarina's sister, Anna-Maria, was sitting talking to a woman in one of the darker corners. She hadn't noticed him enter because she was absorbed in her conversation. He was about to go over to say hello, but thought better of it. He sipped his coffee and went over some of the details of the case in his head.

Lost in his thoughts, he hadn't noticed that Anna-Maria had risen and walked over to his table.

"Pano, what are you doing here," she said, "not your usual beat, is it?"

"No, it most definitely isn't. I just had lunch with a friend. I saw you when I came in, but you were talking and I didn't want to interrupt."

"That's OK, she's a sales rep from Italy. She's gone now anyway. Do you mind if I sit down?"

"By all means. Do you come to this place often?"

"No, never, it was Claudia that suggested it. Her hotel is just around the corner. Katie told me that when you're not around in the evenings with her, she should come up and sleep with me. Is she in some kind of danger?"

"Well, no, not really, but I'm working on what's turning out to be a dangerous case and I might be a bit of a target. It's pretty clear that she and I are close and that might just put her in danger. I thought it would be wiser if she spent the nights with you. I hope you don't mind."

"God no, Pano, I love having her around, although I have to admit I don't understand half the things she talks about, you know politics and stuff. But eventually I get her off that soapbox and we end up talking about shoes and clothes, and me trying to get her to wear sexier underwear and more make-up. Just because you're smart doesn't mean you have to look like a frump. After I've overcome all resistance, I start putting make-up on her and, you know, with a little work, she's damn gorgeous."

"I know," he said, "she's beautiful without any work."

"How bloody romantic of you. Why don't the two of you get married? You can't seem to stay away from each other. You're not gay are you?"

"No, I'm not," he laughed out loud, "although that might be a good explanation for the rest of the world. To be honest, Anna-

Maria, I'm not sure I'd be very good as a husband. There's something in me that freezes up when I think of a relationship getting too permanent. It's been difficult with Katarina because I do . . . I do . . ."

". . . love her?" Anna-Maria filled in the blank.

". . . yes, yes, but . . . there's something . . . maybe . . . well, me being a policeman . . . is it good for her?"

"I know," Anna-Maria said, "sometimes it bothers her, especially when the police do something vile, like those two cops who shot the teenager in Exarchia a few years ago. You should have heard her go on about your lot."

"We've learned never to talk about such stuff and a marriage isn't going to be very good if there are no-go areas that we need to avoid. Know what I'm saying?"

"But that's the way with all couples, isn't it? Or haven't you noticed, you high-minded prig?"

He laughed and nodded his head.

"Pano she loves you, you know. And, believe me, she's even capable of forgiving you for being a policeman. I'll take care of her while you're doing your job, but don't ignore her for long periods."

"Yes, yes, I know," he said.

"She needs you to be around now and again. She gets depressed when you don't call or come around. Is there anything else you'd like me to do?"

"Just be there with her. I don't want her to get hurt in any way. Listen, I'm on the way back to Alexandras Avenue, can I drop you somewhere?"

"No, it's OK, I have to get back to the shop and I've got my car."

"I'll be over tonight, by the way. We're going over to the Koutoulis' for dinner at nine."

"Oh, wonderful," Anna-Maria scoffed, "you can't possibly enjoy listening to those stuffed shirts talking and arguing for hours, can you?"

"I learn things," he answered, trying not to sound too much like an eager beaver student.

"Oh, I'm sure you do."

She stood up and was putting on her jacket when she looked down at him and was suddenly serious.

"You know, Pano, they have more to learn from you than you from them. They may be professors of this and that but they have no idea what you know, doing the job you do. I'm serious. You're a thoughtful, observant man and they would be wise to listen to you once in a while. But they're not wise, they're just good with the fancy talk. Katarina, by the way, can see the difference, even if she sometimes thinks you cops are all fascists."

They kissed on both cheeks and she clickety-clicked her way out of the café with every man and woman in the place watching her shapely form and lion's mane of black hair disappear into the light. Akritas sat back in the chair and wondered what perfume she was wearing. He'd caught a trace of a scent, a very familiar fragrance, as he kissed her cheeks. Then it came to him. It was Argyro, her scent, Voyages d'Hermès.

/14/

At the Koutoulis dinner party that night, Akritas did learn something. One of the guests was a man that he knew about but had never met. A distinguished law professor, the man had been Minister of Justice in the last PASOK regime. Akritas recalled what a breath of fresh air the new Minister brought to the moribund justice system. Bringing in reforms that were long overdue, he was resisted within the cabinet by the Minister of the Interior who thought that the Justice Minister's reforms were far too liberal and far too committed to human and civil rights to be of any use to the police and security services. Indeed, the Interior Minister believed they were obstacles deliberately put in the path of the police to thwart them. It was even rumoured in the press that he had called the Justice Minister a 'traitor' to his face during a particularly heated exchange in a cabinet meeting. But then exaggeration and melodrama are the stuff of party politics. The Prime Minister had to intervene to keep both men at their posts as both had threatened to resign if the other weren't immediately sacked. After the dust settled, they became sworn enemies and the Interior Minister did everything he could to thwart the reforms. Eventually the law professor decided butting heads with an illiterate oaf from Tirnavos was only giving him a migraine and so he resigned and returned to the relative obscurity of the ivory tower, if that graffiti bespattered Faculty of Law building between Akadimias and Solonos Streets could be called an ivory tower.

As soon as Katarina and Akritas arrived at the elegant flat in Neo Psychiko, they underwent the customary hellos, handshakes, and cheek kissing and when things had settled down, he headed straight for the sideboard with the drinks and poured himself a tumbler of aged Kardasi *tsipouro*. It was one of Dimitri Koutoulis's great discoveries, a small distillery in central Greece that bottled it straight from French and American oak casks after aging for two years, so that it had taken on a rich amber colour, unlike the colourless spirit found in the shops. It was absolutely delicious. Whereas the regular store-bought stuff, though not as harsh as *raki*, still burned a little as it went down, killing some of the flavour, the Kardasi *tsipouro* retained all its honeyed taste as it bathed your throat and tongue in a mellow warmth. For Akritas, this was usually the highlight of the evening at the Koutoulis penthouse. With his golden glass in hand, he settled down at one end of a very comfortable sofa and got himself ready for the usual evening, to quote Anna-Maria, of 'fancy talk'.

A short, wide man waddled towards him and dropped heavily right beside him. The sofa exhaled a grand sigh of air as the prosperously fat man sat down.

"Ah, Captain," the man said, "very nice to see you again."

Akritas raked his memory for a memory.

"Ah, yes, professor, how are you?"

This was a guess. The man must be a professor, why else would he be here, Akritas thought. Then as the man spoke, it all came back to him. He'd met him at one of these parties a few months earlier. Katarina had introduced them. He'd been impressed by the professor's very thick glasses and his tight curly hair. She had told him that the man was an important . . . what was it? . . .

anthropologist, no, there was more to it than that. Socio-anthropologist? Psycho-anthropologist? Anyway, there was a hyphen. He'd written an important book, Katarina had told him, about the mental world of the peasant, or something like that. She'd also told him that he'd tried to get her in bed. She'd declined the overture. "He was puffed up like a fat dove," she said. "It seemed to me he'd probably fuck like one," she added.

The entry phone buzzed and it was Søren Lazarides, the law professor and ex-Minister. The Danish first name was his father's doing; the father had also been a professor at the University of Athens, but in philosophy, and his most important contribution to scholarship was a book on Kierkegaard's impassioned existentialist critique of Hegel, the definitive study of the matter in his generation, translated into twelve languages. The son was then burdened with the Danish philosopher's first name and this had caused him a few problems. First of all it sounded strange in Greek and a little too much like a woman's name. It was also thought that the Interior Minister's suspicions about Lazarides's loyalty arose as a result of his queer 'foreignness'. That the Lazarides family had been at the forefront of the war of independence in the 1820s and had given to their country several generations of learned scholars, artists, two brave soldiers, and one rather good winemaker, mattered not at all to the oaf from the north.

Akritas had been one of Lazarides's main defenders in arguments about justice and policing on Alexandras Avenue. For him, the law professor represented the best in Greek traditions of justice and impartiality, of the law as an instrument for the common good, not as a political apparatus for enriching oneself and holding on to power. His support for Lazarides among his police comrades – most of whom had sided with the Interior Minister – alienated him from them socially and politically, and it had also stood in the way of promotions and preferment in the service. He watched the man making the rounds of the other academics in the room and after about forty-five minutes, he came over and sat down beside Akritas.

"They tell me you're a detective," he said.

"Yes sir, I am."

"Please call me Søren. Your name is Panos and you're with Katarina, I hear."

"Yes."

"You know she took a class of mine on law and ethics, about fifteen years ago I believe. She was one of the best of a very good group of students in that year."

"Yes, she's very bright."

"But a little too theoretically minded if I remember correctly," Lazarides said tilting his head and giving him a knowing wink.

"Something like that," Akritas replied smiling, "but she's a lot better these days on the pragmatic side."

"And what about you, Panos? What is it like being in the detection business?"

"I don't know, half the time I'm completely up to my nostril hairs in things, bits and pieces of evidence, and from them I have to construct a theory, well, actually not a theory strictly speaking, but a kind of story, a story in which each of the things has a role to play."

"Yes, detection is a form of story-making from the detritus that remains after the wretched act. Very good. I like that very much."

"Maybe it's a bit more complicated than that," Akritas continued. "The bits and pieces of evidence don't come to you in any particular order."

"They're like a heap," Lazarides said, warming to the subject.

"That's right. The thing is to lay them all out and find the right order."

"That sounds more like a jigsaw puzzle than a story."

"True," Akritas said, "the story emerges only after you've got all the pieces in the right order."

"Yes, I see. What are you working on at the moment, if you don't mind me asking?"

"The death of a man named Nassos Archontas and five others who he was associated with in the war years and during the Junta."

"But he must have died a while ago, he would be very old now."

"Ninety-one to be exact, but yes, he was murdered in his home three days ago."

"You don't say. Hard to feel sympathy knowing what I know. Are you very close to finding his killer?"

"Not yet. There is a trail of things that tells one story, but there are anomalies that suggest something altogether different."

"Do you know that Archontas has a thick dossier in the Justice Ministry about his wartime activities – he committed horrific crimes?"

"No, I don't," Akritas replied, leaning forward and putting down his drink..

"I remember reading the file and wanting to have him arrested but very powerful political people, and not a few higher-ups in the *Astynomia* by the way, threw up a wall around him and we were never able to get him before the courts."

Akritas was now sitting on the edge of the sofa, listening intently.

"Is it possible for me to have a look at the file?" he asked.

"If I were still minister, of course. But the current minister is a shallow, paranoid little man who will think you are trying to undermine him if you make the request. Especially if he didn't know you or what political party had got you your job."

"But I don't belong to any party," Akritas protested.

"That, my friend, would only be evidence that you're trying to hide something."

Akritas sat back and shook his head.

"I'll see what I can do, Panos. There are still a few good people working in the Ministry."

Lila Koutoulis called them in to dinner. Akritas sat with Katarina on one side and a professor of film studies who was also a well-known feminist on the other. Lazarides sat across the table and was soon engrossed in a conversation with the two people beside him.

After dinner, Akritas poured himself another glass of *tsipouro* and sat listening to Katarina and another faculty member discussing something they called 'the political aesthetics of displacement' – it sounded very much as if they were saying the thousands of migrants swimming, rowing, and paddling across the Mediterranean are beautiful people. He swirled the enchanting liquid, took a generous sip, and let it gently stroke his throat. As they talked, Lazarides came up to him and indicated he would like to speak. Akritas excused himself and walked over to a quiet corner of the drawing room with him.

"I'm sorry to interrupt, but I have to leave soon. I wanted to tell you something about Archontas that I remembered from his file. In the years during and after the Junta he was always travelling to Switzerland, at least two or three times a year, and after the fall of the Soviet system in Russia, he went to Moscow almost as many times in the 1990s."

"Was Switzerland on his itinerary for banking purposes?" Akritas asked.

"That's what we presumed. Why else would someone go to Zurich three times a year?"

"Why Moscow?"

"This was more of a mystery, considering his anti-communism in the early years. Only one thing surfaced. Our embassy reported one day that he had been seen on several occasions in the company of an aging ex-Soviet military officer who was suspected of being involved in the theft of the German gold reserves at the end of the war. Those of course had been stolen in turn by the Germans from the countries they occupied during the war, including our country, I might add."

"I thought that there had been a thorough accounting of gold transfers during the war by a technical committee at the Bretton Woods conference."

"You're well informed I see. Most of the transferring of bullion from one country to another during and shortly after the war has been well documented, except for two instances, two shipments one from Germany and the other from Yugoslavia. They left Berlin and Belgrade sometime in the winter of 1944-1945 and disappeared. They have never been traced."

"You think Archontas was involved?"

"When we started to investigate we were never able to establish anything concrete. We were given to understand that there were bank statements that looked as if the Yugoslav shipment had been turned into American dollars at one point but the documents went missing about fifteen years ago from our archives. Reports, invoices, and receipts have also vanished, and the Swiss were their usual helpful selves, or as my grandnephew says, Not! Archontas had many friends. There were constant political roadblocks put in our way by elements in the Interior Ministry. When I left the government, the investigation evaporated like a shallow puddle on a hot summer day. I don't know if that helps you, but there it is."

"Yes, it does help. Very much. Thank you for this information, sir. It's in keeping with the things I've learned recently about this man."

"Well then, goodbye, Panos and good luck. And I'll let you know about the dossier."

Akritas helped him on with his coat. Lazarides said goodbye to his hosts and some of the other guests and was gone. Katarina came up to him and put her arm through his.

"An interesting man, isn't he?" she said.

"Yes. He told me he taught you years ago."

"I learned more from that man in four months than I did from four years with all the others. He seemed to take a real interest in you. What did you talk about?"

"About justice and how solving a crime is like writing a story."

"Really? How is solving a crime like writing a story?"

He repeated some of his conversation but didn't say anything about the Archontas connection. Then they were drawn into a number of conversations with others in the room. Akritas, it seemed, had gained a certain amount of respect from the gathered academics because Lazarides had shown so much interest in him. After several more trips to the sideboard for the *tsipouro*, Akritas was very glad they'd taken a taxi to the party instead of driving.

They got back to Katarina's at 2:30 in the morning, and sat for a while talking in the living room. She was gossiping about things she'd heard at the party. He was listening with one ear and thinking about what Lazarides had told him when his mobile suddenly vibrated and lit up. It was Costas.

"Pano, I don't know whether you're asleep but there's been a development. A petrol bomb was thrown at the front door of Kanellopoulou's building. Not much damage but the whole neighbourhood is in an uproar and she's pretty freaked out. But worse still, our man out front has been killed. He was gunned down first and then the firebomb was thrown."

"Where are you now?"

"At the building. Boutsekes is here as well as a hundred other people."

"Why wasn't I called before?" Akritas demanded. "My phone was on the whole time."

"I don't know Pano, but there's something fishy about this whole episode. Boutsekes and his retinue arrived here within minutes of the explosion. Almost as if . . . I don't know. Can you come down here now?"

"Of course, see you soon."

He clicked off the phone and turned to Katarina.

"Yes, I know," she said, "duty calls. Shall I go up to Anna-Maria's?"

"Yes, I'm very sorry. Something's happened and one of our men has been killed. I'll be back as soon as I can."

Akritas knew what she was thinking. This is what being married to a policeman is all about. Calls in the middle of the night, death and danger. For a moment he wondered if he could get into another line of work. No, he couldn't. As he drove down the deserted streets of the city he was stone cold sober.

When he got to Gennadiou Street the whole neighbourhood seemed to be out in the bright police lights, some dressed, others in their dressing gowns and one bare-chested man in his pyjama bottoms. People were talking quietly in groups and only the occasional police siren broke into the murmur of many voices. Akritas parked his car, spotted Boutsekes, and walked right up to him.

"Why wasn't I called first?" he demanded. "Why are you here? Are you taking over this investigation?"

"When one of my men is killed," came the heated retort, "I'm the one responsible. And why didn't you tell me this whole affair was getting dangerous?"

"Because you already knew it. Sir!"

"OK calm down, Akritas, let's work together here. Why has the prosecutor been targeted again?"

"If we could answer that question the case would break open like a coconut hit with a hammer. There's something very odd about this case."

"Like what?" Boutsekes growled.

"There are things you know that you haven't bothered to tell me. Just like Kanellopoulou."

"Stop being so Greek, Akritas. There's no conspiracy behind the scene here."

"Are you sure? Kanellopoulou held back information until yesterday when the first attempt was made on her life."

"What information?" Boutsekes demanded.

"Doesn't it seem to you that someone is trying to silence her? I wonder who that could be. What is it she knows that makes her worth killing?"

"What information?" Boutsekes repeated, more belligerently.

"It was all bullshit. She was lying," Akritas lied, "but there's no doubt someone is trying to kill her. And I want to know who it is and why."

"Those are excellent questions, and we need to get some answers very soon. This explosion will get into the papers and then the Archontas murder will be brought up and the whole case will get the usual hysterical treatment."

"And what do you expect to tell the media when we know fuck-all about what's going on here?"

"The departmental response to the press is my affair. You start getting to the bottom of what's happening. And you do something about that temper of yours, hear?"

And with that he turned and walked away towards his official vehicle with the police driver and two or three assistants trailing in his wake. Fuck you, Akritas said under his breath as Boutsekes eased his bulk into the back seat. Costas walked up to him and both of them looked at the Chief's car as it pulled out and headed down towards Vasilissis Sofias Avenue.

"OK, who's the man who died?"

"Nikos Seretakos. He's twenty-seven and only been in the force for a year. He's married and has a kid."

"Damn," Akritas said.

"It seems," Costas began, "that the bomber walked up to him and shot him pointblank in the face. Because it happened just after

2AM there were no witnesses. Then, it seems, he threw the bomb at the door and took off. There's no other evidence to be found except for the bullet casing and the bullet that went through Seretakos' head. It hit the wall behind him."

Akritas could see the dead man already zipped up in a body bag. People had begun to drift off as the police investigation wound down. "Have you seen Kanellopoulou?" he asked Costas.

"No, she hasn't come down. There are a couple of women officers up there with her now. Are you going up to see her?

"Yeah, I don't want to, but I guess I have to. Why don't you go home now and I'll see you in the morning."

As the elevator was making its slow way up to the second floor, Akritas wondered what state he'd find her in. One of the policewomen opened the door. Argyro was sitting quietly on the white leather sofa staring at the front door. She stood up when she saw it was Akritas and walked quickly towards him.

"Pano, so good to see you. I'm glad you've come up to see me. Sit down and tell me what you think."

She motioned him to sit down on the sofa. "Would you like something to drink?"

"No, thanks," he said, "I came up to see how you are. I won't stay long. You should get some rest."

"This is another warning to me, isn't it?" she asked.

"Have any idea what you're being warned about?"

After a short silence, she said, "I don't."

Yes, you do, he thought, and wondered what could be done to get this woman to tell him everything she knew. I'll wait, he said to himself, I'll get it out of you yet.

"The two policewomen will stay with you tonight and we'll arrange for a higher level of protection tomorrow."

"They told me the young man downstairs has died. I'm so very sorry. Does he have a family? I can help with a donation if his family needs it."

"We can talk about that later," he said. "Things are getting nasty and we'll need something soon to give us an edge. But why are you a target? Any idea why someone wants to hurt you?"

"I don't know. Maybe someone I put away in the past. Who knows? I'm completely in the dark about this."

No you're not, Akritas thought, as he was going down the elevator. Outside, most of the locals had gone home. Things were wrapping up, but a detail of three men was left to guard the scorched entrance. Explosives and fire investigators would be there again first thing. When he got back to Katarina's, she was still awake. They talked a little, grew exhausted, and finally went to bed just as the dawn was beginning to brighten one end of the street. As he fell sleep he could hear the unwearied murmuring of the horrible grey doves

/15/

As he was driving to the centre in the morning, he remembered the phone number Petros Cleomenes had given him. Theodosis Haniotis had an office in the National Bank of Greece building on Stadiou Street that looked out over Klauthmonos Square. He phoned from work, mentioned Petros and was told to come later that morning. When he arrived for his appointment, he was asked to wait for a few minutes because Mr. Haniotis had someone with him. Ten minutes later he was shown into the banker's office. Haniotis looked up as he entered and presented Akritas with a poker face. He didn't stand up but motioned for his guest to sit in an easy chair a short distance from his desk. He picked up the phone and ordered someone to bring them coffee.

"I presume you'll have some, Captain?"

"Yes, of course."

"While we wait, let me just put away some of these papers and then we can talk."

He busied himself with a pile of documents on his desk, squaring them, then placed some in a tray on a corner of the desk and the rest in one of the drawers. He worked in a meticulous and systematic way. No wasted energy in movement; he seemed entirely self-possessed. There was nothing amiable about him, nor did he seem disagreeable, just intensely concentrated and orderly. Panos for a moment could not imagine him smiling or frowning. This was a man who had embraced neutrality with a passion that Akritas associated with professional gamblers and hitmen. He was neither old nor young; rather average in height, and quite lean so that he seemed to be taller. Short-cropped hair ending in a straight line across a wide forehead made him look a little like a Catholic priest. His was the kind of presence that one soon forgot and wondered if one had seen anyone at all. His eyes were sharp and piercing and Akritas had the impression that they were always open and observant, even when he was asleep. His thin, hawk-like nose gave his whole expression an air of alertness and decision.

When he finished, he looked up and gave him the rumour of a smile. Just then the door of the office opened and a woman brought the coffee on a silver tray. The coffee was standard American issue, with a silver creamer in the shape of a cow and a silver pot of sugar cubes on the side.

"Thank you Diotima, please help yourself, Captain."

"Thanks."

"Now, what can I do for you? I believe that you are interested in a certain Mr. Nassos Archontas."

"Yes, we're looking into his murder three days ago."

"Ah, so it is true. I was told that he had been liquidated."

Interesting choice of word, Akritas thought.

"How did you know, nothing has been released by the *Elliniki Astynomia*?"

"Excuse me, Captain, but the Ministry of Interior is just across the Square and there is very little that goes on there that we here, in the National Bank, don't get wind of. And *vice versa* I should add. No, the rumours started circulating about Mr. Archontas's demise a few hours after you chaps started investigating."

"Good to know our management of information is still working with its usual efficiency," Akritas said drily.

"Our state, sir," Haniotis offered, "is a sieve and all the flour settles nicely in the bowl with only a little shaking necessary, and sometimes none at all. From it one can very often make a relatively tasty cake." Something like a smile flitted across his lips, but there was no twinkle in his eyes. "Now, what do you want to know?"

"Where Archontas got his money."

"This is a difficult question to answer as, perhaps, Mr. Cleomenes made clear to you. To the best of my knowledge, this is what I know. Mr. Archontas was the mastermind behind a gang of former comrades in the wars 60 years ago who enriched themselves by stealing the wealth of others. Their gang began life, as you no doubt already know, as young recruits to a pro-Nazi Security Battalion that operated in the mountainous area west of Lamia, mainly north of Karpenisi and centred on the village of Aghia Triada, which was a hotbed of ELAS fighters and later of the so-called Democratic Army."

"I've heard that they committed many atrocities."

"They did and they were rewarded by the victors with sinecures in what we still quaintly call the civil service."

"You wouldn't happen to know who was responsible for placing these men in these positions?" Akritas asked.

" I'm not the best person to ask about this. Those were political decisions. But I do know that the records won't tell you much. The records of the government of the day are rather sketchy. I've been told that many have vanished or been doctored. But let me continue. Although they were all assigned to different ministries, they remained a tight-knit group, now operating as legitimate agents of a democratically elected government.

"Did they have any official duties?"

"No, none, so they were free to do whatever they liked. Of course, they were not the only ones from the former death squads and torturers who were given sinecures in the bureaucracy. Most of them whiled away their days at the *kafenion*, or in property speculation during the *polykatoikia* boom in the 1960s and 70s, or in other small time business activities, like owning a string of kiosks for example. The Archontas group was the exception. They were after bigger game."

"You mean that Archontas controlled a kind of organized crime enterprise within the bureaucracy?"

"Yes, very much so. They were in the government, therefore immune from proper prosecutions. They were also feared by their political contacts and their so-called supervisors. These men were murderers after all.

"So they had a free hand to do whatever they wanted?"

"Yes, but, more importantly, they had access to information about government funds, the tax records of citizens, especially of rich citizens, the gold reserves in this country and – with the help of former Wehrmacht comrades – the reserves in Yugoslavia and other countries. When communism fell to pieces in Russia they also forged alliances with the new rulers there as well."

"People must have known what they were doing," Akritas said.

"Of course."

"Didn't anyone do anything about it?"

Haniotis looked at Akritas and gave a slight toss of his head and snorted. He seemed to be marveling at an experienced detective's naïveté.

"Nothing was done," Haniotis continued. "The operations really got going under the Junta for whom they performed important security services."

"But after 1974 when the Junta fell, didn't the new government do something about these men."

"Nothing was done," Haniotis repeated. "Your Mr. Archontas knew everyone's secrets and so everyone left him and his henchmen alone. They became one of a number of state groups operating to enrich themselves in whatever way they could. Most of these were small-scale interests, simply relatives and friends of one politician or another making money on the side through influence-peddling. Their self-enrichment tactics were, typically, property speculations, legal manipulation of land-use by-laws, embezzlement, bribery, and when we joined the EU, the funneling of grants and subsidies into their own pockets, that sort of thing."

"I think our commercial crime unit has looked into some of these EU fiddles."

"Has anyone ever been arrested?" the banker asked.

"Not that I know of."

"Just so. Stealing from the EU was referred to as 'commission payments'. One of their primary tactics was getting a relative to set up a phony company, say in Cyprus, that 'advised' those seeking EU grants and subsidies about who to speak to in Brussels and how to fill out applications. For this they charged 'commissions' that varied from 30% to 50% of the funding. But next to Archontas's group this was penny ante stuff. They were the gold standard. In 30 years they had amassed a fortune of about 300 million Euros."

"Good lord," Akritas exclaimed, "you know this for sure?"

"Certainly. We don't know the exact amount down to the last cent and we don't know where most of it is now located."

"Is the money still in Greece?"

"Since de-regulation of international trade and banking in the 1980s, it has become very difficult to know where the very wealthy have their money hidden although I've heard about a law firm in Panama City that specializes in hiding money. But worse still, it is very difficult nowadays to distinguish wealth earned through legitimate business activities and the proceeds of crime."

"I know people who do not think there ever was a difference," Akritas said.

"They exaggerate. But let me tell you one more thing about the Archontas gang seeing that you are a policeman. One of the reasons Archontas was so powerful and untouchable by law enforcement was that he was well-connected with senior levels of the *Elliniki Astynomia*."

"Have you ever heard of Aris Boutsekes?" Akritas asked.

"You mean the Chief of Detectives? Your supervisor in fact? His name has come up in our monitoring of the file you've enquired about. In the Archontas organization, I would guess, if he's involved with them, he must be the gang's contact for security. Although I'm not sure what he does. But he seems to have replaced a man in the police who was caught in the crossfire during a November 17 operation several years ago. Do you remember it? I can't recall his name."

"Manolis Theklas," Akritas said, remembering the man quite well.

He'd been Chief before Boutsekes and had been shot dead by one of his own men who had thought that Theklas was one of the November 17 terrorists. It was recorded as an accident.

"Yes, that's the man," Haniotis continued. "I'm sure you people did a thorough investigation into the circumstances of his death." And the shadow of a smile spread quickly across his face and just as quickly disappeared.

"Why are you telling me all this?" Akritas asked. "I'm with the police, I might be part of the Archontas network."

"Dear Captain Akritas, you come with a solid gold reference. As long as you are not one of Mr. Cleomenes's clients, not one of whom can be trusted with their grandmother's marmalade, you are a man of honour and entirely reliable. Because we are a nation of double-dealers, main chancers, and thieves, we need a code of honour among honest men. Whether you like it or not, Mr. Cleomenes has vouched for you, so you are part of *our* network."

The idea that Petros Cleomenes was an 'honest' man amused Akritas. But who knows, maybe he was, in a Wonderland environment in which nothing is what it seems he could very well be the real Pope and the jolly one in Rome an imposter. If that were so, Akritas thought, you could put wheels on my grandmother and call her a cart.

"Excuse me, Mr. Haniotis, but how do you come by all this information?"

"I have seen a dossier . . ."

"From the Justice Ministry?" Akritas interrupted.

Haniotis hesitated, looked straight at Akritas and nodded his head.

"Yes," he said after a short pause, "it was information gathered by Ministry investigators when Lazarides was Minister."

"You know Dr. Lazarides?"

Haniotis put both of his hands flat on his desk and shook his head.

"No, I don't, but there are others in the Ministry who . . .," his voice trailed off. No more information about his sources was forthcoming and Akritas knew it.

"I suppose you don't have a copy of the file."

"No, I don't"

"Please go on," Akritas said. "What of the other five dead men? What were they?"

"Archontas was the brains, the strategist, the others were under his command. Have you ever patronized the kiosk just outside number 5 Stadiou Street?"

"Well, yes I have as a matter of fact, that's the office address of several professors in the University of Athens School of Media Studies."

"Ah, I didn't know that, but in any case, that kiosk was owned for years, along with many others, by a man named Nektarios Vekres, commonly known by his nickname of Hymous, or Juice. He was the enforcer, the muscle man on the team. He stood two meters in height and weighed well over one hundred kilos. Believe me when I say he filled up that little space in the kiosk handsomely. That kiosk, apart from selling chewing gum to

170

American tourists, was his 'office'. It's where he could be contacted by Archontas. His specialty was terrorizing the people with whom the group was doing business.

"How did he get that nickname?"

"During the Civil War, when the Archontas unit had to deal with prisoners. A man named Xeniades was the good cop, a sweet-talking charmer who promised the prisoner an easy ride for information. Vekres was the bad cop. I'm sure you know the scene, detective. These ELAS men were hard cases and eventually 'Juice' would have to deal with them physically. He would punch them in the face until blood flowed from their mouths, then he would kick them out of the chair. When they were on the floor, he would sit on them, and squeeze more 'juice' through their broken teeth."

"Nice," Akritas murmured.

"They were a very effective team. One of them, an Aleko Echecrates, was the accountant. It is believed he kept impeccable account books of the operation. If we could get our hands on those books we would be able to unravel this knot completely. Christos Hecatos was the liaison officer with non-governmental organizations like the Church. Archontas was a great benefactor of the Church and helped to keep the Orthodox hierarchy looking the other way. The last man, is a shadowy figure who hailed from the Black Sea area, Greek father, Russian mother. His name is Ivan Askisis. He was in charge of logistics and communications. It's through him that Archontas connected with the Russian oligarchs after communism disappeared. Of course, Soviet communism had evaporated years earlier, but the damn word hung around for many decades getting in the way of business. Finally Gorbachev, an unfortunate idealist, did the right thing and began the process that finally erased it from Russian history. Askisis was at Yeltsin's side when his troops fired on the Duma in – what was it? – 1992."

"1993," Akritas said.

"The amazing thing is the coincidence that the group all lived into their eighties. Who would have guessed it? A random group of men all living into their eighties, rather surprising, wouldn't you say?"

"Hmmm, yes. Last question, do you have any idea why they've all been murdered? And who might be responsible?"

"I wish I could help you with some facts, but I cannot. My guess is that as the original group has aged, and others, like your Mr. Boutsekes, have come to realize how much money is at stake, what we are seeing is the typical succession struggle among gangsters. What or who the warring parties are all about, I can be of no particular help. Your guess is as good as mine."

"Oh, one more thing, Mr. Haniotis, do you know someone named Argyro Kanellopoulou?"

"No, I know the family name. Is she related to the Kanellopoulos family here in Athens?"

"I don't think so, because she told me she was from Evrytania, Aghia Triada as a matter of fact, although that might be a lie. She's a prosecutor in Athens, young, in her mid 30s, and was the first official person who wanted to get me involved in this case. Boutsekes was the second. There has been one attempt on her life and a second firebombing of the building where she lives, as a kind of warning I think. Unfortunately one of our uniformed officers guarding the building was gunned down."

"Interesting, but I can't help you with Ms Kanellopoulou."

"Well, thank you very much, Mr. Haniotis, you've been very helpful."

"It was a pleasure meeting you, detective, good luck with your investigation. If I can be of any further help, please do not hesitate to get in touch."

He rose, shook the banker's hand, and walked out, saying goodbye to Diotima. As he cut through Klauthmonos Square towards Christou Lada Street where he'd parked the Opel, he saw a dusty dog sitting quietly in the dirt watching a bedraggled, homeless man who seemed to be in a spirited conversation with some chirruping finches. Good luck to him in winning that argument, Akritas thought as he turned the corner into Karytsi Square. The Opel was across the street from the church. When he got to the car, a man suddenly materialized by his elbow and a pistol, a Makarov, used by the Russian and Syrian police, stuck into his ribs. The old lady in the red dress who always sat under the church walls begging looked over at them and then lowered her eyes.

"Get in the car and drive," the man said in a whisper, "and don't turn around."

He did as he was told. The gunman got into the back seat right behind him. He had not seen the man's face, but he recognized the voice. It was the man from Plaka the night of the attempt on Argyro's life.

"Where to?" Akritas asked.

"Kallithea, get onto Syggrou, take the Thiseos turn and go straight south. I'll tell you when to turn."

They drove in silence as Akritas made all the turns to get onto the main boulevard south towards Neo Faliro. For no particular reason, the name Thiseos reminded him of one night he and Katarina had gone to the Kelari jazz club near the Thissio Metro station and heard a redheaded girl singer bopping with two chumps, one played the piano and then there was the Jesus-faced cello player. Jesus was so into his own sound and tempi he held the other two back. Akritas was fascinated by the girl singer who must have been all of 25 and had the whiskey grained voice of a Julie London. Unfortunately, Katarina noticed his interest, misinterpreted it, and was sullen for most of the evening.

"What's in Kallithea?" he asked.

"Shut up," came the snarly reply.

"OK, listen, I know you're a tough guy, especially with the gun up against the back of my neck, so why don't you drop the play-acting, you're beginning to sound like a cartoon heavy in a B-movie. What's in Kallithea?"

"Someone wants to talk to you."

"Who?"

"You'll find out soon enough."

They drove on in silence, turned down Thiseos and headed southwest towards the coast. At Davaki Square, the gunman told him to turn right on Sivinatidou Street and then an immediate right. Turning into Arapaki Street, he saw a garage door opening near a sign for a German language school on the left and was told to enter. When the door was closed, he was told to get out of the car and not look behind him. A door at one end of the garage opened and a tall, flat-faced man in jeans stood there waiting for them. He was escorted down a long hall to a room with a desk and several chairs. The air stank of cigarette smoke and sweat.

The room looked like some funeral vault. Shallow, ill-lit, a low ceiling inducing claustrophobia. It was placarded with posters of naked women and images of glamorous celebrities fixed to the walls with scotch tape. Akritas imagined himself in some foreign house of the dead with portraits of the deceased covering the holes into which they had been thrust. A paunchy man sat behind a wooden table looking like a devout recluse who had taken up quarters there worshipping Kim Kardashian's ass. A single desk lamp, with a green shade, cast a dim light. A shadowy figure stood in one corner of the room. Akritas was pushed towards a chair in front of the table behind which the pudgy, ugly recluse sat smoking a cigarette. The ashtray to his right was heaped to overflowing. The two escorts stood behind him. He could feel the Makarov still trained on the back of his head.

The ugly man behind the desk said nothing. Thin brown eyebrows made a straight line just above his eyes. A soft mat of pale brown hair looked fake but probably wasn't. Shit brown eyes stared at him.

"Captain Akritas," he began in a soft nasal voice, "welcome. Please excuse the cloak and dagger stuff but we need to have a little chat." He was trying to be amiable but only succeeded in being ominous. Akritas was not cowed.

"You know my name, but I don't know yours."

"Just call me Gareth."

"Gareth! What's that? Are you a foreigner? What kind of name is that?"

"It's Welsh if you must know, I'm as a Greek as you are, but let's say Gareth's my *nom de guerre*?"

"Oh, please, let's get past the theatrics, Gareth. What do you want with me?"

"We need to tell you that Argyro Kanellopoulou is a dead woman and we'd rather you weren't caught in the crossfire. Next time when we have her cornered, it would be best if you just ducked out of the way and let us get on with our business."

"Are you fucking mad, Gareth? Look, you had your chance at the Dioskouroi and you blew it. And then the firebombing of the building was a silly stunt and it got one of our men killed. You think we're just going to forget about it? This isn't New Jersey, you stupid sonofabitch. When one of ours goes down, we catch the bastards who did it and punish them. And if it isn't me, because you decide to kill me, then someone else will come after your fucking ass. Now she's got a three-man detail at her front door and two well-armed policewomen living with her. You're going to need a combat team, Gareth, a little better trained than the chumps who fucked up the Dioskouroi hit."

"Calm down, detective. You're right, we botched our first shot."

"What actually happened there? Why did the guy coming up behind me draw his gun so soon?"

"It was a mistake. He thought a woman further down the hill was Kanellopoulou. His gun was out so he just continued up the hill."

"And the guy in the narrow lane opposite?" Akritas asked. "What's his excuse? He must have had her in his sights before she got behind the metal table."

"He arrived late. The shooting had already started."

"Sweet Jesus! He arrived late? Are you kidding me?"

"OK that's enough of that," Gareth growled.

"So, what does Boutsekes want then?" Akritas asked taking a chance that somehow his boss was connected with all this.

Gareth was silent for a moment. He looked past Akritas to the gunman standing in the back. He thought, shit, this is it, they're going to kill me. He wished he'd had a chance to call Katarina, just to hear her voice one last time. Then Gareth looked back at him and smiled, a fat, pendulous, slug-like smile. Suddenly a mobile phone began to buzz. It was Akritas'. He looked at Gareth and shrugged a question with his hands open before him.

"Don't touch the fucking phone, or Vlassios will put a bullet in your head."

The phone continued to buzz, then suddenly stopped.

"What's your role in all this Gareth? Who do you work for?"

"Let's say I'm the messenger," he replied, "and who I work for doesn't concern you."

"A messenger," Akritas said, 'you mean like Hermes?"

Gareth was beginning to look exasperated.

"Listen to me detective, here's the thing, you're caught in the middle of a war, understand? It was her guys who tried to kill you on Patission the other day."

"Why would she do that? Just a few hours earlier she'd asked me to look into the case."

"Yeah, that's because you're her stooge in this game we're playing. Incidentally, if you hadn't ducked the Dane would have deliberately missed you. She doesn't want you dead. Not yet anyway. She's a wily bitch and she's good at throwing all kinds of distractions out there to confuse matters. She's hunting big game and you, my friend, are a small fish in her pond. Hasn't she tried to seduce you yet? Blowjobs for chumps like you are her specialty, for tangling you up in her web."

Akritas had the sudden urge to tell Gareth to stop with the mixed up metaphors, he was getting dizzy.

"And so," Akritas ventured, "you're on Boutsekes' side and what's the score with that? Are Boutsekes and the bitch going after the same thing?"

"None of your fucking business," Gareth retorted, "we're just telling you that what she says to you and what she's playing at are two different things. She'll sacrifice you once she's sucked out all your blood."

More fucking metaphors. The image of a mosquito dressed in black satin and black patent pumps suddenly went through his mind. He had to struggle to stop himself from laughing out loud. Dangerous situations always had the strange effect of making him want to laugh. It was a nervous reflex

"Fine," Akritas said, "what about the murdered guys, why is the Archontas crew all dead? What have they got to do with this?"

Gareth ignored the question.

"We're going to let you go, detective, but we want you to know that when we get our next shot at her, if you're in the way, we'll kill you. We don't want to do that."

"Is that," Akritas interrupted, "because Boutsekes needs me down at the station?"

"Has anyone ever told you're a fucking irritating smartass? And take this with you. This will answer your question about the dead guys."

He opened a drawer and pulled out a file folder with some papers in it, carefully using a handkerchief so as not to leave any fingerprints.

"Take this. It will tell you all you need to know about Kanellopoulou and why she's involved in this shit. Oh, and don't bother coming down here and busting in, we're just borrowing the space from a guy who doesn't even know we're here."

Akritas took the folder and was about to look at the contents when Vlassios grabbed him by the jacket with one hand and yanked him out of the chair. Swung him around and thrust him towards the door. The other man stepped aside to let Akritas pass and opened the door. Vlassios shoved him out. Then the door was slammed shut behind him. He found himself alone in the dimly lit hall facing the door to the garage down at the other end. Wearily, he walked the ten meters and found the Opel sitting there with the lights still on. Crap, he thought, I hope the battery hasn't died. It hadn't. Then with a smile on his lips as he recalled the absurdity of what had just happened, he pulled out into the dazzling afternoon sunlight of Kallithea.

/16/

"Where are you? I called earlier." It was Costas.

"I'm in Kallithea, driving up Thiseos. Sorry, couldn't answer the phone. Being interviewed by a man with a pudgy face that looked like a clear plastic bag full of yogurt."

"What?"

"His name was Gareth, he said he wasn't Welsh, but I have my doubts. Have you ever seen pictures of Dylan Thomas near the end of his life? I was brought to the meeting by his henchman, Vlassios, who had a Makarov pistol pointed at the back of my head the whole time. Gareth, I should add, had absolutely no idea how metaphors work. In the end he gave me a folder to read."

"Come on, Pano, are you making this up?"

"You can't make this stuff up, Costa, anyway I don't have the imagination. Look it's best we don't talk on these mobiles. Are you at the office?"

"No, I'm having coffee at that little Italian café on Kolokotroni and Praxitelous Street, the place named after the Sicilian detective, the one in the novels."

"You mean Montalbano? I know the place. Is the place named after a detective in a novel? Are the stories any good?"

"Don't know," Costas replied, "never read them, but the young woman who serves here – and I might add seems to have taken a shine to me – she told me. Anyway, how close are you to the center?"

"Just turning onto Syggrou. I can be there in fifteen minutes or an hour depending on the parking. Stay there. We need to talk."

When Akritas walked through the door of the café twenty minutes later, Costas and his young server friend were in deep conversation. They made such a nice couple just sitting there talking and laughing that he didn't want to interrupt them. Costas had been pretty much on his own during the rancorous divorce. Did this *tête-à-tête* have the makings of a new departure, one more turning of the page of life? Jeesus, shut up, Akritas said to himself. As he closed the door behind him the young woman looked up and Costas turned round.

"Ah, Pano, there you are. Here, meet Mara."

"Hi Mara, how are you?"

"Very well thank you. What can I get you?"

"Uhhmm, what's good?"

"Mara makes a killer cappuccino," Costas broke in.

"OK, that sounds good, oh, make it a double and no chocolate. Thanks."

Mara went behind the counter. Akritas sat down and looked at Costas. He leaned closer to his partner.

"Have you," he whispered, "told her what you do yet?"

"Not the whole story, quite yet," Costas replied.

He plunked the file folder on the marble tabletop.

"Gareth gave me this to read. He said it would explain why the six old men had to die. I haven't had a chance to look at it yet."

"So, who the hell is this guy Gareth?" Costas asked.

"My guess is he's got something to do with Boutsekes."

"Boutsekes? Are you sure?"

"No, but it is possible the Chief is mixed up in all this in some way I haven't figured out yet. Maybe Gareth does Boutsekes' dirty work. This really seems to be some kind of struggle for the wealth Archontas and his five comrades amassed over the last forty plus years. I was told about the money by Haniotis the banker." He tapped the file folder. "Gareth gave me this and I'm hoping it helps piece together why these men were killed."

"You can trust what's there?"

"Don't know. But think about this Costa. Kanellopoulou told me about another old man, you know, the guy who owns the Karavias chain of fabric shops, Klopas Karavias, he's the money behind the killings."

"Why? He must be a hundred years old by now."

"Ninety-four. He was a communist years ago, got arrested, tortured, and then recanted his political beliefs and they let him go. He started his business and became rich."

"What, is he a lunatic, or something?"

"It seems he's mad all right, angry mad. Getting his revenge. Kanellopoulou told me he's recruited a gang of young radical leftists for the job. They're the ones who do the killings. How this relates to getting possession of the money, I'm not exactly sure."

He tapped the folder again.

"I'm hoping this helps."

"So," Costas said, "we've got what look like two cases happening, not one. There are the murders and then there's a question of who gets the money. Is that it?"

"Something like that," Akritas said, "but the relationship between the two isn't that clear to me. There's revenge and there's theft. We need to see how the two fit together."

Mara brought his coffee, smiled, and went back behind the counter.

"She seems like a very nice woman," Akritas said.

"Yeah, she is, and there's absolutely nothing about her that reminds me of Stavroula."

Akritas looked at his partner and smiled as he drank his coffee.

"Good. Listen, carry on with the witness interviews. Also can you look into Boutsekes' activities – his finances, friendships, anything you can dig up. Let's not tip him off that our focus in this has shifted. Will you do that?"

"Of course."

"I'm off then to read what's in here."

He tapped the folder for a third time and stood up. He took several more sips of his cappuccino, which was excellent. He finished it, put the cup down, and looked at Mara. She was on the phone. Putting her palm over the mouthpiece, she lip-synched a goodbye. Akritas nodded to Costas and walked out.

Back at Alexandras Avenue, he sat down at his desk and examined the folder's contents. There were nine pages. Two were what looked like a report. Two were a list of names and a chronology, and the last five looked like photocopies of bank statements and pages from a ledger.

The 'report' looked awfully dodgy. Who'd written it? And why? It alleged that Argyro Kanellopoulou had in the course of another investigation come across information about Archontas's wealth. All of it black money. On her own, it seems, she'd looked into who he was and uncovered all the available information about his wartime activities. The dossier in the Ministry of Justice, Akritas thought. Had she seen it? At some point she realized that the Archontas unit was responsible for many of the atrocities up in the area of Aghia Triada, her family's home village, and that they may have in fact been responsible for the torture and murder of her grandfather and his brother. Ah! he thought, the revenge motive. But this is not what the pages he was reading went on to say. The writer said she was only after the money. Not a word about avenging the family honour. He put the pages down and wondered if what he was reading were true. Perhaps that explained her lavish lifestyle. Coming from a village in central Greece and a deputy prosecutor's salary did not add up to the luxury he'd seen in her flat.

Her leaned back in his chair. Is this for real, he thought? He put the two pages down and picked up the next two. There was a list of names, the names of several banks in Athens, Zurich, and Moscow and a dozen or so foreign phone numbers. Beside these there were the initials MF with an address in Panama City, Panama. Among the names, he found his about half way down the first page. There were others he recognized. Boutsekes and Karavias, a Danish name that he presumed was the hitman, then a series of names, six in all, which he didn't recognize. And finally the names of all the members of the Archontas gang with their addresses and phone numbers. There was also a list of what appeared to be ancient vases and artefacts. He reckoned they were the ones in the drawings. The second page had a series of dates that looked like a chronology. A couple of the dates had notations. The first was an AK – Argyro? – visiting KK – Karavias? A little further down one date had Zurich written beside it, some German names, and an Air Aegean reservation number. Further down still, Moscow, a reservation number, and a Russian name – Anatoli Seskov. There was also the name of a bank in Beirut, but some information beside the name was blacked out. Finally, there was the name of a bank in Panama City, a man's name, Señor Adelberto Mendoza-MacLeod, and what looked like an account number. At the very bottom of the second page there were two circled letters AS.

So, here's the raw data, he thought. Why have I been give this? It certainly shines a new light on Argyro Kanellopoulou. But could all this be trusted? Was he being set up by someone like Boutsekes in the same way he'd been led astray by Argyro's stories when they first talked? He turned to the last five pages. They were photocopies of bank transfer notices for millions of Euros, Swiss francs, and British pounds from banks in Zurich, London, and Moscow. The name or names of the receiving institutions were blacked out. The senders were all impressive sounding corporate entities. Akritas was no forensic accountant but they looked like typical commercial transactions. The largest amount was for 105 million Swiss francs from a Zurich bank, the others for lesser but still quite large amounts. A quick calculation put the figure at around 300 million Euros. Haniotis came to mind again as the man who'd journeyed up the murky river of this financial jungle. Maybe he'd see things in these documents that were invisible to an amateur's eye.

Money-laundering? Bank transfers through third parties, to where? Panama? Lebanon? He put the photocopies down and leaned back in his chair. A headache was coming on. The light outside was fading fast and he wondered what Katarina was doing. He could hear the traffic noise on Alexandras and someone speaking loudly down the hall. Looking around the room with its beaten up desks, stained walls, grime-streaked windows, he suddenly felt old and dead. He wasn't tired, just empty and hapless. He thought of the €43 in his trouser pocket and then of the millions of Euros and Swiss francs and British pounds flowing from bank accounts in one continent to accounts in other continents. From one fatcat millionaire to another. He felt suddenly nauseous. It was a world that made you want to vomit. Then the crime scene photos of the dead men's corpses, slashed and bruised, flooded his brain and he shivered. How was all of this civilized? How was it superior to, an improvement on the broken-down drug addict scoring in Karaiskaki Square at this very moment, then hurrying into an alley, a brothel light gleaming in the night, and shooting up so that his evening might pass cuddled by mother smack instead of doubled over sweating and weeping among the fat dogs sleeping in the weed-choked park? Meanwhile in Panama City some fat men were sitting around a teak table smoking Cuban

Fonseca cigars and drinking thirty-year-old scotch. He looked towards the window. His city was dark and he knew it was full of pain.

Vibrations woke him from his reverie. The phone was buzzing.

"*Ela*," he said wearily.

"You OK, mate?" Greg asked.

"Greg, hi, hi, I'm fine, just sitting here thinking about a case."

"Look, Pano, I'm on my way over to Oscar Wilde. Meet for a drink in half an hour?"

"Yeah, OK, I'll see you there."

He clicked off and picked up the landline and called Katarina.

"Hi, darling," she said, "how nice to hear your voice again. I was just thinking about you."

"Greg just called me," he said, "and asked me to go have a drink with him. Are you busy later on tonight? Or maybe you want to come to the centre and meet us at the Irish place."

"I'm in the middle of something. Why don't you come over when you and Greg are finished?"

"Yes, I'll do that. It'll probably be in a couple of hours."

"That's fine. I've got at least that amount of work to do. See you after 9 then."

"I've missed you Katarina, many kisses," he said.

He could hear her smiling as she hung up the phone. His mobile buzzed again. Costas' number flashed up on the tiny screen.

"Yes?"

"Pano, you still at the office?"

"Yes, anything new?"

"Do you need me for anything tonight?" Costas asked. "Mara and I are getting together after she finishes work."

"One thing. Can you call all the others and have them meet us here at 10 tomorrow morning. I need to hear about the interviews. Can you do that?"

"Of course. Ten tomorrow then."

"And," Akritas added, "don't say too much about what we know so far. OK?"

"Yes, sure, sure."

In the elevator, Akritas flipped through the folder again and decided he'd better keep it to himself. He wondered what Boutsekes had to do with all this. Was it possible he was after the money too or was he just someone else's dummy? And why was a rich man like Karavias involved in all this crap anyway? It didn't really make sense.

Greg was sitting talking to Jimmy, the Greek-American bartender from Detroit, when Akritas arrived. He slid into the seat beside his friend and listened to Jimmy describing some erotic encounter he'd had with an American schoolteacher from Tulsa who was in town with a Baptist tour group visiting Biblical sites. They'd just arrived from Thessaloniki and were at the Areopagus as Jimmy was walking around the Sacred Rock on his way to work from Makrigiannis. She'd wandered away from the group and wanted to see a little more of old Athens. Jimmy brought her around towards Thissio pointing out all the sights. Finally arriving at the pub, he'd asked if she was thirsty and would she like something to drink. She came in, sat down and was still there at closing time. Jimmy walked over asked her where she was staying and offered to make sure she got home safe seeing as it was 2AM. When they got to the Hotel Carolina, she more or less dragged him into her room and started to undress him.

"Yeah, of course she was drunk," he said, drying a glass slowly. "She was begging me to do her. It was hard to resist, but you guys should be proud of me. I undressed her, put her in bed and left. I didn't touch her."

"Bravo Jimmy, you did the right thing," Greg said.

"I might give the hotel a call later and she how she's doing. Hey, hi there, Pano. You arrested that bastard, the Prime Minister, yet?"

"Not yet, Jimmy. Can I have a Black Barrel, no ice, no water? Greg, how are you my friend, any more problems with the lawyer?"

"After she thanked me for the €500, no receipt, I probably won't hear from her again for six months, unless she's short of cash and dreams up one more obstacle we need to clear. What are you up to?"

"I've got this tricky case and every time something happens or I find something out, I'm no closer to busting it open than when I started. Each bit of evidence raises more questions than it answers. I fucking hate these cases. They're too much like life. Everything gets more complicated the older you get. Hey, can I ask you something?"

"Sure."

"If you had a pile of dirty money, you know black money, and you wanted to put it in a safe place, I mean a bank, not in the back of your fridge, which bank would you use?"

"If I was in Britain either HSBC or Barclays. I don't know why they've come to mind, but it's maybe because they've had to pay fines for sleazy business practises. If I was here in Greece, I'd probably go with Eurobank, just from the fact when you go into one of their branches it's so dilapidated and dirty it's got to be a front for something shady. Otherwise, I'd use some sleazy financial institution in either Cyprus or Lebanon."

"Lebanon? Why Lebanon?"

"Ever since the civil war, the banks there have become the financial wing of organized crime in North Africa and the Mideast."

"How do you know?"

"Some mates who made a bundle in Iraq used Lebanon as a way of whitening up the cash so they could bring it into the UK without raising any suspicions and without getting Inland Revenue on their case.

"Did it work?"

"Sure did. They only had a fifteen percent commission to pay the guys in Beirut. British tax would have been in forty plus range. Well, that's what they told me and I know they're not bullshitters. Hey, they're from Brum."

"What were they? Contractors?"

"I don't really know, Pano. These are guys you don't ask questions."

Akritas took a sip of his drink and looked at his watch. It was 7:38. He had an hour to kill before he made his way to Katarina's. He ordered one more Black Barrel. Greg ordered another sleeve of Kilkenny Red.

"How's Katia?" Akritas asked.

Greg launched into a long complaint about his relationship with the woman of his dreams. This was all familiar terrain. They'd been together for five years and obviously loved each other but to hear them talk about it, you would have been excused thinking they were in the last, desperate throes of an ugly divorce. He ended the lamentation with the surprising news that they were going to be married in the summer.

"About fucking time," Akritas snorted. "You two will go to your graves complaining about each other but you'll have the goddamned undertaker put you in the same coffin. The poet says, 'none do there I think embrace', but you two will figure out a way."

Greg leaned over and put his arm around his friend's shoulders and gave him an awkward man-hug that was just barely this side of drunken.

"Pano, I know, the booze has loosened my tongue, but I have a stone sober suggestion."

"Yeah, what?" Akritas said, expecting humour.

"Why don't you ask Katarina to marry you and then the four of us can all get married together?"

Akritas put his drink down.

"Nothing would give me greater pleasure, my friend, if only this voice in my head would stop warning me not to go there."

"You're talking in riddles, Pano. It's like that silly joke about short-term memory. 'Not only is my short-term memory horrible, but so is my short-term memory'."

It took Akritas a moment, then he laughed.

"If the idea gives you pleasure," Greg said, "how can you even hear the voice?"

"Greg, Greg, I love Katarina, but the idea scares me."

"You think your fear is too much to overcome? Read, man, read. The things that torment us the most are the very things that connect us with the people who matter most. All the great writers know that."

"Any suggestions?"

"We're in his house getting drunk. How about *The Picture of Dorian Grey*? Or even better anything by Kazantzakis. Listen to me, when you want to trick yourself, concoct a thoroughly credible ruse."

"Now, you're not making any sense."

He paused. A thoroughly credible ruse. Then the crimes he was trying to unravel came into focus.

"Wait," he said, "yes, you are making sense. You're a genius Greg."

Now it was his turn to give his friend a hug.

They talked for an hour more and then it was time for Akritas to go. As he got up he realized that the gunman who'd taken him to Kallithea was sitting in a corner of the pub near the door. After saying goodbye to Greg, he walked over and looked down at him.

"How you doing Zorba? Any chance I can lose you for a few hours while I visit my girlfriend?"

"Fuck off," was the sullen reply.

Akritas laughed and went out. He walked up Asttigos Street and ducked into a dark doorway. His 'tail' came out of the Irish pub, looked both ways and turned in the opposite direction. Akritas waited for a few minutes, then came out, found the Opel and headed north for Maroussi. Katarina was happy to see him when he arrived. She asked if he was staying the night and when he said yes, she took him in her arms.

"I love you *morro mou*. Let's go to bed early tonight."

"You mean now?"

"If you want to," she said, "but I was thinking sometime before 11. Do you want something to drink? Or eat maybe? My mother made some chick pea soup."

"What I'd really like is a glass of *tsipouro* and maybe a bit of feta with that nice bread from down the street."

"Do you want me to cut up a tomato?"

"I'd love it. How're your parents?" After the day's events all he wanted was to be immersed again in normal, every day life.

"They're fine. My Dad's gall bladder seems to be acting up again but he knows what he's got to do to keep it in check. But you know what he's like, can't give up his favourite foods or sweets. I'm a bit worried about Anna-Maria, she seems to be staying out all hours and also trying to work at the shop. I can see that it's affecting her health."

"She's an adult. She can take care of herself. I think she's tougher and smarter than you think."

"I hope you're right," Katarina said gazing into his face.

She crossed herself three times quickly, looking as if she were strumming a banjo, but after the open palm on her chest, she still seemed anxious.

Akritas too was anxious because of the complications of the case. His only comfort these days was Katarina's arms. After the *tsipouro* and feta, they talked for a while and then, hand in hand, they wandered slowly down the hall to their place of rest.

/17/

When he walked into the detectives' room the next morning at nine thirty, the whole team was already there.

"Good morning. Let's go down the hall to meeting room D."

As they trooped down the hall, Costas came up beside him and indicated that he wanted to speak to him privately. They stood outside the door.

"Someone who works for Boutsekes told me earlier this morning that he's been having financial difficulties for the last six months. It seems the crisis has hit him rather badly. He had bank stocks that have fallen through the floor. Because he was leveraged to the hilt, his cash flow hasn't been able to keep up with his liabilities. He's been forced to sell quite a few properties and at a discount as the property market has tanked. He's managed to keep most of his troubles secret, but he's very worried that the higher-ups are going to find out and he'll be canned."

"The bastard is too well connected for that to happen. And he's got everyone's dirty little secrets as insurance."

"Also, and get this, someone broke into his flat and stole some private papers. They have information about his financial dealings that could be used to blackmail him. All this happened about two days before the firebombing at Kanelopoulou's building. It occurred to me that maybe the two events are related. What do you think?"

"Yup," Akritas mused, "could be. The person who told you all this, how do they know?"

"She's been having an affair with him but she found out that while he was screwing her he was also screwing some tart over in Sepolia."

"Is this Afroditi whatshername?"

"Yeah, how did you know?"

"Everyone knows. She's probably in the best position to know all this shit about him. Anyway, thanks for the information, very useful stuff. Let's go in."

When they entered, the uniformed officers were chatting away about football. Statiris was playing around with his phone. Akritas sat down and asked the uniforms to report on their interviews. Nothing much of interest had come up from the peripheral witnesses like cleaners, cooks, and building concierges. Then he turned to Tolio.

"The six people I talked to were all pretty tight-lipped. I didn't get much more from them than we already knew, or at least what was written in the reports. However, one thing did strike me as weird, that wasn't mentioned in the reports. They all seemed afraid, scared, as if they had been threatened maybe. One of them, a grandson of Ivan Askisis, was sweating the whole time I was speaking to him. He was also tongue-tied and hesitated for a long time before answering any question. It seemed to me he was making up porkies as we were going along and had to work out some line of consistent bullshit. I guess that's about it."

"I had the same impression with my people," Costas said.

"Anything else, Costa?"

"A granddaughter of Vekres had a diamond ring the size of a golf ball on one of her fingers. When I commented on how beautiful it looked, she seemed embarrassed and said it was gift from her husband. Then she did her best to hide her hand. I think she was kicking herself for not taking it off before meeting me."

"That reminds me," Statiris broke in, "the grandson of Evangelos Xeniades arrived at our meeting in a silver Lamborghini Gallardo. It was beautiful, but jeez who the hell can afford that kind of ride nowadays? Also he had a good-looking blonde in the passenger seat who couldn't have been more than 18. He looked like he was in his late 50s."

"I see," Akritas said, "anything else from any of you?"

One of the uniformed officers said a maid for Mr. Hecatos told him about an interesting change that echoed what the others had just said. The great-grandchildren of Mr. Hecatos would come over to the house a lot. Over time they all started wearing expensive clothes and shoes with lots of jewellery and expensive looking electronic gear. One of them the maid remembered especially because she once saw Mr. Hecatos give her lot of cash in €100 notes, maybe twenty or thirty. When she first started coming over she must have been about eighteen and had just started at one of the private colleges. She'd usually take the Metro and bus, but after a while she started showing up in a BMW and instead of the jeans and the cheap H&M blouses she used to wear, she would come in expensive slacks, cashmere pullovers, and a Gucci bag where before she'd only had an Adidas backpack.

"It seems that the fortunes of the families of the victims improved with time," Akritas said. "Let's see if we can pinpoint when exactly this change began to happen. And did it happen at the same time for all the families?"

They went over more information from the interviews and the picture of increasing wealth emerged more clearly than ever. If the Archontas gang were beginning to repatriate the money then their families were also reaping the rewards. No wonder they wanted to keep quiet and to have the investigation over and done with as soon as possible. Akritas wondered if they had a local banker who facilitated the transfers from the other cities where the bank accounts listed in the folder were located. Another question to ask Haniotis. After an hour or so, Akritas gave them some new orders. When the group was gone, he called Diotima and made an appointment to see Haniotis later that day.

In the meantime, he called Argyro's mobile and asked if he could come over to see her. She said, yes, of course. As he drove towards Kolonaki, he wondered how far to go in revealing what he knew. In the end, he decided to play it by ear. First, of all he didn't really know whether all the information about her in the folder was true or not. Maybe it was disinformation put out by the people who were trying to kill her. He decided to tell her about Gareth and what he'd said about her. When he arrived at her flat, a policewoman opened the door after checking his identity with the guards downstairs. When he'd been let in, he told the two policewomen to go out for a coffee. Argyro came out of her bedroom in a gold coloured silk dressing gown and it seemed pretty clear as she led him into the sitting room that she had very little on underneath. Her black hair was heaped up high and held in place with the ebony hair sticks, stray curls hung around her neck and she had a gold necklace with what looked like a solid gold pendant nestled in her ample cleavage.

"Can I get you something to drink, Pano?" she asked.

"A coffee would be good."

"Anything stronger? I have some very good Scotch."

He laughed.

"Hey Argyro, you've been trying to get me to have some of that single malt Scotch ever since I saw you in your office. OK, why don't you bring me a coffee and a very small taste of that fine Scotch you have."

She nodded her head in approval and smiled. She disappeared into the kitchen. He looked around the room. It was tastefully furnished and reeked of money. After about five minutes she emerged with the coffee and the glass of Scotch. She leaned forward and put them on the coffee table in front of Akritas. Without meaning to, he looked straight down into the valley between her breasts. OK, he thought, here goes, time to throw the dice.

"Argyro, can I ask you something?"

"Of course, Pano, go ahead."

"I hope you don't think this is forward of me but I know you're a civil servant. I don't know how much a deputy prosecutor makes but it can't be that much, so how can you afford a place in Kolonaki and with what looks like very expensive furniture, art, electronics, clothes, and other stuff?"

She smiled and looked pleased with herself.

"I've had some very generous benefactors," she said. "I don't mind telling you that I've got a career ahead of me in politics and it's interested some people who want to help me make a difference in our country. They've been very open-handed in supporting my plans."

"Yeah, but you're PASOK and they're toast. So, how are you going to get into politics with a party that's headed for the dustbin of history?"

"PASOK may be done," she said eagerly, "but that doesn't mean the political process is over. Process and timing are everything in politics. What we see today will be gone tomorrow and people will be dealing with an entirely new situation. What you were yesterday won't count for much when they see what you are today. Do you understand? I'm moving on Pano, not standing still."

"But, how are you going to finance it? If PASOK is a dead letter what party are you going to go to next?"

"What if I told you I might form my own party?"

"My first reaction would be that you're dreaming in technicolour."

She laughed out loud and her breasts shook under the silk as she tossed her head back and exposed her throat. Akritas looked at her and realized that perhaps he was blind to the majesty of her genius. Or at least the majesty of her sensuality.

"Look, Argyro, don't you think the people have memories? Won't they remember what you were and find what you've become a bit of a con? I hope you don't mind me being blunt?"

"Of course, Pano, what do you take me for? A fragile little *neraida*? People will believe of me what they believe and none of it will be flattering, but in the end they will get behind the leader who seems to have the most personal authority, the leader who has a grasp of things, a grasp of reality. They will follow me if I am confident enough and convince them that their individual fates, as diverse as they are, rest in good hands. Mine."

She looked at Akritas and gave him a sweet little smile that said, if you hitch your fate to mine you'll be well taken care of. He could see the sort of power she had. Aimed at a weaker personality her magnetism would be overpowering.

"Now I know," he began, "why they want to kill you."

"What do you mean? Have you found out who wants to hurt me? And why?" she asked.

"Yesterday, I was taken at gunpoint to see a fat man named Gareth – no it's not a joke – Gareth is responsible for trying to kill you at the Dioskouroi and the firebombing. He wanted to warn me that if I tried to protect you, he'd kill me too. For some reason Gareth and whoever he works for don't want me dead. Not just yet anyway. He said that the attempt on my life was your doing and that you brought the Danish hitman to Athens, not the Karavias gang. That your story about Karavias and revenge was a smokescreen for something else. But I said that it was you who'd first suggested I get involved in the case, so why would you want me dead the very next day? He said the Dane would have deliberately missed me had I not gotten down in time. That you want me alive, for now. Any idea what all this means?"

"Did you believe him?"

"Are you kidding? This case is so full of anomalies and false trails that I don't believe anything anyone says. Even you, Argyro, I have to take with a grain of salt.

"You don't mean that, do you?"

"I have to. An investigation is just like watching a film. Only it's as though you always get in ten minutes after the movie started, and no-one will tell you the plot, so you have to work it out all by yourself from the clues. But in this case, it seems that I arrived a half hour late and there seem to be two movies playing at the same time.'

"I'm not following what you're saying. What two movies are you talking about?" she asked, beginning to look a little alarmed.

"Here's the thing. The suggestion is that you've got some scam going and that all this revenge stuff is rubbish to make it more difficult to get the drift of the real plot. To be honest, I would have thought Xiloudes was doing just fine. Had no clue what was going on. Unless, of course, he was a little too clueless. If we do have a puppetmaster here, it's important that the investigating officer read the evidence in the right way, the clues that will lead to a plausible, but totally irrelevant conclusion. Plots and stories of imagination tend to elude those without one, don't they?"

"OK, Panos, you've got a great imagination but let's get to the truth. Your boss, Boutsekes, wants me dead because he's worried that I'm going to have influence in politics and that I'll represent and promote everything he hates."

"Do you really expect me to believe that? That Boutsekes has a team out there looking to murder you because you might, one day, represent a political idea that he disagrees with?"

"And why is that so hard to believe?" she asked sounding both belligerent and wounded in equal measures.

"Let me be very honest, Argyro, I don't believe a word of it. He's after something else and you are too probably. I presume you're both after the same thing. In my line of work if the reward isn't revenge or sex, it's about money. I think you'd better start coming up with something that sounds a little more plausible. No-one in this country is that interested in politics for its own sake. We're interested in what politicians can do for us. Period. What can you do for me? How much money can you put in my pocket?"

"Your pocket? Are you asking for a bribe or something?"

"A bribe? Me? I don't want anything, Argyro. Money means nothing to me. Can you understand that? I used to believe in things like justice and law and that it was possible to make this that kind of orderly country. I no longer believe that. Then, I wasted some time not believing anything, finding a little satisfaction in irony and black humour. All I want now is to get to the bottom of this case. Fuck everything else. The only thing that matters is following through on the work, making the work count for something and the work for today is trying to figure out why you're giving me nothing but bullshit. Why does Boutsekes want to kill you and who is he working for? He's too stupid to be doing this for himself. And where the fuck did you get all this money?"

And with that he drank down the two fingers of the finest Scotch money can buy and looked at Argyro who was sitting there, with her legs crossed and the dressing gown laying her leg bare half way up her thigh. She was staring at him. He couldn't tell whether she was trying to control her temper or whether she was about to throw off the silk gown and offer herself to him. She did neither. She took up her coffee and had a sip. She replaced the cup very carefully in the saucer and looked at him again.

"You know, Panos, where I get my money is really none of your business. And why Boutsekes wants to kill me – if that's true – I have no idea. Yes, he is stupid, so how you think I'd ever be involved in anything that has him anywhere near it is, frankly, insulting to me."

She spoke calmly and without emotion. It was a practiced gambler or actor's demeanour. Akritas looked at her steadily.

"You know, Argyro, you're good, you're very good. And to be honest if I didn't know you as one of the most impressive liars in Greece, I'd probably vote for you in an election."

"Are you trying to provoke me, Panos? Because if you are, it won't work. Look, let me explain something to you. Everything I've ever wanted or liked best has been a fucking fistfight. Everything I've ever gained has been because I could fight. And win."

She paused. It had all come out in a hot rush. She could see the sudden show of heated vehemence had taken Akritas by surprise.

"Do you hear me?" she zeroed in. "I know what you're doing. You've run into a dead end with the case and now you'd like me to open a door so that you won't look like a fool. Well, I can't. I've told you all I know. I think Karavias is the person you should be insulting, not me. I'm innocent of whatever you think I've got hidden somewhere in the background."

For a moment there was silence. Her eyes burned with a cold flame, scorching, devouring, commandeering.

"You know what I've learned being a cop?" he began quietly. "It's probably not worth doing something or pursuing an idea unless someone, somewhere, would much rather you weren't doing it."

He looked at his watch.

"OK, I've got to get somewhere. I'll send the two women up when I get downstairs. On Monday when you go to work, the two women will accompany you and we'll provide an escort car just in case."

"Fine," she said, looking strained, angry, and unhappy, and having, in the meantime, closed the gown completely.

"I'll be back," Akritas said, not caring if it sounded like a threat, "and we'll carry on our conversation. But remember this, Argyro, I know the truth is out there somewhere, but the lies are always inside our heads."

As he was going down the elevator, Akritas, thought of the *nerantzaki*, the orange-like fruit that grows everywhere in Athens. It looks delicious, sweet, and juicy, but inside it's dead bitter. Argyro, he said under his breath, you'd better add a lot of sugar to the bitter fruit, to make the syrupy treat people like having with their coffee. When he got to his car, he took a deep breath and pulled out into Gennadiou Street and headed for the wide boulevard down the hill, turned right, towards Syntagma and Stadiou Street for his appointment with the banker. The sky above was a blue dome as he crossed the wide boulevards. It was like changeless metal and beneath only complexity, mire, and blood. As he was passing the National Library building on Panepistimiou he heard an EKAB ambulance behind him. Siren on and lights flashing. It was accompanied by two motorcycle police units. They raced past him and turned down Pesmazoglou Street towards Stadiou. A police car, siren on, shot by and by the time he'd turned towards Stadiou Street following the ambulance and police units, he realized something of some consequence was happening.

At the front of the National Bank of Greece, with its striking façade that hadn't yet made up its mind whether it was neo-classical or baroque, there were several police cars, motorcycle units, and two ambulances. Cops were rushing in and out of the building, blue lights were flashing, and a big crowd had gathered across the street looking on. He parked the Opel and sprinted towards the door of the bank. He identified himself, ran across the lobby and took the stairs two at a time to the third floor. The commotion on the third floor was just as chaotic as out on the street. It was all focussed on Haniotis' suite of offices. He was out of breath and his lungs were burning. But he managed to get to the door, showed his warrant card, looked in and saw Diotima sitting at her desk weeping. Then his phone started buzzing loudly, over and over again. He ignored it.

"Diotima," he said between breaths, "what's happened?"

She looked up at him, wild-eyed, and between sobs tried to speak.

"Mistah Ka ... Ha ... Haniotis," she began, "he ... he .. dead."

He looked past her desk into the office and saw the banker's sprawled body, riddled with bullets, looking as if he were trying to swim through a pool of blood.

His phone buzzed.

"Pano," Costas said, "I've been trying to reach you. Something's happened."

"Yes, I know, Haniotis is dead. Shot."

"Haniotis the banker?"

"Yes."

"But that's not what I want to tell you."

"Well?"

"Get ready, this is bad. Katarina has been kidnapped."

"What?"

"Sorry to break it to you over the phone, Pano, but it's true."

"Wait. Did you say kidnapped? What happened?"

"Witnesses say that three men stopped her while she was walking on Akademias Street near Sina, bundled her into a grey BMW, and drove off into Kolonaki. It happened about 45 minutes ago. I was just told."

"How did they identify who it was?"

"People say her handbag fell to the ground in the scuffle. It's more likely the kidnappers let it go deliberately. She had her briefcase over her shoulder, but national ID and a couple of credit cards and some other papers and stuff were in the bag. I have it here with me. Someone upstairs decided it was part of our case."

"I'll be there as soon as I can."

He clicked off the phone and sprinted down the hall to the stairs, going down two steps at a time. Outside there was still pandemonium, but he zigzagged his way to the Opel, jumped in and was off, almost running over two tourists who were standing in the street taking snapshots. He cursed them and gunned the car towards Syntagma and the wide boulevards that would take him to Alexandras Avenue. As he drove, his heart was beating fast and not from the physical exertion. He immediately thought of Argyro. Was this her doing? If she had Karavias' squad of young killers at her beck and call, then maybe they were responsible for killing the banker. His earlier confrontation with her may have forced her hand. Looking into his rearview mirror, he suddenly realized that he may very well be a real target now instead of an extra in Argyro's little drama. He half expected the Dane to be following him on a red motorcycle. Don't jump to conclusions, he said to himself, let's look at all the evidence first. Soutsou Street was slow and with each passing minute his anxiety increased, then his anger.

He thought of how Katarina might be feeling in captivity and he suddenly felt a spasm of rage – murderous rage. If Argyro was responsible for this, he'd pursue her to the ends of the earth. Was it punishment for letting Argyro know that he suspected her of something? If Xiloudes was unable to pick up on the right storyline, perhaps he was only too able looking past the obvious and finding the little anomalies and contraries in the scripted tale. He was Panos Akritas after all, the cleverest detective of them all, he thought bitterly. Yeah, so damned clever he'd forgotten to protect Katarina, the sweetest and most innocent woman on earth. He banged the steering wheel of the Opel with his open hands as he waited.

But it was true, he'd not been fooled by the smokescreen, because he'd seen odd, anomalous shapes drifting in and out of it. Too much of the evidence was vigorously and self-consciously pointing at itself, waving its arms in his face. Look here I am, follow me down this path. Two and two is four, see? But instead of four he kept coming up with 300 million. Things didn't add up after the evidence insisted the sum had already been calculated. He had finally reached the place where there was no longer a way forward on the neatly paved road. It was time to get off the main track and head across unmapped terrain. What was it the ancient rhetoricians used to call that experience, yes, *aporia*, a puzzle that leads to an impasse, that stops the unfolding story in its tracks. *A-poros*, 'no passage this way' is what it meant in the old language. With it came the feeling you get when you are at a loss, unable to work through a problem, cross a place, or reach a person. He'd been troubled by that feeling from the start. In the end, the fog had lifted and he could see more clearly the rough ground ahead. But now the adversary was on to him.

Xiloudes was allowed to go off to Xanthi to live with his mother. No, Akritas wasn't going to be given a pension and sent off to Patras to tend his mother's grave with little *arybolloi* of olive oil and flowers. They'd put a bullet in his head first. And then he could be laid beside her in the family plot. And who would place little bottles of olive oil and flowers on his grave? He felt cold, then angry, frustrated and bitter, lingered awhile in utter despair, then the polar winds blew through his body again.

The grimy elevator up to the eighth floor seemed slower than usual. As the steel box passed the fourth floor he banged his palm against the grey steel wall. Costas was out in the hall waiting for him. He grabbed his arm and pulled him into the detectives' room. Smell of human sweat infused the air. There was no-one else about.

"Any more news?" Akritas asked, trying to control his desperation.

"Not yet, but wait, there's something else. Listen. Boutsekes did not come into work today."

"Fuck Boutsekes, Costa, what about Katarina?"

"Just hold on, listen to me. A police general, I think it was Solovos, called his home. His wife said he left for work as usual. That was around eight this morning. The general asked if there was anywhere else he might have gone, like a café for breakfast. The wife then said that he had a mistress in Sepolia who he visited most mornings on his way to work. She gave name, address, and telephone number and before you ask how she knew, she had a private detective tailing him. Anyway, there was no answer at the flat and Boutsekes wasn't answering his mobile. A unit was sent over there. They broke in and found Boutsekes and the woman dead. They were on the floor of the bedroom naked and they'd been shot execution style in the back of the head."

"Boutsekes dead? And the poor tart too? What about Katarina?"

"Nothing yet from whoever took her."

"Let's get our team together as soon as possible and call Solovos upstairs and ask him, no, tell him to assign three more motorcycle units to us for the day. We're going to pay Klopas Karavias a visit. We're going to search every inch of his house. Also we'll need to start leaning on the relatives. They're all hiding something. Finally, we're going to bring Argyro Kanellopoulou in for interrogation here, not in her flat or her office. We'll wait until she's at work tomorrow morning and then we'll go in and detain her in full view of everyone in the building and we're going to take her out in handcuffs. Got that?"

"Are you sure, Pano?"

"Never been surer."

Pulling the team together to raid Karavias's mansion took about an hour, except for Tolio who was not in the building. Eventually Costas contacted him and told him what was happening. He was told to meet the group at the Karavias house in Plaka. It took a few minutes to get everyone in position around the house on Nav. Nikodimou Street. Tolio was left outside with two uniformed men locking down all the entry and exit points. He argued strenuously to be allowed to go into the house as well. Akritas refused. When they had the outside covered, Akritas gave the signal, walked up to the front door knocked and, without waiting, had the battering ram driven into the double doors. They splintered and one immediately came off its hinges. When Akritas, Costas and four uniforms entered they found a startled maid standing at the far end of the front hall with her fist to her mouth and eyes wide open.

"Spread out and start searching," Akritas ordered, "and you over there sit down in that chair and don't move. Who's in the house?"

The maid was frightened into speechlessness.

"Come on, come on, who's in the house?"

"Just the cook in the kitchen and the master," she blurted out, pointing up the neo-classical staircase with its small baroque *putti* leering at nothing.

"Anyone else? Are you expecting anyone?"

"The master said that Melina is coming over sometime today."

"Who's Melina?" Then he remembered. "You mean his daughter."

"Yes sir, her."

"Is his wife here?"

"No, she's at the house in Kifissia."

"OK, stay there and don't get up. Where's Karavias now?"

"Up in his study, beside his bedroom."

"Where's that?"

She pointed up the stairs and said it was the hall to the left. Second door was the study. When Akritas entered the old man was sitting in a brown leather armchair. He was looking at the door, obviously having heard the commotion downstairs. A book rested face down on his knees. Klopas Karavias was a collapsed man. White hair looked as if a high wind had just blown through the book-lined study. Watery eyes set in a bony face stared unsteadily at Akritas. His chest was sunken and his breath coming in short wheezes. He looked dazed, but not frightened. One frail hand came up and shaded his eyes.

"Who . . . who are you? What do you want?"

"Captain Panos Akritas of the *Astynomia*. We're searching your house because you've been named by a prosecutor as being involved in the murders of six men. Nassos Archontas being the latest. The others were associates of Archontas and we know you've known them for a very long time. I can give you their names if you want. You should know that my men are now searching your house. There have also been three more incidents related to these murders. We suspect your involvement in them as well."

The old man was silent and for a moment seemed to be semi-conscious. Then with what seemed an act of will he came widely alert. Finally he spoke with surprising firmness.

"Yes, I know these men. They were fascists in the dark years and if they are dead it is all they deserve. May they rot in hell."

"You have been accused of recruiting and supporting financially the killers of these men."

"If anyone had come to me asking for money to assassinate those bastards I would have given it willingly. But no-one came. So, I deny your accusation."

"Do you know Argyro Kanellopoulou?"

There was the slightest hesitation. Then he spoke, less steadily than before.

"I kno . . . know the name. If she's related to the former prime minister then I know the family, but if she's not, no, I … I don't know her. Who is she?"

Costas appeared at the door and called to Akritas to come with him.

"You wait here. I'll be back."

Costas led the way downstairs and into the sub-basement. One of the uniformed men was standing beside a table with a briefcase lying on it.

"We found this down here," Costas said. "Do you recognize it? Could it be Katarina's?"

Akritas looked at it. Although he'd seen her with a briefcase often, he'd never paid much attention to it. He couldn't be sure.

"If it is hers, her fingerprints and DNA will be all over it. Bag it and send it to the lab. That's the only way we'll know for sure. It was empty, I take it?"

The uniform nodded.

"Anything else down here?"

"Nothing yet," Costas said, "but it's a bit of a labyrinth."

Back upstairs, Karavias was still sitting in the armchair, with his eyes closed, when Akritas returned.

"Mr. Karavias, can you tell me how you knew Archontas and his men?"

The old man opened his eyes and looked at Akritas as if he were a stranger.

"Ah, detective, you're back."

"Did you hear my question? How did you know Archontas and his men?"

"It was during the Civil War, I was in the Democratic Army and was captured in late 1948. I was taken to the prison island of Gioura and then transferred to Makronisos. I was there for five years. Xeniades questioned me and Vekres beat me up on several occasions. Archontas would come in now and then to watch and in the end he offered me a way out. Sign the recantation paper and go free, or stay on the island for several more years. I was tired. I wanted to see my family again. I signed. But in my heart I didn't recant. Months later they let me go. Archontas himself saw me off on the boat and he even gave me 100 drachmas and a pat on the back. I hated the man."

"Did you have any further contact with Archontas or any of his comrades?"

"No. I saw Vekres once or twice at that kiosk on Stadiou Street. I don't think he recognized me. Archontas I saw in Plaka once drinking coffee with several other men including two police officers in uniform. But by that time I had started my business and wanted to forget about the past."

"Do you know a man named Aris Boutsekes?"

"No, never heard of him."

"Did you sell your company recently to a Dutch firm?"

"Well, detective, you're very well informed. Yes. I did. What of it?"

"Where's the money you made?"

"What? Why are you asking? It's really none of your business."

"Listen, it's either you tell me now or we drag you out of here in handcuffs and you tell me on Alexandras Avenue."

"I am not scared of handcuffs, sir, I have been in them before. But if you must know I kept enough of the profit to keep me and my wife going in our old age and I gave the rest to my children."

"Have you recruited and paid for a group of young extremists and used them as a death squad?"

"Are you mad?"

"Have you?"

"No."

"Stay here. I'm not finished with you yet."

Akritas went out in the hall and called Costas. Nothing. He started down the stairs when Costas came bounding up from the basement. The maid was still sitting in the front hall, hands in her lap and a frightened look on her face. It was getting late in the day and the room was falling into gray dusk. Akritas looked at the young woman.

"Go turn on some lights on this floor, then come straight back and sit down."

She did as she was told.

"Pano," Costas pleaded, "you've got to come down here. We've found something."

Akritas followed Costas down the stairs, along several hallways, past several rooms. They came to a doorway, in what would have been the central chamber if this were a labyrinth. Costas opened the door. The room had no-one in it, but an armoire had been moved from its position against the wall. Akritas peered behind the piece and looked straight into a dimly lit chamber. They walked in and found one of the uniformed men holding an AK47.

"What's this?" Akritas asked.

"Look around, it's a weapons cache," Costas said beaming. "There's half a dozen assault rifles, twenty or so pistols, body armour, night-goggles, and a military ammunition box with hand grenades. The grenades are NATO issue. I remember them when I was in the army."

"Well, well, well," Akritas murmured, "I think we got the old bastard by the balls. Let's bring him down here and have him explain this. Go get him Costa. I want to take a closer look at this stuff."

Twenty minutes later Costas returned with the old man crumpled awkwardly in a wheelchair.

"Sorry it took so long, but Mr. Karavias has trouble with stairs. We had to take the elevator in the other part of the house. He wasn't sure where the wheelchair was."

Once they were all in the room with the arsenal, Akritas asked Karavias why he had all these weapons in his house. The old man looked genuinely surprised. He shook his head and just looked around the room. He was shown some of the weapons and he just shook his head.

"I don't know," he began, "I don't know."

"Don't know what?" Akritas asked.

"I don't know what this is. Where did it all come from?"

"Are you saying you didn't know this was down here?"

"I never come down here. I haven't been down here for a long time. Why are they here?"

"That, sir, is the million dollar question."

The old man was wheeled back upstairs and Akritas called for a police van and more men to collect the weapons. He then started looking into every one of the rooms in the basement. They were all finished with expensive wood paneling, fireplaces with mantelpieces, and furniture. Some were bedrooms, others looked like studies or offices. There were at least eight rooms. When he entered one, he saw a single bed and armoire, and one of the uniformed men was going through the drawers of an ornate bureau.

"Hi, there, Spyros, what have you got on your belt?"

"Hi, boss, it's a scarf that I found wedged between the wall and the bed. I also found this bracelet down there too."

"Let me see them."

As soon as he saw the scarf he knew that Katarina had been in this room. The bracelet too was hers. Akritas recognized it instantly because he'd given it to her when he'd come back from Istanbul about a year or so earlier. It was a delicate thing with intertwined threads of white and yellow gold. He wondered whether she deliberately left the two items there thinking that perhaps he'd find them. Clever girl, he thought. So, the Karavias house was being used as a weapons depot and safe house. Maybe the old man didn't know, but perhaps the maid and the cook knew something.

He walked upstairs to the front hall and told the maid to get the cook. They both returned and he motioned them to go into a sitting room off the front hall. Costas came down the stairs and they entered the sitting room and closed the door.

"Who uses the downstairs bedrooms and offices?" Akritas asked the maid.

"Now only visitors, but nobody usually. Except recently there have been a bunch of people coming and going from downstairs and the master said it was all right. He'd arranged it with a friend of his for them to use the basement rooms."

"Who's the friend?"

"I don't know his name sir, but he's a friend of the master's daughter."

"Would you recognize him or any of the other people if you saw them again?"

"Yes, some of them but not all."

"Was there anyone here today – a young woman with black hair – that was brought in who've you've never seen before and might have looked like she was being taken downstairs against her will."

"I was upstairs most of the day helping Mr. Karavias. So, no I didn't see anything different. People were coming and going though and some seemed in a hurry because they were slamming doors and talking loudly. They were rushing about a lot."

"Did you hear anything of what they were saying?"

"I'm sorry no. Just words here and there."

"Like?"

"'Call the boss,' was one of them. I heard the word 'Sepolia' because my sister lives up that way. But nothing else really."

The cook had been in the kitchen all day and had seen nothing at all. He let the two of them go to attend to the old man. Akritas then gathered all the police in the front hall and asked if they'd found anything else. One of the uniformed officers said there was an art book open on a desk downstairs with drawings of some of the pictures in the book.

"Show me," Akritas said.

When he saw the book open to the picture of the small sculpture with its head on backwards and then a few pages on a picture of the funeral *stele* with the open hands, he smiled to himself. Yes, this is the command centre for the gang. But how did they come and go without arousing any suspicion? The old man was not entirely gaga but he was clearly unable to move around the house easily and the stairs of course were a problem, so people could come and go in the basement rooms without exciting any notice. Who was giving the orders? Could it be the old man?

"Bag all this stuff and bring it back to the office."

He went up the stairs, found the maid in the sitting room. He looked at her.

"Have you ever seen a red motorcycle parked outside or belonging to any of the people who are coming and going?"

"Yes, but not lately. I don't know who it belongs to. It was parked on the pavement by the wall for a couple of days. One of the men who clean up outside asked me if I knew who it belonged to. I haven't seen it lately."

He wished he had a picture of Argyro to show the maid. If Argyro was somehow involved in all this, and she was the one who had put Akritas onto Karavias, she might have actually visited the old man's mansion.

"Tell the old man his door is broken down and he should get someone in to fix it today. Send the invoice to the procurement office in police headquarters."

The old man would be reimbursed in about a year. Or never, which was more likely. The *Astynomia* did not, as a matter of course, volunteer reimbursements unless someone made a big stink and got a cabinet minister to put pressure on the Chief of Police. Out in the front hall the bagged evidence was piled up in a heap awaiting the police van. Akritas looked at the stuff.

"Is it all here from downstairs? Is there anything anyone found that I haven't seen yet?"

"No," Costas answered, "that's it."

"Anything happening outside? Call the guys in here."

When Tolio and the two uniforms came in, he asked if they had anything to report.

"There were a few bystanders," Tolio said. "They were wondering what was happening here."

"Did you say anything to them?"

"No, not really."

"Tolio, what the hell does that mean?"

"Well, there were a couple of guys who approached Jason and asked what was going on. I intervened before he said anything and told them it was just a routine police investigation and that they should move on. Which they did."

"Don't forget the woman," one of the uniformed men said, "who came towards the house, saw us, turned and walked away quickly. I went after her but she'd disappeared down one of the side streets by the time I got to where she'd turned off Nikodimou."

Melina, the daughter, Akritas guessed.

"Yeah, that's right," Tolio said, "I forgot about her."

Akritas could see that Tolio was agitated about something. It was probably because he'd had to do the donkeywork of standing around outside locking down the perimeter. As Akritas turned to leave, Tolio's mobile started buzzing and he walked off to answer it. He saw Costas standing in the busted doorway.

"Time to go, Costas," he called, "leave three men here to guard the place and let them wait for the van to pick up the stuff. They should stay here until we get some relief for them the rest of the night. The new guys will be relieved in the morning. Bring the briefcase with you, also the scarf and bracelet that Spyros has."

As they were leaving, a silver Mercedes drove up and a portly woman in a cream-coloured pantsuit heaved herself out, leaving the car in the middle of the road. A scarlet gash where a proper mouth should have been disfigured her face. Ten thousand hours of sun had tanned her skin to the consistency of a cow's hide. Her neck, wrists, and fingers were swaddled in chunky gold necklaces, bracelets, and evil-looking rings. She was a heavy load of nasty trash.

"Excuse me, who's in charge here?" she called out.

"What's it to you?" Akritas asked. "And move your car before I have it impounded."

"My name is Blana, Nancy Blana, I'm Mr. Karavias' lawyer. What's going on here?"

"Your name is what?"

"Blana, Nancy Blana."

"Right, Ms Blana. Go inside and talk to your client, he'll explain it all to you. But move your car first."

And with that Akritas turned, walked briskly to the Opel, got in and drove off, wondering the whole time what kind of weird name Nancy Blana was. Could it possibly be Greek? Maybe Albanian?

Back at Alexandras Avenue, Akritas gave Costas the key to Katarina's flat in Maroussi and told him to take one of the crime scene guys to pick up her fingerprints.

"And while you're up there go to Karavias' house in Kifissia and bring the daughter Melina down here. Put her in a cell for the night. I'll talk to her tomorrow."

"What charge?" Costas asked.

"Unlawful possession of illegal weapons and explosives and leaving the scene of a crime."

"Right."

"Oh, and Costas send the briefcase down to the lab to have it dusted for fingerprints as well.

He suddenly felt very tired and decided to bed down for a couple of hours on one of several camp beds that were there for the night guys. With Katarina gone he knew he wasn't going to be able to go to his flat and sleep. What could they possibly want with her? The thought kept him awake until he slipped into a state of restless stupor.

/18/

At midnight, he woke with a start. He looked around the darkened detectives' room. The traffic on Alexandras Avenue snarled its way east and west. It was Friday night and the strident yells and curses of young people out partying reached all the way up to the camp bed where he lay on his side contemplating the lights crisscrossing the ceiling like tracer bullets in a night battle. The shabby curtains that neither kept out the light nor ennobled the human spirit with their beauty flapped dejectedly in a light, cool breeze from the east. What could they possibly want with her?

In the filthy bathroom down the hall, he washed his face and realized he needed a shower and a change of clothes. He called the night commander and asked if anyone had been assigned to the Boutsekes case yet. The answer was not yet, because the higher-ups were not sure how to proceed in such a sensitive case. Sensitive my ass, Akritas thought, as he listened to the explanation. He asked if the night shift had the key to the apartment where Boutsekes and the woman had been gunned down. Yes, they had it. He said that he'd be by to pick it up in a few minutes because he thought those murders were related to the Archontas case. He was told it was irregular for someone, even a police officer, to enter a crime scene without the proper authorization. The apartment was being guarded, he argued, so what could possibly happen if he went over and had a look around? Eventually the night guy relented and Akritas went down to the second floor, picked up the key, and was on his way to his flat in Galatsi to clean up and change clothes before heading for Sepolia.

He arrived at the murder scene at about 1:30 in the morning. The two men stationed at the door had been alerted by the night commander that he would be by. When he got off the elevator on the second floor, Akritas recognized one of the men.

"Hey, Louka, how are you? Wife and kids ok?"

"*Geia sas*, Pano, we're all fine, How are you?"

"Bummed out really. You know that Katarina has disappeared?"

"Yeah, I heard, you must be gutted?"

"Yes I'm fucking angry and scared. But I've got to keep going. It's related to this Archontas case. And I think what happened here is also part of it. Can I go in?"

"Of course, of course. You got the key? Hey, Pano, we're all pulling for you getting Katarina back safe."

"Thanks, Louka."

He produced the key and let himself in.

"You guys want to come in with me?"

"Nah, we'll stay out here," Louka replied.

The apartment was dark, but the shutters had not been closed and lights from an active neon sign down below where playing dimly across the walls and ceiling, first green, then yellow, and then a smudgy purple, repeated *ad nauseum*. He flicked on the overhead light and found himself in a small sitting room. Sofa, armchair, antique coffee table, a bureau with some knickknacks on it and photographs of children and an elderly couple. The door to the only bedroom was to the left and on the right there was a small hallway to the kitchen and bathroom. Across from the kitchen there was another room that had a dining room table and four chairs. The bedroom door had an official police notice stuck to it.

Slipping on his latex gloves he opened the bedroom door gingerly. The bodies had been removed but the signs of the murder were still there. Mainly dried blood on the wooden floor and the beige rug. The bed looked like an overturned cupboard, dark red billows of satin cloth spilled out. A little carpet at the foot of the bed was blood-soaked and crumpled. It looked as if Boutsekes and the woman were in bed when they were surprised by their executioners. Dragged out of bed, they were made to kneel and then shot in the back of the head. He could see the bedclothes on one side had been partly pulled onto the floor. He looked around the room carefully. He went up to the low bureau with the mirror and opened the top drawer. It was filled with women's underwear, panties, bras, stockings, a camisole or two and some men's stuff as well. Boutsekes, Akritas thought. He moved the clothes from side to side. The second drawer had some women's pullovers and sweaters. He rummaged around there as well. The bottom drawer had more clothes, but at the very bottom there was a large plastic envelope, blue, with a string that secured the flap. He wasn't sure what he was looking for but this might prove interesting.

    He pulled it out and placed it on the bureau, carefully unwound the string and opened the flap. Inside he found a sheaf of papers. There was no room on the bureau to look at the papers. He walked back out and down to the dining room. Taking out the sheaf, he placed the papers one after the other on the tabletop. There were exactly 17 leaves. They were photocopies of what looked like a bookkeeper's ledger. A name at the top of the third page immediately caught his eye, Aleko Echecrates. The accountant, he murmured. And there it all was. The accounts kept by Archontas's man. They only covered a period of about a year and a half but it was clear that these were the accounts that Haniotis had mentioned. There were more somewhere, no doubt, but here was the part of the evidence of how the money was made and where it was deposited and under what names. The money trail looked circuitous, but a Finance Ministry forensic accountant would make sense of it. Akritas straightened up and looked at all 17 sheets lying before him. Should he return them to the drawer or simply take them with him? It took him five seconds to decide. He replaced the empty blue envelope in the drawer where he found it. Tucking the papers in his belt at the back and letting his jacket hide them, he walked back into the bedroom and looked around carefully. Finding nothing else, he went into the sitting room, took one last look around, switched off the light. Just as the yellow neon was turning into the sickly purple, he walked out of the apartment. Louka and his partner looked up as he came out into the hall.

"OK, Louka, I'm done. Take care eh! See you down at the station."

"See you, Pano, and good luck getting Katarina back safe and sound."

He drove back to his flat and placed his find in a pile of other loose papers on his desk. He'd read Edgar Allan Poe's 'The Purloined Letter' so he didn't bother to hide them anywhere more secretive. He only wished that Poe would be proved right if anyone should come looking. It was now three in the morning. He wondered where Katarina was being kept. Why did they want her? Why had he even been brought into this case? What was the connection between Argyro and Boutsekes? Argyro and Karavias? Why did Boutsekes have the photocopies of the Echecrates ledger? Why was Boutsekes killed? Or Haniotis for that matter? It was obvious that the killers had no idea what was hidden in the mistress' flat. But where was Katarina? He felt sick thinking about what she was going through. Did Anna-Maria know? Maybe not. That particular party animal was probably not even home yet. It was Saturday after all and, crisis be damned, all the yuppies in Athens flock down to Glyfada, Voula, and Vouligmani for the dozen parties that the bars down there specialize in. Maybe Tolio was down there too, licking his wounds after being made to stand guard duty at the Karavias mansion while the men did all the real work.

Akritas disliked shallow-water paddlers like Tolio and maybe Anna-Maria was a bit like that too. They have a daring desire to jump into the deep end and swim, but when they take the plunge they are relieved that the water only comes up to their knees. Any deeper and they'd drown. But the shallow water is all they know and having taken the plunge what do they do? Transform their so-called daring into a show of artistry. Paddle around in circles and figure eights and impress their fellow paddlers with their turns and flutterings, always waiting for the applause. But maybe he was being unfair to Anna-Maria. At four, he suddenly felt tired. He lay down.

At nine he woke with a start, glad that the dream he'd been in was not real. He'd been out in a village somewhere south of Patras with Katarina. It had something to do with the first case he'd ever solved when he was a rookie detective in his hometown. For some reason the whole time they were there he was worried that Eleni Konstantinou, his old university flame, was there too and he didn't want her to see them together. Katarina had a lot of luggage with her that she was making Akritas carry. At one point she went off to the car and left him in what looked like a fairground with all the bags. An hour passed and then another and still she didn't return. He grew anxious. He couldn't remember where the car was parked. There were lots of people around. He took his coat off. As the weather was hot he saw a kiosk a little ways off and walked over to buy some water. On returning, he found his coat on the ground. When he looked for his wallet, he realized his two credit cards were gone. One had been replaced by a piece of cardboard that looked like a credit card but advertised a trip to Manhattan. The other one was also cardboard but was an exact duplicate of the real card even to having his name printed on it. The village men standing around looked at him with knowing smiles. They were all in on the theft. He'd also had an envelope in one of the jacket pockets with 400 euros in 50s. It too was gone. One man with a smirk on his face walked over and said, 'why don't you take the bus back to Patras'. He had the distinct feeling that Katarina was not going to come back, that she'd met another man, taller and more handsome and smarter than he, fallen in love, and had left him. He grew increasingly agitated and angry, the words 'career move' kept repeating themselves as the men in the vicinity walked away laughing, leaving him alone under the remorseless sun with all the baggage. Then he woke up in a cold sweat.

He wondered what the dream meant and why he'd dreamt that Katarina seemed to be betraying him with another man. This was out of character for her, but perhaps this was his secret fear. Was this the unconscious impediment that stayed his tongue? He'd taken for granted that she loved him and all he needed to do to gain her consent for marriage was simply to ask. And yet he hadn't. Why? In the dream, her love was not such a certain thing. This was new. Sometimes he thought that he loved her because she was like a defenseless animal in a cruel world. She needed him and he was the kind of man who wanted to be needed. Maybe he was wrong. His character had been shaped by the fact that he'd struggled against his own family when he announced he wanted to be a policeman. His natural inclination to defend and protect had been rejected by those closest to him. Their reasoning was twisted and wrong and the innocence of his feelings negated. This made his resolve stronger. But it also made him reticent to a fault. It was a paradox that few ever understood. Persons attracted him in proportion to the possibility of his defending them, rescuing them from states of distress, and he had to resist an inclination to think badly of the privileged and self-contained. This had affected his personal relations. A keen-eyed observer, able to follow the twists of his character, might have noticed that he was more likely than many less passionate men to love a woman without telling her. His greatest fault was a tendency to keep aloof even from those who, in feeling, he felt close to. Greg, his British friend, had sometimes laughed at him for having something of the 'knight-errant' in his character. It would have been more telling if Akritas had known what the Engish expression, knight-errant, meant.

/19/

There was still no word from Katarina's kidnappers. It was early Sunday and the city was quiet. He called Anna-Maria's landline. She answered after a dozen rings.

"Oh, it's you Pano. Sorry I only got in a couple of hours ago. Are you downstairs with Katarina?"

"No, I'm not. But I'd like to come over. I have something to tell you."

"Can't you tell me over the phone, I'm really tired."

"No, I can't, it's too important. I'll be there in half an hour."

He had to buzz her three times before she let him in.

"Sorry," she said, as he got off the elevator into her flat, "I fell asleep again."

"I should probably apologize for waking you up, but this can't wait. Katarina has disappeared."

Anna-Maria was suddenly wide-awake.

"Say that again. Did you say she's disappeared? Why?"

"I don't know. We haven't been notified by those who took her."

"What?" Anna-Maria cried out. "She's been kidnapped?"

"Yes. Yesterday on Akademias Street. By three men who took off in a BMW."

Anna-Maria slumped down into a chair. She looked stricken.

"I'm pretty sure it's related to the case I'm working on, but I just don't know what purpose taking her is supposed to serve. Are you all right?"

"No, I'm not all right. How could she possibly be involved in some police case? Did you get her involved in something? If you did, I hate you, you fucking bastard."

"She's not involved in the way you're thinking. Please listen to me, Anna-Maria. This is a way of putting pressure on me. But for what reason exactly, I'm not sure. I know I should have done more to protect her and I hate myself for not seeing the danger more clearly."

"OK, OK, Pano, but what are you doing to get her back?"

"We can't really do much until the people who have her contact us and make whatever demands they have. It's some kind of pressure tactic. Maybe to get me off the case. I seem to have opened up something they want hidden."

"Well, what are you waiting for? Just get off the fucking case."

"The thought has crossed my mind, believe me, but who do we tell that I'm off the case? We have no idea who has her."

"I see," Anna-Maria said quietly. "Is there anything I can do?"

"Nothing that I can think of for the moment," he replied.

"Do you want me to tell my mother and father?"

"Maybe not just yet. Let's see what happens over the next 48 hours."

Anna-Maria started to cry. Akritas did his best to comfort her.

"I know you're going to do what you can," she said between sobs, "but please, please Pano, get her back. Please."

"I will. I'll get her back safe."

He was going to add 'don't worry' but realized as the words formed in his head how stupid that sounded.

"Oh my God, Pano, what if she's been hurt?"

"Don't think about such things. Look, there is maybe something you can help me with. Did you and Katarina have any secret word or phrase over the years to communicate when you didn't want other people to know what you were saying?"

"Yeah, of course…"

"Tell me."

"Whenever we were bored with what was happening, usually some stupid family get-together, one of us would say, 'yes, but consider the novel' as if we were having a conversation about literature. That would be the signal to start making for the door. The other thing we'd say if we wanted to warn each other was 'I think I've got a cold coming on'. Usually when some idiot man was about to hit on one of us. But when one of us was trapped in some situation and we wanted to say, sit tight, I'm working on something to get us out of this mess, we'd try to work 'rubber boots' into the conversation."

"Thanks, 'rubber boots' sounds good. I'll call you if there's any news."

"Could you just call me anyway even if there isn't any news. I don't want to be alone. I'll just worry."

"Yes, yes, I will."

As he was driving back into the centre, he called Costas on his mobile. His partner was at home getting ready to head down to headquarters. Akritas asked him if he had plans for the day. Mara was visiting her family in Zakynthos where her brother, an architect, was having woman problems. He'd made a Serbian woman pregnant while she was on the island for a holiday. The family was trying to figure out what to do. Maybe you should have gone to help out, Akritas suggested, and Costas just laughed. No thanks, was his only comment. They decided to meet for lunch and discuss what next steps they should take in the case. Then Akritas had a brainwave. He dialed Anna-Maria again and asked her if she wanted to come along for lunch. She said yes right away and thanked him.

He decided to take a look at what was happening on Gennadiou Street. At Argyro's building the work on the door hadn't yet started, plywood panels and canvas covered up the scorched glass and walls. The three police guards were in place and Akritas assumed that the two policewomen were upstairs with Argyro. He parked a ways up the street so he could see what was going on. To his surprise the two policewomen emerged from the burnt out entrance and walked over to the officers. They had a tray of coffees and brioches for all of them. It looked as if the two women were going to stay downstairs while they had their coffees. That would take an hour or two once the chatting started. Did this mean that Argyro was going to go out?

He got out of the car and walked around the back of the building. There was a garage entrance there. He found a convenient vantage point and waited. After half an hour the security gate started going up and Argyro's steel blue BMW came slowly up the ramp and into the lane. She stopped and waited for the gate to close. Then turned towards where Akritas was hiding and turned right on Evzonon Street going west. He raced back to the Opel, jumped in and followed the route she'd taken. When he turned left into Evzonon, he saw her turning left on Anapiron Polemou and climbing the hill slowly up to Souidias and the Gennadius Library gates. She turned left towards city centre. He went up in a hurry, turned left and there she was, stopped at a red light. He came forward slowly and slumped down a little so that she wouldn't recognize him.

He followed her through Kolonaki along Solonos Street staying well back. There wasn't much traffic this early on Sunday. He kept her in sight without too much effort. Eventually she arrived at Patission and turned north, drove into the suburb known as Nea Filadelphia and parked on a short side street. She got out, walked towards an apartment building, and let herself in with a key. That's interesting, he thought. The glass door swung closed behind her and she disappeared. She must be expected, he thought. He wondered what to do. As he sat parked in his car, he looked up and down the street and suddenly realized that he recognized one of the cars. He'd seen it a few times at police headquarters. But he knew who it belonged to. It was a late model green Alfa Romeo and not that hard to spot in a street full of cheap grey compacts. So, she was visiting him. How damn interesting, he thought, they know each other. He wondered for a moment if that was where Katarina was being held. Unlikely, he thought, that Argyro would visit the place where a crime was in progress. Deciding it was better to go than to give himself away, he drove off after making a note of the address. As long as Argyro didn't suspect he knew something very important about her contacts, she would leave things as they were.

"I've got Melina Karavias in a cell downstairs," Costas said when Akritas arrived at headquarters. "You want to talk to her?"

"Right. We'll go in together and you ask her some questions about her family, friendly-like. Then I'll come in with a question about the weapons."

Melina Karavias appeared depressed when the woman officer brought her into the grimy interrogation room. She had a sallow, fawn-coloured face. It may have been naturally sunned but looked too orangey, more like some stuff out of a tube. She was thin like a bulimic model and a little disheveled after a night in custody. Her earrings were in her bony hands when they entered. She would have been beautiful in a haunted sort of way had she been able to apply make-up. This Sunday morning she looked underfed and under the spell of some sort of malaise. Her manner implied that the quite ordinary burdens of life were well beyond her strength. She didn't just stand or sit. She posed, taking up attitudes one after another as if she were weary, exasperated, and sunken. The poses were simple and easy to grasp. There was something confused, blurred, half-baked about her. Akritas and Costas sat facing her across a wooden table.

"When can I see my lawyer?" she demanded.

"Soon," Costas said, "as soon as you've answered a few questions."

"What questions? Do you know who I am?"

"Yes," Costas said, "we know who you are Melina Karavias. Do you live in Kifissia or at the Plaka address with your father?"

She looked at Costas and then at Akritas. She played with the earrings in the palm of one hand.

"I live in Kifissia."

"Do you have any brothers and sisters?" Costas asked.

"Two brothers. Both live in America." She looked around the room as she spoke, a gesture meant to convey her boredom.

"What do they do there?"

"One is a mathematician at a university, the other is in business in New York." Why are you asking me these questions? What do they have to do with why I'm here?"

"Did you visit the Plaka house yesterday?" Costas asked a little more pointedly.

Melina hesitated for a moment. "And what if I did? But no, I did not."

Akritas leaned forward. He'd had enough of the cat and mouse. "Miss Karavias," he began, "you were seen approaching the house yesterday and when you saw the police, you turned and fled. Why?"

"I was nowhere near the house yesterday," she spat back.

"That lie will be found out when we get to court."

"What are you talking about?" she said leaning back in her chair. "I haven't committed any crime."

"We'll see about that," Akritas stated. "Why is there a cache of weapons and explosives in the basement?"

Melina's face grew noticeably whiter. It was clear she had not anticipated the discovery. Slowly, she reached forward and put the earrings on the table.

"Well," Akritas said.

"I know nothing about it," she said quietly.

"Neither does your father according to him. Is he lying then?"

A short silence ensued.

"My father has nothing to do with it," she said looking down at her empty hands. "A friend asked me if he could store some things in the basement room."

"What's his name?"

"His name is none of your business," she said with a note of defiance in her voice. "You can take me to Makronisos if you want, but you'll never get his name out of me."

"The torturers of Makronisos have been relieved of their duties for some time now," Akritas said letting a little acid creep into his voice. "The place is a tourist attraction these days. You're just simply going to go to jail. Is that what you want?"

"Do you clowns know who I am? If you think I'm going to spend any time in jail, you're out of your minds. I'll be out of here as soon as my lawyer comes. People like me don't go to jail. Understand?"

"Do you know a man named Aris Boutsekes?"

"Who's he? No, I do not?"

"How about Argyro Kanellopolou?"

"That jumped-up little slut! Yes, I know who she is. What has she got to do with anything?"

"How do you know her?" Akritas asked.

"She's a vulgar nobody from a village who thinks that because she's a lawyer she can wriggle herself into the right social circles."

"How can she do that?"

"She thought the men who run New Democracy would have her. But all they wanted to do was fuck her. Stupid bitch took a long time to figure that out and, when she did, she switched to PASOK. That and SYRIZA are where all the sluts end up these days."

"What was your friend going to do with the weapons?"

"I don't know. I didn't even know they were guns."

"Stop lying, Melina, what was your friend . . ."

"Shut up. I've said all I'm going to say. Where's my lawyer? The Chief of Police is going to hear about this. This is bloody harassment."

Akritas leaned back in his chair and looked at Melina's lean face. Her eyes were hate-filled, flickering like two bright candles.

"OK, Costa, that's it. Let's get her back in the cell."

"We'll talk again," he said looking down at Melina.

Maybe he was mistaken. Perhaps Argyro was not involved in the murders of the six old men. Perhaps it was Melina who held the key. Perhaps perhaps perhaps.

After Costas returned, Akritas asked him to check on how long they could keep her in custody and whether a lawyer had been summoned. Akritas told him that he'd meet him at the restaurant later. Back at his desk, he started making some notes. Something with a concrete shape was slowly emerging in his mind. Several things that hadn't made sense before began to fall into place. When it was time to go to lunch, he drove through the streets, now more congested than before, feeling a whole lot better with himself. Finally, a real break had come his way. Melina was hiding something. Clearly it wasn't her father. It wasn't Boutsekes and it wasn't Argyro. It was a man.

The restaurant was in Exarchia on the corner of Emmanouil Benaki and Valtetsiou Streets. The Apollonia, a very nice, quiet place with good food, was run by two gay men and a transgendered chef. Born Simon on the island of Sifnos, where he'd learned how to cook, she now presented herself as Simonetta in the city. Her grilled sardines served on a bed of lentils with spinach, cranberries, and *katiki* from Domokos were legendary. Costas was already there when he arrived.

"Costa," he said, "I hope you don't mind but I've invited Anna-Maria, Katarina's sister, along as well. I saw her earlier and she's pretty shook up. I thought it would be good for her to be with us. The usual people she hangs out with are flighty, you know Voula people, like Tolio, but without the gun."

"It's OK with me. I think I've only ever met her once, maybe twice, but I liked her. She's bloody gorge . . ."

And at that moment Anna-Maria, without makeup, or stiletto heels, or skintight jeans, her cleavage covered by a modest white blouse and her hair tied back in a long, dark ponytail, came in and greeted both of them. Without the glamourous camouflage, she was more beautiful than ever. The two men both stood up.

"Anna-Maria, I think you've met Costa before," Akritas said as she sat down.

"Yes, we have met," she replied looking at Costas.

"Yes," Costas added, "you and Katarina came by headquarters to pick up Pano. We were introduced then."

"Yes, I remember, you were talking to him out on the street."

"I'm sorry about Katarina," Costas said.

"With you two on the case, I have nothing to worry about," she replied trying not to sound bitchy but with a wan smile on her face.

From the back Simonetta emerged with her hair piled up and held in place by pretty light blue ribbons. She was dressed all in white, like a proper chef, with a bright crimson heart sewn on the white fabric over her right breast.

"Back for more of my poison, eh Pano, can't get enough of it, can you? How's Katarina? I'm Simonetta," she said looking at his two companions.

"She's fine," he lied, "can't make it today. This is her sister Anna-Maria and my colleague Costa. What have you got for us?"

"Let's see, there's fresh trout from Epirus grilled with rosemary leaves and olives, I have Katarina's favourite, rooster in a light sage and thyme tomato sauce with tagliatelle, there's a very herby lentil dish with the best sausage, a neighbour in Sifnos makes it especially for me, there's rabbit cooked *alla Milanese*, without tomatoes, but with plenty of onions and mustard, and finally for the odd tourist who falls in here by some error in the judgment of heaven, I have my special *moussaka* that, as they say in America, will 'knock your socks off'. I'll never understand why having your socks knocked off is so widely admired in that forlorn land. Or if you don't like any of that but insist on staying, I can make you 'steak frites', *a la Français*. Then there's the usual assortment of side dishes, *horta*, my mother's wonderful recipe for *taramasalata*, *fava*, some absolutely delicious *keftedes* just like we make them on the island, *et cetera, et cetera, et cetera*. And just for you Pano we've brought in more of that very nice white wine from Limnos. Ah, yes, if you're vegetarian, I can recommend a very nice little bistro with no customers just up the street. They will be glad to serve you a bean or two. Nice to have met you Anna-Maria and Costa, but I have to get back to command central and so I'll leave you in the capable hands of Apostolos to place your orders."

"She's rather tall for a woman," Anna-Maria said as Simonetta retreated to the small kitchen.

"Yes, they grow them that way on Sifnos," Akritas said, looking at Costas.

"It's quite an island, sometimes you can't tell the women from the men," Costas added.

"Now, you're both pulling my leg," she pouted goodnaturedly.

The food and drink were superb as usual but it was difficult, under the circumstances, to fully enjoy it. Every attempt at conversation ended in gloom. They were all thinking of Katarina and what might be happening to her. They talked about the case and brought Anna-Maria into the picture. Akritas wasn't sure about telling them what he'd seen following Argyro. In the end he didn't, because there were a couple of other things he wanted to check out first. He was coming up with a plan of action and he needed to work it out in all its details before bringing Costas into it. As Anna-Maria ate and talked, he even began to think of a way she might help in finding Katarina. Finally, they were done. They paid and got up to go. Simonetta blew them a kiss from the kitchen. They said their glum goodbyes on the street outside the restaurant and each walked off in separate directions to their cars. As he approached the Opel, his mobile started buzzing. He looked at the little screen, but it read 'private number'.

"*Ela*," he said.

"If you want to see your girlfriend again, you'd better do as I say."

"I've been waiting for you to call," Akritas said trying to keep calm . "Is she all right?"

"Yeah, she's fine and you'll do what I say or she won't be fine for long. Understand?"

"I want to talk to her before we make any deals."

"That's not how we're playing this game," the voice said. "You listen first and then if we have a deal, I'll call you back and you can talk to her for one minute. Understand?"

"Yes, yes, go ahead."

"You know that Boutsekes and his whore are dead. Correct?"

"Yes."

"Well, he's going to take the fall for the murder of the Archontas gang. Here's how. He was after Archontas's money. His three stooges decided to cut him out. They liquidated him."

There's that word again, Akritas thought.

"We have them in custody."

"Wait," Akritas interrupted, "what do you mean 'in custody'? Are you in the *Astynomia* or the security police, or Delta? What?"

"It doesn't matter who we are. We're going to hand you the solution to your murder investigation on a silver plate. Listen. We have the three men in custody. We'll let you know where they are. We'll give you enough evidence to show in your report that you had the killers."

"Had?" Akritas asked.

"Yes, had, because you're going to go in and find them dead. You're going to say they were killed resisting arrest. Understand?"

"Hey, buddy, make sure you don't kill them execution style. It'll make us look bad."

"We know what we're doing. You'll then take the case to the deputy prosecutor with a report that the old men were murdered by these three dead guys under the command of Chief Inspector Aris Boutsekes in order to steal the money Archontas and his men had stashed in their homes."

"What money?"

"You know what I'm talking about. You'll be able to recover most of the cash. About four million euros. It will be a triumph for you and you'll be able to expose your former boss as the corrupt shit he was, and you'll avoid a very embarrassing trial."

Four million, Akritas thought. That leaves about 296 million unaccounted for. Interesting.

"One thing. What do I say about the weapons cache that we found at the Karavias mansion?"

"You will say that one of the men was fucking the maid and she let them come and go from the house."

"Is this true?" he asked.

"It doesn't matter, she will have committed suicide by then. But that's the story you'll tell. I will be in touch in a few days with the exact details of the operation. Do you understand?"

"Yes. Now can I talk to the woman?"

"Not yet, you have to accept what's being offered."

"I take it this conversation is being recorded."

"No, it isn't it."

Liar, Akritas thought.

"OK, I'll do it. Let me talk to her."

"Hang up and I'll call you back in ten minutes."

He waited and waited. Twenty-five minutes passed. Then his phone buzzed.

"*Agape mou*," Katarina said, "are you all right?"

"No, I'm not because you're in danger. How are you? Are they treating you well?"

"Oh, I'm fine. They let me keep my books, so I've just been sitting in this room reading and wondering when they'll let me go. Do you think that will be soon?"

"Have you seen their faces?"

"No, they wear those ski mask things over their faces whenever they come in with food and water."

"It's a real swamp, this case is," he said, "but I've got my rubber boots on so's I don't get my feet wet."

She hesitated for a moment.

"That's good, you wouldn't want to catch a cold."

She understood him! Then he heard a voice speaking in the background. Time to go, he thought.

"Good-bye darling, I love you," he said.

There was no answer. The line was dead. He clicked off the phone, opened the door of his car, and sat in the driver's seat for a moment. They were setting a trap and they were going to kill him when they had what they wanted. The useful idiot had become a danger and there was too much at stake to let him walk away into the sunset with his girlfriend. They needed him for the last act but he had to die before the curtain fell. And probably Katarina too. Sitting in his car, he realized that he'd gone off script, their script. Now he was going to be forced to improvise his lines. And his executioner? The Dane no doubt, and this time he wouldn't miss.

Afternoon light was throwing sharp shadows on the graffiti spattered wall opposite. Dark triangles sliced up the painted agony of faces and contorted limbs in ways that brought out all the hideousness of this sad and brutal age. But, on the other hand, the rectangle of sky above was unblemished, blue and far away, and innocent of any intentions. He sighed. It was going to be a fine evening with one of those magnificent sunsets over towards the Oros Egaleo. Wisps of grey-pink clouds in the darker part of the sky, light shading down, hue by hue, to that orange belt just above the red band where the sky meets the land. He loved autumn and the case was now coming clear to him. Katarina was still in danger but he could just make out a way forward and the voice on the telephone had given him a small opening. He gripped the steering wheel, took one last look at a gruesome purple-green face staring at him, started the Opel and was gone.

/20/

The next morning he arrived at headquarters and found Costas poring over a map of Athens.

"What's up, Costa, why the map?"

"I saw a show last night on TV about a cop in some city in Canada who believes that you can find out a lot about a series of related crimes, like a serial murders, if you diagram the episodes on a map. They'll reveal a pattern and that might allow you to predict future events. Of course, our case isn't quite like trying to bag a serial killer, but I thought maybe if I mapped the various murders and attempted murders, something might jump out at me."

"Anything?"

"Not yet."

"Listen put that aside for a minute, I want to fill you in on some things. Let's go to the café, I don't want anyone else to overhear us, accidentally or otherwise."

When their coffees and water were brought to them, Akritas started by describing the telephone call he'd received after they left the Apollonia. Boutsekes was definitely involved in the struggle for the Archontas fortune. After the talk with Melina they now knew there was someone else. They were either in it together or they were rivals. In the end it didn't matter. The mystery man was going to pin the murders on Boutsekes, no matter what deal they had. But whoever he was, he wasn't about to let Boutsekes live long enough to tell anyone about the money. Boutsekes had three men working with him. The murder was going to be pinned on them and then they would all be killed before they could be brought before a prosecutor. If any did get to speak, the whole plan would be blown. So, they have to die, 'resisting arrest'. Akritas' role was to be the shining knight, who not only survives a fake assassination attempt on his life and solves the case, but also recovers about four million euros for the government treasury. The money was a sop for the media to show how well the *Astynomia* was doing its job. The relatives of the dead might make claims on the money, but the treasury has a way of deferring payment so far into the future that it vanishes like a ship disappearing on the far horizon. They will say they'll pay but the timeframe will be so vague that claimants will all be dead before any money comes their way. It's the special genius of the state bureaucracy.

Akritas then explained his plan for bagging the lot of them, including the mastermind of the whole operation. He told Costas to keep everything he said to himself, including not telling the other three members of their team anything about what he'd just learned.

"Not even Tolio?"

"No-one, not even Tolio. For now, it's just between you and me. I have to wait for them to call me again. They said in a few days. After they call with how things are going to work from their end, we'll figure out the details of how we're going to set the trap."

"Are we going to tell one of the higher-ups about what's happening? The whole thing could blow up in our faces."

"Have anyone in mind? To be honest, Costa, I don't trust too many of them up there. Do you?"

Costas hesitated, mentioned Solovos as an exception, and then just shook his head. He seemed nervous and Akritas tried to assure him that if they kept things simple and tied up any loose ends, they'd make the arrests stick. Then it was up to the prosecutors to do their bit. The system was not so corrupt that their efforts would come to nothing, especially as it would be all over the media. Akritas gave him a sly wink. No fear, he implied, it would definitely be all over the media. He gave the address where he had followed Argyro the day before and asked him to get all the details on who lived there, the owners and how long they'd been in their flats.

As it was Monday morning, Akritas thought he should call the prosecutor's office and enquire whether Argyro was working today. She was and she was accompanied by two police guards to protect her. He then called the Ministry of Finance and asked for a reliable forensic accountant to be assigned to his case. He was put through to a Ministerial assistant to whom he explained the financial complexity of the murder investigation. The man he spoke to seemed co-operative and promised to have a decision in an hour. About two hours later, the assistant called back and said an accountant was on her way to Alexandras Avenue.

When his phone rang again a few minutes later he thought it was the Ministry of Finance, but no, it was Petros Cleomenes.

"I'm very sorry about the death of Haniotis," Akritas said. He knew his friend would have been devastated by the news.

"Yes, it's bloody tragic. There was no finer man in the whole of Athens. He will be missed. But that's not why I'm calling. Well, let me put it another way. It's because of his murder that I started doing some investigating of my own. I have contacts that may not be available to the *Astonymia*. People who will talk to me but not you."

"Why am I not surprised? What have you got?", Akritas asked.

"That woman you mentioned to me at lunch, Argyro Kanellopoulou, she's come up in some fascinating conversations with certain knowledgeable people. Are you interested?"

"Of course."

"Meet me in the bar of the King George hotel in half an hour."

After they were settled with their drinks. Cleomenes began his recitation.

He began by echoing what Gareth's file had alleged. Argyro Kanellopoulou had in the course of another investigation come across information about Archontas's wealth. At some point she seems to have realized that the Archontas unit was responsible for many of the atrocities up in the area of Aghia Triada, her family's home village, and that they may have in fact been responsible for the torture and murder of her grandfather and his brother.

"Someone who knows her," Cleomenes continued, "says that she often talks about revenge for what happened to her grandfather and his brother. But, it turns out, she never actually knew them."

"What do you mean?" Akritas interrupted.

"She's too young to have had anything to do with them. For her, they were shadowy figures, more like characters in a novel than real people. It was the epic tale her father and his brothers spun out over *tsipouro* and grilled meats on hot August evenings back in the village. You know what village life is like. But the money, now that was all too real, and when she looked more closely at how much there was of it, she saw the dull sheen of the brass ring hanging there before her eyes."

"Oh, I see, that's how she was going to get into politics."

"Of course, but not because she had any particular passion for public service or social justice. No, nothing like that. It also didn't matter which party. She wanted to be queen of the hive. She knew that politics was how you made your mark and accumulated a great deal of property and wealth in the process."

"Did she think New Democracy was the path to glory?" Akritas said.

"They are the money people, aren't they?" Cleomenes said. "As far as she could see their only interest was using the state as a way of making more money for themselves, their relatives, and political and business associates."

"But how could she move in those circles?" Akritas asked. "She was a nobody from somewhere up north."

"Just so," Cleomenes replied. "The New Democracy families are all Athens born and bred. They live near each other in the right neighbourhoods, socialize with each other, they've all gone to the same private schools, universities abroad, married each other, and are mutually supportive of each other's business activities."

"Sounds like Argyro, as an outsider, didn't have a chance."

"Right. But she was smart enough to realize it."

"Have you ever met her?" Akritas asked.

"No, but I understand she's rather beautiful."

"Well yes," Akritas began, "in a hard, glittery way. Let's say she knows how to show herself to the best advantage."

"Which is why," Cleomenes interrupted, "my informant told me that when she appeared on the fringes of good New Democracy society up in Kifissia and Paleo Psychiko she met with two reactions. The men simply wanted to set her up in a flat for their occasional amusement and pleasure. And the women simply wanted to scratch her eyes out."

"Is that why she turned to PASOK?"

Cleomenes laughed. He looked past Akritas and waved a greeting to someone standing at the bar.

"Of course, of course, socialism had nothing to do with it. I don't have to tell you Pano that social democracy and conservatism are just labels that mean very little."

"If you mean that it's pretty much the same mentality and culture in both parties, then, yes, I know very well what you're saying."

"PASOK does, or should I say did, have a few more idealists, but Argyro steered clear of them. All they would do was drag down a young woman on the make. She stuck with the movers and shakers, whose sole interest in 'social democracy' was, like their opposite numbers in New Democracy, self-promotion and self-enrichment."

"Wasn't she surprised what close social connections there were between the two parties?" Akritas asked. "I imagine that as a complete outsider, she'd always thought the two parties, one capitalist, the other socialist, were sworn enemies. I think that's a mistake I made when I was first aware of politics."

"It certainly sounds like that when you hear them vilify each other in Parliament or when they shout at each other on the big political talk shows on TV. She, like many people, hadn't realized how much of it was theatre."

The two men paused in their conversation to order two more drinks. When the young barman had set their scotches on the low table before them and left, Cleomenes continued with his story. It seems the light went on when she learned that two prominent men, one a New Democracy minister and the other, his PASOK shadow in the opposition, were the best of friends. They had roomed together at Princeton, played tennis with each other every weekend, and their families holidayed together at the latter's villa on Corfu. The revelation didn't anger her or turn her away from politics. In fact, it re-assured her. She saw very clearly what she was dealing with. New Democracy was old established money, closed off more or less to outsiders, certainly to outsiders without means. They were well connected to the old established families in other European countries. PASOK was more new money, cosmopolitan, better educated, and more connected to European intellectual circles. But they were very much like their New Democracy opposite numbers in all the essentials. The 'socialists' seemed a better bet for a smart young woman like Argyro. Their fringes overlapped with artists, musicians, and other bohemians; they were more hip, more artsy, and more 'progressive'. This was the word they used to characterize their politics, having picked it up in America when they were being groomed for governing in some expensive Ivy League college.

"So, PASOK," Cleomenes continued, "was clearly the shining path for the outsider from an obscure village in central Greece."

"I suppose," Akritas said, taking a sip, "the fact that her grandfather and granduncle had suffered at the hands of the fascists didn't hurt."

"Didn't hurt at all. It was a card she played with great skill. She had the right pedigree for the progressive cadres in the party. A love affair here, a favour or two there for party members after she'd occupied the prosecutor's office and, of course, her very good looks marked her out as a comer in party circles."

Cleomenes warmed to his narrative, relishing the twists and turns of the plot. Argyro, it turns out, also knew that unless she could manage to get her hands on some money, lots of it, a further career in politics was going to be very difficult. Marriage might be the ticket, but most of the rich men she was introduced to were such vermin that even an opportunist of Argyro's rapacity balked. She was still on the lookout for an acceptable male benefactor when the debt crisis hit the country. She was appalled to discover that the New Democracy and PASOK leadership were so deeply involved in feathering their own nests that they had no idea how to deal with a real economic crisis. The usual fantasy world they spun out for the people in the media evaporated and these clowns were left looking at each other like people who'd got off the train at the wrong station. Not only didn't they know where they were, but they couldn't speak the language of the locals. Men and women in the parties that she'd respected as movers and shakers were shown to be bumblers, parasites, and, in terms of the interests of ordinary people, near enough to being traitors that had she had a few grams of idealism she might have started prosecutions against them.

"But idealism was never her strong suit," Cleomenes said. "What she saw was that the royal path to glory through PASOK was finished. New Democracy held on for a time, but even their core voters began to ditch them when it became clear the old money was as stupid as the new money."

"What about SYRIZA then?"

"To a friend, she once described that bunch of loony leftists as angry children. And on that point I agree with her entirely. Their anger is part real and part opportunist faking. Like children, they don't seem to know whether they mean what they say or know only too well they're spouting claptrap. Anyway, SYRIZA is no use to her because she's already identified with PASOK and they're nowhere these days. Speculation is she wants to take a new path."

Akritas remembered that Argyro had said at their last interview that she might start her own party.

"How could she start her own political party without money?"

His friend lowered his glass to the table and a wry smile broke his face open. "Guess," he said.

"Archontas?"

"You got it in one, dear boy! With the old fascist's money she'd be able to finance a run for Parliament and, if necessary, to start her own party. The money would make her invulnerable and give her freedom of action."

"I see," Akritas said, nodding his head. "After the crisis crushed PASOK, New Democracy, and SYRIZA, she could present herself to her countrymen as something new and fresh. You know something resounding like Hellenic Sunrise, on the model of Reagan's Morning in America."

"Right again. I can see it all now," Cleomenes mused, raising both hands unfolding a panorama. "She would campaign against the antiquated party men, the *palaiokommatistes*, and take control of the state, especially its finances and the patronage system. The country might have to default on its debts, go bankrupt, cut pensions. Without the Archontas fortune, she would be in the same meatgrinder as everyone else. But with it, she would not only survive but be positioned, later when the garbage had been taken out of the kitchen, to order up some tasty *pasticcio*.

Akritas sat back in the comfortable armchair of the King George hotel's bar. "Are you sure this is all true?" he asked.

"It's what I've been told by persons who usually have all the political gossip in Athens at their fingertips."

"Murders, thieving, and conniving are usually simpler than this. What you've told me is like stuff in a bad thriller. At least the Jason Bourne films my friend Greg has dragged me to have great music. I can't imagine what the music of Argyro's political life sounds like."

" A lot of schmaltz, interrupted by gunshots, a good deal of backroom murmuring, and maybe some slurpy sounds from the bad sex," Cleomenes declared with a note of triumph as he drained his glass.

Back at headquarters Akritas waited for Angeliki Forck, the forensic accountant, to arrive. Finally, he was called down to the lobby to sign her into the building. She seemed very young for someone with technical knowledge of accounting, maybe about twenty-five or thirty at the most. Even though he had his doubts, there was something about the young woman that inspired confidence. Perhaps it was her self-assurance, a kind of controlled poise, no unnecessary fidgeting or looks of alarm. Or perhaps it was just the way she carried her brown leather briefcase. Dressed in a charcoal pant suit, without a single ornament, and with the whiteness of her skin set off between her light-brown coronet of hair and her violet blouse, she did not seem like a woman who needed to be looked at or required any external testimony to secure her well-being. He enquired about her odd name and was told she had a Greek mother and an Austrian father. He had died when she was seven and she'd been brought up in Athens when her mother returned home as a widow.

Akritas suggested they go for a coffee. He filled her in on the case and then showed her the photocopies. She took a quick look and said that she'd need a place to work, so she could go through them in detail. Back in police headquarters, he found a small office for her. He emphasized that she was not to show the documents to anyone in the building. Confidentiality was crucial for the proper conduct of the investigation. He also asked that she keep the door locked and to call his mobile if she needed to go out or when she had something to report.

While waiting, he phoned the team members one by one and asked them to come in for a meeting later in the afternoon. At 12:30 PM, Costas came back with the information about the address.

"Pano," he said with some excitement, "you'll never guess who lives at that address."

"Let me guess, Tolio?"

"Yeah, how did you know?"

"When I followed Argyro, that flashy car he drives was parked out in the street. Does he own the flat?"

"Yes, he does, and he bought it six months ago, by bank transfer from a bank in Beirut. He paid the full amount in cash."

"I see."

"OK, you'd better tell me more because this case just got more confusing. What has Argyro got to do with Tolio?"

"They're obviously working together and I suspect she's pulling the strings. That's why he can drive an expensive sports car, wear €200 loafers, and €150 jeans. What I don't know is if they're lovers or whether he's just in it for the money. Costa, I'd like you to tail him for me in the evening. I know he spends a lot of time down in the Glyfada-Vouliagmeni area clubbing and partying."

"Pano, I don't know anything about that scene. I'd stand out like a sore thumb."

"Yeah, I know, that's why I'm going to team you up with someone who'll blend in and be able to tell us more about Tolio."

"Who's that?"

"Anna-Maria."

"You can't be serious. That's endangering her, isn't it? Do you want to take the risk?"

"What option have we got? I know that she wants to help get Katarina back and she knows what happens there better than anyone. She may have already run into him at a party or club. If she can tell us more about him, who he hangs out with and whether he's in the market for sex or whatever, we'll have a better idea of what we're dealing with. She doesn't have to ask him questions or do anything, just make herself available and see if he bites. He'll have no idea she's connected to Katarina or us. Anyway, you'll be just around the corner if she needs your help."

"Well, OK, but I'm still a little leery about this."

Akritas called Anna-Maria and asked if she could take a couple of days off from work and help him with the case. She said of course, and agreed to meet him later at his favourite café in Psirri. After he hung up, his phone buzzed. It was Angeliki.

"I think I've found something quite interesting," she said as he entered the office.

"Good, tell me."

"Look at these transfers. They're payments to the individuals listed here, pointing at the list of the five Archontas comrades on one of Gareth's other photocopies."

"How can you tell? There are no names on the transfers."

"It's the four numbers beside the names. See these numbers, how they correspond with the accounts over here. The men have been identified by taking every other digit in the account number as their particular code. It seems to me each got an equal share from Mr. Archontas. Twenty million each. Total of 100 million, see, the figure there. From these other photocopies, that would have left something in the order of 200 million for whoever controlled access to the money and I presume that was Archontas. Now the really interesting thing is that all that money which was housed in a Swiss bank, and banks in Panama City and Moscow, found its way into a bank account in Beirut where I assume it still is, unless there are other documents which say different. In any case, I presume that the money is still in Archontas's name with a Mr. Mohammed al Hadi as the contact in Beirut."

"But now that Archontas is dead, what's happened to the account?"

"Someone else must be listed as the account holder. Mr. al Hadi seems to be the go-between or trustee in this case. There's an ambiguous amount over here, amounting to about 15% of the total that seems to have been paid to him and the notation in accounting talk has him receiving a commission. So, if the amount is 200 million, minus 15% commission, I suspect the account holder now has about 170 million."

"What you're saying is that it looks as if Archontas paid each of his former comrades 20 million each and now that they're dead, the relatives are suddenly much richer." And that's why, he thought, they didn't want to say too much when questioned and why they were just interested in getting their relatives buried and forgotten.

"I see," he said, "thank you so much for untying this knot for me."

"Not too fast," she said, "these are fragmentary documents, and I'm making some surmises that could be wrong, although I think I've got it all straight in terms of what you've shown me. But there are still little mysteries. The circled letters AS on this document doesn't mean anything in accounting speak. And there are other incomplete transactions that I'm not sure what they mean. Do you know if there are more photocopies?"

"If they exist, I'm not sure where they are. Will you be available to look at anything else that turns up?"

"Oh, didn't they tell you from the Ministry? I've been seconded to you until you send me back, so, Captain Akritas, I'm all yours for the duration."

"Really," he said smiling, "welcome aboard then. I guess I'd better figure out something for you to do."

"Nah, don't bother, I'm going to go online and see if I can find my way into the Beirut bank and take a closer look at their records."

"You mean hack into it?"

"I wouldn't call it hacking, detective, just 'due diligence' in the pursuit of a criminal investigation. I'll also give the Zurich bank a try. The one in Panama City should be easier."

"Do you have some computer geek in the Ministry to do this for you?"

"You're looking at her. I have three university degrees, two in accounting, and one in computer science with a major in 'due diligence'."

He was beginning to like Angeliki Forck more and more.

"But there is something else I wouldn't mind you doing for me," said Akritas. "Find out what you can about a banker named Theodosis Haniotis who was murdered a couple of days ago. He was the one who really opened up the financial side of this case for me. I'm not sure why he was shot, but it probably has something to do with this money."

"What was he and where?" she asked.

"Senior executive with the National Bank. He had an office at Stadiou Street."

"OK, I'll see what we have on him."

"Where do you want to work? Here?"

"You must be joking. Look at this place. No, I'll work from my office."

"I've been in the Ministry of Finance and it's no Hilton either."

"Well," she said with a smile, "it's less shabby than this and it doesn't smell like sweat and beer. But seriously, I need to use my own computer. It's specially tuned up for due diligence."

"Is it secure? Can anyone get to you in the building?"

"It's fine. Anyone coming into the Ministry these days who doesn't work there has to show ID, prove they have an appointment, and go through a metal detector."

"I'd like to assign a man to accompany you there. Just to be on the safe side. I don't anything happening to you."

"No need, Captain Akritas, no-one knows I'm working on this case except a ministerial assistant and he's completely reliable."

Akritas hesitated but finally assented. She stood up and was gone.

Yup, he liked this Ms Forck a lot.

/21/

Down at the personnel department, now called rather sinisterly 'human resources', he was able to get the employment file with a photograph of Tolio Statiris. He'd entered the service about twenty-four months earlier as a uniformed officer, then without any further explanation in the file, he'd been promoted after nine months to detective. Boutsekes, Akritas thought, when he was still working with Argyro. Now he realized why Boutsekes had assigned their boy detective to work on the case. Looking at Tolio's photograph, he was surprised to see how much he'd changed since entering the *Astynomia*. In the picture, he looked a little bit like a hick from Epirus, in fact he was from Komotini in Thrace. Bad haircut, cheap nylon shirt, a little on the chubby side from his mummy's cooking, and bad teeth. The transformation into gilded Vouliagmeni-man was extraordinary. The designer haircut alone got most of Komotini out of him. Argyro, the Archontas money, and the dental work had erased the rest. Would Anna-Maria recognize him in Glyfada? The basic face was pretty much the same, it was the accessories that made the difference. Anyway, Costas would point him out in a crowd if necessary.

He arrived at the Styl café in Psirri early. Up in the loft area he found a table and comfortable sofa near the back door, sat down and ordered a double espresso and glass of Black Barrel. Quiet and on his own before Anna-Maria arrived he felt a pang, a tightness in his chest, and an ache through his whole body. He hadn't seen Katarina for a couple of days now and he realized how frightened he was for her safety. How much he missed her! And doubly so, because of the danger she was in. God, he had to get her out soon. He felt helpless. Then angry. His descent into despair was halted by the arrival of Anna-Maria. Beautiful as ever, she was made-up and dressed for work. Smart-looking, but sexy, tight skirt, just enough cleavage to look interesting but not enough to put off the women customers in the shop. Big chunky jade ring on her middle finger, left hand, a snaky gold thing on her right thumb. She looked down at Akritas as she was taking off her light jacket.

"This is the place Katarina told me about. I've never been here. You and her come here all the time, right?"

"We've been coming here since we met. I come here alone sometimes. It always makes me feel closer to her."

"You two are romantic little lovebirds, aren't you?"

In the past, he'd noticed that she was always sarcastic and sour after a day in the shop. Shop owners spent all day being pleasant to customers with their delusions of grandeur and impossible demands, dealing with a multitude of self-important skinflints. People always wanted a palace for a pittance. The forced bonhomie and tolerance of the shop owner built up behind the agreeable façade a backlog of vitriol as the day progressed. It was a little like a dam being built every day devastating the pleasant valley upstream. Then when the shop closed, the dam would burst and the waters would turn to yellow bile.

"Have a drink," Akritas said, "sounds like you had a rough day."

She put her hand on his arm and moved closer to him. He embraced her and kissed her forehead. She was crying. They held each other for a while as her emotion subsided. When she looked up at him her make-up was a mess. Mascara and eyeliner running in black daggers down her cheeks. Her eyes were red and she needed to blow her nose. She extracted some wet tissues from her bag and using a mirror cleaned up the mess around her eyes and cheeks. When she turned to Akritas, she was human again, most of the mask had been wiped clean.

"You're a good man, Pano, I think I know why Katarina loves you. Is there any word?"

"When I talked to her, she said she was ok. I'm just hoping it's true."

"Why did you want to speak to me?"

"I'm going to ask a big favour of you, Anna-Maria. It does involve some danger. But it will really help if you can do it. I want you to go clubbing in Glyfada tonight and for the next couple of nights."

She laughed out loud.

"Me, go clubbing in Glyfada? I am the number one party animal on the south coast. It's the only way I can regain my love of humanity after a day in that fucking shop dealing with the cheap dolts we seem to attract. Sorry to sound bitter, Pano, but the last two days, with Katarina gone, I've had my patience tested to the limit. Of course, I'll go to the clubs. Hell, I was going to go anyway. Is there anything in particular I'm supposed to do? Or be?"

"Here, take a look at this picture."

She studied Tolio's photograph and looked up at Akritas.

"Except for the fact that the face has some babyfat, and I wouldn't use the shirt to wipe down my kitchen, and the haircut is pure hillbilly, I'd say it looks like Tolio Statiris."

Akritas leaned over and kissed her full on the mouth.

"Come on now, Pano," she said chiding him.

"Anna-Maria you're great. You recognize this guy?"

"Yes, he showed up at the clubs about a year ago. Good looking guy. Lots of the girls were enchanted. Still comes around, mainly during the week, don't see him too often on the weekends. Why do you have this grubby photograph of him?"

"He's a cop and he's working on this case with me, but I think he's bent and is in with the bad guys and probably knows where Katarina is."

"Fucking bastard! I'll kill him."

"Not just yet," Akritas said, putting his hand on her shoulder. "Does he know who you are? Does he know that you have a sister?"

"He knows me, yes, but we've never had a thing together. He doesn't know me well enough to know anything about my family. The only conversation we've ever had was when someone told him about the shop. It seems he bought an apartment and wanted some new furniture and stuff. He said he'd drop by and see what we have. That was about seven months ago I think. But he's never been in. At least not when I've been there."

"Have you ever heard of Argyro Kanellopoulou?"

"No, who is she?"

"Does he ever come to Glyfada with a regular date, a very good-looking woman, mid-30s, with lots of black hair, sexy but hard looking, and always very well dressed? Usually with plenty of bling."

"Not sure," she said, "the description could fit any dozen people. He sees women for a while and then moves on. I don't remember any woman in particular lasting more than a few weeks with him."

"Remember anything particular about him? The kind of car he drives? That kind of thing."

"To be honest, Pano, I don't pay much attention to him. He's a bit cartoonish and not really my type. Good-looking but a little rough around the edges. I think someone told me he comes from up north somewhere."

"Komotini," Akritas said.

"OK, that explains it. So, what am I supposed to do?"

"You're not going to be alone. Costa will be with you but he'll have to stay out of sight, he exudes cop from every pore and anyway Tolio knows him. What I'd like you to do, if you can, is engage him in conversation. Furniture for his new apartment might be a good place to start. Ask him a question about the place, how big is it, what does he like, stuff like that."

"Yes, I know what to ask. I know the places where he hangs out. There are only two where he's a regular."

"Ask him about previous places he's lived and what he had in them. Maybe make it sound like you might be romantically interested and see how he reacts. He'll probably have to admit that he's a cop."

"He probably won't. He'll make up some bullshit about how important he is. That's Glyfada style."

"Maybe after first time you talk, tell him you'll be back at the same club the next night and see if he's there. Remember always to stay in a public place with him. If things aren't working well or you feel scared, leave right away. Costa will be just outside."

"All right, that sounds easy enough. When do I start?"

"How about tonight?"

"It's Monday, Pano. God made Mondays so that partygoers would have a day of rest just like Sunday for the people who go to church. Tomorrow night is a better bet."

"OK," he said, "tomorrow night it is."

They talked for another hour and at one point Anna-Maria held his hand tightly with both of hers.

"I'm scared, Pano. Not about Tolio, but about what's happening to Katarina."

"Me too. I can't sleep until we have her back."

Round about midnight, they left the café and Akritas walked her to the Peugeot. It was parked on Ermou. They chatted for a minute or two more as she was searching for the key in her bag. Two kissed cheeks later, she drove off. He looked across the street and thought that maybe Greg would be at the Oscar Wilde. He walked in just as a big football match from England was wrapping up. The place was crowded and smoky. The hell with it, he thought, he turned and hadn't walked more than a hundred feet from the pub entrance that he noticed someone had left the bar and was following him. Maybe it was his old Plaka and Kallithea friend, Vlassios. Walking just quickly enough to see if it was just his mind playing tricks on him, he managed to get around a corner and slip into the deep shadows of a doorway protected by a wall from the street light. The guy walked by at a quickened pace and Akritas watched him go about 25 meters before emerging and starting to follow him. The man soon realized he'd lost Akritas. He looked around momentarily and then continued to walk all the way to the Monastiraki Metro stop. Akritas followed him down to the platform going south towards Piraeus. As the platform had a long curve it was easy staying out of his line of sight.

The tricky thing was going to be getting on the same carriage and not be seen. As the train arrived and the crowd on the platform moved forward, Akritas edged his way towards where the man was standing. When the guy got in one end of the carriage, Akritas managed to squeeze in at the other end. He could see the man's back. He still didn't have a clear view of his face. Not surprisingly the guy disembarked at Kallithea and Akritas followed him along the platform and up over the bridge spanning the tracks into the streets leading to the main drag, the wide boulevard called the Thiseos by the locals. It had another official name but he'd forgotten what it was. The follower and followed crossed the Thiseos at Davaki Square. On Ifigenias Street, the man walked up the steps of an apartment block, opened the door and got into the single elevator in the lobby. Akritas saw from the indicator light above the lift door that he got off on the 4th floor. Making a note of the address, he stepped back on the street and looked up. It was all dark. The shutters were all drawn and there was probably no need to hang about.

Just as he was getting ready to go back to the Metro, a car pulled up in front of the apartment block and Akritas recognized Gareth and Vlassios getting out. They went into the same block and took the elevator up to the 4th floor. Maybe Katarina was being held there. He was uncertain what to do. Would it be better to jeopardize the whole operation by pulling in a tactical unit to storm the place right now, or should he wait? He wanted to bust in and rescue her but he also knew that without knowing the layout of the place, which room she was in, how many people were there, or even if she was there at all, he'd be asking for trouble and undermining the investigation. Best to hang tight, he thought. He waited for another half hour in the shadows. Then he left hoping that tonight he'd be exhausted enough to get some sleep..

/22/

The next morning Akritas called Petros Cleomenes. He thanked him for all the information about Argyro.

"I meant to ask if you knew anything more about the Haniotis murder," Akritas asked. "

Cleomenes seemed subdued and disheartened.

"Don't know for sure," was his glum response. "Someone had told me that Haniotis found something which implicated people in high places. They just rubbed him out before he could act on what he'd found.

"How high?"

"Don't know," replied Cleomenes flatly.

"OK. Will you call immediately if you hear anything more? Thanks, my friend." Akritas clicked off his mobile. Within a few seconds, the phone buzzed. It was Angeliki Forck.

"Yes," he said, "how are you?"

"Fine, fine. Are you in the building?" she asked.

"No, I'm at home. Have you got something for me?"

"Yes. Where shall we meet?"

"The Montalbano on Kolokotroni, number twelve, in forty-five minutes."

"See you there," she said.

Driving towards the centre he was reminded how much he hated graffiti. It was everywhere, uglier and more sinister than usual because of the anxiety he felt about Katarina. The wall daubings put everyone in a perpetual state of depression. He learned about the graffiti 'community' from his twenty-something girlfriend, Eleftheria, some years ago. These so-called alternative artists spray-painted everything in sight. They were little more than no-talents who resented the fact that they were ignored by society. They had some vague sense that they deserved attention, the attention of others. This was, he thought, one of the psychological problems in his country. Those who thought they had something special to offer, artists, writers, designers, architects, intellectuals, they all needed an audience. Not just any audience mind you, it had to be the right audience. This was so they would be recognized as brilliant geniuses and invited on the TV talk shows, to book launches, panels, university meetings. Everyone was a big star in their own heads and they spun out conspiracy theories to explain why they were being ignored.

Of course, these so-called artists had no idea what a life in art was really all about. They did not burn with the longing, the desire that would have made them devote themselves to their art whether anyone was standing around watching or not. It was not engraved in their character. He remembered his old professor, the mercurial Yorgos Koukougiannis when he had spoken once long ago about the word 'character' – character he had said is something engraved coming from the old Greek, *charassein*, or *charasso*, meaning to 'make pointed', 'sharpen' as well as 'engrave'. Morality, he had said, is character. And so, Akritas had thought and still thought, so is law. And so is art. It has nothing to do with what people acclaim as brilliance or genius, it is something engraved, inescapable, and true. It must manifest itself no matter what conditions, favourable or otherwise, prevail. Morality, art, and the law, these were either engraved on one's character or not. Everything else was cleavage and bling. The hideous wall spatterings included.

The problem was that even if the gifted one was the new Pablo Picasso, he or she may very well be ignored anyway by the obtuseness of those who'd clawed their way to the top of the social pyramid. You couldn't really rely on the notion that the cream always rises to the top. It was the graspers, the well-connected, the conmen who often rose to the top and stayed there. And with that unpleasant thought, he turned from Athinas Street onto Kolokotroni and made his way along that grim road, full of memories of the young Eleftheria, to the Hot Hot Burger Bar and the Montalbano next to it.

Angeliki Forck was waiting for him when he got there. Mara was surprised to see him and even more surprised when, after greeting her, he went and sat down with Angeliki.

"Oh, you two know each other," Mara said.

"Yes," Akritas replied, "how are you Mara? Meet my colleague Angeliki."

"Hi, what'll it be, Pano?"

"How about a double cappuccino, no . . ."

"No chocolate, I remember," Mara said smiling at him. "Is Costa coming too?"

"Not that I know of, but you never know. He could just wander in unannounced."

After Mara went off to prepare the coffee, Akritas turned to Angeliki.

"So you've found something."

"The man in Beirut, al Hadi, specializes in moving black money around the world. He seems to be well known in the organized crime world. If you need to launder dirty money, he's your man. It seems Archontas was referred to him by a law firm in Panama City that specializes in setting up offshore shell companies and accounts. It's been implicated in money laundering and tax evasion. We have a list of about 470 Greek citizens who've used their services. The MF notation in the documents refers to them. Al Hadi is now providing the same service for his successor. The numbered account in Beirut that belonged to Archontas amounts to €159,673,108. Two days ago the money was transferred to a new account in the same bank – listed on the bank's books as a numbered account, but I managed to get into the system and find out the name: Kanellopoulou, Argyro. The personal banker handling the account is Mr. al Hadi. Remember the fifteen percent from the other day? He's already taken his commission it seems. He charges a further fee for making wire transfers."

"Excellent work, Angeliki, how does she access the money? Do you know?"

"She sends al Hadi a message and he wire transfers the money to one of five accounts she has. Two accounts in Greece, one in a bank on Cyprus, one in Moscow, and another in Zurich. The two accounts in Athens are with the National Bank and Alpha Bank. They are in her name. Now this is where the story gets interesting. The man you asked me to investigate, a Mr. Haniotis, began monitoring her National Bank account the day before he died. His computer hard drive shows that he was checking the account every hour on the hour. When he was killed the activity stopped."

"I wonder how Kanellopoulou found out he was suspicious?" Akritas asked.

"I don't know. Is there a way of finding out?"

"Wait, this is a long shot but let me try." He dialed Haniotis' office number. The phone was answered by a familiar voice.

"Hello, Diotima, this is Captain Akritas. I'm a little surprised to find you at the office. Why didn't you take a little time off after the tragedy?"

"Oh, Mr. Akritas, I just couldn't sit at home doing nothing. Mr. Haniotis was my whole life. Twenty-five years I have been his assistant. For more than twenty-five years. I can't bear the thought of him gone. And there were many things we were working on that needed our, I mean, my attention."

"I'm very sorry for your loss. Did he mention anything to you about the case I brought to his attention when I met with him the other day?"

"Well, yes, I put a call through to your office at police headquarters the morning he was killed. I left a message for you with a detective I spoke to. Mr. Haniotis had some information for you about a woman named Kanellopoulou."

"Do you remember the name of the detective you spoke to?"

"I think it was Stathis, something like that, if I remember correctly."

"Was it Statiris?" Akritas asked.

"Yes, that's it, Statiris, yes."

"Did you mention Kanellopoulou to Detective Statiris?"

"Yes, of course, he said he was your partner in the investigation."

"That's right, thank you very much for clearing this up for me."

"You're welcome. Goodbye."

He clicked off the phone and shook his head.

"I know why Haniotis was killed. He was about to let me know that he'd seen the Kanellopoulou account. But unfortunately he told the one person who would have known what this meant. They swung into action within a couple of hours to silence him."

Back at headquarters he sat down and began to sketch out the story so far, at least as he understood it. First it was important to understand why and by whom the Archontas gang had been murdered. During the war and after, Archontas was the mastermind and the others loyal soldiers. They were war criminals who had escaped judgment in a Greece that was immediately plunged into the Cold War before the hot war was even over. They were rewarded by the rightist victors with bureaucratic sinecures. During the period of the dictatorship in the 1960s and early 1970s, they used their positions to steal enormous amounts, including turning gold reserves stolen by the Germans into cash which they deposited in a number of banks in Europe, Russia, and central America. He wondered how Archontas had got his hands on the gold reserves. Perhaps it was the shipment that disappeared when it left Belgrade. That gold trail was cold but who knows maybe the Serbs knew something. In any case, the total amount accumulated was approximately three hundred million Euros harvested over a forty-year period. One hundred million was paid to the five Archontas accomplices, each receiving twenty million. Archontas then consolidated the remaining cash in Beirut with the help of a local personal banker in the Lebanese capital. The banker had taken a fifteen percent commission and the remaining, one hundred and seventy million Archontas kept for himself. This had all happened about five years earlier.

Recently two more actors had appeared on the scene, Kanellopoulou and Boutsekes. Kanellopoulou, who had been investigating the former political activities of the Archontas gang, discovered accidentally the leader's large fortune. She saw a great opportunity to get rich. The relationship between Kanellopoulou and Boutsekes was still a little obscure, but the two seemed to have decided to cooperate in order to get their hands on the money and then to share it. They were surprised to learn that Archontas and the five other members of the old Security Battalion unit were, amazingly, all still alive. Kanelopoulou about six months earlier had recruited a third member of the team, rookie Detective Anatolios Statiris, and he was tasked with organizing a kill squad of six. They used the basement rooms in the Karavias mansion as a kind of HQ, at least their arsenal was located there. How they came to have access to the house was clear. It was Melina Karavias, the old man's daughter. But Akritas still didn't know why she'd co-operated. Karavias was known for his fabric shops, but his story as a former leftist, a man imprisoned on Makronisos and then released, had been splashed all over the newspapers a little bit earlier by an up and coming young journalist who had managed to get the old man to break his silence and admit he'd never really recanted his beliefs. The old man with the communist background was no doubt one more piece in the revenge theory of the murders, one more useful pawn. Each of the squad members was promised a generous payment when the job was done. They began the systematic killing of the old Archontas gang. The relatives were advised, privately, that if they wanted to see the considerable amounts remaining from the twenty million each man had received, they would be wise to stay quiet as their fathers and grandfathers were being liquidated.

Then Boutsekes seems to have got greedy and talked Statiris and three members of the kill squad into trying to betray Kanellopoulou, but what he hadn't realized was that she and Statiris had become lovers. Statiris told her what Boutsekes was planning and the two then made their own plans to get rid of him. At first Statiris pretended to go along with Boutsekes. But eventually Boutsekes began to suspect that something was up and a kind of underground war had broken out between the two camps.

The original plan had been to make the murders of the old men look like revenge attacks for things they'd done years before. The men were old, the relatives were inheriting fortunes, and who really cared that old war criminals were finally being punished for their evil deeds? A series of false clues were manufactured to lead investigators to the wrong conclusions. All this in the interests of hiding the true motive, which was simple theft. Andreas Xiloudes the original investigator was not far wrong. It was all about robbery, but not in the way he thought. His lack of imagination meant that he didn't notice the false trail that would have made revenge the motive. He was removed and Akritas brought in. Kanellopoulou and Boutsekes both realized, separately, that Akritas had the intelligence to pick up the trail they'd laid for him.

But, in the end, he also was the wrong man for the job. He had picked up the scent of the real motive and at that point the plot began to unravel. Eventually Kanellopoulou took control of the whole operation by turning Boutsekes's men against him. It was easy. Her looks and large amounts of cash had done the trick. Boutsekes was also liquidated.

Akritas then turned his attention to the present danger. Although there was now sufficient evidence to begin making arrests, Statiris and his kill squad were holding Katarina hostage, presumably at an address in Kallithea. He then went over the deal he'd been offered. Three of the gang members, probably the ones who stuck too long with Boutsekes, were going to be sacrificed by Kanellopoulou and Statiris. He speculated that the three chumps were Gareth, Vlassios, and the third man present during the earlier meeting in Kallithea. Akritas had been offered the safe return of Katarina, the three kidnappers to be killed during the fake rescue by Statiris and the remaining three members of the original murder squad. The police would have the culprits who had killed the old men and stolen whatever money they'd found in the dead men's homes, about four million in total. That money would be recovered by the police and the hostage rescued. The police and the presiding deputy prosecutor, none other than Argyro Kanellopoulou herself, would be congratulated for having solved a difficult case. The state would have recovered four million for the treasury and everyone would have what they wanted and that would be that. Kanellopoulou and Statiris would then quietly enjoy the Archontas fortune, safely deposited in a Lebanese bank.

There was only one loose thread, Akritas himself. His death would come soon enough. Perhaps he'd be killed during the arrests, like Manolis Theklas, his old boss, years before, or perhaps they would wait until he was re-united with Katarina and liquidate both of them in one go. And just in case, they'd probably gun down Costas as well. That task would probably fall to Tolio. He felt cold all over, the room frigid like the icy vaults where they keep the carcasses in a meat processing plant. The person who had telephoned him the day before said to wait for a day or two and he would be contacted again. The next part of this little drama was going to be very tricky.

Akritas leaned back in his chair, put his hands behind his head, and thought about evil. He remembered accompanying Katarina to a conference on good and evil at Oxford last year. She'd been busy with the sessions and he'd had an opportunity to call and visit some old British acquaintances from his time at the UK policing college twenty-five years earlier. It was late summer and Oxford was particularly beautiful. It was in the final burst of summer flowerings, the last full bloom before the sodden English winter set in. He recalled one rapturous walk they'd taken in the deer park of Magdalen College. They'd leaned up against the parapet of a little bridge and talked about themselves and their future. Beneath them, a single swan silently navigated the dark water. They let their bodies press against each other and Akritas recalled that he had never experienced such perfect bliss. It wasn't just love of Katarina, the perfect harmony dazed them – the green park, the distant tawny deer grazing, leaf-heavy trees, the swan's slow glide, black water flowing, finches and robins chirruping, the sun somewhere up above the leafy canopy, the light falling through the trees like golden coins dropping from heaven, and the gentle breeze rustling the foliage. It was paradise.

He remembered that once in a pub one of his British colleagues, a former student there, raising a pint of ale to his lips, had said that the problem with finding oneself in Arcadia was that one never wanted to leave. With lowered eyes, he had said "unfortunately one must" and Akritas remembered the regret he heard in the man's voice that day. It was like being evicted from the Garden of Eden, he said. On that bridge on that September afternoon, he knew what the man meant. And, then, just as Akritas and Katarina could not conceive that a greater perfection was possible, the unexpected happened. A wasp landed on Katarina's sandaled foot and stung her. She cried out in pain and the idyll collapsed. He hurried her into one of the College buildings and found an elderly porter who helped her with a little ice, some ointment, and a plaster. He also gave her a cup of tea and a biscuit and told them that in late summer the wasps get rather aggressive, it's as if, he said, evil cannot abide so much goodness and must do what it can to hurt it. All that evil really possessed, he said looking at them both intently, was the power to sting us, to make us aware, again and again, of its presence, but it did not have enough power to destroy the world. The pain subsided and the porter shook Akritas' hand in farewell and much to his surprise Katarina, eyes shining with tears, hugged the kindly old man and kissed both his cheeks. You Greeks, he said smiling as they were leaving, you are a wonderful ancient people.

Ancient perhaps, Akritas thought straightening up, but maybe not that wonderful. If anything happened to Katarina he would never forgive himself. He would resign from the force, take whatever pension was due him and go live on an island as far away from the mainland as he could get. He looked around the detectives' room. It was empty. But the noise of the city outside roared on in its relentless pursuit of . . . what? Night was approaching and he wondered how Anna-Maria was going to get along down in Glyfada. He had developed a new admiration for the woman. Under the mask of the party girl with the cute little girl voice, she was all woman with a mind of her own and a degree of courage that surprised him. Anna-Maria loved her older sister and believed in her relationship with Akritas. Perhaps she could be forgiven her tight clothes and the jeweled cascades of gold and amber. His mind went blank for moment. What was he supposed to be doing? Time to go home and get some rest. Tomorrow would be a dead loss. The day after, he sensed, would prove to be the day of reckoning.

/23/

Two days passed and then at 9:31AM the third day, his mobile began buzzing. He put down the spoon with which he'd been having some yogurt and honey with orange slices on the side and looked at the tiny screen. Private number.

"*Neh*," he said.

"Ready for instructions?" the voice asked.

"Shoot."

The voice explained in detail what was going to happen and how he was going to fit into the little drama. He was told his movements and his lines. And he was told how to handle the aftermath, including the release of Katarina. The key thing was to show up at the Kallithea apartment at exactly 4:30PM in the afternoon.

"Any questions?" the voice asked.

"No, it's all pretty clear. But remember if anything happens to the woman, I'll track every last one of you down and kill you."

"Fuck you, just do what you're told and don't be an arsehole."

Driving to Alexandras Avenue in the Opel, he thought about how he was going to deploy his team for what was to come. As he waited for a red light in Kypseli, he dialed Costas and told him to be at the station in 20 minutes and to bring the two uniformed officers with him and two more from the group that had searched the Karavias mansion. He was assured there was no sign of Statiris in the building. When he arrived, his team was waiting for him. He told two of the officers to ditch the uniforms and go in plain clothes to Statiris's apartment, make themselves invisible and watch to see who was coming and going. The other two, also in plain clothes, he assigned to watch the apartment in Kallithea where he suspected Katarina was being held. Costas was to go to Gennadiou Street and keep an eye on Argyro Kanellopoulou and to follow her if she left the building. When they'd all set off, his mobile rang. Anna-Maria's number lit up the screen.

"Hi, Pano, I'm on my way to town to see you. I've got stuff for you."

"Where are you now?"

"Kypseli," she said. "Let's meet at the coffee place where we ran into each other the other day. About 30 minutes?"

"OK, see you there."

When he arrived there was no sign of her. He ordered a double espresso and waited. She came in about ten minutes later looking very professional rather than her usual glamorous mask and costume. Hair pulled back, only the merest touches of make-up, a mauvy red on her lips and tailored charcoal skirt that reached almost to her knees. Grey nylons and black shoes with medium high heels instead of her usual stilettos.

"You're looking good," he said.

"You're not so bad either Pano, especially if you get rid of that shapeless sports jacket you're always wearing."

She settled herself down, ordered a cappuccino and then told him her story.

"OK, I arrive at the club called Planet Bourbon Street, which is the place Tolio frequents the most. Costas stayed in the car across the street. I waited for about half an hour having to beat off the attentions of half a dozen jerks, when I saw Tolio walk in. Luckily he was alone. I immediately went over and said hi, remember me, we were going to discuss furniture for your new place. Oh yeah, he said, how you doing? Come, I said, let's have a drink and a little discussion about your new flat. Since we last talked, he said, I've actually finished decorating it. Oh, I said, so there's no point in talking about it then. I'll let you get on with what you were doing. No, no, he said, stay, I've got another, older place, that really does need a make-over as far as furnishings are concerned. Where's that, I asked. Kallithea, he said. I had it on a lease but then I came into some money and bought it. I rent it out now because I've got the other place. I get some income from the Kallithea flat so I'm going to keep it. But I could charge more if the place was up-dated, you know painted cool colours, new furniture, new drapes, and wooden shutters instead of those clanky metal ones. Well, I can help with all those things, I said. I'm free tomorrow why don't you and I meet over there and I can give you some ideas about fabrics, colours, style of furniture, etc. etc. No, no, not tomorrow, he said, looking a little anxious. Can't do it tomorrow or the next day or even the day after that. No, it'll have to be at least a week from now, if not longer. Look why don't I give you a call when I'm ready to show you the place. OK, I said, here's my card. I'll write my personal mobile number on the back so you can get straight through to me. When you're ready, call, I can give you the highest quality furnishings at a great price. What do you do Tolio, sounds like you're doing well? I'm in the security business he says. You know consulting, setting up systems, stuff like that. You mean alarms, I say. No, more high end stuff, personal security for politicians and businessmen and their businesses of course. Wow, that must be pretty interesting work, I say wide-eyed. You haven't seen any dip in your revenues because of the crisis then. No, I haven't, he says, looking as if he were conversing with my tits, no the exact opposite. The people I deal with haven't suffered much, they never do, but they feel more exposed now that others are doing so badly. Also they're afraid of leftists in power. They're paranoid. They think a radical left government will call out its attack dogs and threaten them. Oh, really, I say. I hadn't thought of that. Then he says, hey Anna-Maria are you waiting for somebody, because if you're not let's you and me go to the The Panic Room – that's another club – and have a drink there. They have live music. So, we go. He's pretty chummy by now, putting his hands on my arm and shoulder. When we get out I can see Costas starting the car and following us as we walk a block or so to the other bar. After Tolio has put away a couple of rum and cokes – yuck – I can see he's getting very chummy. Now, he's brushing my breasts as if it's accidental and at one point he puts his hand on my hip and gives me a little love rub. This goes on for about an hour. Then he says, hey Anna-Maria, why don't I show you how I decorated my new place, maybe you can see what sort of taste I have. Yeah taste, I think, and I remember the picture you showed me with the hillbilly haircut. OK, I say, I have my car, why don't we meet there. He gives me the address. I wait until I see him driving off in his Ferrari or whatever that green thing he drives is. I go over to Costas and tell him what's happening. He tries to talk me out of it. I say, don't worry, I pull out a small bottle of sleeping pills. I need them sometimes to get to sleep. I crush two of them into a powder on Costas' dash and put the powder in a small square of waxed paper. I get to his place and Tolio is there. He has a rum and coke already poured for himself. He asks me what I want. Some white wine would be nice. He goes to the fridge in the kitchen and I can hear him pouring the wine. While he's out I pull out the paper and drop the powder into his drink. Remember we haven't eaten anything so the stuff is going to work pretty fast. Just one of these pills will knock you out for 6 hours. He comes back we start talking. He shows me around his place and I can hear him slurring his words and getting very relaxed. I say let's sit down on the sofa and he makes a half-hearted attempt to put his hand between my legs. By the time he gets halfway up my thigh, his eyes are closed and he's out like a light. The pills and booze will do it every time."

"Wait a sec, how often have you done this?"

"Don't be shocked, my innocent-as-an-April-shower-detective, once or twice is all. We girls have our various methods of self-protection when assholes make a nuisance of themselves. And you know some of the men in this city are jerks, possibly even most of them, even if they do drive Ferraris. Anyway, there I am in his flat. He's out on the sofa. So, I look around a little and guess what I find?"

"What?"

"This!" She pulled out several handwritten sheets. "Don't worry, I didn't take anything from his place. But I found some papers and I copied out what was written on them. I used some blank sheets that were by his printer. I know exactly where the originals are in his place, should you want to bust the bastard. I think you might want to seize his computer when you do bust him. I didn't get into it because it was password protected, but there were some emails from Argyro Kanellopoulou that he'd printed out and left on his desk. I copied them out as well. Here take all this stuff, I hope they help you put this bastard and his bitch behind bars forever."

And with that she handed the sheaf of papers to Akritas. He looked at them, then up at her and he could see under the tough-broad smile on her face, the Zofianou tenderness and vulnerability that was so much a part of Katarina's character.

"Anna-Maria, you're amazing. Really I mean it, you are one smart, brave, good-looking broad and if I didn't love your sister, I'd . . . I'd . . ."

"No, you wouldn't Pano, you're not my type."

"OK, you're right," he said, bowing before her greater wisdom. "So, let's take a look at what you've got."

"Pano, there was one more thing I found that I didn't take because if Tolio had checked his things when he woke up, he'd know I took them. So, I left them for you to discover. I'll tell you exactly where they are. You can find them yourself when you search this guy's place. It's a series of photographs of dead men, old guys, they must have been taken by Tolio because the woman, Argyro, was in them standing over the bodies, looking as if the corpses were her trophies. But, and I can't understand evil like this, she's naked, her hair is all a mess like she and Tolio have just had sex. There's at least ten of these. I have to say I've never been so disgusted in my life. And believe me I've seen some shit. I almost threw up."

"I wonder," Akritas mused, "why they had a kill squad, if they did the murders themselves?"

"Maybe they didn't," she said, "maybe they came in after the killers had left, just to make sure the job was done right. I mean I always do that after a flat has been furnished or renovated to make sure my guys have done what they were told. I always take a few photographs for the shop's Facebook page and Instagram. It's good advertising."

"Argyro seems like such a pro, why the hell would she indulge herself in this crap?" Akritas asked.

Anna-Maria shrugged.

"They probably took a few trophy photos of the corpses for those quiet winter days by the fire when you're very old and you pull out the old albums and look back fondly at all the crazy stuff you did when you were young."

"Yeah," he chuckled, "you're probably right."

"Listen, I've got to go," she said getting up. "I'm meeting a couple of girlfriends, good friends. You look at what I brought you. Call me if you have any questions. Sorry about the handwriting. I was working fast. I didn't want to be around when that fucking cockroach woke up. Oh, by the way, I left him a note, saying that it's too bad he fell asleep just when things were getting interesting. But I'd probably see him again when he called me about the Kallithea apartment. Do you think that Katarina is there?"

"There's a very good chance, but I'm not completely sure. Anyway, ciao, and talk to you soon."

He watched her walk out, when she got to the door, she turned, smiled, and blew him a kiss with the palm of her open hand. Quite a lady, he thought. Looking down at the papers, he began to read. Here it all was. The wire transfers into Argyro's account were listed. A note from Tolio to Argyro, he presumed, telling her that he'd had to lean on Melina Karavias who was getting cold feet when she found out what the basement of her father's mansion was being used for. Even suggesting that she might have to have an accident'. There was another note from him saying that it was time to get the operation over with so he wouldn't have to fuck that 'animal' Melina any more. She was a disgusting whore and he was sick of her. The two short emails established the connection between Argyro and Tolio without a shadow of a doubt. Although in a trial, attorneys had a suitcase full of doubt which they plunked on a case whether there was any doubt or not. And then when he thought of the photos Anna-Maria had seen, he knew that when they were made public, they would clinch the case and these two would end up in jail for life. If they were kept out of public notice, Kanelopoulou and Statiris, because of the vagaries of the legal system, might just wriggle out of the clutches of the law.

The Greek legal system was morally elastic, uncertain, easily distracted. You could steal millions from the state treasury, take bribes, use your influence to give a friend a state contract, perjure yourself non-stop, lie through your teeth to Parliament, the media, to your wives and mistresses, even gun down several migrant farm workers when they have the temerity to ask for some of their back wages, but if you said that you did it for something noble, like your family, because, at the end of the day, you're a good father and husband, most everyone would understand and most probably you'd be forgiven and walk free. He remembered the case of a minister of finance a couple of years back who deleted the names of three of his relatives from a list of wealthy Greek tax cheats given to him by the French finance minister. He was caught, went to trial, the panel of judges scolded him, and he walked away, got into the limousine and was driven right back to his mansion in Kifissia. There was only one kind of crime that the Greek legal system could not abide, flagrant and shameful sexual misconduct or criminality, but, then, only if it was made public. As long as it was kept private, the legal system would look the other way if the perpetrator was well enough connected. It really had nothing to do with the law. Gross indecency and sexual violence splashed on the pages of the newspapers and television was an affront to that abstract honour code imprinted on the national psyche. Keep the whole thing out of the public eye and evil didn't enter into it. In fact, for all intents and purposes evil didn't exist in Greece. Look at how the Archontas crew got away with murder for decades and grew rich on the proceeds while occupying sinecures in the bureaucracy. And it wasn't as if no one knew a thing about it. In this environment of an essential lawlessness, you could, if you played your cards right, quite easily be a moral monster and have a statue raised in your honour after your death.

/24/

By 2PM, everything was in place for the final act. Akritas knew that the killing of the three unsuspecting 'sacrificial lambs' he presumed were guarding Katarina in Kallithea would happen between 3:30 and 4PM. He was supposed to arrive with his men at 4:30PM and pick up all the pieces to 'solve' the case. But Akritas was not going to arrive at 4:30PM. He was going to strike two hours earlier in four places. He knew that Katarina was usually locked up alone. If the Delta assault team could get in quickly enough at 2:30 they'd be able to deal with the three 'sacrificial lambs' before they could react and before their executioners arrived to get them ready for the fake rescue. At the very same time another Delta team would be breaking into Tolio's new flat. They presumed it would be empty. But no-one was taking any chances. They were going in fully armed and ready for a battle. They would secure the place until Akritas arrived later with Anna-Maria to search for the laptop, documents and photographs. Tolio Statiris would be called to headquarters at 2PM, arrested and kept incommunicado. At 2:30PM Akritas and Costas would enter the deputy prosecutor's suite of offices in the Court of Appeals building and arrest Argyro Kanellopoulou. There were the three executioners from the kill squad that were unaccounted for. Akritas did not know where they were located. They were probably in the vicinity of the Kallithea flat ready to go in sometime between 3:30 and 4 to kill Gareth and the other two. Melina Karavias would be arrested and brought in for more questioning. Nothing would be announced to the media until Katarina was safe.

As 2PM approached, Akritas grew increasingly nervous. Was Katarina at the Kallithea flat? He wondered what he would do if she wasn't. This was a calculated risk, but they were under a deadline. They had to act before 4:30 or else . . . what? He couldn't predict what would happen. At 2PM Costas arrived. They went down to the Opel and drove over to the Court of Appeals and Prosecutor's building. The taxi drivers outside were still waiting for the victims of the legal system to come staggering out and be driven to their homes and there to wail in solitude or to shout abuse at family members. They parked and sat in the car. There would be two uniformed police officers guarding the office of Argyro Kanelopoulou. The charade that she was still under threat had to be continued in order not to alert her to what was about to happen. They waited. At 2:20, they entered the cavernous marble lobby of the building and stopped to get a clear view of what was happening. There were a few people walking back and forth and one group consulting a lawyer over to the side. There weren't two guards by the prosecutor's office, but three. Costas was the first to notice and the first to say that it was odd. Only two had been requisitioned. Why were there three? They looked at the three men and realized they didn't recognize any of them. They were also carrying assault rifles that were not regulation *Astynomia* weapons. Akritas realized these were the three missing killers. It was now 2:28. The operation at the other locations was about to begin. Fuck, Akritas said out loud.

"Costa," he said, "talk to me for a few seconds, then let's shake hands as if we're parting. You go to the left and I'll go to the right. We're going to come at those three fuckers in a pincer. They're wearing body armour, so we'll have to take headshots. If it happens fast enough, they won't know what hit them. Once the three are down, we go right in and grab her. OK? All right, let's shake hands and go. It's exactly 2:30."

Akritas started walking down the side of the big lobby. When he got to one of the doors near Kanellopoulou's office, he stopped pulled out his gun and quickly walked right up to the guard closest to him and killed him with a shot to the head. Crimson splashes streaked the white marble. The other two turned beginning to raise their weapons. Then Costas took down the guard closest to him. The middle guard had his AK47 up and just as a bullet from Akritas' gun hit him square in the temple, he let off a burst of gunfire into the ceiling. Before he'd hit the ground, Costas was in the office, pointing his pistol at Kanellopoulou. She was standing up and had her hand in a drawer. She pulled out the pistol but Costas fired a shot right by her head missing her by inches deliberately. She dropped the pistol and put up her hands. Akritas came in.

"You fucking moron," she spit out venomously, "what the fuck are you doing? You are a piece of shit. I should have had Larsson kill you when we had the chance. You lousy dumb fucker.

"Argyro Kanelopoulou, you are under arrest as an accessory to the murder of Nassos Archontas. When our investigation is complete you may be charged for other crimes. Please come out from behind the desk, keep your hands up. Costa, the handcuffs please."

As he was cuffing her from behind he whispered into her ear.

"You shouldn't have posed for those photos."

He left Costas to guard her. Out in the lobby he called the team leader at the Kallithea apartment. There had been a firefight. Two of the kidnappers were dead, one badly injured. Two of his men also wounded, and no sign of Katarina. Shit, shit, shit, Akritas shouted in the marmoreal splendour of the lobby. The echoes died out after a few seconds. As soon as the shooting started everyone in the lobby had vanished. Then he called the team at the other apartment. They said the place was empty, no sign of Katarina. Fuck fuck fuck he yelled at the top of his voice. The building yelled right back at him. At headquarters, Statiris had been arrested but he wasn't talking. Just demanding he have a lawyer present. Where the fuck was she?

On returning to the office of the prosecutor, he had to endure another burst of venomous insults. He was trying to figure out a way of getting Katarina's location out of her without showing that he had nothing to go on.

"You'll also be charged with kidnapping," he told her.

"Oh yeah, who the fuck am I supposed to have kidnapped, you dumb fuck?"

"Katarina Zofianou."

"You mean your bitch, that tedious slut," she said spitting out the words like one might spit out food that's gone off.

"She'll testify that you were involved."

"Look, you moron, she doesn't even know who I am."

"When Tolio was fucking her, he mentioned you were behind the whole thing, not him."

"Do you really think I'm going to believe that?"

"I don't give a fuck whether you believe it or not, you'll have to sit there in the court and listen to Tolio selling you down the river. You don't know an eighth of what your Tolio's been up to."

"The only thing the court is going to hear is what an incompetent moron you are. You don't even know where your bitch is, do you?"

"Oh, we found her all right and you're the one who's going to have to do all the explaining to the court."

She hesitated. He realized he'd hit a raw nerve.

"Fuck off," she spat, "get me a fucking lawyer, I've had enough of your bullshit."

"Costa, let's get the lady over to headquarters and make sure she gets a chance to call some slimeball lawyer."

When they emerged with her in handcuffs, the staff and employees in the building were all beginning to come out of their offices. They watched as the handcuffed deputy prosecutor was marched out towards a police vehicle. An ambulance crew and people from the medical examiner's office were already dealing with the three dead men outside her door.

At headquarters, General Solovos was down in the holding area and he told Akritas that he hoped he knew what he was doing.

"Yes, yes," Akritas said, "just trust me, boss. You'll see soon enough."

Out in the Opel, he called Anna-Maria and told her the bad news. Then he asked her to meet him at Tolio's flat. As he drove over there, he wondered what had made Argyro hesitate. He played the conversation over and over in his head. When he arrived, Anna-Maria was already there talking to one of the Delta cops securing the flat.

"No sign of Katarina?" she asked in a calmer voice than he'd expected. "Is she in danger, do you think?"

"Kanellopoulou and Statiris are in custody. The three guys at the Kallithea apartment are either dead or in hospital. Costa and I killed the other three. So, unless we're dealing with someone else, she's somewhere on her own."

Then he realized there was one more person involved he'd forgotten about, the Dane. Was that why Argyro had hesitated, because she knew that Larsson, the Dane, was with Katarina. He wondered if the hitman from Cophenhagen realized what had happened. Maybe not yet, it was only 3:30PM. The operation wasn't supposed to start until 4:30, so they had an hour. He said nothing to Anna-Maria.

"Let's go in. Please show me where you found those documents and photos."

After twenty minutes he and several of the Delta team had bagged up all the evidence. He said goodbye to Anna-Maria and started driving back to headquarters, wondering what there was in Kanellopoulou's flat. Should he go over now, or should he make some effort to find Katarina? But what could he do? He didn't really know where to start and there was only 40 minutes left. At the outside he'd have an hour before the Dane would begin to wonder why he hadn't heard anything from Argyro. He called Costas and had him find the key to Argyro's flat in her handbag and to meet him there as soon as possible.

Twenty minutes later Costas drove up and saw Akritas waiting for him near the entrance to the building.

"OK, let's go up," Akritas said, "we're going to search the place for documents, photos, her computer, anything that we can use. You know what I'm afraid of Costa, remember the Dane and the fake assassination, I have a feeling he's the one with Katarina and he's somewhere probably waiting for a phone call from Argyro or Tolio to either release her or kill her. We've only got twenty minutes before 4:30. I'm at a dead loss right now. Let's go in and see what we can find."

They entered the building and rode the lift up to the fourth floor. The recessed lights cast their silvery glow of wealth and privilege, bringing out the metallic gleam of the stainless steel fittings and trim. The door of the lift closed quietly behind them.

"There's her door," Akritas said, lowering his voice. "I'll go in first, you wait out here to make sure no one comes in."

He pushed the key gingerly into the lock and turned it. Pushing the door slowly, he realized the lights were on. Someone was already there . . .

"Is that you Argyro?" a heavily accented voice asked.

Akritas pulled out his pistol and thrust the door wide open, pointing the weapon at a man who was already disappearing into an adjoining room. The door slammed shut. He paused, looked around. He heard movement and murmurs.

"Hey, Hamlet, come out, police, we've got the place surrounded. You can't escape. Argyro is not going to be here for a very long time. Come out."

Akritas looked back into the hall and motioned for Costas to enter and to have his pistol drawn. The two of them were standing in the glassy, metallic vestibule when the door to the room began to open. Two people emerged, Katarina first, with a man's arm around her shoulders and neck, followed by a tall blond guy with a pistol pressed up against Katarina's temple.

"Is this it you're looking for?" the blond man asked in a marked Scandinavian accent. "And let down your guns." He spoke with a mechanical rattle, like most Danes.

"Are you all right?" Akritas said, looking into her eyes.

"Shut up, don't tell fucking words," the Dane shouted into her ear.

She closed her eyes. Katarina never did like people shouting.

"Let them down now!" he bellowed.

Akritas ignored him. "OK, Hamlet or whatever your fucking name is, this is the story. You can't escape. Kanellopoulou and Statiris are in custody. Five of the six others are dead and the sixth is in critical condition in hospital. Melina Karavias is also in custody. Right now you're not involved in the killings as far as I know. We can keep it that way if you surrender. You'll have to go to trial here of course but I'll see to it that you get the minimum sentence. We'll also support your lawyer's application to serve the sentence in Denmark. You wouldn't want to spend five minutes in one of our prisons let alone three years or, perish the thought, life. Do you understand? If you kill the woman, my partner and I will gun you down here and now, and you'll never be able to walk your grandchildren to school. So, you just take a moment and have a quick think. A few years in those Club Med prisons you got up there in Denmark or you can go face down here oozing blood on that nice white carpet. What will it be? Oh, and by the way, if you don't die right away, we won't finish you off to ease the pain. You'll lie here and watch me personally shoot your pecker off and your balls."

The Dane didn't move. Katarina opened her eyes wide and looked straight at Akritas. She was trying to tell him something. Then she did something unexpected, she dropped straight down. The Dane had clearly loosened his grip while he was thinking. His gun went off but it missed her head by inches, just singeing her hair. At that very moment, Costas fired a round and hit the guy in the shoulder. Just as he was trying to gain his balance and take another shot at Katarina, Akritas fired and hit him just above his right eye, opening up his skull and tossing him backwards against the white leather sofa. The Dane's pistol went off once more but the bullet hit a large mirror shattering it. He was thrashing on the sofa when Costas walked over and finished him off. Akritas rushed to Katarina, who was crumpled on the floor, and wrapped his arms around her. He could smell burnt hair. She looked up at him and much to his surprise she smiled.

"It took you long enough to find me. And where did you learn to talk like a guy in an American gangster movie?"

He held her close as she began to tremble.

About half an hour later a crime scene unit arrived, followed by a medical examiner and a doctor with an ambulance. While the doctor was checking Katarina, Akritas called Anna-Maria and told her that her sister was fine and that maybe she could drive down in an hour or so and take Katarina home once her statement had been taken. Akritas could hear Anna-Maria sobbing as he clicked off the phone.

Back on Alexandras Avenue, Katarina was interviewed by the psychologist. Once it was established that she was well enough to give a statement, Costas recorded the details, the psychologist remaining in the room and Akritas watching from behind the one-way mirror. When Katarina was abducted, she had a hood put over her head. Her handbag was ripped from her shoulder. They drove through city streets for about 15 minutes. Their movement slowed down and for the next 15 minutes or so the car seemed to be winding its way very slowly through narrow streets. That was Plaka. Eventually they stopped and she was brought out and taken down some steps into a basement, walked through some corridors, and pushed into a room. The Karavias mansion, Akritas thought. A man in a ski mask came in, said nothing, and emptied her briefcase on the single bed, mainly books and notes. He left taking the empty briefcase with him. She wondered where she was but thought it might be a good idea to leave something of hers in the room in case anyone came there looking for her. She jammed a light scarf down in the gap between the bed and the wall and also the bracelet Akritas had given her.

 About an hour later, two men in ski masks came in, dropped the hood over her head again, and walked her out to the car. They drove slowly for a time and then must have got on a major road because the car was moving very fast. In about half an hour, they stopped and she was taken up some stairs and then into an elevator to the 4th floor of a building. She couldn't tell which part of the city she was in. She was there for two days. That morning, she'd been moved again, to Argyro's flat, where she was put in a rather luxurious room and guarded by the blond man, until Akritas and Costas arrived. She was left alone most of the time. Only one of the masked men seemed dangerous to her. He had said when he came in the room on the second day that if she started suffering from 'Stockholm syndrome' he'd been more than happy to oblige. Then he'd reached down and put his hands on her hips and pressed his groin against her. He stopped and looked around at the door when they heard a woman's voice outside. He left and never returned. All she remembered was that he was wearing very expensive shoes.

After the statement, Akritas and Katarina had some time alone while they waited for Anna-Maria to arrive. He told her about his memory of Oxford, their walk in the deer park and how the wasp sting had ruined it. She smiled as he spoke and said that she often remembered that day and how perfect it all was.

"I've never forgotten it," she said holding on to his hand. Her natural contralto was a pitch higher and a little more rapid than usual as she spoke. "What the old man said about that wasp and how it's like evil. It inflicts pain to remind us that it's always there, but that's all it can do. It can't destroy the world because deep down and radically so, the world is ever only good. I believe that. Look how the wasp that stung me ruined our wonderful afternoon in that beautiful park. But in the end, when we left the old man, didn't we feel that the wasp's sting had actually created something good? Didn't we feel a new kind of perfection? It's what Mephistopheles in Goethe's *Faust* says about himself, 'I am part of that power which eternally wills evil and eternally creates good'. I think that's what he says, I'll have to look it up. Evil is always extreme, Pano, you see it every day when you work, but listen to me, it is not radical, it has no depth. It's all on the surface, it's like the wasp's sting, it causes pain and a redness on your skin but it cannot hurt your heart."

He could tell she was rambling. Shock probably. Some people go mute, others want to talk. All he could do was look at her as she spoke and nod his head. He wasn't sure he understood exactly what she was saying but he suddenly realized he wanted to believe. To believe again. Then, Anna-Maria was there and the two women were in each other's arms. They held on for a long time. Anna-Maria turned and looked at Akritas, took his arm and pulled him into their embrace and the three of them clung to each other as if they would never let go. When the emotion had settled, they began to get ready to part. Anna-Maria would be taking Katarina home and Akritas would stay to complete all the necessary paperwork. As the two sisters were leaving hand-in-hand, Katarina turned and looked at him.

"Will you come tonight," she asked, "when you're finished here?"

"Yes, I will. I'll call when I'm on my way."

"I kiss you."

"I kiss you too," he replied.

Then they were gone. He turned back towards the offices and realized he had one more thing to do.

He went back to the room where they kept material evidence. He looked through the boxes that contained the items collected so far. He found the plastic envelope with the photographs Statiris had taken of Argyro and the dead men. He looked at them one more time. Taking his phone from his jacket pocket, he scrolled through his contacts and found the number of Philolaos Manolakos, the one journalist in Athens that he trusted.

"Hey Phil, Panos Akritas here. How are you?"

"Pano, nice to hear from you. It's been a long time. I'm fine. And you?"

"Couldn't be better," Akritas said. "Just busted open a big case that I think might interest you. There's going to be a press conference tomorrow to make announcements and to say that we've arrested the perpetrators. Can we get together soon? I have a couple of things to show you."

"Is this about the Archontas murders?"

"Yes, it is."

"You've got the killers then?"

"Yes, and I've got some additional stuff related to the murders. I need your advice on how to handle it, the way we present the case to the court and to the public. To be honest, I think this stuff is going to be decisive in getting convictions."

"I'm intrigued," the newspaperman said.

"Meet you at Montalbano at 6?"

"Good, see you there."

As he parked the Opel, he saw his journalist friend entering the café.

"Pano, these pictures are dynamite!" Manolakos said. "You know that our media will not touch them, right?"

"Why?"

"They're too pornographic and the newspapers and TV stations will suppress them for various reasons. Like for example the people you've mentioned, the prosecutor, the chief of detectives are identified with certain political parties and powerful people who will not want their good names dragged into the mire. They control their media outlets totally and the owners will decide what goes in or is kept out. If there's any chance they might be made to look bad, they'll just suppress the whole thing. As one of my colleagues says, our media is not in the information business, it's in the political influence business."

"And your paper?"

"My editors will say this is tabloid stuff. They'll report it but they won't actually publish any of the photos. Their power to astonish people will be lost."

"What about the alternative media?"

"Sure, but no-one will believe them. People will say the pictures are fake, doctored, photo shopped, or what have you, so their impact will be minimized."

"So," Akritas asked, "what do you suggest?"

Philolaos Manolakos looked at his friend, flipped through the photos one more time, and explained to Akritas what he had to do.

/25/

"You know," Akritas said looking at Argyro, several days after the arrests, "it'll be the photos that he took that'll get you sent down for a long time. Why you let him do that, I'll never really understand."

She looked at him for a moment her face expressing scorn. She was standing by the window in the dull green interrogation room. Without her stilettos, she looked smaller than he remembered when she stood above him in her office feeding him lies.

"We'd get you for some of the financial stuff," he continued, "but you know how the courts deal with money crimes."

"No, how *do* the courts deal with money crimes? Damn, I was *only* a prosecutor, how the fuck would I know how the courts deal with money crimes."

"They never take them seriously, well, not seriously enough, especially if you argue you did it for your family's honour, or just for your family because you love them so much, or if you get an accredited psychologist, especially a foreign-trained one, in Vienna, or Paris, to say you're simply suffering from depression or some such bullshit. You know what I mean, the Viki Stamati-defense. You'd get three years at most and most of that under house arrest. But the porno shots with the corpses right there, that will do you in. The Church will make sure of that."

"Is that a fact? Why don't you just shut up," she said looking out of the window.

"Why you screwed up your career as a prosecutor I also don't get. Had you played it straight, you might have had that career in politics when the economy gets back to normal. All you had to do was stick with prosecuting until the worst was over."

"What do you know about it?" Argyro exploded angrily, turning to look at him. "You don't know what I had to deal with in the party. When I was twenty-two, I was a star. All those fat fuckers wanted to fuck me. And I didn't give it out too cheaply either. But when I turned thirty-five, they couldn't get it up for me anymore, even if they sucked back the whole bottle of Viagra. Every morning when I got up I could see the sag setting in one millimeter at a time. And then there was always a new parade of twenty-two-year-olds with their tits and their asses for sale. I had that to deal with, and believe me, this new bunch are wiser than I was at their age. They've seen enough porn by the time they hit their sixteenth birthday to know what the fat fuckers want women to do to them. Those bitches can suck ten years off a man's life. So, please don't patronize me. Stick with your bitch girlfriend and leave the adult stuff for adults. You're a schoolboy, Panos, you'll never grow up."

With that she turned away and looked out the window of the interrogation room, her face drawn back into a tight grimace, her hands fidgeting with the draw string of the blind. Akritas read a little more from the papers in front of him and looked up at her. She was staring at him.

"You know," she began, her face blank again, "if you'd played ball with me, we could have gone a long way."

"What about Tolio?" he asked. "That's another thing I don't understand. Why him? He's an idiot."

"Yes, but a useful idiot," she said. "The years I spent sucking cocks in the party taught me a lot about useful idiots. You need them to do stuff, like get the coffee, clean up the messes, and amuse you when you need amusing."

"Is that what the photographs were? Amusement?"

"If you must know, they were my idea. The fucking after the photo shoots was something else. But you wouldn't understand, you're such a fucking boy scout."

The weird thing for Akritas was that he did understand, but it was better if she thought he was a boy scout. He realized then and there why he wanted to be with Katarina. He needed her innocence, the idealism, even the silly, airy-fairy theories. Her unapologetic naïveté dissolved the venom that poisoned Argyro's world.

"I can maybe understand Tolio, at least he had something on the ball," he said, "but Boutsekes seems a stretch, how did you ever get involved with him, he's a New Democracy man?"

"Come on, you don't actually believe these party labels mean anything, do you? "But Boutsekes?"

"Boutsekes and I have known . . ."

"Had known," Akritas corrected.

". . . each other ever since I got in the prosecutor's office. He'd brought cases to me and so there was a kind of professional understanding. We both knew our different political stances were, more or less, flags of convenience."

"You mean like tramp freighters?"

"Fuck you. One financial fraud case involving Xeniades led us to a Archontas bank account in Moscow with over 45 million euros in it. When we saw that, we both looked at each other and thought the same thing. The numbers amazed us. The Archontas organization had accumulated a huge amount and it had been wiped clean by being moved around through Switzerland, Russia, and Panama. It had finally all landed in Beirut. We made a deal with al Hadi and he turned the money over to us after he got a better percentage from us than from Archontas who was a bit of a tightwad it turned out. The old man didn't really know what was happening with his money because al Hadi lied to him. But a couple of the other old men, Xeniades and the one called Aleko Echecrates, got wind of what we were doing, so they had to die. But we couldn't just kill two of them, all had to go. Boutsekes recruited the kill squad mainly from low-lifes he'd met in his years in the police. He put Tolio in command. Three of them were former police officers who took bribes and had been sacked. He thought they would be loyal to him. Then that limp fuck got greedy. He thought he could cut me out. It was easy as hell turning the squad against him and, well, you know the rest."

"What about Karavias? Why was he involved?"

"That old turncoat had nothing really to do with it, specifically. He was another useful idiot. Rich, but still an idiot. We needed to pin the revenge motive on someone with money and after I read that interview with him by that journalist, I thought, yeah, here's a guy who had a 50-year grudge against people like Archontas. I know that Karavias tried to make himself out as some kind of anti-fascist hero but believe me he wasn't. Tolio started fucking Melina the slut daughter. She would have done anything for him. We just used the basement rooms in the mansion for storage and as a safe house. If it had all worked out as planned, Karavias would have been the fall guy. Our guys would have disappeared with their very generous fees in their pockets and we would have planted all the evidence you dunces needed to convict the old man. At his age and his position in society and especially as he would have been accused of killing war criminals as a crime of 'political' passion, do you really think our notoriously understanding Hellenic judges would have done anything to him? Well, convicted him maybe, but to serve his sentence comfortably in his mansion for the rest of his life. Which is what would have happened to him anyway. At his age, he wasn't going anywhere. And don't be fooled by that interview with him. To save his skin, he informed on other communists that he knew and told Archontas where they were to be found. He was an opportunist and we just used him because he was a shit all his life."

"Speaking of dunces. Why did you pick Xiloudes to lead the investigation?"

"I didn't. Boutsekes assigned him to the case because he thought Xiloudes was smart enough to pick up on the vengeance stuff but not smart enough to see what was really going on. Xiloudes has a one-track mind and it got stuck on the simple robbery idea and couldn't be budged, even when we were waving evidence in his fucking face. So, when Archontas was killed we needed someone who'd at least get a hold of the obvious."

"Yeah, but why did you choose me? There are others. Psarros for example, Or Zantidis, Alkinous, Palios, others. Why me?"

"Believe me, you weren't my first choice. I was going for Zantidis. He's just sharp enough, but not so's he'd upset the tomato stand. But I let Boutsekes talk me into it. He said you had a good reputation and when you came up with the revenge angle people would believe you. You know what people are like in this country. No-one ever believes anything anyone is saying unless they have a rock solid reputation for honesty. And you can count that bunch on the fingers of one hand. But I was still doubtful. And I was right. No smokescreen is perfect. There'll always be things that don't add up. But if they're small and seemingly insignificant, most of your dumbass colleagues would ignore them and go with what they'd see as the preponderance of evidence, wouldn't they?"

"I'll tell you what almost convinced me that it was revenge," he said, "the drawings with the corpses. When I saw them I knew simple robbery, like Andreas thought, was not it. Were they your idea?"

"Well, yes. I didn't know Xiloudes like I know you. I'd never worked on a case with him like I have with you and I presumed, wrongly, that he was a little like you. I thought he might be more convinced of the revenge idea if he had to figure it out, if there was a teeny weeny puzzle to solve. But I was wrong. What does that dolt have for a brain, something teeny weeny like a fucking period at the end of the sentence? You picked up on it fast enough. Congratulations."

"And Hamlet, the Prince of Denmark, whose idea was that?"

"You mean Gunnvald Larsson. He was mine. When I began to suspect that Boutsekes was going to try and fuck me over, I brought in Gunnvald for protection. He was recommended to me by a man I put away a few years ago and then got him released early. He expressed his gratitude by giving me Gunnvald."

"And the fake assassination on Patission?"

"I wouldn't have bothered if we had Zantidis to deal with. I needed one more detail, I thought, that might steer you away from the robbery idea and on to what I wanted you to think."

"Well, I have to admit you had me pretty confused for a while. Did he kill Haniotis?"

"Yes. Incidentally, how did Haniotis know about me?"

"I was talking to him about Archontas and as I was leaving, I asked if he'd ever heard of you. It was a bit of an afterthought, but by that time I was beginning to get suspicious. He said no, but he must have checked your name and up popped the account at National Bank."

"What's happened to the money in Beirut?" she asked.

"We put out an international arrest warrant through Interpol for Mohammed al Hadi. But he must have been tipped off by his pals in the Lebanese *gendarmerie* because he left Beirut three days ago and surfaced 36 hours later in Grozny. The Archontas money has disappeared with him and he's probably paying the guy who runs things in Chechnya, Kadyrov, a handsome sum for protection."

At that news, Argyro fell silent and looked out the window again. A dark evergreen treetop like an open sooty hand was waving slowly back and forth in the bright sunlight. It was early October and the weather was very fine. Warm, with a light southeasterly breeze, and many flowers still in bloom. The cooler weather wouldn't set in for several more weeks. She continued to stare out and up at the blue sky. Not a cloud in sight.

"The only thing I regret," she said finally, with a tenderness that surprised Akritas, "is that I probably won't ever see Folegandros again. I love that little harbour at Karavostasis and the white hotel. The front room with the terrace looking out over the bay always made me feel like a child again, it was so beautiful. I would sit with my legs drawn up so that I could rest my chin on my knees and look out across the Aegean. I would love to catch the local bus again and spend the ten minutes bumping up towards the town and walk among the white houses and sit under the plane tree in the square and have the sultan's omelet and a salad and glass of white wine. It was where I was going to spend my old age, would you believe it. Me the only woman Prime Minister of Greece, giving up the high life in Athens and retiring to a small island home. Not Santorini or Mykonos or any of those other filthy places, with all their noise and hollowness. My little house wouldn't even have to overlook the sea. I would walk to the seashore with my towel and sunhat and swim for two hours and then rest and return to eat in the shade of that wonderful tree. I would have died a happy woman."

She fell silent and Akritas was sure that she was seeing an unusually clear day in the Kyklades. The little white passenger ferry following the horizon heading for the harbour. At noon the white stones down there on the bare shore would grow warm with the sun's heat and the gleaming blue bay would look inviting. He knew that she was seeing herself at rest, in no hurry at all, but finally rousing herself, going down there to enter the sea.

For a moment he felt sorry for her, her softening voice, or was it her final sigh, luring him into the white maze of her blue imagining. Then he remembered the photographs and he suddenly saw her for what she was. He knew that she was in for a rough ride. The photographs, suitably cropped for family viewing, would be appearing, on Manolakos' advice, the next morning in three newspapers, three tabloids, one in Italy, one in Germany, and one in Britain. He did not trust the Greek media. The PASOK media would not run the story, neither would the New Democracy media because of the Boutsekes involvement. The KKE would only draw ideological lessons from the whole affair, dirty capitalist shenanigans blah blah blah, and probably not even bother with the photos. They were above such things. But if they appeared in foreign papers first and caused a stir, as these no doubt would, the Greek media would have to pay attention, especially when the story and the photographs would be all over the Internet in a few hours.

He knew this was her *psychostasia*, the weighing of souls in Hermes' scales just like in the drawing. She was the figure on the lower scale about to fall off, to be dismissed by the indifferent gods. They'd lost interest in her. They were ready to move on to new heroes and new villains, all of them full of that energetic spiritedness the ancient Greeks called *thymos*, that sometimes, among the villains, tilted towards *hubris*. The latter brought you down, the former raised you up to tackle the most difficult tasks – to swim into rough seas to rescue a stranger, to sacrifice yourself on the battlefield, or, in this case, to wrestle for that glistening pile of blood-spattered gold that you believe can set you free. The struggle was over and she was done for. She was already, an *eidolon*, a shadow of her former self. There's no accounting for the caprice of the gods.

He looked over at her in the frumpy prison clothes she was now being forced to wear, no make up, no lacy underwear, no jewels, cheap trainers on her feet, and her body already beginning to show the prison sag that eventually weighs down all inmates. It was the angry, aggressive wasp dying in autumn, its venom exhausted, its power to sting spent.

/26/

"Hello, yes, this is Captain Akritas, could you put me through to Mr. Cleomenes."

"Yes, Pano, how are you? I'm sorry I couldn't stop and chat at Haniotis's funeral. Thanks for coming. He had told me after you talked to him that he thought you were a fine man."

"Good, but I still feel guilty for turning him into a target."

"But Pano, it was just bad luck. He could have got onto a plane and disappeared over the Indian Ocean with a couple of hundred other people. Just bad luck, my friend. Don't fault yourself. Are you calling about something specific?"

"Well, yes, I am. Do you know anyone you, or I, can trust in Grozny in Chechnya?"

Cleomenes paused. Akritas could hear him turning pages in a book.

"Why do you ask?"

"The Archontas money is in Grozny with a man named Mohammed al Hadi. I presume he's used some of it, probably a good deal of it, to buy himself protection there. But I would like to see if we can recover what's left. We've already started proceedings against the family members who profited from the murders of the five Archontas gang members. They're being charged with withholding information and obstructing justice. We're going after as much of the money as possible and we're hoping to put pressure on the government to use it to set up a fund to help any surviving former inmates of Makronisos and the other prison islands or their relatives. Melina Karavias, after some persuasion, has given several million already from her father's fortune. Is there anyone?"

"Yes, his name is Pavel Klesmer and he can be reached at 8712 65 71 44 and the country code for the Russian Federation. Seven I think. He works for the Federal Unity Bank in Grozny. Tell him I suggested you call him. He has many contacts in the Russian banking system and he'll do what he can to help you."

"Thanks Petros. Any chance we can have lunch any time soon?"

"Of course Pano, how about next Tuesday at 2:30? To Kafeneion?"

"Of course."

"We can dedicate the first cocktail to the memory of that very fine man, Theodosis Haniotis, and all the honest men and women who still make this a great country."

"Perfect."

***

When Tolio Statiris was brought in he looked grey and used up. The fashionable haircut was turning to scruffy. He was beginning to resemble the old Tolio in the photograph taken when he first joined the police, a little chubby and sallow. Must be the prison food, Akritas thought. The €200 shoes were gone and he was shuffling around in cheap, no-name trainers.

"Sit down," Akritas said. "You're being charged with murder and a half dozen other felonies. You're going to be put away for a long time and we want to put Argyro Kanellopoulou away for a long time too. We have enough on both of you to do just that, but we want to make sure that she goes down for the maximum sentence. You can shorten yours by cooperating with the prosecutors. They're just outside and will come in after you and I are finished to interview you. OK?"

Tolio said nothing, just looked blankly at Akritas' face.

"I've been asked to speak to you because you were a serving police officer. If you cooperate, they're willing to offer you a deal. They'll explain what it is when they come in. Do you understand?"

Still nothing.

"If you don't cooperate, they'll go for the same sentence for both of you. You should know that Kanellopoulou has already spoken to the prosecutors and she's putting a good deal of the blame on you. That you forced her to take those photographs because you're a sick pervert. That you liked killing people and were primarily responsible for the murders and that you personally killed Haniotis . . ."

"I didn't," he blurted out. "It was the Dane."

"You and I and the wall may know that, but she's going to testify that it was you. The Dane is no longer around to confess and they want someone to pin it on. You'll do.

"She's fucking lying, dammit."

"She wants to seem like she's cooperating and you know Argyro, she'll lie and weep and look pretty and bat her eyelashes innocently at the panel of judges and they'll probably fall for it. They'll end up giving you life and her 10 years with a chance of parole after 5 for good behaviour and you know how good an actress she is."

"How do I know you're not lying to me?"

"That's not the question, Tolio. The real question is, are you willing to take the chance?"

Akritas paused for a moment.

"OK, you think about it," he continued. "The prosecutors will be here in five minutes."

***

Four o'clock in the afternoon is always the quietest part of the day at the Oscar Wilde pub. Akritas and his good friend Greg were at the bar drinking scotch. Jimmy, the bartender, was leaning up against the dishwasher talking to the pretty young woman they'd just hired to help in the evenings when the place was packed. Akritas and Greg were both privately thinking it was about time to find another place to drink. The Wilde had become too popular. It was getting too crowded, too smoky, too noisy, and it was full of very young Greek men and women, some little more than teenagers, instead of the weary older ex-pats and middle-aged Greeks like Akritas. The younger crowd seemed to think it was cool being in what they took to be an Irish pub environment. Of course, it wasn't anything like an actual Irish pub. Most people wouldn't want to be seen dead in one of those, but the Oscar Wilde management put up a damn good front. There was a picture of Oscar on the matchboxes. Quotations stenciled on the paper napkins and more photos of Oscar decorating the walls. You could not pass an evening there without hearing, at least once, someone say 'I have nothing to declare except my genius'. And this, always garbled, from a 20-year-old Greek guy with a cigarette in one hand and his other hand making free with his girlfriend's thigh. There was also a rather large photograph of the Liffey and, incongruously, a framed copy of the first edition cover of James Joyce's *Ulysses*.

"Has Katarina recovered from her ordeal?" Greg said. "I haven't seen her for ages."

"You'd be surprised Greg, how well she came through it. She was very shaken by the whole experience. But she also seemed able to stand back from the direness of the situation and look at it in a detached kind of way. I think this is her scholar side. You know, turning the whole thing over in her mind as if it were a subject of intellectual interest. It probably helped her stay on an even keel."

"You mean she never thought those guys in ski masks might actually kill her?"

"She obviously didn't think it was a lark, but she did stay calm, well as much one can under the circumstances. It wasn't until Hamlet almost blew her head off that the threat really hit home."

"What about some counselling? I know she's a therapy nut. Every time Katia and I are quarrelling, she wants Katia to go see her therapist in Halandri. I don't think she understands the difference between a quarrel and a 'quarrel'."

"To be honest, Greg, I don't think I understand it either. She's seen Christini the police psychologist several times and that seems to have helped. They've become quite good friends actually. In fact, they're meeting for coffee this afternoon."

"How's she managing the media attention and interviews?"

Akritas laughed and shook his head.

"She's not that good with the one-liners and when they ask her that stupid question about how it felt to be kidnapped, held prisoner for three days by desperate criminals, and almost shot in the head, she never says what they want to hear. Instead of saying how stressful and traumatic it all was, she always talks about what it means to have feelings and what current theories of trauma have to say. Then she quotes Cornelius Castoriadis or some other philosopher and you can see the eyes of the interviewer glaze over. She's getting fewer media calls."

The two men laughed out loud and Jimmy looked over.

"What's so funny, you guys?" he shouted.

"Nothing Jimmy, nothing," Greg called back.

"You know, Greg, it was something you said to me a few days ago that really made me see more clearly what I was dealing with in this case."

"Really, what was that?"

"It was when you suggested a double marriage. Remember?"

"Oh, yeah, but how did that help?"

"It was what you said about a credible ruse, or something like that."

"I said something about a credible ruse? I didn't realize I was so clever. Go on, tell me how clever I am."

"At first, I didn't get what you were saying and then a half-formed thought I had in my mind about my case suddenly stood out as clear as the moon in an empty sky."

Greg nodded slowly, still not sure why his words had made a difference, but as long as his friend thought he was a genius, he was fine with that. They drank in silence.

"Greg, how are things with Katia these days. Making plans for the wedding?"

"Yes and no. We're not actually talking to each other these days because she wants to have the wedding on Spetses, you know where her mother has a house, and I want to have it in Birmingham, where my mother lives."

"Greg, are you kidding, is there a choice here? Spetses is beautiful. Birmingham has its own kind of peculiar beauty, but it lacks something, don't you think?

"You mean like warm weather, flowers, sunshine, and the deep, blue sea? Well yes, you have a point. But the whole thing has to do with what Katia is going to wear. She wants to wear something light and diaphanous with those ornate sandals she bought on Lesvos a couple of years ago. She says that in Birmingham, it'll be cold and grey, wet and gloomy, she'll have to wear some itchy wool thing and horrible shoes. She says that the dress she wants to wear will show off her figure better. My God, Pano, she's 50 years old."

"Greg, what the fuck are you talking about, a woman after 40 is just coming into her own. At 50 she's in full bloom. What do you want, a teenager? Good for Katia, she should show off her figure. I have a new respect for your intended."

"You do?"

"Of course. Do you know what the difference is between a mature woman, a woman who is all-woman, and a . . . what's that English word . . . a stripling? Listen, when the stripling walks into a room she has to concentrate all her energy in that self-control that makes her appear gracious. She has to remember to do this and to do that. She has to modulate her voice so that it's low and languid and totally delightful. All of this has to be remembered and rehearsed. A real woman, a woman of 50 who's seen a bit of the world and is settled comfortably in her own skin doesn't have to concentrate on appearing gracious, she is gracious. She doesn't have to remember and rehearse how to speak and how to move her body. She speaks and moves and is herself. It's all so fucking effortless man. Your Katia, she's got it. I think my Katarina has her own version of it as well. It really is what I find attractive about her. And what makes her different from every other woman I've ever been with. It took me a while to learn how to understand it and appreciate it."

He paused, lifted his glass and brought it to his lips. It was a gesture of homage.

"You know what you need to do Greg?"

"No, what?"

"You need to develop something you English lack almost entirely, except maybe for some of your aristocrats."

"What's that?" his friend asked.

"You need to develop the perfection of relaxed reverence."

He paused. Greg had been looking at him intently the whole time.

"You're not pulling my leg, are you?"

"Not at all."

"I'm not sure what you mean but I I think it means it'll have to be Spetses then, won't it?"

"Yes, it will," Akritas replied, laying his hand on his friend's shoulder.

"Pano, do you mind if I just go right now? Sorry, but I need to talk to Katia."

"No, go, go, go to her, man, tell her that you've made up your mind about the island. Let her make plans, see to the dress, get excited, want to give herself to you, let her find herself in a woman's paradise where all your nonsense is adorable."

Greg disappeared without another word. Jimmy came over.

"He took off pretty fast," Jimmy said,

"He had to see a woman about a wedding."

Jimmy smiled and went back to chatting up the new barmaid. Akritas looked down at his drink and wondered where all that guff he'd just said had come from. Probably some novel read a long time ago, he thought.

***

"How are you, Panos," Police General Xenophon Solovos said indicating a chair near his desk.

"Fine, sir, I hope you're well."

"Yes, good, I've asked you to come and see me because I'd like to sound you out about something."

"What's that, sir?"

"Now that Boutsekes is gone we need a new chief of detectives on the eighth floor and I'd like to offer you that post."

Akritas looked at the General. Solovos was about the only higher up that Akritas still respected. The rest seemed to be politicians and time-servers. Solovos was a law-man. He was a serious and dedicated policeman. Akritas knew the man had struggled to professionalize the *Astynomia Elliniki*. He had made progress but there was still a long way to go. He needed people, like Akritas, in positions of authority to change the culture of the police service, to make it a service and not a police *force*. He knew that if he refused, he would disappoint the General.

"General Solovos," he began, "this is a great honour, that you think so well of me that you would consider me for the post. But I have to say I'm not really the man for the job. I'm an investigator, not an administrator. I'm not patient enough to deal with management and personnel matters. Please don't take it as a snub. I have the highest respect for you and the kind of changes you're making in the service, but I'm not the kind of man who will be diplomatic enough to do what's necessary. I hope you understand."

"I do, Panos, and I half expected that this would be your answer. So, let me ask you then if there is anyone you might recommend, internally, for the position?"

"I would say my partner Costas Psarros will make an excellent chief sometime in the future, when he's had a little more experience. I'm not sure he's ready yet, but he will be. He bears watching. As for the rest of the detectives, no, I don't have anyone that comes to mind immediately. I've heard very good things about a man in Thessaloniki whose last name is Famellos I believe. He might be well worth looking at more closely."

"Thank you, I'll make a note of the name and I'll contact someone I know in the prefecture up there. Incidentally, congratulations, the prosecutors say we'll have convictions from the way you put the case together."

"It wasn't just me working on the case, Psarros contributed, and uniformed officers as well. On the day we made the arrests there were at least two-dozen men involved. And two civilians, both of them very brave women, also provided us with information that clinched the case."

***

When his phone buzzed again he was trying to finish the last of the report. He picked it up and looked at the screen. He didn't recognize the number.
"*Neh*," he said.
"Pano? This is Spyro down at the garage. Your Skoda is ready for pick up."
"Great, how much is it going to be?"
"The boss told me to give you a 35% discount, so it'll be €177."
"That's all? Hey thank Fotios for me."
"There's one more thing," Spyros said hesitantly.
"What's that?"
"Your front brake pads are down to 5-10%, you'll need a brake job soon. The back brakes are good for a while."
"How much is that going to cost?"
"Regular, it would be about €400. But Fotios will probably give you a discount."
"OK, thanks for letting me know. Can you do the brakes soon?"
"I can do them right now and you can pick up the car at about 6 tonight."
"All right, see you at 6."
He clicked off the phone and said, quite distinctly, "Damn it to hell."

***

"Will they give you a little time off after all the excitement?" Katarina asked.

"Yes, probably, Solovos is in charge until they appoint a new chief and he likes me, so I can probably get a few days. Why?"

"Why don't we go somewhere while the weather's still good? Like maybe an island? Or somewhere else."

"Sure, but can you take the time off, won't Dimitri and Lila miss you?"

"Don't be sarcastic, Pano. It annoys me when you're like that."

"Sorry."

"The course that Dimitri gave me doesn't start until the new term and everything else I'm doing can be put off for a few days."

"Where would you like to go?" Akritas asked.

"I was in Rome once as a child with my parents and I've always wanted to go back."

Akritas thought about Rome. Some years back he'd spent a month there working with an Italian detective, a guy with a funny name who came from Venice. They worked on a case that involved some Greek gangsters who'd moved in on the territory of some Italian gangsters. The struggle between the two gangs got ugly and they had started shooting each other up and of course killing and wounding innocent bystanders caught in the crossfire. Akritas and the Italian detective – what the hell was his name? – had got along very well. He wondered if the guy was still there. He'd have to look back at some of his old case notes.

"Yes, Rome in October will be wonderful. Let's see if we can spend a week there," he said, suddenly eager to get going.

"Can you take a week?" she said.

"Yes, I'm sure I can."

Her smile was lovely and he pulled her towards him and kissed her on the lips.

"Shall I start looking for a hotel?" she asked.

"Nah, don't bother. When I was there a couple of years ago working on a case I stayed in a great place near the Piazza Navona. I have the guy's number still in my mobile. Andrea was his name,

Andrea Marchi, wow, I still remember it. He was a schoolteacher, all bright and keen, and always rode his bicycle when he came by. He would announce his arrival by ringing the bell on his bike. I'll call him and see if we can stay in this little apartment he's got, which is great. It's small, but it has a huge bed, a roomy modern bathroom and a little kitchen with everything we need to eat in if we don't want to go out. The only thing is that it has no windows, but it's bright because the ceiling is opaque glass or something and the light comes down from above. I know it sounds a little bit like a dungeon but, you'll see, it's not. I loved the place.

"Were you alone in Rome?"

"What do you mean," he asked?

"You weren't there with anyone, were you?"

"Of course not, I was working on a case with an Italian cop."

"So, you never had another woman in that 'dungeon'?"

"Katarina, please, do you think I would take you there, if I had?"

"Well, I just wanted to make sure, *agape mou*."

And then she touched his arm and looked at him with that smile that always voyaged, through all the dark cities, straight to his heart.

About the author

John Xiros Cooper was born in Athens, Greece. He turned to fiction writing after thirty-five years as a university professor of literature in Canada. The Panos Akritas series adds a new voice to the tradition of Mediterranean noir

Printed in Great Britain
by Amazon